LOOK WITHIN
YOUR HEART

LOOK WITHIN YOUR HEART

Margaret Graham

BANTAM BOOKS

LONDON · NEW YORK · TORONTO · SYDNEY · AUCKLAND

LOOK WITHIN YOUR HEART
A BANTAM BOOK : 0 553 40817 8

Originally published in Great Britain by Doubleday,
a division of Transworld Publishers Ltd

PRINTING HISTORY
Doubleday edition published 1994
Bantam edition published 1995

Set in 10/11pt Linotype Sabon by
Phoenix Typesetting, Ilkley, West Yorkshire.

Bantam Books are published by Transworld Publishers Ltd,
61–63 Uxbridge Road, London W5 5SA,
in Australia by Transworld Publishers (Australia) Pty Ltd,
15–25 Helles Avenue, Moorebank, NSW 2170,
and in New Zealand by Transworld Publishers (N.Z.) Ltd,
3 William Pickering Drive, Albany, Auckland.

Reproduced, printed and bound in Great Britain by
Cox & Wyman Ltd, Reading, Berks

For Shelagh

Acknowledgements

My thanks to my Aunt Doris who spent twenty years in India, and to her son, Tony, who also spent many years there. My thanks also to all the staff of Bath Travel who went to great lengths to help me plan my tour of the First World War battlefields, and then Crete, where the owner, Maria Zafiropoulou, of Cretan village, Ayios Nikolaos, lent me her father's desk – he was also a writer. And thanks also, to Beamish, The North of England Open Air Museum and, as always, Sue Bramble and her staff at Martock Library.

BOOK ONE

1

'Your father's coming back from the war at last Connie,' Belle said, kneeling on the lawn of the grey stone vicarage, her arm round her eight-year-old daughter. It was July 1919 and she had received her husband's letter this morning.

Connie stopped counting, took her hands from her eyes and swung round, her blue eyes widening, her pale skin flushing. 'He's coming home, here. When?'

Belle kissed her daughter's fair hair, aware that the colour matched hers exactly, though Connie's had more curl, or was that just because she wore it in plaits during the day? She didn't want to tell Connie what else Walter had written but she must. 'No, not to the village, darling. He wants me to meet him in Newcastle this afternoon. You see, he might want us to live there.'

Connie stiffened then said, 'But we live here. His church is here, our house is here. You must tell him, Mam. Revd Driscoll's been looking after it for him, he knows that.'

Belle looked helplessly at Mrs Driscoll who was sitting on the terrace, shading her eyes from the sun which glinted on the mullioned windows behind her.

She watched as the old woman pushed a strand of grey hair back then pulled her straw hat further forward. Mrs Driscoll called, smiling, 'Don't worry about it now, Connie dear. Let your mother go to the city and talk to your father. Then, and only then, do we really know what's happening. Now, Boy is down there by the roses, or has he gone behind the runner beans beyond the laburnum arch? He's waiting for you to go and find him. In fact, he might even be in the greenhouse, but I hope he's not picking the tomatoes.' Her voice was not as firm as usual. She removed her spectacles and polished them on her skirt.

Belle stood up, pulling Connie with her. 'Go on, he'll think you're showing off and counting to one thousand. Either that, or that you've fallen asleep.'

Connie ran down the steps. She ignored the paved path, running instead across the grass, side-stepping the circular beds brimming with roses and the alyssum she had helped to plant. She turned. 'Anyway, I've forgotten Da, I don't know who he is any more, so who is he to take us away? He's only a face in that photograph. Tell him I can't leave Rempton or Boy, they need me.' Her voice was high. Soon there would be tears.

Belle started after her.

'No, leave her. She'll feel better with Boy.' Mrs Driscoll replaced her spectacles and stood up, feeling older than her sixty-odd years as her heart broke for this young woman whom she had grown to love and could not bear to lose. 'Come and sit with me. You'll have to go in a minute and those tears won't look well as you walk through the village.'

Belle took the handkerchief that was offered, smiling but not speaking, fearing that if she did she would cry again. Her hand shook as she drank the lemonade that Mrs Driscoll offered. The fragments of lemon were tart on her tongue.

She looked across the garden and watched her daughter, and Boy, Mrs Driscoll's four-year-old grandson, throw a ball against the wall which surrounded the vicarage grounds.

She searched for control and finally found it, saying, 'He hasn't been home since August 1914. I have so longed to see him and now he wants us to leave. He can't mean it?'

'You won't know whether he does until you go and talk to him, and you *do* want to go.'

'Yes, of course. But, Helen, he knows we've been given permission to stay in the Rempton living indefinitely because of his war service – how can he ignore that? He must know that the thought of Rempton in peace time is what has kept us all going throughout this dreadful war. I can't believe he doesn't feel the same. He must just be overtired. Oh, why did he refuse all leave in order to stay at the front? He must come here, it's what he needs, it's what the village needs.' Belle dug in her pocket for Walter's letter. 'I mean, you and I and James have held his village together for him, we've prayed for the men of his parish who'll never come home, we've nursed their grieving parents, even polished his pews. I just don't understand. See if you can.'

Belle thrust the letter at Mrs Driscoll who looked at this lovely, slight woman with hair the colour of wheat. Then across the lawn at Connie. Had a mother and daughter ever been so alike, from the deep blue of their eyes to the tone of their skin and the clear sound of their voices? She sighed and read aloud.

> Dearest Belle,
>   I shall be in Back Dock Mission, Ellis Street, Newcastle on 16 July at 2 p.m. Come to me there. Just you, not Connie yet. I long to see you. It has been so very long. I have permission from the Bishop to start a shelter here for ex-servicemen, and any others in need. Meet me, Belle.
>   Your Walter.

Belle rolled her glass backwards and forwards against her cheek. 'Has he forgotten that you and James came out of retirement to help me look after all this for him? Has he forgotten that he loves you, that his best friend all through his school-days, and after, was your son Philip? For heaven's sake, Walter stayed with you when his parents were abroad. You were his mentors. Surely he remembers that presiding as vicar here, as James did, was all he ever wanted? Why hasn't he come to Rempton to talk to us about this – why?'

Mrs Driscoll returned the letter, patted her mouth, swallowed and watched the children. Would this be the last time she would sit here with Belle as Connie played with Boy? It couldn't be.

Belle touched Helen's arm. The fragile skin was cool. 'I'm just going round and round, driving myself mad, and probably you. I'll go now. I'll ask him to start his shelter here. The men would like the fresh air and could walk to Longdale and watch the skips taking up the slag.' Belle pointed across the meadows to the winding gear of the neighbouring pit village which shimmered in the morning heat. 'There might be pit jobs they could take, or farm work here. They could walk to the beck here in Walter's village – because it is his, can't he see that?'

She put her glass down, wiping her hands on her skirt. The church clock was chiming. She set her hat straight.

Helen Driscoll said, 'You look too young to be thirty. He'll be so pleased to see you, and you to see him. You'll both realize how much you love one another, how lucky you are to have a life together. Just hold hard to that while you talk. But remember to listen too, Belle.'

Belle kissed Helen Driscoll, hugged her, called to Connie, 'Be good. I'll make it all right with your Da, if I can.'

She blew kisses, then said softly to Helen Driscoll, 'You see, I'm nervous because the last words Walter and I spoke were in anger.'

She walked through the house, scarcely noticing the panelling in the hall, the wide staircase, the gleaming irons by the large fireplace. She waved the maid back. 'I'll see myself out, Maud.'

She shut the door quietly behind her, and walked down the steps onto the gravel drive. She stood for a moment looking at the profusion of roses and marigolds, the staked hollyhocks and delphiniums, all of which continued into the garden of the East Wing where she lived. It, like the front of the main house, was covered by Virginia creeper but in addition she had grown honeysuckle around the wrought-iron porch.

He must come back and lie with her in the bedroom above, and smell its fragrance mingling with the smell of hay as the sun lowered in the sky, then he'd never want to leave.

She and Walter had talked of growing it when they had first arrived and she remembered his lips on hers, his laughter as he had swung her over the threshold that first day and she could almost hear his voice as he said the words she had never forgotten. 'Now it begins. Our life, and our work here, where I have always longed to be, with the woman of my dreams.'

He had chased her then and they had run in and out of the sitting-room, the dining-room, the kitchen, heedless of the nanny's stare, then they had pounded up the stairs, in and out of the bedrooms, until he had thrown her on their bed, and she had hurled pillows at him as he wrenched her shoes off to blow on her feet.

One pillow had burst and feathers had floated high into the air, then onto the dressing table, the wardrobe, into the grate, into their hair, their mouths, and he had leapt round the room quacking like a duck until she had thought she would die from laughing.

That night they had made love, and talked of the scent of the honeysuckle they would one day grow.

Walter sat on a bench in the hall of the mission, his hands quite still. He listened to the sound of the docks, the hoots, sirens, the shouting – but no guns.

Paper littered the floor, dust was thick on the benches, chairs were piled against the green walls, tables were shoved together, some with broken legs. Would she come?

'If you come, will you stay, Belle?' he asked aloud, his voice echoing in the emptiness. 'You must, I can't live without you, not now.'

He looked at the door which led from the hall to the church. His church. He should at least go in. But he could not. Instead he put his head in his hands and wept.

Belle lowered the train window, secured the leather strap and waved to the porter as the train lurched from Longdale. She looked across to Rempton which seemed so crystal clear today. It was so unchanging, so beautiful with its village green and pond, where the children collected frog-spawn and water-boatmen, carrying them to their homes along the main street past the baker, the butcher, the co-op. She saw the neat cottages with gardens full of phlox and roses, hens and the odd pig, and the school which Connie attended.

On the hill behind the village sat the squire's house and all around were the fields of corn, the haystacks, the potato fields and to the east the beck with its clear water, its stepping-stones.

She leant out, waving again to the porter, as the train moved past the sidings of Longdale, the slag-heap, the rows of houses, and was grateful as she always was that Rempton was agricultural, that there was no seam beneath them.

She sat down and in time the countryside turned from a mixture of fields and slag-heaps and distant sweeping hills into colliery villages and towns, which were so numerous they seemed to merge one into the other. There were rows of black-stained houses and factory chimneys which belched grime and filth, but still there were the hills in the distance.

She smelt the sulphur from the engine and was assaulted by a hammering of sound as the train swept through tunnels again and again until, after two hours – which seemed more like a lifetime with every passing minute – they entered Newcastle.

Over by the Tyne were more chimneys, more grime and a pall seemed to hang leaden in the sky. She slammed the door shut at Central Station and walked along the wide streets with their imposing buildings, appreciating their elegance, especially the Assembly Rooms, but longing for Rempton.

She took the tram towards the south-west of the city. The tram jerked, clanked and rattled past a tatter shouting, 'Rag 'n' bone', past straining brewery horses, and people jostling. Where was the sunlight?

It seemed that there were only houses which crowded the road, and streets which ran off at right angles, their terraces huddled together. There were ships' masts in the distance, bridges, huge arches, darkness. There was a factory, there were shipbuilders, an abattoir, there was chaos.

What was going to happen to them? How could they live here when at Rempton there was light and comfort and a sense of belonging. But her husband was here – how could she belong anywhere he wasn't? She thought again of the honeysuckle, of the feathers which had fallen, of the laughter, and didn't know what she was feeling.

She stepped off the tram at High Road uncertain of the way, but over there a woman scrubbed her step. Over here, another wiped the grime from the window-sill.

'Is this the way to the mission?' Belle asked. The woman looked up from the sill, her face pallid, her eyes sunken. Her apron was filthy. A child clung to her leg.

'Aye, straight down, turn right, left, right again. New vicar there.'

Belle smiled. 'So I gather. Thank you.'

She walked slowly now, longing to see him, to feel his arms around her, but wanting also to return home. She bunched her hands and dug them into her pockets. This is your husband, you know him, he knows you, you love him, he loves you. She stopped, put her hand on the wall. A woman approached, stared, went on.

'I can't even remember what he looks like, let alone whether there is love. There was so little when he left, too much had happened between us,' she said aloud.

She felt the roughness of the brick through her glove, dusted it off, continued to walk, turning right, then along, not wanting to go on, to face the man she had fought on the cricket green on the evening that war was declared.

'You are mad, a warmonger not a man of God. You have gone too far along the Driscolls' path,' she had shouted desperately into his shocked face after he had urged his cricket team to march to war, his face full of the self-righteousness she had watched him acquiring as the weeks and months passed at Rempton, their earlier joy forgotten.

For what Belle and Walter hadn't realized was that the Driscolls had become set in their ways as age overtook them. They proved to be censorious and overbearing in those early months, determined to mould the new vicar in their image.

Walter had succumbed; more than that, he had embraced their strict authoritarian legacy brushing aside Belle's objections explaining that there was virtue in order, in standards. It led to certainty. It led to approval.

But not hers. No, never hers, she thought now.

It had taken the death of the Driscolls' son just after the Christmas Truce of 1914 to shock Helen and James out of the veneer of dogma.

Belle shaded her eyes, looking for the mission, looking for Walter, half-fearful, half-longingly because she could still remember the hate she had felt for him when he took the team away. That hate had remained until the Somme, when six of them died. Then an echo of love had stirred, and grown to full bloom as shock and grief had stripped him of cant, and his letters at last became full of the old humanity. Oh Walter.

She stopped again. There was a church ahead, adjoining a large hall attached to a house. A man stood on the steps – and was so still. He was watching, waiting and was so thin, so drawn. She put her hand to her mouth – it was Walter's father, surely it was his father, surely that drawn, bowed, white-haired man was his father. But Walter's father was dead.

She walked on again. My darling love, you should have come home, she thought, running now, love overwhelming her, her arms open. He moved, calling, 'Belle, Belle, you came.' His voice was that of an old man too.

Then his arms were around her, his hands on her hair, his lips on her cheeks, her eyes, and then her lips. 'Oh Walter, what have they done to you?' she whispered against his mouth.

'You came,' he repeated, pulling away, pushing her from him, his hands on her shoulders. His eyes searched her face. She had forgotten how brown they were and how thick his eyebrows, and how full his mouth. 'You came. Thank you.' His voice was almost formal, but his lips trembled.

She reached up and touched his cheek – it was so smooth. And how tall he was, and though his shoulders were bowed they were still wide and would one day be straight again – surely. She felt the weight of his head as he leaned against her hand and now she saw the tiredness, the emptiness in his eyes. 'Let's go inside,' she murmured, her voice breaking, 'It's been so long.'

The paint was peeling on the door that Walter pushed open. He pointed to the end of the passage. 'That leads into the house, though there is also an external door. Here is the hall.'

He led the way, moving without his old grace. Belle eased off her gloves and felt the dull, dirty, green walls pressing on her.

Walter walked further into the hall.

'Please Walter. I want you to hold me, to feel your arms around me.' He stopped, half-turned, looked at her and the emptiness was gone from his eyes, and in its place was agony. She moved towards him, her hands outstretched. 'Walter, I love you.'

'The kitchens are there. Behind them, and above is space for dormitories when they are needed. We already have some beds set up.' He pointed to an arched door, 'Through there is the church. I minister to the whole parish, not just those whom we help here, and Belle, I already have my first ex-soldier. There will be many others – for they come to cities, not to villages.'

The agony was gone, the emptiness had returned and Belle's arms dropped to her sides as he looked at her across the distance his words, and his movements, had created.

She whispered, shocked, 'So, if you are talking like this you have obviously decided already. Has nothing changed between us?'

She must feel him against her, she must feel his arms around her because the anger which was rising in her mustn't be allowed to live. She reached for him and still he didn't move and now anger broke through. 'Come to me, let me hold you, then you may tell me why you made the decision about *our* future before I even arrived, before I could talk to you of your daughter's wishes, of mine. Come to me, Walter.'

He flinched, and it was because of this she went to him.

'Why have you done this, my love?' she asked, all anger gone, only desperation and confusion remaining. She felt his breath on her hair, and his body so thin beneath his clothes. Now his arms moved and he held her but only for a moment, for he pulled from her, putting his hands up as she moved to hold him again.

How did a husband speak of a soul that was disfigured by war, of a despair that drove everything and everyone into a grey distance? 'I prayed for the team's deliverance, Belle, but one by one they died. Just one was all I asked for. Just one, and for a while I *did* have that one. It was Archie. Do you remember our fine upstanding schoolteacher? Do you, do you?'

Belle nodded slowly. 'Yes, I remember Archie, but why do you look as though you hate him? Oh Walter, what's happened to you?'

'I held him in my arms as he died, and heard his confession. Dear God, that confession.'

She moved towards him. 'I don't understand.'

He held his arms up as though to ward her off. She stopped. He looked at her beautiful face, her eyes shadowed with tiredness.

'What has happened is that my faith has gone – I lost it in the mud of Flanders, and what does a man of God do, when there is no God?'

Belle stared, all thoughts of Archie gone. She could say nothing.

'It's not prayers but the sound of leather on willow which haunts my days, and the cricket team who come to me at night. They stand just as they did on that hot August day. Oh, it was hot, wasn't it, Belle?' His voice was cracking.

She nodded. 'Yes, my love, it was hot.' She could hardly speak as she watched this man who had once been young struggle to find words.

'They stand, alive, laughing, young as they did on the eve of war. They leave me as dawn breaks, one after the other, no longer young, laughing, alive, but mud-covered, silent, weary, hopeless, bloodied.'

'Walter, don't.'

'I must. You need to know because although they leave, I still hear that leather ball on the willow bat all day.'

Belle gripped his trembling hands, and saw the horror and pain on her husband's face as he continued to force the words out.

'You were right to shout at me that day, and every day until we left. I should have listened, then they would be alive. How did you know that war is dirty, agonizing, relentless, when I did not? All I knew was that I was right, that we were fighting in God's name, that it would be a glorious sacrifice we would all be honoured to make, in Christ's image. I actually told my men that on the eve of the Somme, Belle.'

He was laughing, a harsh bitter sound and Belle wanted to put her hands to her ears, her eyes, but his were gripping hers and so the tears ran from her cheeks to her neck, and soaked her dress.

He continued. 'I wouldn't listen to you. But now, I ask you to listen to me. I can't go back to the village, or the cricket pitch, or the homes where my lads lived, or the lanes they will never again walk along. I have no right to feel the Rempton ground beneath my feet.' He was panting, gasping for breath. 'I lived, they did not. Can you understand?'

Belle kissed his lips, his eyes, holding him so tight that he felt he could hardly breathe though he could smell her skin and feel its softness against his cheek, and knew for a moment, but only a moment, that he loved her as deeply as he always had. And felt, for a moment, but only a moment, as though he had come home, as though he could rest, and now he wept, as he had not yet allowed himself to do.

Why was it that men's crying was so much worse than women's? She stroked his back, his neck, she kissed his cheeks and tasted the tears, and forced her own to stop.

'I love you so much,' she said as he began to shake. 'It's all right, my love. I shall be here with you, and so will Connie. We will help you and you must remember that war is man-made; God can only do so much, we do the rest. We are all responsible for our own actions. One day you will find your God. Look, you've remained within the church, that must mean something?'

He was no longer crying, and his voice was almost a whisper as he said, 'You see, there's such a darkness, such a hole. I try to climb out, but I can't. I call for help, for forgiveness, but all I hear is the laughter, the sound of the cricket match, then the cries, and then the confession – Archie's confession. And yes, remaining within the church means something, it means that the mission is financed.'

'But what confession, Walter? What can be so terrible?'

* * *

That night, in Rempton, Belle looked from her bedroom window across the village well lit by the moon, breathing in the scent of honeysuckle, listening to the bullocks coughing, watching the bats swoop.

Walter should have been here, with her, or she with him in the mission, holding one another, loving one another, but instead he was searching the streets for the local girl Archie had made pregnant – the girl Walter had banished from the village as a lying whore as war broke out.

2

Belle scrubbed at the grease and dirt on the green wall. Thank heavens they were almost finished. Sweat ran down her back, her hair dangled in her eyes. They'd been here a week; it felt like a year.

'Connie, will you move my hair, darling?'

Connie was squatting, wiping the suds from the wall.

'Quickly, it's going to make me sneeze.'

Connie pulled the hair to one side. She wore an apron which Mrs Driscoll had made in the rush before they left. 'It will remind you both of the fields,' she'd said.

Belle looked at the roses, the poppies and the corn-flowers. They didn't need reminding, they would never forget. She dropped the brush into the bucket and pushed herself to her feet, hauling Connie up and hugging her.

'Urgh, you're all wet, Mam.'

'We couldn't have done this without her, could we, Sandy?' Belle called up to Walter's first ex-serviceman, Sandy O'Neil, as he clambered down from the ladder, his long legs taking two rungs at a time.

'That we couldn't and bye, she'll have built up a thirst.' He brushed his moustache which was as flecked with grey as his mousey hair. He squatted, tied his boot-lace and the muscles of his arms and shoulders moved powerfully beneath his shirt. There were deep lines of strain to the sides of his mouth but there were also also laughter lines around his hazel eyes as he grinned at Connie. 'A spot of lemonade, lass?'

'We could all manage some of that,' Belle laughed. 'I've some in the house kitchen. We'll go through.' She looked round the hall at the partitioned alcoves they were building as quiet areas for the men, and at the walls. The green was cleaner but, but—

'There's so much to do, and it's still so depressing,' she murmured.

'It looks just like sick,' Connie said.

Belle laughed. 'Wrong colour, but yes, the room definitely looks unwell, and since those partitions will have to be painted anyway—'

She looked at Sandy.

'I was afraid you'd say that,' he grinned.

Belle and Sandy followed Connie across the passage into the house. 'Will you help paint the walls, Connie, or are you going to play with the children we saw in the back lane?' Belle asked.

Connie shook her head. 'I'll help.'

In the kitchen Connie drank lemonade which had been standing in a bucket of water and was cool. She listened to Belle and Sandy talking of the colour they would use.

'Cream,' Connie interrupted. 'It's warm, like Daisy's milk.' She slouched through to the scullery, then the wash-house, and finally into the yard. Could Boy still be watching the cows, was the beck still running, the slag buckets churning, even though she had left? She couldn't bear to think of it.

Belle gazed after her as Sandy said, 'Good idea, white's too harsh.'

Belle nodded. 'Would you mind fetching it? We've an account at the store. And Sandy—?'

'Aye, don't you fret, I'll be helping, but we'll need more than the two of us. What about the Revd Symmonds?'

Tension tightened her shoulders. 'He's not strong enough but look, it'll be time to put the water on for tea in the hall. There'll be men coming in. You get the paint, I'll sort out the tea.'

Belle watched him leave. It wasn't just that Walter wasn't strong, it was because he was still too busy trying to find Archie's child, and the mother of that child, and through them, some forgiveness. Why couldn't

Archie have taken his confession to the grave with him?

But no, that wasn't fair. A great wrong had been done in that August of 1914 and now she no longer saw the clippie mat, the range, the tea-towels drying. All she saw was her husband's face, his cassock, the stained glass window behind him, as he berated Binnie, the pregnant village girl for fornication, and worse, for bringing the name of the village schoolteacher into disrepute – a man who insisted he had done nothing but guide and nurture her until she left.

For this man, Binnie claimed, was the father. But she hadn't lied as you swore to my husband, had she, Archie? Belle thought. You did indeed nurture her, but too damn well. She bit her lip.

Why hadn't she fought harder for Binnie that dreadful day? She moved to the window, looking out at the shadows. Why? Because she hadn't known what Walter intended to say, that was how estranged she and her husband had become.

She had fought him afterwards though. 'Look at yourself,' she had raged. 'Look at the man you have become. Can't you see it's cruel, this girl deserves succour and there is a far from blameless man somewhere, or are you claiming this as an immaculate conception, Walter? Perhaps you feel your God would honour you with this in your parish?'

He had shaken her then, glaring, his lips tight, certain of his judgement, before striding from the wing to the main vicarage which the Driscolls had bought on their retirement.

Belle had said nothing more to him, but had gone to Binnie's house. 'She's left for Newcastle,' her mother said, her eyes red-rimmed.

Two days later war was declared and Binnie was forgotten. 'How could I have forgotten a frightened girl?' Belle murmured. 'And will we ever find her now? We must, if either of us is to have any peace.'

The clock struck the hour. Walter was with the church authorities, checking through records again. Later he would traipse the streets, looking for the girl and the child he had cast out in God's name, so sure that he was right to do so.

Walter's voice had risen almost to a scream last night as he said, 'Archie and I talked of the mysticism of the Song of Songs, we walked the meadows behind the lines, crouched beneath the path of shells, grieved together. We shared so much, but not the truth, Belle. He only told me the truth as he died. Oh God, what have I done?'

He then whispered, 'When I buried Archie I hurled the mud and stones onto his face, but it was me I wanted to hurt – all this – for no God. All this, for my own glory.'

Connie sat on the wash-house steps, her head on her knees, her finger tracing shapes in the earth. She could feel the sun through her dress and her hair. She smiled at the memory of the drawing Boy had done of her with wheat instead of hair and violets instead of eyes. What would he think of this place?

She looked up now at the broken bottles, the nettles, weeds, papers, the broken lavatory, then felt the touch of her mother's hand. Connie clutched it and leant against her as she sat down.

'I think we'll make this a garden, then we'll bring some of the country here, to us, shall we?' Belle said, wondering if Binnie had a son or daughter, holding her own child tight. 'At least we have a home, friends who love us and you have a father, darling girl.'

'He's not like a father. He doesn't smile, he doesn't read to me, like you said.' Connie's voice was muffled as she pressed her face against Belle's shoulder. 'And even if we make this yard nice, it still isn't the country. I hate him for taking us away, Mam.'

Belle stroked her daughter's face. 'It's very difficult

being grown-up, you know. Things happen to you, they change you. Listen carefully to me now, Connie. Sandy was telling me of things your father did in the war – he was very brave and the men loved him very much. He stayed with them in the trenches when the guns were firing, rescuing some of them. He learned first aid, he arranged concerts to cheer them up.'

Connie pushed away from Belle. 'He doesn't try to cheer us up. He won't even let the harmonium be mended in the church. Everyone drones and croaks because there's no music. There's no choir either. Almost no congregation.'

Belle sighed. The sun was glinting on the broken bottles. 'I don't know why he hates music now, so we'll have to try and find out. But he's not well, you see, Connie; he wasn't wounded by a gun, he was wounded by what he saw, by the friends he lost. Imagine how you would feel if you lost Boy.'

Connie put her head down on her knees. 'I have lost him.'

'No, darling. Imagine how you would feel if Boy died.' She was looking carefully at Connie now. 'Or Mrs Driscoll, or Revd Driscoll. We didn't like them for a long time, do you remember? They were cross and difficult and then Boy's father died and it changed them. We love them very much now. You will love your father again.'

'They got nice, Da's got horrid.'

'No, not really. He's very tired inside, and very sad, but one day he'll be better.'

'Do you promise me?'

Belle smiled. 'Yes, I promise.' She hoped that she was not lying. She took a deep breath. 'I promise.'

Connie looked at her. 'I'd die if Boy died.'

'No you wouldn't, you'd have to go on living. That's what Da's doing, and he's trying to find the best way of doing it. That's why we're here. You must ask him to explain it properly.'

'How can I? He's never here, and when he is, he doesn't see me.'

'He'll be back this afternoon and believe me, he'll want to spend time with you. He said so last night.' He hadn't, but she would make sure that today Walter Symmonds talked with his daughter.

'Now I'm going to show you something that you can write to Boy about, but tell him not to do it unless his mother or grandmother is with him. Who knows, it might be something you can show the children out there in the alley.' Belle nodded her head towards the noise. 'Come with me a minute.'

She walked into the yard, then crouched down, holding a piece of broken glass over the paper she put on the ground. 'Watch it carefully.'

They waited, and Connie felt the sun on her, heard a bee, and saw a cabbage white linger over the nettles. A ship hooted, the pigeons next door cooed, then she saw the paper brown, smoke, and a small, neat hole was burned.

Belle said, 'It works much better with a magnifying glass, but ours is still packed. My mother showed me. She was a teacher but died before you were born. Do you remember Revd Driscoll showing his scouts how to start their cooking fires?'

Connie nodded. She did now. 'They put a bit of hay down, used glass then added twigs to it once it caught. They cooked us potatoes.' She sat back on her heels. 'Tell you what, I'll show Boy when we go back. We will go back, won't we?'

Belle nodded. 'Oh yes, at first for holidays, then, when our work is finished, we'll go home for good. Because it has become our home, hasn't it? Now then, we'll burn up the rubbish later and cook potatoes in the ash, shall we? Newcastle will think that Bonfire Night's come early.' She stood up. 'Come and help with the tea in the hall, or you could start to clear the garden, or plan the beds, but don't touch the glass.'

Connie stayed in the garden, walking to the gate at the end of the yard, peering through the knot-hole, smelling old creosote. The children were there, playing marbles. She could see them flicking the number ones just as she and Boy had done on the terrace of the vicarage. The children were laughing now. She turned away and looked at the yard, then shouted at the house. 'How can you make a garden out of this muck and how can an old man like Da be so horrid?'

She waited, wanting her mother to hear, but then was grateful that she had not. But how dare he come into their lives? He should have stayed in his trenches. Connie kicked at the rotten planks of wood.

'I hate you, I hate you, do you hear me? You've got a face like a wet weekend, your hair is white. It used to be black, and my mother is working, scrubbing away, when she's done enough, all through the war. I don't care what you did. I just don't care. I hate you.' She was hissing into her fists.

'There's no Boy here, there's just kids who call me a penguin's daughter and chase me down the alley when I go out with my marbles.' She lifted her dress to see the bruise the stone had made. 'You didn't get wounded. I got hit the first day I got here.'

Belle put the kettle on the mission stove. The heat wafted out at her as she wiped her hands on her apron. She looked through the hatch. There were eleven men now – word was being passed round by the army chaplains, and from one soldier to another. They looked lethargic and weary.

Sandy came into the kitchen. 'The lad'll bring the paint at closing time,' he said, pouring milk into the mugs.

On one table the men were playing cards. Their faces were immobile, their movements slow.

Belle said, 'I taught the village schoolchildren to knit sleeping helmets in the war, Sandy.'

'I probably wore one.'

She smiled. 'If it had dropped stitches, I probably knitted it. We sewed sandbags too.' Belle looked at her fingers – how sore they'd become. 'It helped the children to feel as though they were contributing. Come and look at these men.'

She moved to one side and Sandy joined her.

'Fine body of men there, just sitting about,' he said, his face impassive.

'Quite. I haven't any khaki wool, but there are some very lonely paintbrushes. What do you think?'

Sandy laughed. 'If I want to live I suspect I need to say yes. Will you tell them, or shall I?'

'Tell them what?' Walter's voice was tired and Belle spun round. She hadn't heard him come in. Her eyes met his and knew from their emptiness that he had not found Binnie.

Belle moved to his side. 'I'll write to Helen Driscoll again – she might have found out something. Come along, sit down. Let's have this jacket off.' She eased it from his shoulders, nodding at Sandy as the kettle boiled. He poured the water into the pot.

'Keep the tea-leaves, won't you, Sandy? We'll bank both fires with them last thing.'

Now they could not afford help in the house she had to remember to do these things, and to smile nicely at their neighbour, Mrs Gribble, who had always cleaned for previous vicars, and whose nose was severely out of joint at the new incumbent's penny-pinching ways, or so she had sniffed to her friend in Belle's hearing one day.

'Who and what are you going to tell?' Walter repeated, leaning back before taking the mug that Sandy offered. His hands trembled as he raised it to his lips.

'Would you take the tea to the men, please, Sandy?' Belle waited until he left, then said, 'I'm going to suggest that they help us paint the hall. It's so dreary—'

'No.'

'But it needs painting, Walter. It's too miserable.'

'Then you and Sandy can paint it but not these people. They're not hired help.'

Belle was outraged. 'Sandy and I are not miracle workers, neither are *we* hired help. Just think about it – Sandy helps because he wants to, it gives him a measure of self-respect to feel he is earning his keep. Why should any of those men feel otherwise? People want to contribute.'

She fought to control her anger. 'I'm sorry, Walter, but you said we've got to become functional as soon as possible. Don't worry, I'm not going to force anyone. I'll just ask for volunteers, and I'll also see if there is anyone who can help with the partitions. You said men from the trenches like small, enclosed areas but are these too cramped? They'll take two chairs and a table.'

He shook his head. 'They'll do.'

She said gently, 'Believe me, my darling, it is better for people to feel they are doing something. Look how you feel you must walk the streets.'

His eyes were empty again, his shoulders slumped. He was too tired to speak, always too tired, he thought, not caring any more who painted, who sawed and hammered, because the hole was so deep.

Belle touched his face. 'I can talk to the men, can I?'

'Yes.'

'Now will you go and lie down?'

He shook his head. 'I have to go out again. Parish work. I can look and ask about Binnie at the same time.'

'Not so fast, you must lie down first, but when you go, please take Connie with you.'

Walter struggled to his feet. He reached for his jacket, shaking his head. 'No, she resents me, barely speaks to me and who can blame her?'

Belle bit back her irritation. She wanted something positive from this man but that was a very long way off.

'Please take her. You need to learn about one another and she needs you, she's been five years without a father.'

'Binnie's child has been that long without one too, and that is my fault.' He walked towards the passage. Belle ran after him, holding him back.

'We don't know that. She might have married and that is beside the point. Here we have a situation you can do something about *now*, or don't you care about your family?'

He said, 'I'll take her.' He was too tired to argue.

Connie walked with Walter along the front of the houses in their street, past a rope hanging from a lamp-post. She'd have liked to swing from it but didn't dare. They passed another at the end of the street and here a gang of children poked out their tongues, nudging one another, pulling faces. Their feet were bare, their legs dirty. She looked down at her dress, her shoes, then up at Walter's black suit, his white collar and longed to be with them, not with her father.

They walked alongside a wall, then past a blacksmith, then into another street. Her father entered a shop. She waited outside and rubbed dirt on her shoes. She followed behind when he came out, down street after street, as he posted letters through doors.

He pointed to the tram sheds. 'When you're older you'll catch a tram to the grammar school.'

She thought of the village school and missed it with a fierce pain. She hated him. She looked at his hand which trembled. What were the trenches like? She looked at the terraces either side, so close they seemed to fall on her. She looked up at the sky.

'You don't see the whole sky here, do you? You just see the lines of sky. It makes it dark,' she said, falling in beside him, glad her shoes were dirty and dull.

He stopped and looked down at this child with the fair hair, suddenly interested that she should say such a thing. His father had had fair hair. He put out his hand and

33

touched hers. Connie looked up at him but said nothing. Her eyes were as blue as Belle's.

He looked up at the sky and began walking again, saying, 'You get used to seeing the sky in strips in the trenches. You get used to small places, to walls around you. Space can be frightening.'

Connie didn't want to ask him if he had been frightened. Grown-ups shouldn't ever be scared. If they were scared who was there to look after you?

'This is just like one big trench then, is it, to you? You feel safe here, do you?' she asked.

For a moment he saw her need.

'Yes, my dear. I feel safe here, with these walls, you, and your mother.' He smiled.

Connie stared. When he smiled he reminded her of someone. She thought for a moment, then something caught in her throat. Yes, he looked like Boy when he wanted to make her happy.

She reached up and placed her hand in his and they walked for what seemed like miles together, until they reached a bank beyond which lay water, turgid with debris and timber.

'This is the slacks, where they store wood for the sawmill.' Walter struggled to keep his voice level. 'It empties when the tide goes out. Those sleepers are used to keep the timbers together.'

They said nothing more, but felt the warmth of their touching hands. They walked again until her legs ached and they reached a narrow lane which led to the quayside. There were warehouses on the left and old shops and houses on the right. Merchant ships were berthed at the quay and seamen were walking down the gangplank of one with huge clogs on their feet. Connie felt the wind in her hair, tugging it, and her dress, as she pulled at her father. 'Look at them.'

Walter said, 'Those men are from Holland. It's a very flat land with windmills, and they make round cheeses and grow tulips.'

'I'd like to travel one day.'

'I spent the first eighteen months of the war in Egypt – there was lots of space, but I felt safe.' Dear God, how safe, but he mustn't think of that.

They turned down street after street, passing the bakery with its sweet smell of bread and the brewery horses which struck sparks as they slipped on the cobbles. She could hear the leather harnesses creaking.

'Were the guns noisy?' she asked.

He paused, then said, 'Very. It's still strange to find all this so quiet.'

She listened to the street with its clatter of carts, the horses, the people, the trams. How could this be quiet? She looked up at the sky again. How could anyone live in slits in the ground? She thought of Boy, of losing him, of him dying, of burying him.

'Did you bury your friends?' she asked. 'You're a vicar so you must have done.'

He dropped her hand and didn't answer. She looked up and saw the sadness in his face and knew that he had. She put her hand into his again because she would feel wounded and ill if she had to do that to Boy. Her mother was right, he needed looking after and somehow she must remember that.

'Mam said you'd explain to me about the mission.' They passed a school. The bricks were dark red, the windows high. She didn't want to think of school. Those children would be there. 'Talk to me, Da.'

Walter dragged himself away from the guns of the Somme and Tyne Cot and looked at the child tugging at his hand. 'War is nasty, cruel and painful. I think a country fights because it doesn't know the other country very well. Once you know and like someone, you don't want to hurt them, do you? Or take things from them?'

The school was behind them now, and on their left was waste ground where boys were kicking a ball and shouting. It seemed so light suddenly.

Walter stopped talking.

'Go on, Da. So what will we do at the mission?'

'We'll give shelter to any ex-soldiers in need – all races and religions will be welcome. We will raise money and bring Germans to our mission so that people can see they are just people like us – we will send our men over there. It's a very small way of trying to stop war, but it's all I can think of to encourage tolerance.'

'Does God think this is a good idea?'

Walter said, 'I expect so.' But how could something that did not exist have an opinion?

The clock chimed midnight as Belle climbed the stairs. She could still smell the ash and tea-leaves she had thrown on the fire. She rubbed her roughened hands with Vaseline in the bathroom. They would be paint-covered tomorrow but it didn't matter because the men had agreed, laughing and joking as they put the cards away and looked at the alcove partitions. Two knew enough to help and would teach the others.

She stood in the bath and sluiced her body with cold water. The previous incumbent had installed a geyser but economy was all-important, Walter said. She smiled as she thought of Connie's arms around her neck as they had kissed good night. 'Da isn't well but I held his hand and he told me that he wants the world to be friends. We'll help, won't we?'

Belle dragged on her nightdress; her skin was still damp. She ran her hands over her breasts, her thighs. She longed for her husband and wondered if tonight, for the first time, he would hold her. At least just hold her.

He did not. He lay still and she touched his arm. 'Never mind, my love, we'll find her, you'll see. And when we do, we'll make it up to her.'

One step at a time, she told herself. Today it was Connie, tomorrow it would be the painting. And please God, let it one day be Binnie, then her husband might learn to live again, and love, without the burden of guilt which was driving him deeper towards the darkness.

3

The fire was crackling in the Driscolls' sitting-room as the flames teased the coals. It was so good to be back, even if it was only for a few days.

'Belle, did you stay up and welcome in the New Year?' Helen Driscoll asked.

'Yes, indeed, Connie too. And the men in the mission stayed up very much longer, then had sore heads yesterday. That's right, isn't it, Connie?'

Connie was playing snap with Boy near the grand piano. 'Yes, and Sandy still had one when we left this morning. Oh, say "snap", Boy.' She pushed him gently.

Belle looked at the clock. It was not yet nine and she sank into the comfort and peace. Would Walter remember to eat? She frowned, then relaxed. Sandy had promised to keep an eye on him and for the next few days there would be no fires to bank, no meals to cook.

She listened to James Driscoll playing the piano, gently, softly.

Amelia, Boy's mother, looked up from her embroidery. 'Do you remember the canticles in church every Christmas, Belle, and Helen's organ recital?'

Belle smiled. 'How could I forget? I just wish we had music at the mission. The carols seemed flat and joyless this year.'

'Haven't you had the harmonium repaired yet?' Helen asked.

Belle shook her head. 'I found someone who'd do it, but Walter turned him away.'

'But why?' asked Amelia in surprise.

'We've tried to find out but he just gets upset and insists

that there is no music. It will be something to do with the war and there are enough echoes of that destroying our lives as it is.'

Amelia and Helen exchanged glances, then looked at the clock. Amelia straightened. 'It's well past the children's bedtime.'

'I know, I'll take them up,' Belle started to get up.

Amelia waved her back. 'Sit down, for heaven's sake, I'll do it. You've only been here two hours. Come along, Connie, let's get this tiger up that wooden hill.'

Belle grinned as Connie heaved Boy to his feet then kissed her, saying, 'I won't be long, I'm tired too.'

Boy ran to James, pulling his hands from the piano. 'Come and read to us, Grandpa.'

They climbed the stairs. Connie counted them, as she always did, following Boy, hearing his laugh. She stopped on the landing, looking at the door to her room. Tonight she would lie in bed and watch the moonlight; she wouldn't sleep, she'd just hug to herself the thought that there was no school tomorrow, no gang waiting to chase her with their taunts, their sneers, sometimes another stone, another bruise.

Belle looked at Helen, then at the familiar prints, the curtains, the ornaments on the shelves.

Mrs Driscoll asked, 'Does Connie miss Boy as much as he misses her?'

'Oh yes, and as a vicar's child it seems so difficult for her to make new friends. We set her apart somehow.'

'You're right, we found the same with Philip but he was so soon away at school that it didn't matter so much. Will you arrange a boarding-school for Connie?'

Belle shook her head. 'No, I couldn't send any child away, that's not why I had her.' She pulled a face at Helen then closely examined the dark red brocade of the armchair. They both laughed as Helen shook her finger, saying, 'We always did argue about this.'

'Only this?' Their laughter deepened, then Belle thought of Walter. 'If only we could find Binnie.'

Helen steepled her hands and looked over her glasses at Belle. 'He's no better then?'

'He won't be until we find her.' Belle suddenly felt tired, then impatient, then desperate. 'Good heavens, Helen, someone in the village must know where she is? She must have had some friends but who were they? Oh damn – if only her mother was still alive.'

'You can hardly blame that poor soul for not clinging to life for your convenience.'

Belle shook her head. 'You know I don't mean it like that – or do I? Am I becoming a monster?'

'You always were, and no doubt will continue to be so, especially when you get the bit between your teeth.' Helen peered over her glasses and again they laughed.

'But is this a bit that is worth biting on?' Helen murmured at length.

Belle started, all laughter gone. 'Helen, how can you say that – you know how important it is to Walter.'

Helen stared at Belle, searching her face, then she looked into the fire. 'Yes, I suppose I do know that, but I had hoped he would have improved to the point where we no longer had to find this – oh, this girl. I'll try to discover who took her to Newcastle. I gather it was a man.'

Belle leaned forward, her hand held up. 'Wait a minute. You said in your letters that you'd already asked in the village if anyone knew anything – so who will you ask, if they know nothing? Helen, what's going on? Have you lied about already trying?' Real anger was in the air.

Helen sat up straight, her eyes cold. 'I have tried and I'm not lying.' Then her voice softened. 'I meant that perhaps someone will remember if I try a different tack, so calm down and listen to me.' She fixed her eyes on Belle. 'You were right to ask about Binnie's friends but think back carefully and you will remember that she had none.'

Helen heaved herself to her feet, leaning heavily on her stick as she poked the fire, then she rearranged the photos on the mantelpiece.

The fire was too hot now. Belle moved to the piano. 'There must be someone.'

'There isn't. She preferred men to women and women are the ones who keep in touch and have up-to-date news.'

Belle pressed the keys softly. 'Then why haven't you asked the men?'

'I have but most won't even admit to knowing her.'

'Poor Binnie.'

'Perhaps.' Helen shook her head. 'Look, there's no point in going all over this again. I'm just repeating that it's not going to be easy to trace her through the village.'

'No, you're trying to tell me something else as well. You're trying to warn me about a wretched pregnant girl. We're back to August 1914 and the righteous indignation of you all.' The anger was back; she paced backwards and forwards. 'For heaven's sake, what are you really trying to say?'

'Very well, then, but stand still, I can't afford another carpet.' Helen's voice was sharp too. Belle stopped and glared. Helen murmured, 'And if the wind changes you'll stay like that.' Then she smiled but Belle couldn't.

'Helen, just tell me.'

'Very well.' Helen took a deep breath. 'You see, Binnie was friendless because none of the village can forget what she did years before the pregnancy. The reason for that sounds petty in the clear light of day but it wasn't at the time and it still affects our attitude to her. Do you remember the Sunday School Party we had every year?'

'Yes, but what—?'

'Do you remember the Christmas tree, with a fairy on the top? Well, when Binnie was about ten, the fairy was stolen. Binnie said that she had seen Rachel Billings take it. Before I could stop him, little Rachel was given the strap by her father and then I found the fairy in Binnie's school "treasure pocket". We were still using them when you came, do you remember? I somehow knew it would be her, and I knew she had intended Rachel to be strapped.'

'But why?'

'Because Rachel had been chosen as Mary in the Nativity play, and Binnie had wanted the part – she actually told me this. She was a very envious child, though she was no poorer than anyone else. I often wondered if it was because her father was a drifter, always chasing dreams or greener grass. Either way, I could never care for the child again. Every time a toy went missing, or was mysteriously broken, it seemed Binnie was near by, with that look on her face. I always felt she wanted what belonged to someone else. It was very wrong of me, I can see that now. It was also wrong to be relieved when we thought she had publicly lied again and we could get rid of her.'

A coal fell from the fire. Helen reached for the tongs. 'Yes, it was impossibly cruel of us all.'

Belle almost laughed with relief. 'For heaven's sake, I thought you were going to tell me she had committed a murder, and you're right, it's absurd. Binnie was a child then; are children not allowed mistakes?'

'I shouldn't have brought it up at all. I'm sorry, forgive a ridiculous old woman. I veer between being ashamed of myself and feeling confused. I'm overtired and I'll be glad when the Longdale minister takes our parish under his wing. Perhaps I just needed to clear my head. I just wanted you to – oh, I don't know.'

They sat in silence, drinking the cocoa when it came. It was thick and sweet.

'Daisy's milk?' Belle asked softly.

Helen Driscoll smiled. 'Of course.'

As they left the room and climbed the stairs together Helen put her arm through Belle's. 'I'll find the name of the man who took Binnie to Newcastle if it wears out my shoe leather. I've been so foolish.'

'Why stop there? I've worn away my feet, and Walter's up to his armpits.'

They smiled. Their friendship could survive worse disagreements than this evening's.

Helen watched Belle walk to her bedroom, her smile fading. She loved Belle, and would never forget how Belle had cared for them after Philip's death in spite of the fact that she and James had been as arrogant and self-righteous as they had encouraged Walter to become.

Philip's death had changed them both, brought them closer to reality, made them better people, she hoped. So perhaps Binnie had also changed – having a child was almost as thought-provoking as losing one.

Belle lay in the high bed with Connie, her headache easing as she held her daughter, watching the moonlight on the carpet, seeing the reflection of the room in the tall mirror. She was so weary, she was almost beyond sleep and already she could barely remember Helen's words. Would she become as suspicious when she was old? Surely not, but she hoped she was half as wonderful.

As Easter approached Belle sat at the kitchen table reading Helen's letter.

> My dearest Belle,
>   We might be closing in on Binnie. At the Longdale/Rempton Whist Drive, Mrs Winters, who lives near the pit, remembers her son saying something about a seaman. He'd met him in a public house in Newcastle, or rather, had a fight with him, and then, weeks later, had seen him in a cart heading into Rempton. It could have been the August Bank Holiday when Binnie left.
>   The Winters boy took off to the war and was killed before he could be returned to the pit. She's trying to think of the seaman's name. It's the only lead so far. I'll keep trying.
>   Here, there is still ice on the water-butt in the

*morning but it is a joy to see the spring sunshine,
and the snowdrops. Have you and Connie made
plans for your little garden yet? I ask you this
because Boy has just told me that Connie is chased
each day by a gang, on her way home from school.*

*She feels you have too much to do, and to worry
about, and it is their 'secret'. I know you would
wish to be told. Get that garden dug, Belle, sow
your grass, your soot-defeating flowers. Give her a
cause!*

*I will write again as soon as I have any news.
Your devoted friend,
Helen.*

Belle looked out of the kitchen window. Connie was in
the yard, hanging out the doll's clothes she had washed,
standing on her toes to reach the line Belle had strung.
The rotting wood was piled into a heap but had not been
burned. Belle pressed her fingers to her mouth.

She hurried into the yard, forcing herself not to take
her daughter in her arms, forcing her voice to sound
calm, natural. 'It's high time we planned this garden,
you know. Shall we turn it into a copy of the vicarage
wing?'

Water was running down Connie's arm as she pegged
the last skirt. She looked up, surprise and delight on her
face. Water flew as she shook her hands. 'Oh Mam,
yes, but aren't you too busy?'

Belle squeezed water from the clothes as they hung,
dripping. 'I'll wring your clothes for you next time too,
Connie, and remember, my darling, I'm never too busy
for you, never. If I don't hear you the first time, just poke
me.' She hugged her daughter. 'I'm never too busy, do
you hear, madam?'

'You're hurting, Mam.'

Belle laughed. 'I love you, Connie Symmonds.'

They walked into the house together. 'Go and cover
Betsy, it's none too warm. Then, I think it's about time

we made toffee apples, young lady.'

As Connie bent over the pram and kissed the doll that Helen Driscoll had given her for Christmas Belle watched. Why hadn't she been the one to notice that her child was still too often alone, how could she be so stupid?

She hurried now, finding pans, sugar, butter. 'Sticks, we need sticks.'

Connie pulled out the kitchen table drawer. 'Can we use these wooden skewers?'

'Indeed we can, they're ideal.' Belle tied her apron, throwing one to Connie, dragging more out of the drawer. 'Fetch ten apples from the store.'

'Ten, are we giving some to the men too?'

'No, to the gang out there. It's time you all got to know one another.'

Fear drenched Connie. She dropped the skewers onto the table. 'They won't want to, Mam,' she said quietly. 'They're – well, they've got themselves, that's all they need.'

Belle lined up the wooden skewers and counted them. 'Just one more, Connie. Try the scullery cupboard.'

'Mam,' Connie shouted. 'Don't ask them. They won't want to.'

Belle looked at her daughter. 'How do you know?'

'I just do.'

'Philip Driscoll had difficulties in the village at first, did you know that? I think it's time we put an end to your bad times.' Belle was putting more coal onto the fire, riddling it.

'But they don't like me.'

'But they've never met you properly, have they?'

Belle waited.

'They don't like my clean shoes. Theirs are dirty, they have cardboard in them because of the holes and sometimes they don't wear shoes at all in the alley. They don't like my nice dresses. Theirs are old.' Connie's voice broke.

44

Belle wanted to pick her up and carry her away from here, from the gang, back to the fields and beck of Rempton, but all she could do was hold her, as she did now. Then she said, 'Put on that old apron of mine. I'll turn it up.' Belle rummaged for her needle and thread. 'Stand still. Then go upstairs and put on the oldest dress you have, and the boots with the broken laces. I know it seems like cheating, but believe me, darling, money is getting tighter so it soon won't be.'

Connie looked at her mother as she knelt, sewed, then told her to turn a little. 'They've chased me, they've thrown stones but I suppose it's because they don't understand us.' Connie paused. 'Don't tell them I've told you.'

Belle finished, broke the thread, replaced the needle, then, when she could trust her voice she spoke. 'I won't tell them, but I really do think we must stop this particular war breaking out. Now, go and change.'

As Belle walked down the garden she could hear the children. She opened the gate; the hinge grated. She walked towards them. They stopped their marbles; their hands were red from the chill, their eyes were wary.

Belle smiled. 'Come on, we're making toffee apples. I thought you'd like to join in.'

The older girl stood up, her face suspicious. 'Can we eat them when we've made them, missus?'

'Well, of course, Sadie, now come on in.'

She walked back. They didn't come. She called, 'Well, come on.'

There was a pause, the sound of lowered voices, then they emerged and followed her into the heat of the kitchen. They looked at the table, at Connie, at the fire. 'We don't have that much coal on our fire,' a young red-haired girl said. Connie stiffened.

'I've just put more coal on it, Susan, because we need to make the toffee. It is Susan, isn't it?' Belle asked. 'And we need to make people cups of tea, when they come to tell us their sad stories. We need to make calves-foot jelly to take to people who are ill. I made some for your grandmother, Sadie, don't you remember, and for your cousin, Susan? It's our job, just as it's your parents' to look after you. Now, come along, who's going to measure out the sugar? But everyone, first wash your hands – you too, Connie.'

No-one moved. The gang looked at Sadie. She looked at Connie for a long moment, then said, 'You'd better show us where, then.'

By twelve the toffee was made and one by one, the children dipped the apples into the pan, turning them this way and that, their hands becoming sticky in spite of the sticks. They dipped them into the bowl of water to set hard.

'Let's leave them on the rack for a moment.' Belle sat down, licked her fingers, and watched the children do the same, laughing along with them. 'Go on, clean out the bowl, we'll have to wash it all up soon.'

Connie groaned. 'Oh Mam, can't you?'

The others looked at Belle until she nodded, then they laughed again and bent over the pan. It was going to be fine, Belle thought. At least this problem was going to be solved.

But then the door to the passage opened and Walter came in, black-suited, his white collar stark. He frowned. Belle moved quickly, holding up a toffee apple. 'Look, Walter, we've been busy this morning.'

The children fell silent. Walter looked at it, then her, then said, 'For heaven's sake, Belle, you shouldn't be in here, you should be in the hall. It will soon be time to dish out the soup. What are you thinking of?'

Belle smiled at the children, though her shoulders had tightened at the tone of his voice. The children did not smile back. Connie paled.

'Walter, I'm busy. Making toffee apples is an extremely important business, isn't it, children? And right now we have a pan to wash.' She raised her eyebrows at them and Sadie looked from her to Walter.

When Walter spoke his voice was sharp. 'Don't be so

flippant and absurd. Now off you go, you children. Go on, off.' He waved his hands at them.

Belle was stunned, then started forward. 'Walter! Children!'

But it was too late. They had run out, tearing off their aprons, throwing them in the yard, slamming the gate. 'Bloody old penguin,' they shouted.

Connie's eyes were full of hate as she watched Walter leave the room. Belle saw, threw down the apple and rushed after him, forcing him to stop.

'How dare you? Did you see your daughter's face? Did you? How is she going to face them? Are you insane or just cruel? Oh Walter, how could you?'

He wrenched away, brushing at his suit. 'You have made my suit sticky.' There was distaste on his face. 'I have a man out there sobbing. He keeps hearing his brother out in a shell hole taking three days to die. I have to get back and the men need their soup, which it is your job to provide. Then I have to go out to see the Bishop about the German exchange. I do not have time for toffee apples.'

Belle's distress grew. 'We've a daughter who's been forced to live here. We should be busy looking after her, making plans for her as well. Forget the men for a moment, and your never-ending plans. Can't you see what's happening? You don't deserve your daughter, and neither do I.'

Connie stood in the doorway and looked across the yard. She had taken the toffee apples out to the alley and just left them on a plate. The plate had been thrown over the wall. It broke on the old lavatory. The toffee apples had gone.

'I hate you, Da, I hate you,' she hissed.

*   *   *

47

On Connie's birthday in June, Mrs Driscoll sent doll's clothes for Betsy, and a letter for Belle.

> *'Try the name of Rogers,'* she wrote. *'Mrs Winters thinks it was Ted Rogers who collected Binnie. And I hope Connie has the strength to fight for acceptance, because, as you say, she will have to. Life isn't fair, my dear, you are so right. I'm glad the grass is growing, try ferns in the shady areas.'*

On Saturday of that week Walter and Belle walked through the workhouse gates where Binnie Rogers was registered. The gates were huge, the drive was gravelled. The windows of the dark, grey building were like dead eyes.

They said nothing to one another as they entered. What could they say? They both knew that when a mother entered the Institution her children were sent to the Cottage Home. They knew that the mother could only visit once a month. They knew that the mother wasn't free to leave the workhouse until the child was old enough to work for itself. They knew that they had condemned Binnie to this. What could they possibly talk to one another about? What could they say to Binnie?

Belle stood dry-mouthed as Walter talked to the supervisor, reminding her of his earlier meeting with her. 'It's visiting time anyway, come in here.' The woman's voice was crisp, cold. 'I'll get her. She knows you're coming.'

The room was large. There were tables, chairs, people sitting. They sat next to one man, one woman. Belle looked away from the raw misery she saw on their faces. 'Is Binnie's husband in the men's section too, do you think? Does he also come visiting? Oh Walter.'

Walter was silent. He must look at his hands, not around the room at the girl begging her parents to take her away, or the man clinging to his wife's hand. He must not look at anything, because if he did he would know that Binnie could never forgive him, and give him his peace.

The supervisor entered. Binnie walked behind. She was pale and thin, her hands were red and rough, her eyes were heavy with tiredness. Belle clenched her hands. 'I want to die.'

Binnie stopped; the supervisor left, her keys jangling. Binnie sat down and placed her hands on her lap. The veins were swollen, the skin of her wrists chapped.

Belle said, 'We've been searching for a long time, Binnie. We must get you out of here. We know you didn't lie. Archie confessed, he wanted Walter to find you. We feel so ashamed of our actions – where is Mr Rogers? Where is your child?'

Walter spoke now. 'Forgive me, please forgive me.'

Binnie just looked at them, her eyes heavy-lidded. Belle reached across and touched those rough hands. 'Please will you let us help, Binnie? Not only do we owe it to you, but we want to.'

Walter was shaking; his whole body was moving and now Belle put her hand on his arm, and looked at Binnie, waiting for an answer, trying to read her face, but she could not.

4

Belle wiped down the cooker in the old curate's flat at the top of the house and called through to the bedroom. 'Open the window, Connie, there's a good girl, and check that we've enough pillowcases.'

She put the pans in the cupboard. 'Oh, what else?' She rushed into the small sitting-room and polished the brass fender. 'Quick, your father will be bringing them soon.'

She couldn't get the sight of the workhouse out of her mind, or the smell of it. She opened the window, looking out over the roofs. At least here it was light. Oh, poor Binnie. It had seemed an age before Binnie had spoken, and then her words had come out slowly, haltingly, as though she was unused to speech.

'I've got a girl, she's called Dora. I married a seaman. He was kind, the only one who was kind. He died, you know. I tried to look after meself and the bairn, mind. I tried so hard but I couldn't, we was starving. I had to come in here, what else could I do? I work in the laundry. The poor bairn doesn't know what the hell's going on. Doesn't know that Rogers wasn't her father either.'

Her voice had risen then and Walter had reached out. 'Forgive me.'

Belle had wanted to silence him. Forgiveness seemed trivial in this place. For heaven's sake, all they had thought about these past months was finding this poor girl, and taking from her something they wanted. It wasn't enough, not nearly enough.

She had said, 'Binnie, we run a mission in Newcastle for men who have been scarred by the war. We are trying to give them a bit of peace to sort themselves out, then we try to find them jobs. We need help, Binnie. The men do what they can, it makes them feel better. But we need an assistant.'

There was a question in Walter's eyes. Belle ignored him. Did he think they could just walk away from here, once Binnie had said the magic words, 'I forgive you.'? But he couldn't think, not with this darkness; she knew that. She must think for both of them.

'We can offer you that job. There is a flat at the top of the house and there will be wages of course, the usual ones.' She put up her hand as Walter began to speak. 'Or we can help you to find a job elsewhere, perhaps as a housekeeper.'

Walter squeezed her hand, and smiled, but Belle kept her eyes on Binnie because this girl must leave this place.

Binnie spoke at last. 'I'll come with you please. I need people I know, people who care. It's been so hard. I love me bairn, you see. I'd do anything for her. She's like Archie, she's got grey eyes like his.'

Walter started. 'His eyes were blue.'

Binnie's chin came up, her voice was harsh. 'No, not when he kissed me.'

Walter flushed, his grip tightening on Belle's hand. 'Of course, I didn't mean I didn't believe you. We should never have doubted you all those years ago.' He didn't want to think of Archie's body on this woman, or the mud he had shovelled onto his face. He should tell Binnie that, he should confess. It would help, it would lighten the darkness.

Belle said, 'I'm glad you are coming. Now, I'm going back to the mission to make sure the flat is aired and ready. Walter will go with you to fetch Dora. That's all we need to do.'

'No,' Walter said. 'I need to know if you forgive me?'

Again Belle wanted to plead with him for silence but Binnie said, 'Yes, I forgive you. You weren't to know he was lying. You wouldn't expect it of him, but the whole village would expect it of me. They've always hated me since I did wrong years ago. They can't believe that a child can do something and change, can they?' Binnie looked at them, and all Walter heard was 'I forgive you.'

But Belle heard everything and said, 'They know they've made a mistake, they are all sorry.' She paused. 'Would you rather go to the village?'

Binnie shook her head. 'Oh no, I must come to you. I couldn't go anywhere else now that you've found me.'

Belle heard Connie say now, 'Come on, Mam, we'd better put some tea on. I've put the doll you bought Dora on her bed.'

They closed the door to the flat.

'Will Binnie mind working here?' Connie asked.

'No, she chose to. You see, I didn't want her to think we were offering her charity; it often offends.'

'Where will we find the money?'

'Oh Connie, you must let me worry about that. There should be enough from the mission funds and we do desperately need staff.'

Connie was leading the way down the stairs, then past bedroom after empty bedroom. She stopped and pointed to one. 'I hate it on this floor, it's so dark and dreary. There are probably ghosts in there.'

Belle laughed. 'Get along with you. Come and have a look, there are just cobwebs.' She opened the door. Motes danced in the light from the window, and there were cobwebs, and a butterfly trapped behind the window.

'Where do they come from?' Belle murmured, pushing open the window, letting it escape.

'Where does Binnie come from?' Connie asked as they looked at the sky.

'Our village. She met a man, had a baby and the man died. She had nowhere to live.' Belle leaned her head against the window.

'So was she living on the street?'

'No, in a place called the workhouse. It's where people go when they have nowhere else. Their children have to go to a home; they can't live with their mothers, their mothers can't live with their fathers. It's all very wrong, very sad.'

She closed the window, and they said nothing more. They hurried past the other six bedrooms, and then down the stairs to the next level where they slept.

'There must be lots of other mothers and babies,' Connie said.

Belle nodded; she had just been thinking the same with dismay.

Connie held her mother's hand. 'We have lots of empty bedrooms.'

Belle had been thinking the same, and now she smiled.

Connie said, 'It'll be grand to have Dora, but I loved it when Boy was a baby, and I could bath him. We could look after the babies together, Mam, you and I. It might make us laugh again.' Connie leaned against the landing wall, one foot on the other, trying to wear her shoes down, as she was always doing.

Belle leaned on the opposite wall. Could they afford it? She saw the eagerness on Connie's face, the anxiety. She thought of the workhouse, the tears of the girl sitting on the next table whose visitor had been the married father of her child. A child she only saw once a month.

She grinned at her daughter. 'Yes, you're right, it would bring laughter and joy and somehow I'll raise the money. It would wipe out the past. We could look ourselves in the eye again.'

Connie frowned. 'What do you mean?'

'Nothing, my darling. Just don't say anything to Da until I give you the nod. Until then it's our secret. It might just be too much for your father; we'll ask Dr Scott's advice.'

Connie ran on ahead. 'I won't say anything, but talk to the doctor soon.'

Belle called after her, 'But remember, although you will have Dora, and some babies, you still need to make friends of the girls in the gang. They're the only ones of your age around here. We must sort that out too.'

Connie ran down the stairs. She didn't need friends now and she wanted to shout it out loud.

Binnie closed the door to the flat, looking at Dora as she stood in the centre of the room, holding the doll she had found on her bed.

'But Mam, it's not as big as Connie's. That's not fair.'

Binnie caught her by the arm and slapped her face. 'That's enough, you silly little cow. When they give you something you smile, you simper, you kiss their bliddy feet if you have to, got that?'

Dora rubbed her cheek, flinching as her mother lifted her hand again.

Binnie hissed, 'Now, you just listen to me. As far as that lot downstairs are concerned, we were living in a poky little room, no bigger than that hole there.' She pointed to the kitchen. 'We've not had anything, not for years. I don't want them to know we was turfed out of that bugger's house.'

'Me da's, you mean?'

'Yes, your da's, but they think you're someone else's, but that needn't concern you. You just remember to keep them sweet. Now get to bed.'

She looked at the cupboards, full of pans and crockery. She lit the gas cooker, put the kettle on, took a Woodbine out of her pocket. Well, well, that bloody old fool Archie. She'd always wondered if he'd realize he'd been too drunk on the beer she'd given him to get his leg over. She dragged on the cigarette, then went through to Dora and said again, 'You just remember the story, mind – your da is supposed to have died, not thrown us out. Bloody good job he's gone down to Southampton or he could blow the lot.'

'Yes, Mam.'

Binnie dragged at her cigarette again, tasting the nicotine. 'He was a stupid bugger anyway.' How was she to know he'd come home early and catch that Dutchman with his pants down. She grinned at Dora. 'We're out of the workhouse anyway. Thank God I was looking so bloody awful when that Belle and Walter came. Never thought I'd bless a bout of bliddy influenza. Now get to sleep.'

'Yes, Mam.'

Binnie made herself tea, poured it into a mug, then into a saucer, blowing on it, slurping it.

Strange to be back here with the bloody vicar. Better remember Archie's eyes were blue. Thank God Dora's were too, but there was no doubt about her being Ted's; it was after that time she'd met him in the pub.

She looked round. Not as nice as Rogers' place but then she could milk it here. Lots of stores in that kitchen to sneak out and sell off. Bound to be money lying around. She'd have to be careful though.

She sat down on the sofa, putting her feet on the table, shoving off the lace coasters. Oh yes, my fine vicar, there'll be a lot of pickings here, and you're not bad youself; nice body if you put a bit of flesh on it, but a daft mind. All that rubbish about earth on Archie's face. Who the hell cares when they're dead?

And what about all that tripe about forgiveness? Lots of scope there; she'd have to keep all that on the boil. She nodded. She'd work on him and who knows – why stick at the flat when there's the whole bloody house here, and a man too – one who thinks he owes you the earth.

Belle brought cocoa up to the bedroom and eased into bed. 'Are you feeling better now that we have found Binnie?'

He leaned back against the headboard. 'I can still hear her words, "I forgive you." And yes, I feel so much better. You were right to bring her back here, Belle.'

'Have the sounds faded?'

He nodded. 'Yes, a little, but only a little.'

Belle bit back her disappointment. 'It will take time,' she soothed, 'but I promise you, you will improve. Shall I take your cup?'

As she reached across, her hand brushed his. He flinched. She said desperately, 'I'm sorry, I was just reaching for your cup. But Walter, why can't you bear me near you – I'm your wife, I want to help you.'

He stared at her. 'Then help by doing something worthy, not by demanding what I cannot give.' He lay down and pulled the sheet up. 'I don't want to talk about this. We are here to work and rebuild our lives. We have found Binnie. It has made me stronger, I'm sure of it, and now I'll be more able to concentrate on the men.'

Belle stared at his rigid body, then at his cup, then round the room that was dark and gloomy. The oil lamp lit up the samplers she had worked on when she was first married and Walter was kind, humane, selfless.

She gazed at the contours of his body beneath the blankets. This was the man that had kissed her lingeringly at their wedding reception, ignoring totally the tuts of amazement. It was only when they had to draw breath that he threw back his head, hugged her to him, and laughed, drawing everyone into their happiness. Then he had kissed her again and danced with her until it seemed they had blended one into the other.

This was the man who had continued to kiss and laugh and dance with her, even when she was pregnant with Connie. She remembered how he would leap to his feet when they sat in the garden on warm summer evenings, bowing before her, taking her hand, singing the music, whirling her across the grass, telling her of his plans to help the community once he had his own parish, telling her of his love, his joy, his happiness.

This was the man who had invited all the tramps into their kitchen to eat, and visited the poor and unloved even on Christmas Day, coaxing her along, building up her confidence, telling her that this was *their* job, they were a team.

This was the man who had chased her through the house until feathers floated. She smiled at the memory, at the echoes of joy. One day that man would return – must return.

And now determination set in, and impatience, and beneath it all, anger at the self-absorbed prig she shared her life with. He seemed to see Binnie's rescue only in relation to his well-being. This man must go; the old Walter must return. She could not wait to talk to Dr Scott; she must speak now, while the memories were with her, giving her impetus. But she must choose her words carefully, oh so carefully.

'Walter, you are quite right, we must put ourselves aside and think of others, and I have an idea that might help you to feel even more that you are not only repairing the past, but building for the future. Have you thought that there are other Binnies around, being thrown from their homes, only to be separated from their child when it is born? We've found Binnie, we've helped her to escape; we could do something for these other women.'

Walter stirred, then sat up. 'Yes, you're right. We can have a collection I suppose.'

Belle took a deep breath and said quietly, 'No, that's too easy. We need to *do* something, and we can. We have the room. We need to take these girls in, make sure they can stay with their children then help to place them in jobs, as you are placing your men.'

Walter turned and looked at her in amazement. 'But Belle, don't be absurd, we're only interested in victims. That is what my men are. Girls who become pregnant are not.'

Belle looked again at the sampler, hearing in him the Walter who had been in the pulpit. Her voice was cold as she said, 'As I've said before, years before if you remember, babies are not produced out of an immaculate conception. And don't shake me this time, Walter.'

He flushed, looked away. 'I would never touch you, Belle.'

She wanted to laugh. Did he think she didn't know that? But perhaps after all, a shake would be preferable to the nothingness of their personal lives, but then she felt ashamed again. For heaven's sake, she should have been more patient and remembered this man was ill. She shouldn't be discussing this tonight, before she had spoken to Dr Scott. Was she mad? She drew a deep breath and tried to speak, but he continued.

'And what about my Germans? I was going to put them on that floor when they came. No, it won't do. We've done enough. I already feel better, I've told you.'

'Sandy said they could go in the attic dormitories over the hall, and this is about more than your redemption.' Her voice was sharp again and this time she had made no effort to restrain herself, for heaven's sake not even depression gave any person the right to such selfishness.

Walter stared at her, then lay on his side, dragging the sheet up. His voice was muffled as he said, 'Oh, it's obviously all decided so why did you even bother to ask me?'

Belle wrenched down the sheet. 'Don't you turn your back on me, Walter. The girls might not be victims in your eyes but what about the babies?' She stormed from the bed, over to his side. 'Don't you dare close your eyes. Think of those babies, think of those empty bedrooms, think of the example you are setting Connie.'

Walter sat up again. 'All right, so there are empty bedrooms if the Germans use the dormitories, but how will you fund it? It's bad enough trying to raise the money for the Germans.'

He was shouting and Belle had not heard his voice raised in anger since 1914 and she suddenly smiled, held his face, kissed his forehead, because for once there was something more than agony or emptiness in this man. It was what Dr Scott said might one day happen. 'He has to come alive,' he had said. 'He has to show some emotion, it doesn't matter what.'

This time she didn't mind when he pulled away from her. 'If I raise the money, and get church approval, will you agree to me going ahead?' she persisted.

Walter still felt the warmth of her hands on his cheeks. God, he was tired, there was so much to do tomorrow and suddenly the anger drained out of him.

He drew his knees up, hugged them, looked at her. 'Yes I'll agree, but you must also get approval from the neighbours.'

She smiled and touched his cheek. 'Thank you, my darling.'

She returned to her side of the bed, holding the memory of that brief glimpse of feeling, even if it had been rage, because it might be the start of Walter's return journey. She would talk to Dr Scott, and if he agreed she would go forward with the women and the babies. For everyone's sake.

Walter lay in the dark breathing deeply and gradually he realized that the sounds in his head had finally stopped. Binnie had helped him to climb further out of the darkness and soon he would have his Germans in the rooms above. They would help him also towards the light.

He heard Belle twisting and turning. He knew she would never raise the finance, and if she did, the neighbours would never agree. Didn't she see that there was no room in their lives for her ideas? There was so much to do for the men first.

It was only when dawn came that he heard the men, laughing, joking, their faces young and fresh, the sun on their hair, their skin, in their eyes, in Archie's blue eyes. How could blue eyes become grey? What did it matter? They were back, and he despaired. But then he lay still, because they were not as loud as before. Thank God they were not as loud. How could he ever thank Binnie?

*   *   *

59

Connie looked out of her window, across the darkness of the city. She picked out Sadie's house, and Susan's, Betty's, Flo's. Tomorrow she would be able to show Dora the terrace they were making, the flower-beds they had dug. Dora could put her doll in the pram, wheel her up and down the path and when the babies came, they could help look after them.

She looked again at Sadie's house. But the gang were still out there.

5

Belle settled in the garden chair she had placed on the new terrace, sighing with contentment. It had been worth heaving the rubble and slabs until she could no longer count her blisters. She shielded her notepad from the September sun and heard Connie laugh as Dora pushed the pram along the clinker path towards the tent they had made out of a sheet. All the effort had been worthwhile. The garden was perfect, though the alyssum hadn't liked the soot in the air and hadn't thrived.

Belle studied her list again. The men had helped repaint the bedrooms and bathroom, and set up a kitchen, and at last the finance was assured. The church authorities had this morning agreed to partial funding for the unmarried mothers, and the Driscolls insisted on making up the difference.

She chewed her pencil. She had caught Dr Scott as he was leaving the mission last week and invited him for tea on the terrace. He had laughed when he saw the grass, the paving stones, the lavender. 'So, you've brought the country to Newcastle. What a determined woman you are, Mrs Symmonds.'

'I'm thinking of bringing pregnant girls to the vicarage too,' she'd said, pouring him tea in the silence that fell. 'But only if you agree that it would help Walter.'

The silence had continued until she had feared he would object, but he did not. He had agreed on the condition that she accepted his services free, feeling that the area, and Walter, both needed the project. 'It might break the hold of the war,' he'd said.

It was only the neighbours who still pursed their lips.

What had Mrs Gribble said? Oh yes, 'Who knows what it will encourage? Why should girls, who are no better than they ought to be, have help?' Would she have been more supportive if they had kept her on to clean the vicarage? Probably not, Belle thought, after all, some people just loved to lead a charge of angry women, and Mrs Gribble was one of them. Perhaps Belle should talk to her of the dangers of idle hands. She grimaced. Perhaps not.

She heard Sandy cough. He stood in the doorway, his hands on his hips, his lips tight.

'That Binnie's not in the kitchen again, Belle. She's always late. The soup should be ready, and it isn't.'

Belle tucked her notebook in her pocket. 'I'll come.'

'But Belle, you're paying her to do the job and you've already been at it since dawn. I don't know why you put up with it. Anyway, there's something about her.' Sandy stepped out into the sun, lowering his voice, 'She's not just lazy; she don't look at you straight.'

Belle turned her pencil over and over. 'Would you, if you'd been in the workhouse?'

'What's the war, if it's not like the workhouse? No choice, no dignity, and it hasn't stopped me working me guts out. And look at you, bonny lass. Life's no picnic for you.'

She tossed the pencil onto the table and squeezed his arm, not wanting to think of her life. 'I'll keep an eye on her, and, Sandy, please come and tell me earlier another time. You've done the soup, haven't you?'

Sandy nodded.

'Well, you mustn't do that again. Call me immediately and I'll deal with it there and then. She seems to be permanently tired. I fear she might be depressed, though the doctor doesn't seem to think so.'

Sandy grumbled, 'Just needs a boot behind her.'

'I'll pretend I didn't hear that, Sandy,' Belle said, looking across at the children, chuckling, because she too, wanted to kick Binnie up the backside. She was so slow, so tardy, and always *there* – asking Walter to teach her

62

to read, to play chess, to explain the Bible. She shook her head. No, she mustn't resent Binnie; she must just think of the good it might be doing Walter, and after all, they both had a great deal to make up to the woman.

She and Sandy watched the girls come out of the tent, and run over to the pram. Connie picked up Betsy, hugging her whilst Dora watched, not taking out her own doll.

Sandy said, 'D'you remember how Dora cried when you gave her that doll. She wanted a big one like Connie. She's from the same mould as her mother.'

'Sandy,' Belle said sharply, 'now come on. She understood when I told her that one like Betsy would be just too big for a six-year-old.'

Sandy grimaced. 'She still said, "Will you get me a big one when I'm nine?" ' He mimicked her voice. 'Trouble is, she wants what other kids have got.'

Belle looked at him. Where had she heard those words before? She tried to think, but just then Walter approached saying, 'Belle, I spoke to Mrs Gribble after communion this morning. She's still not happy about you taking in those girls. I haven't spoken to one of the near neighbours who is.'

She crossed her arms, stifling her irritation. 'Perhaps you could try to—' she began but then they heard a cry. She turned. Connie was putting her hands to her mouth while her doll lay broken on the bricks which lined the path. Belle ran, with Sandy and Walter close behind.

Sandy breathed, 'Dora damn near threw that doll. I saw it with me own eyes.'

Dora was staring at them, backing away. 'I thought Connie had the doll. It was in me hand, and then I thought it were in hers.' She began to cry but there were no tears from Connie who was pale and rigid as she stared at the doll – its head split open to reveal eyes that stared up from their wires.

Belle hugged her. 'What happened?'

Connie said nothing for a moment, then crouched

down to touch Betsy. 'I dropped her, Mam, it was my fault. Dora handed her back to me, but I just didn't hold her safe enough.'

Dora was still wailing and Belle wanted to scream at her to be quiet. She looked at Walter and asked him to go to Dora but sweat was beading his forehead and he was staring at the doll. She asked, 'Walter, are you all right?'

He turned and walked away as though he was an old man.

'Walter,' Belle called, but Sandy shook his head.

'Let him go.' Impassively he wiped Dora's face with his handkerchief.

Walter walked to his study. Alec Green's head had looked like that when he had found him near the ruined Cloth Hall at Ypres after he'd left him with the chalice, the hymn books, the harmonium – the bloody harmonium which was untouched.

In the flat Binnie bent down until her face was against her daughter's. 'Don't you ever show your hand like that again. I told you you'd have all the dolls you want one day but if you go on like this we'll be out of here and it'll ruin me plans.'

She slapped Dora hard on her back, again and again, where it wouldn't show. 'That's to remind you to keep your mouth shut and your bliddy manners up front. Now go and say sorry to that spoilt brat, and stop that noise.'

In the afternoon Connie walked down the path. She stopped where Dora had thrown Betsy, because that really was what she had done. She was angry, but she shouldn't be, not with a girl who had been in a workhouse.

She heard the children out in the alley. Sadie gobbing the others. She looked through the knot-hole. She'd have to run home from school again next week because of them, because of her Da who'd brought them here, and who was useless, who went white and walked away from

64

a broken doll and then cried behind his locked study door, and wouldn't open it, though her mam begged him.

The anger deepened.

Connie opened the gate. She walked to Sadie and the gang. They stopped their marbles match and watched her.

'You broke my mother's plate when you threw it over the wall,' Connie shouted, pouring out her anger. 'I hate you, I'm glad I'm not the same as you and don't you bliddy dare chase me any more.'

'We'll chase you if we want to, bliddy little penguin swank, and we'll throw more than plates over the wall into that bliddy field you've made. We'll come in one night and pull up all the flowers, and I'm glad that Dora smashed your doll. Should have seen your Da's face. White face, white face, matched his bloody collar! We see everything you do.' Sadie pointed to the knot-hole.

'So that's why your nose is so bliddy long, is it?' Connie shouted. 'I'll grab it next time and stuff dirt up it, then you'll die and good riddance. You're just a silly cow.' Connie was dragging up all the words they'd called her; they sounded good in her mouth – strong.

Suddenly Sadie was on her, tearing her hair, kicking her, and Connie was glad and pushed, pulled, punched and swore, 'You bliddy bitch.'

The breath rasped in her throat and she grabbed Sadie's dress, holding her, pushing her onto the ground, then Sadie was on her, punching her chest. She threw her off, wanting to smash her into the ground, hitting her again and again.

Then she felt a hand on her shoulder, a big cold hand. It pulled her, lifting her from Sadie. Sadie was being dragged up too – her nose was bleeding and Connie was glad. She tried to push off the hand so that she could reach Sadie again.

'What on earth is going on?' It was Walter and his voice was louder than she had ever heard it. 'Who started this disgraceful exhibition?'

Sadie hung her head, squirming beneath his grip. Connie stood quite still, her breathing shallow, her anger gone, leaving a strange tiredness. She looked at her hands; they were covered in blood from Sadie's nose. Was it snot too? She wanted to be sick.

Her father shook her. She felt the bile rise. He turned to Sadie. 'I'll take you back to your mother, young lady, and warn her to keep you away from the back of our property. Look at you, you're filthy from the dirt you've all been kneeling in. Have you no decency, and after we allowed you to make toffee apples too?'

Connie felt her anger come again and wanted to be sick all over his black suit to make him shut his silly mouth. 'I hit her first. And I called her a silly cow. Just leave her alone, you stupid man.'

She was pleased at the shock on her father's face. He released Sadie, who ran back down the alley, picking up the gang before disappearing round the corner.

'You did what?' He put his hand up. 'No, don't say anything. Haven't you any thought for others, don't you know what I'm trying to do here? Isn't it hard enough to sort it all out without this? I need peace and quiet to think.'

He wanted to strike her, to push her against the wall as he had wanted to strike the Germans. But padres were men of peace, therefore they had no outlet for their pain and rage. The heat was in his face, his hands were throbbing. He saw her fair hair, her face smeared with blood and now he took himself in hand, as he had always done. 'Just get inside and wait for your mother to return.'

Belle came to her room, a wet flannel in her hand. She wiped the swollen eyes, the bloody lip and listened as Connie said, 'I called Sadie names, then she hit me, but I wanted her to, so I could hit her. That's why I told Da I did it first. But he shouted at them before I could even say that.'

'In that case I think you were right to take the blame.'

Her voice was calm. 'There will be no further punishment, my love. Black eyes are not a pretty sight.'

She wasn't calm, though, when she entered Walter's study and shouted at him for treading again on her daughter's hopes of ever becoming part of the children's world which haunted the alley. Walter said nothing because his anger was coming back, and he must not allow any feelings to surface or he would suffer as he had when the last of his men died.

'You haven't heard a word I've said,' Belle cried 'You are deeper inside yourself than ever.'

The next week Dr Scott called and asked Belle if she could take the first of her pregnant girls.

'I'm telling you now that this girl, Mary, is introverted and very quiet. I knew her mother, a nice woman, but she died and Mary has come to me for help, just today. I thought of you. I know you still have to convince your neighbours and Walter, but I need somewhere for her, if she is not to go to the workhouse. She's with my wife at the moment. Can you take her?'

'When is the baby due?'

'In six weeks.'

Belle smoothed her dress while she looked at Connie who was nodding. 'What can I say, but yes? The neighbours will just have to accept it.'

Dr Scott asked, 'And Walter?'

Belle looked at him. 'Just bring Mary tomorrow. Everything will be ready, Walter too. Perhaps all this has come at the right time.'

That night in bed, Belle told Walter – she didn't ask – then she turned on her side and pulled the sheet up, as he had so often done, and didn't think of her husband, his lost God, his darkness. Instead she thought of the new life there would soon be in this mausoleum of a house, and of Connie who would start her new term the next day, and of the feathers which had floated in the bedroom at Rempton.

*　　　*　　　*

Connie pulled Dora along the back alley out into the cobbled street. 'Come on, hurry up, we'll be late.' They wouldn't be, but she was frightened and looked for the gang at every corner as they crossed the tramlines, kicking aside the coal that had fallen from the carts as they jolted and rocked across the junctions. 'Come on, Dora.'

'Me mam said I should have new clothes on me first day at school.'

'That'd only make things worse. We've got to try and fit in, not stick out like sore thumbs. Anyway, my mam hasn't got that sort of money any more; we've got too many men coming into the hall and staying put. There aren't any jobs for them.'

She looked down the road to the docks, seeing the men leaning against the slimy walls, their hands deep in their pockets, hoping in vain for work. She turned right, then left beyond the second-hand shop, always listening for the shouts and jeers above the noise of the trams, the carts, the two cars that chugged past.

'Your hand's all wet,' Dora complained, pulling away.

Connie grabbed at her, hauling her along. 'Oh come on. It's hot, that's why.' But it wasn't the heat, it was fear. She began to run. If Sadie was waiting behind the co-op with a stone she might not hit them if they were going fast. But there were no stones; there was no gang.

She slowed. 'Sorry Dora, I forgot your legs aren't as long as mine. I just don't want to be late.'

The Infants School was at the head of the street, the Junior School next to it, its dark red bricks and tall windows seeming to suck the light from the street. Connie straightened Dora's hair, checking the ribbons on her plaits. 'You look really nice. Are you nervous?'

Connie looked over her shoulder as she spoke. Dora said, 'No, it'll be grand after the one near the workhouse.'

They walked on into the playground, heading for the lines that were already forming. She left Dora with the teacher who was ringing the bell, then ran into her own playground, towards her own lines.

Sadie was there, standing in line, looking at her, but not even sneering – how strange. Connie licked her dry lips. She must be waiting for home-time, saving it all up.

Connie looked across at Dora's school, then ran out of the playground into hers, heading for Dora's line. She shouted, 'Hurry up after school. Meet me at the gate. Run so we can get home in the crowd.'

On her return she was given thirty lines to write by the morning. 'I must not leave my line.'

At lunch-time she helped the teacher set up the art class. In the afternoon she painted carelessly. In history they learned about the Kaffirs of Africa, and Red Indians of North America but her breathing was quick and shallow because she knew that in fifteen minutes there were the streets and corners – and Sadie and the gang.

She watched the clock as the large hand jerked away the minutes. She watched Sadie who sat with her head resting on her hands, looking at Mrs Anderson, her eyes half-shut.

She heard the bell, saw Sadie move. 'You may leave, children,' Mrs Anderson said, putting down her chalk. Connie rushed for the door, not looking back.

'Be there, Dora, be there,' she chanted as she ran out of the gate, into the infants. Dora wasn't there. She didn't come until all the children had gone.

'What kept you?' Connie shouted, pulling her out of the playground, waiting, looking both ways. 'We can't hide in with the other kids now.'

'Why do we need to hide? And don't pull me.' Dora shrugged from her grasp.

The coast was clear. Connie took a deep breath. Dora mustn't know they might be chased; it would frighten her, it wasn't fair. 'Look, we might have to run. There's a game some of the older kids play. Just do as I tell you, right, pet?'

Connie tried not to hurry and she made herself listen

as Dora said, 'We had this story, it was about this elf, you know. He had nowt to eat, he was found by an owl who made clothes out of feathers.'

Connie nodded, watched, listened, crossing the street, ducking down Victoria Terrace to avoid the Co-op. 'But why were you so late?'

Dora skipped ahead. 'Me mam said to be nice to the teachers, they're the nobs, so I helped tidy up. Got this an' all.' She brought out a piece of yellow chalk.

Connie laughed. 'Well, old Silvers must like you to give you anything except a dirty look.'

Dora looked round at her and laughed. ''Course she does. Don't you go saying anything though, else all the kids'll want some.' Why tell Connie she'd nicked it?

Connie called her back now. 'Wait there, while I look.' She peered round the corner by the bookies. Men lounged against the wall. 'When I say run, we'll cross the road, and go down the back alley. Do what I say, whatever happens, and get in the house.' Connie checked the entrance to the back alley. She couldn't see Sadie. She gripped Dora's hand, taking a deep breath. 'Ready?' she asked. 'Run then, Dora.'

They took off, running past the men, then over the cobbles, down the alley. 'Come on, Dora,' Connie was pulling the girl. She reached their own gate. It was open. Belle stood there smiling but her eyes were anxious.

Connie stopped, her breath pounding in her chest, laughing, almost crying. She hugged Dora. 'You can run really fast, you're a clever girl. Go and show your mam the chalk.' Dora ran inside, and Connie said to Belle, 'We were having a game, that's all, just a game.'

Belle shut the gate, her hands felt stiff. 'I was a little worried because you were late.'

Connie walked down the garden. Why hadn't they been there? Was it because Dora had been with her or was it because she had fought them and they were frightened? Sadie hadn't looked frightened. She stopped by the old pram.

'I'm going to give this to Dora,' she told her mother.

'But why, you love that pram?'

'Because we weren't chased, and it was because she was there, or because I fought them, and I fought them because I was angry with her. She's the reason it's stopped, for now at least, and she ran ever so fast, Mam.' Connie paused, and kicked at the clinker.

Dr Scott brought Mary Brennan to the back door as Belle was drinking tea and checking Connie's lines. He called out as he came through, 'I wanted to show Mary your garden, to prove you were a giant of a woman who can move the country to this grime, and who can sort out every problem.'

Belle looked at him. But not my husband's, or not yet, she wanted to say. She didn't, but rose quickly and held out her hands to the girl. 'How pleased we are you've come, aren't we, Connie?'

Connie said, 'I've dusted your room and put chrysanthemums in the vase, and there's a cot in there too, and I can't wait for you to have the baby. You see I've bathed—'

Belle laughed, shooing Connie back to the table. 'Forgive her, she's so pleased. She's had to leave her special friend behind in the country and she used to bath him every night.' Whilst she talked she guided Mary to a chair. 'Come along, get the weight off those legs. Oh heavens how tired mine were when I was pregnant.' She nodded to Connie. 'It was one of the happiest times of my life.'

Dr Scott carried an old paper bag, from which clothes were spilling. Belle gestured to the sideboard. 'Put it there. We'll freshen the pot, and then sort everything out. We're celebrating.'

Dr Scott raised an eyebrow.

'Tell him, Connie,' Belle said, wrapping a tea towel round the handle of the kettle, before pouring water into the pot. She felt almost young again as she heard Connie tell the doctor how the gang had ignored her. 'They didn't chase me, just let me come home with Dora.'

Dr Scott ruffled her hair. 'That's the best news we've had in a long time, isn't it?'

Belle turned to Mary. 'You see, Connie is seen as different because she's the vicar's daughter and it's led to problems.'

'They've thrown stones, shouted at me, but not today.'

Mary paled and clutched her handbag. She whispered, 'Why do folk have to be such cruel beggars and hate any who're different?'

Dr Scott looked at Belle, who hurried across and put her arm round the girl. She was as fragile as her voice, and Belle was moved, because there had been almost as much pain in this girl's eyes as there was in Walter's.

'It's not as bad as Connie makes it sound. Don't let it upset you so – though when you're pregnant, things do, I know. I remember myself with Connie. But my dear, you must treat this as your home. We are your friends, your family, and we are here to help you. Now Connie, pour the tea.'

Connie poured for them, and they ate the biscuits Belle had made with some of the men during the afternoon.

They were soggy. Connie bent hers and laughed. She told Mary about Rempton, Boy, Daisy the cow, and while she imitated James Driscoll marching as a Special Constable in the war, Dr Scott motioned Belle to the scullery.

'Mary's overwrought, too sensitive. It's as though she's expecting a disaster at any minute. You can see how she overreacted with Connie. Try and get her to talk, Belle. Ask Walter to try as well. Remember to involve him, my dear. I'm certain it's what he needs. Now, Mary is also malnourished, and exhausted; she's been working far too hard in a laundry. You did say she could rest, didn't you? I don't want her doing any hard work.'

Belle touched his arm. 'Just enough to make her feel useful, and not a bit more.'

He walked back into the kitchen, picking up his hat.

Mary half-rose. Dr Scott said gently, 'Sit down, hinny. Finish your tea and relax. You're in good kind hands and no-one is going to hurt you.'

Mary looked down and said quietly, 'How can I thank you?'

'By looking after yourself. Lots of lightly cooked liver.'

Connie grimaced. 'Urgh.'

Dr Scott laughed. 'And you, young miss, make sure you go on keeping out of the way of that gang.'

Belle and Connie showed Mary the sitting-room and the small kitchen. 'But until we have other girls here you must feel as though you are part of the family, eat with us, sit with us. When others come I think you'd prefer to cook, shop, and be more independent. I thought I could guide you, teach you some child care, and after the birth we'll place you in a job you like, one that takes the child too.'

Mary stood at the doorway. 'But what if no-one wants a bairn, one who's a mite different?' She was looking at her hands.

Belle stood quite still. 'I moved the country to the town, so believe me, there will be no unwanted babies while I'm around.'

Mary tucked a strand of hair into her bun, straightened herself and smiled gently.

Belle said, 'Now, come into the hall. Sandy will be there. He is a very kind man and has suffered a great deal; he'll be a good friend to you, as he is to us all.'

Belle drew a deep breath before she opened the door into the hall. Would Walter be pleasant to this young, frightened woman? He must be. The noise of banging, talking and laughing greeted them. Belle nudged Mary into the room and pointed out the carpentry class at the bottom of the hall.

'We have a carpenter amongst us for now, so we're using him to teach the others. I believe they start with a "house-joint",' Belle raised her voice, 'isn't that right, Sandy? Come and meet Mary.'

Sandy tweaked Connie's nose, shook Mary's hand, his eyes staying on her face, his embarrassment at her swollen belly obvious to Belle. Was it to Mary?

'That's right, Belle. Come on, I'll take you down there. Keep away from the saws, though.' He led the way, talking to Connie until they reached the bench.

Belle interrupted him. 'Where is Walter?'

Sandy looked at the carpenter and then the man pummelling a punch-bag; anywhere but at her. His voice was hesitant as he said, 'He's gone to see the Bishop. He asked if you could do his evening shift.'

Belle closed her eyes for a moment. Walter knew that Mary was coming and not only was he absent, but he had made it impossible for her to spend the first evening with the poor girl. She said nothing for a moment, then forced her voice to relax, saying, 'All right, I'll be here for the evening meal.'

Sandy said, 'We could get Binnie.'

Belle shook her head. 'No, it's all right, she's done her shift, she was even on time again this morning, wasn't she? We don't want to rock the boat.'

Sandy rubbed his face, introducing Mary to the men playing cards, then saying quietly to Belle, 'Yes, she was on time. After all, it was Walter's shift, wasn't it?'

Belle looked at him, not understanding, then Connie called, 'Come over here, Mary, and tell George about the baby.' Connie turned to George, who was teaching another man to mend shoes. 'We're going to bath him when he's born. He hasn't got a da, you know. The postman has magicked him inside the wrong mother.'

Belle said quickly, 'We'll talk to George later. He's busy and I must get on with our supper. Don't worry, Sandy, I'll be back in time, but after I've had a little word in someone's ear.'

Mary peeled the potatoes while Belle helped Connie to clean the pram in the garden. As they worked she told Connie how babies were made, adding, 'Babies are a gift of love, but sometimes love dies, and the woman and the baby are left alone, and to talk of it, as you did to George, reminded Mary of the sadness.'

Connie looked at her, then finished straightening the bedding of the pram. 'Then I'm half of Da, am I?'

Belle nodded.

Connie said, 'I don't think he remembers that, do you?'

In the hall, Belle asked for a team of volunteers to help make the pies. She said to Sandy who was cleaning a cupboard, his face creased in concentration, 'The more skills they have the better and let's face it, none of them are going to make a living baking bendy biscuits, but they might cooking lunches.' They laughed together and she was glad she was busy because Walter still wasn't back.

Sandy set out the bowls, smiling and joking to the men as they gathered, then stepping back as Belle explained the procedure. George put in too much water. 'Bendy pastry too, eh?' Sandy said, laughing at Belle's face. There was flour in his moustache.

'Are you turning completely grey within the first few minutes of baking practice?' Belle muttered, then burst out laughing as he tried to brush the flour out, only adding more.

They cut up rhubarb and made crumble, then the men laid the tables as Belle pushed her hair back from her forehead and asked Sandy, 'When will you leave us? I can hardly bear the idea of it, but you must go when you're ready.'

He wiped the table, saying nothing for a moment, then turned to her, the laughter and fun gone from his hazel eyes, the lines round his mouth seeming deeper. He dropped the cloth onto the table. 'Do I need to go? Can I stay and help, just for me keep?'

Belle put her hands behind her and leaned back against the sink. 'But Walter said you had a wife, and two boys.'

Sandy rubbed his hands together, scratching at the

crumble, not looking at her. He swallowed and when he spoke his voice was unsteady. 'In a way I have but I was reported missing, believed killed, though all the time I was a prisoner. The missus set up with someone else and now the boys don't remember me, and she's got another bairn. So I can't go back. I want to stay.' Now he looked up at her and his look of distress and uncertainty contrasted sharply with the strength and power of his body.

Belle checked the vegetables, searching for composure. Was there no end to the sadness the war had left? 'I'll arrange it with Walter. We need you, and want you here so much, and Sandy,' she looked at him closely now, 'do what you can to ease the situation for the pregnant girls, will you? You know, with the men, the neighbours. They'll need your help too.'

They served and the men groaned at the pastry, and Matt, the carpenter, said his table could do better. 'Tomorrow night you can prove that,' Belle retorted, making a mental note to tell Walter that a new craft was well on the way.

After the dishes were washed, Belle took down the cocoa tin, prised off the lid and gasped. 'Sandy, how many people have we here at the moment? Are there a lot of one-nighters – there's hardly any left?'

Sandy looked over her shoulder. 'No, just them damn great mice again, or one anyway.'

'What do you mean? Oh Lord, we'll have to try and raise some more funds if I go on underestimating like this.' Belle spooned it out.

She looked again at the clock and finished the cocoa mugs, not wanting to understand Sandy, not wanting to voice her own suspicions. Binnie wouldn't do this to them, and it was only cocoa anyway for goodness sake – they were all tired and making mountains out of molehills. Yes, it was nonsense. She looked again at the clock, finished the cocoa mugs and thrust the tin back in the cupboard. 'I must hurry, Mary's in the kitchen, and Connie's waiting to be kissed good night.'

Connie was lying in the dark and Belle kissed her, holding her close, telling her she loved her, her da loved her, and pretty soon, Sadie might love her. They laughed. 'I don't feel so scared, Mam, even if they are waiting. I've had one day when it's been all right.'

Belle smiled at her. 'How is Mary? Did you have a nice talk to her?'

Connie kissed her mother and pulled the sheet up. 'No, she was in her sitting-room. Binnie sent her there, said Mary'd like some peace.'

Belle tucked in the bedclothes and hurried downstairs and into the girls' sitting-room where Mary sat in the dark and the cold. Belle chafed her hands. 'You silly girl, you should have lit the fire, and the gas mantel. Come along, into the warmth, I meant you to stay there. Whatever was Binnie thinking of?'

She opened the door into the kitchen and saw Walter bending over the newspaper with Binnie, his finger tracing the headlines, spelling out the words. Their heads were so close together that his white hair intermingled with her red.

Belle stood still, then spoke. 'Binnie,' her voice was sharp. 'How could you leave Mary in the sitting-room? I thought I made it perfectly clear that she was to remain with you until the other girls were here. Now perhaps you could make us some cocoa, then I think it is time you went to bed.'

Her voice was too loud, too sharp. She wanted to ask why her head was so close to her husband's, why the tin of cocoa was so low? But instead she smiled and led Mary to Walter. 'Mary, I'd like you to meet my husband. He's the man who is behind all the good works in this house. He started the men's side as a result of his experiences in the war, and then found he wanted to help women too, as a result – well, as a result of the war too. He's a wonderful man.'

She stared at Walter, daring him to be rude, to be cruel, begging him to respond, and all the time tension knotted her stomach. He stood up, motioned to the chair next to him where Binnie had been sitting. 'I'm glad you've come. Come and talk to me, tell me about yourself.' His smile was kind but his eyes were bleak when he looked at Belle.

Binnie slammed the door of her flat, shoving Connie's pram into the wall. Dora called for her to be careful.

'Stupid little bugger, how can you be pleased with their cast-offs? Bliddy insult. You deserve something new from them.'

She slumped into the chair. Bloody bitch of a woman, telling me to get that trollop some cocoa. Who'd she think she was giving orders? Well, soon she'd learn just who she wasn't. Binnie lit a Woodbine, thinking of Belle's face, knowing she must be more careful when she was with Walter, or she'd be rumbled. She'd even stop taking the cocoa for a week, and just cream off the shopping money. Jesmond was where they'd go. He could get a nice little parish there.

Belle lay in the bed, hearing Walter's breathing, feeling again the sharp stab of jealousy. She remembered the bleakness of his eyes when he had looked past Mary to her and lay on her side, and wept without noise or movement.

6

Belle looked anxiously at Mary as the girl worked on the clippie rug stretched across the frame Sandy had made. It was a Saturday in late November, her hands were puffy and the baby was overdue. Dr Scott had said he would call in later. 'Has she talked to anyone?' he'd asked.

But she hadn't, and was still so quiet. Even Walter had taken her to his study and tried to get her to talk, but only once.

'I've tried,' he'd said, 'that is enough.' Dr Scott had murmured, 'Patience,' when she'd told him.

Belle saw that Claire and Anne, the two girls who had joined her in October, were watching her. She smiled. 'Goodness me, Mary will burst soon. Keep an eye on her please, Claire. If there's a problem come and find me, or if not me, Sandy, or if not Sandy, Walter.' She laughed and the girls did too. 'I'm on late shift in the hall. I'll be in our kitchen if you need me.'

Mary looked up and smiled. 'That's grand, Belle.'

In the kitchen Binnie was slurping tea from the saucer and Belle said, 'I thought you were supposed to be in the hall kitchens?'

Binnie looked up. 'I was but I wanted to talk to you. I'm not managing, you see, on the money you give me. I need a rise.'

Belle gripped the back of the chair. It was the one Binnie had sat on every evening for the past month. The one that had been pulled close to Walter's. 'But you earn more than Sandy and he manages.'

'I have Dora to keep.'

'But for goodness sake, you share our food, you eat

79

with us, even though you have your own kitchen.' Belle knew her knuckles were white. She gripped the chair tighter. 'We have no more money. We simply haven't. We are getting through more and more food in the hall kitchens, though it slacked off for a while. There are so many men using us, the shopping is increasingly expensive. Binnie—'

Binnie smiled suddenly and interrupted her. 'Look, of course I don't want any more if that's the case. You've been so good to me. I'll try and manage on less, and let you have some back.'

Belle felt her mouth slacken with surprise, then Walter spoke from behind. 'My dear Binnie, surely no-one is suggesting you should take less money?'

He walked to the fire, warmed his hands, tapped out the pipe he had taken to smoking, looking from Belle to Binnie.

Belle looked at neither of them, just shrugged. 'No, no-one was suggesting that. I'm glad we've straightened it out, Binnie, but while we're talking of work we'll compromise – I'll take over the shopping. It'll give you one less job to do.'

Stick that in your pipe and smoke it, she wanted to add. She called to the two girls who were playing in the garden. 'Come along, we'll go to the quayside to have a look, then on to the food market.'

Binnie said, 'But what about Mary? I didn't mean you to take on any more work. Let me keep on the shopping for you; you work too hard.'

Belle helped the girls on with their coats. 'You've been through childbirth, so you can help her while Sandy goes for Dr Scott. Meanwhile there's the cleaning; help Claire please.'

Belle swept the girls out of the house, into the back alley. She shouldn't leave Mary, but she had to get out. She patted her handbag. Now she'd see just how much Binnie was fiddling or indeed, if, she was fiddling. She had to sort it out, one way or another.

'What if Mary has her baby while we're away?' Connie asked.

'She won't. Even if she starts we'll still be back in plenty of time.'

At the City Road end of the quayside they heard a clock strike ten.

'I saw some Dutchmen getting off their ship here,' Connie told Dora.

'That man I thought was me da was a seaman. We lived over there until he threw us—' Dora stopped.

'What did he throw?' Belle asked quietly.

'Until he threw us a fit,' Dora said quickly, trying to remember if that was what her mam said he'd died from, trying not to think of her da's face when he'd punched that man, and tipped their belongings into the street.

Belle looked at her. What had she really been about to say?

They walked in the shadow of the bridge, past traders selling from suitcases, some from handcarts, one from an old pram. A man walked out of an alley-way wearing a sandwich-board. 'Repent for the Day of Judgement is Nigh.' Belle grinned wryly. There'd been so many months, hours, seconds of repentance from Walter, it must make up for all those who never ever thought of the word.

They browsed amongst the second-hand clothes then approached the café. The girls looked at one another in excitement, and Belle nodded. 'I think we could all do with a treat.'

They sat next to a table of Africans. 'Their skin's so black, it's almost blue,' Connie whispered.

There was a woman at another table in curling pins. She wore an apron with big pockets and jingled her money. 'Are her fingers grey like that from the pennies?' Dora asked.

Belle nodded.

They drank tea from large mugs and Belle sighed. She had forgotten there was a world outside the vicarage.

She listened to the girls talking and laughing and smiled because Connie looked so much more relaxed and she no longer ran home from school now that Sadie and the gang ignored her, neither smiling nor scowling. It was an improvement, but not enough.

Belle counted her money. They were so short these days and winter was coming.

'How can we heat the house, the hall, the dormitories?' She leaned back in her chair. 'Perhaps we could make and sell toffee. There are all sorts of house shops being set up now times are so hard, perhaps we could sell cakes? Get the men going on that?' Connie and Dora nodded in reply, not really listening.

Belle fingered the wooden doll that Matt the carpenter had given her. 'We could make more of these and sell them.' She was thinking aloud really. The children had finished their tea. Hers was cold. She wasn't thirsty or hungry.

They walked out into the cold air, smelling the smoke on their clothes, took a tram to the big market, and Belle felt a surge of anticipation, almost hope, that she would find that she had change after the day's shopping, unlike Binnie. It would prove her suspicions were correct; it would allow her to step between that woman and Walter.

Binnie sat in her flat, counting the money she'd put on the horses. Would that bitch notice the difference in the shopping? Would she see there was one pound in change which never reached her? Binnie felt a prickle of sweat down her back. She shouldn't, because Binnie always shopped last thing and got the cheaper scrapings and the left-overs, and Belle didn't know that.

Belle staggered in through the back gate, the shopping almost pulling her arms out of her sockets. The girls carried one bag between them.

They put it on the scullery floor and Mary helped

unpack as Binnie came in and stood, her chin up, her shoulders defensive. Belle handed the sugar to Mary, smiling at Binnie, feeling guilty at her mistrust, but disappointed too, because there was no more change with her than with Binnie.

'We had a cup of tea, Mam,' Dora said. 'There were these black men at the next table.'

Mary dropped the cabbage. Belle looked at her. 'Are you starting?' Mary was pale. She shook her head. 'No, just tired.'

Binnie pushed the cabbage with her foot, looking at Belle. 'So, did you get any bargains?'

Belle shook her head. 'Just the sugar. It was from the bottom of the sack, otherwise it cost the same as always. We must shop at the same stalls, Binnie.'

Mary said, 'If you go late in the day you can get it cheaper. Might be a good idea?'

Binnie glared. Belle was stacking the margarine and butter, and now distrust re-emerged, and with it hope, again.

On Monday Belle's shoulders ached from heaving the poss-stick up and down and her hair hung lank in the steam. She rested against the tub as Claire and Anne chattered and rubbed the clothes on the scrubber then possed, and at first she didn't hear Sandy.

He shouted again. 'Parcel here from Rempton, Belle. Shall I give it to Mary to deal with?'

'No, she's lying down. Binnie's there, though, making tea. Give it to her, please, it'll be the used clothes Helen promised for the men, and us. Ask Binnie to sort them out.'

There was silence for a moment, then Sandy said, 'It'll keep. Mary can do it later.'

Binnie protested and called through, 'I'll do it, Belle, let the poor lass sleep.'

Belle worked on, then checked the fire beneath the boiler; it was low. The coal bucket was empty. She hurried through to the kitchen, reaching for the scuttle, saying, 'It's too cold to go out, I'll pinch some of this.'

There was no answer. She looked round. Binnie was no longer in the room.

Sandy came through into the kitchen, looking at his pocket-watch. 'Where's that Binnie? She's late again.'

'She must be taking the clothes to the airing cupboard.' Mary came in. 'I heard the front door go.'

Belle looked at the coal-scuttle in her hands, then at the brown wrapping paper screwed up into a ball. 'Check that there are some extra clothes up in the airing cupboard, will you, Mary?'

She watched as Mary walked towards the door, then stopped her. What was happening to her, how could she send one woman to check on another? She disgusted herself – she was persecuting Binnie just as much as the village women had done, just as much as Walter had done and she was ashamed of herself. Mary was waiting.

Belle said, 'I'm sorry, forget I said that, just make us a cup of tea.'

She carried the coal into the wash-house. She must stop this side of herself coming out. She must make herself laugh with the children, make herself see the sun when it came out, not just the clouds; she must smile when she didn't feel like it. Everyone depended on her and she must not let them down, especially Walter.

That night, Mary went into labour at last, and Dr Scott carried out his examination while Belle stroked her forehead.

'Early days yet,' he said gently, looking round the room at the cot and the airer hung with sheets and towels. There was a vase of flowers on the chest of drawers. 'This looks cosy.'

Belle smiled. Mrs Driscoll had sent the sheets and the material for the layette.

'The last thing we sewed were the sandbags, do you

84

remember, Belle dear? I have made one nightdress but it looks most odd. What a shame babies aren't square. Do try to make a better job of it.'

Belle sat up with Mary all night before making breakfast for Connie and Dora. 'There might be a baby when you come home, but I can't promise. First ones can take ages.' She looked at Binnie and for a moment there was an understanding between them.

Binnie said, 'If men were to have them, there'd only be one child in every family.' Belle laughed gently with her. It was only later as she climbed the stairs with warm water to wash Mary that she thought of the other babies she would love to have, and which looked an impossibility.

Connie walked round the playground at lunch-time, hunched against the cold, her hands in her coat pockets. Her eyes watered from the wind and she didn't see the girl throwing the hopscotch stone until she bumped into her. It was Sadie. They stared at one another.

'Why don't you chase me any more, are you frightened of me now?' Connie asked, pulling her muffler from her mouth.

Sadie turned from her, laughing, throwing the slate, jumping it, hopping from one square to another, picking it up on her return.

'Scared of you? You must be daft.'

Connie caught her arm. 'Then why?'

''Cos you didn't squitter to your da that I thumped you first. You took the blame.'

Sadie handed the stone to Susan. 'You have a go. I'm bored.'

Connie shook her head in surprise, watching the girls, watching Sadie. She moved near her. 'Can I be in your gang then?'

Sadie laughed again. 'Why you?'

'Please, I can tell you something you don't know.' Connie thought of Mary's baby.

The girls all drew round and Sadie said nothing for a moment, then pushed her. 'Go on then, tell us.'

Connie said, 'You mustn't tell your mams.'

Sadie shook her head. 'Why would we tell the grown-ups anything? They just clout you for nowt. Get on with it then, the bell'll go.'

Connie told them then about the way a man's seed goes into the woman, and the baby grows inside her. 'The baby's not brought by the postman, you know.'

The girls were squatting on the ground, their breath visible in the frost-sharp air. 'My mam says your mam is going to have bastards in her house. She says it's not nice,' Sadie said.

'My mam said that an' all,' Flo shouted, wiping her nose on the back of her sleeve. Connie saw the streak and swallowed. This was all going wrong. There was a silence.

Sadie said, 'I don't believe men put a seed in you.'

'Only when you're older, and only if you let them, my mam said. Don't tell her I told you, my da will be really angry.' Connie spoke quietly, wishing she had said nothing at all, looking round at the girls who were all too close, who might not let her get up and away, but now Sadie stood, and the others scrambled to their feet. The bell rang and the gang ran. Connie stood there watching. Sadie was trailing behind; she stopped and turned.

'Come on then, keep up. You can be in the gang. You've done something you shouldn't have, so that's all right.'

Connie didn't believe her for a moment, then she tried not to grin as she walked towards her, though she could feel her face creasing, and then as she reached Sadie she knew it was a full smile. Sadie nodded, then smiled too, and Connie wanted to run home and tell Belle and she knew that if she did she would not even be out of breath because the happiness she felt would let her run miles and miles today.

*　　*　　*

They walked home together and Connie told them that Mary might have had her baby. 'I hope your mams aren't going to be horrid. I hope you're not, not now.'

Sadie said, 'They will be horrid, but we're a gang. We don't care where babies come from, or who has them. Be here tomorrow, we'll walk in together; you can bring her too.' Sadie pointed to Dora. 'She can belong as long as she's with you.'

Connie told Dora as they walked down the path where babies came from. 'You ought to know, if the whole gang does, but don't tell anyone I told you. Now let's see if Mary's had the baby.'

The evening passed into a dark cold night with frost whitening the garden, and ice forming at the edges of the water-butt though in Mary's bedroom the fire glowed. Belle wiped the sweat from her forehead. 'It won't be much longer.'

Mary groaned, panting and gasping, gripping Belle's hand so tight that it hurt.

It was taking too long. Belle took the jug from the room. 'I'm just going to fetch more water. I won't be a moment.'

She shut the door and rushed down the stairs, into the kitchen. No-one was there. She ran into the mission hall. Sandy and Walter were clearing up after the Whist Drive. They looked at her and Sandy dropped the brush. 'What's gone wrong?'

'Nothing, it's just taking so long and she's very tired. The midwife's gone off to someone else. Fetch Dr Scott, and be quick, Sandy.'

Sandy was gone before she could finish, running out of the front door without even a coat. Walter said, 'I put Connie to bed tonight.' He was leaning on his broom. 'We made a pound from the Whist Drive and the cakes you made. It'll help with the food.'

Belle nodded, really only hearing that he had put Connie to bed, feeling warmth steal over her. 'Did she tell you she has made friends? Oh Walter, it's so important she's happy. Did you read to her? She so enjoys it.'

He nodded. 'Yes, of the pyramids in Egypt. I explored them when I was there.' Silence fell and they looked at one another and there was neither emptiness nor pain in his eyes, there was – what?

Claire ran into the hall. 'Please come, Belle. It's Mary.'

Belle looked back at Walter, and now there was only emptiness. 'I'm glad you spent time with her. She misses you.'

Walter said nothing.

Belle made Claire stay in the sitting-room. 'Don't come up, I can manage. Just send the doctor. She's frightened, that's why she screamed. She will be fine.'

She forced herself to climb the stairs at a normal pace until the first landing, then, once out of sight of Claire, she ran, bursting into Mary's room, rushing to her side. 'I'm here, I'm here.'

She rubbed the girl's back until the contraction subsided.

'How far apart now?'

'Five minutes,' Mary whispered, her face drawn.

Belle reached for the jug of water. Damn, it was downstairs.

She moved quickly, but quietly, to the bathroom. She grabbed the other jug, filled it, hurried out, seeing Connie sitting on the top stair. 'Off to bed.'

'Why did she scream?'

'Because she's frightened, and because having a baby can hurt, but it's really fear. Now madam, off to bed.'

Connie rose and opened her bedroom door. 'Da read to me.'

Belle returned her smile. 'I know, now go and think of those pyramids. You could find out more about them from him tomorrow.'

They nodded at one another and Belle dared to hope that this baby had brought a new beginning to them all.

After another half-hour the pains were coming every three minutes. 'Not long now, Mary.'

Sandy knocked and called, 'The doctor will be here within the next twenty minutes.'

Belle opened the door. 'Make sure Binnie and the girls are boiling up water.'

He nodded, his face almost as drawn as Mary's.

Belle sat back in her chair, smiling at Mary. 'That lad has a soft spot for you, my lass.'

Mary turned away. 'He won't have, not once I have this bairn.' Her hands were limp on the sheet, and almost as white.

Belle leaned over and held them. 'He's accepted that you're pregnant, so he'll accept the baby.'

'Not when it's born.' Mary was twisting and turning as the pains came again, and she screamed, pushing Belle away, drawing her legs up.

'You must try and relax, give in to the pain. You must help your baby.' Belle leant over, trying to hold Mary's arms as they flailed.

'I don't want the baby. No-one will want the baby,' Mary shouted as pain twisted her face, then eased. She lay silent.

Dr Scott came, his young face calm, his voice easy, reassuring as he examined Mary. 'Not long now.' He and Belle stood by the bed, then moved to the window.

'It's almost as though she's holding on to it. She's just said she doesn't want it,' Belle murmured.

Dr Scott smiled. 'Most women say that at this stage.'

Belle laughed softly. 'I know, I certainly did, but I wonder.'

Dr Scott turned back, watching Mary. 'Has she talked to you at all, are we any the wiser?'

Belle shook her head. 'She's very private; she holds her problems to her, but once the baby is born it will release her, I'm sure.'

Another contraction came and soon Dr Scott and Belle had no time for talk, and the sweat was pouring from them both as they shouted again and again at Mary to push, but she couldn't, wouldn't, until Belle held her face, made her look into her eyes.

'This baby will die. He's your baby. You're tired, but not that tired. One more push, come on, Mary. For me, for Connie. She wants this baby. I want it, you want it. Now push. Come on, push.' She was shouting, 'Push, push, push.'

At last Mary's grey eyes focused. She looked from Belle to Dr Scott. 'Push!' they both shouted. She did. Belle held her hands now. 'Push, push.' Again and again.

'I see its hair. It's darker than yours,' Dr Scott called. 'Careful now, don't push yet, not until I tell you.'

'I must,' whimpered Mary.

'No, not yet,' urged Belle. 'Pant.'

'Now push,' called Dr Scott. 'Good girl, come along. She's coming, keep going.' Mary's face was screwed up with effort, and then it was over.

'You have a boy, a beautiful boy,' Dr Scott said, lifting the child. Belle hurried to him, taking a towel from the airer, hearing the baby's fragile cry, feeling the tears coming, taking the baby which was so black against the white of the towel. She met his eyes, both of them knowing now why Mary had been as she was.

Dr Scott said quietly, 'So this is what it's all been about. Aren't your friendly neighbours going to have a field-day over this one? My word, this will be a challenge for Walter, with his views of prejudice. Will he rise to it, I wonder?' He raised his voice. 'Only a few more pushes, now, Mary. I warned you a mother's work is never done. Just the placenta now. Take her son to her, Belle.' His voice was gentle.

Belle touched the child's hair and smiled at Mary, whose eyes were wary and who turned from her as she approached.

'Enough of that, Mary, your son needs you. He's beautiful and he is very welcome here.'

Mary turned and Belle placed the baby in her arms

and now there were tears running down Mary's cheeks too, as she held the child. She touched his fingers, his nose, his hair and Belle saw the love appear. Mary said softly, 'I'll call him Joseph, his father's name. He was a Nigerian seaman. He died.'

Belle bent over, kissed them both.

Mary said, 'I thought you'd send me away if I told you. Will you now?'

Belle shook her head. 'No, never. This is what we are working towards, an end to fear and suspicion. But you should have told me, I could have helped so much earlier, you silly girl.'

Later, when Dr Scott had gone, Walter and Binnie brought Connie and Dora to see the baby. Connie put her finger against Joseph's fist; he opened his hand and gripped her. She looked up at her mother. 'He's just like Boy was.'

Dora wouldn't touch him. 'He's dirty, he's all dark, like them blackies.'

Belle put her hand on Mary's shoulder. 'Yes, isn't he lucky, he's a mixture. He's part of one race and part of another; we're lucky he's been born to us.'

She looked at Walter and saw the shock as he looked in the crib and saw the child against the whiteness of the sheets. She said gently to him, 'It confirms why we're here. We must help her; it's a challenge, my love.'

He stood and looked at the child, then touched the black hair. He smiled at Mary. 'He's very lovely. We're all very lucky.'

Binnie said nothing, just stood by the door, her face impassive.

That night Belle lay in bed, remembering how Walter had held her close on their wedding eve, how he had entwined his limbs with hers, kissing her body, stroking it until she could scarcely breathe, until she couldn't bear it any longer and had cried to him for more, but more of what she didn't know. Then he had entered her, gently, tenderly and she had thought she would die of love, and desire. Connie had been born nine months later. Did he remember? She turned towards Walter, laying her hand on his belly.

He turned, shrugging her from him. 'I fear the rest of the house and hostel, not to mention the neighbours, will not welcome Joseph. We can tackle the hostel, but I told you you should have gained the neighbours' support. What are you going to do about them?'

7

Belle walked alongside as Mary pushed the pram towards the mission. A potato rolled from the box beneath the pram and Belle stopped it with her foot, laughing at Mary. She called to Mrs Gribble who was working on her front step with her beige rubbing stone. 'They should pick me for the football team, Mrs Gribble.'

Mrs Gribble sniffed. 'It'd give you better things to do with your time, right enough.'

Belle put her hand on Mary's. 'I'll give you a hand to push. Merry Christmas, Mrs Gribble,' she called back, then made Mary laugh by telling her about the lights the Special Constables in Rempton had insisted mothers must fit on their perambulators during the war. But it was a weak laugh.

They reached the front steps of the house. Belle carried the box of vegetables up the steps, feeling her back take the strain. 'Wait there, I'll come down and help with the pram, Mary.' She hoped that Sandy would come to help. He did not, just as he had not spoken to Mary since he had seen the colour of Joseph's skin.

'I just can't stand the thought of her with a nigger seaman,' he'd said and Belle had wanted to shake him.

They bumped the pram up the steps, Belle laughing though Mary was silent until they reached the top. Then she said, 'I'll leave. You said you'd find us jobs. I'm making it all too difficult for you.'

Belle picked up the vegetables, leading the way into the kitchen. 'No, we need you here to help with the girls. I've already told you that Binnie is too busy in the hall. I am busy in the parish, as well as the hall, as well as the girls, as well as Connie – need I go on?' She dropped the box onto the table. 'Which reminds me, I'm off to the Board of Guardians with Mrs Ellis.'

She picked up her handbag. 'You can see for yourself, we've Claire due after Christmas, Anne two weeks later, Norah coming next week, on December the twenty-seventh. I can't cope without you, I just wish I could pay you what you're worth.'

'You pay me more than enough.'

Belle walked down the street, wanting to shout through every letter-box that they were unchristian bigots who needed their heads examining, and not just for dickies. She should have checked them when she'd done Dora's and Connie's last night.

She called in at Mrs Ellis, despairing at the sight of the damp cold room. 'Bye, it's a cold one,' Mrs Ellis said, dragging her two girls with her as they left the room. 'That lav's broken again.' She peered down the landing, towards the half-open door.

Belle draped her own scarf round Elsie, the younger girl. 'Didn't you get the scarf I sent?'

Mrs Ellis nodded. 'Aye, but we had to eat that day, pet. I put it in the pawn.'

Belle took Nancy's hand. 'I'll find another and let's hope we get something from the Board this time.'

They weren't seen until four in the afternoon, and then all they were offered was an official who would investigate the claim and call to check their means.

Belle protested. 'There's only one room and a broken lavatory down the hall and a husband out of work, what is there to investigate for heaven's sake? I'll write to the Bishop.' It did no good.

They walked back silently and as they entered Mrs Ellis's room Belle gave her five shillings for coal and food. 'I'll see if we've someone who knows about plumbing at the mission.'

Mrs Ellis smiled at her, lifting the blankets on the bed for the girls to crawl beneath. 'The landlord should do it.'

'A lot of people should do a lot of things.'

Belle hurried back to the mission, calling in at the hall. 'Sandy,' her voice was curt. 'See if we've a plumber. If we have send him to Mrs Ellis, 15a Bunston Terrace. I'll pay him.'

She didn't smile at the man who had turned his back on Mary. She marched into the kitchen. Binnie was there, pacing up and down in front of the roaring fire. Belle pointed to the coal. 'Why did you put so much on? It's wasteful, unnecessary. We can't afford it.'

Binnie put her hands on her hips. 'We can't afford to have our children growing up as sluts either.' Her voice was loud, aggressive.

Belle flung down her hat, ripping off her gloves, unable to remove the image of Mrs Ellis from her mind, or Sandy's sombre face. 'What on earth are you talking about now, Binnie – have you yet more complaints?' She was shouting, but she didn't care. The whole world was mad, and unpleasant, and this woman epitomized it. 'Go on, tell me.'

She leant against the table, waiting.

'You told that girl of yours about babies and how they're born, and she's gone and told the neighbourhood and my Dora. It's rude and disgusting. My Dora cried.'

Belle straightened and laughed but it was bitter and unamused. She had been working all last evening whilst this woman and Walter played chess, she had been out all day sorting out problems while the fire burnt high for just one woman. 'For God's sake, Binnie. It might stop her making the same mistake you made.'

She wanted to slap her, forbid her to eat with them ever again, sit with her husband ever again, tell her to be on time for everyone's shifts, not just Walter's. She put aside the vision of the poor pregnant village girl; it had worn too thin now. She opened her mouth.

'Belle!' Walter's voice cut across her. 'I'm surprised at you.'

She spun round. 'Good, at least I've made you feel

something. Now I'm taking Connie to Jesmond, and we're tatting up and down the posh bloody roads for clothes, food, presents, to make up into parcels we will give out at the Christmas service, at which, I presume, there will be no music yet again. And you might like to know that I've been pounding on the Board's table again, when it would be better if you did. But I presume, again, that you've been too busy writing to the bloody Bishop about your bloody men. You couldn't have been out talking to the neighbours about poor Joseph, that would be too bloody much to ask.'

Walter recoiled, paling, but Belle just stormed past him. 'I thought not, now you two can sit and tut while I get on with more bloody work.'

She and Connie knocked on the front doors of the houses, while two of the mission men pushed the barrow and waited outside. She spoke to the maids, refusing to go to the tradesmen's entrance, explaining that she was the wife of the minister of Back Dock Mission, collecting for the Christmas Fund, naming the Bishop as their patron.

At nine p.m., their hands and faces frozen, their voices sore from singing carols with the men, and their ribs aching with laughter at Matt's antics, they stopped at Mrs Ellis. They left three blankets, and Belle noted the coal on the fire, and confirmed that the plumber would be there tomorrow. There would be no charge.

They returned to the mission, and Belle put Connie to bed, then came into the kitchen. It was empty, the fire was banked. She walked along to Walter's study, entered, and stood there as he looked up at her.

'Can we talk?' she asked.

He balanced his pencil on his finger. 'About what – there's no point. Everything would have been perfectly all right without the babies, there would have been none of this emotion.'

Belle looked at the low fire in the grate. 'I thought it would help everyone, you and me too.'

'You were obviously wrong. It's just made everything more difficult.'

He leaned back in his chair. She turned and left, sitting at the kitchen table until long after she heard him go to bed, looking all the time at the Christmas decorations that Connie and Dora had made.

'God in heaven, I can't go on like this.' She held her hands over her face. 'But what can I do about any of it?' How could she bring him out of this morass, how could she bring him towards her – or was all hope gone on both counts?

She lay that night alone in the bed, hearing him tossing and turning in his dressing-room which was where he chose to sleep now. The nightmares would begin soon, but the last thing she must do was to comfort him. Perhaps she should go and get Binnie, damn her.

She clutched her pillow and pictured the feathers floating in the Rempton bedroom and heard echoes of their laughter, and felt the sun on their faces as they danced in the garden, and the pressure of his body against her, and the love which had encompassed them. She rose, looked out of the window. No, she wasn't finished yet, she would think of something; she had to she still loved him so much.

Binnie drank from the bottle. The beer was thick and warm; the Woodbine rasped her throat. She wiped her mouth with the back of her hand. Bloody sums with Walter tomorrow, but it would all be worth it.

The next morning Belle looked for Sandy in the kitchens. 'I need a tailor to make Joseph's christening robe.' Her voice was sharp.

He pointed to a grey-haired man smoking and playing cards. 'Jim'll do it.'

She spoke to Jim, then showed him the sketch Mary had drawn up. She talked to Matt, telling him what she wanted, adding, 'I need the figures to be large, at least a foot, and ready by Christmas Day. Can you do it?'

He nodded.

Belle said, 'I'll make over an alcove. Don't tell anyone. And Matt, I shall love you for ever for this.'

'Then promise me you won't try the descant next time we go collecting.' They laughed.

She told Sandy; she did not ask him for the use of the first alcove. Her voice was crisp, her face cold.

She entered Walter's study. He was working on his German and French exchange plan and pushed the papers into the file.

Belle sat opposite, her hands loose in her lap, glad that the desk was between them and that she could pretend that her husband was a business partner, because she must keep her distance, she must be very careful, since this plan had to work. She was drained, almost finished.

She spoke. 'I must apologize properly for my behaviour yesterday. I was tired, but I was also wrong. Connie should not have told Dora, I should not have shouted at Binnie, or at you. It was unforgivable.' She went on, 'I realize that I have perhaps jeopardized your work by setting the neighbourhood against us.'

She saw the query in his face and gestured towards his file. 'We have a half-caste child who has been born in this house. You are trying to bring together the Germans, the French, the Belgians and the British, but how can you bring such people here, when all they will see is a hostile neighbourhood? I am the cause of that. I insisted on taking in these girls.'

She saw his eyes drop and hoped it was for shame. Was she still smiling, looking contrite?

She told him what she had asked Matt to carve. He listened.

'Will your sermon on Christmas Day support me? Will you put around the message that there will be parcels? People will come then, even Mrs Gribble. They will come and they will listen, and it will help your cause.'

She looked at her hands as Walter agreed. She left, her head still bowed, or else he might see too much love, too much hope, too much fear.

On Christmas morning Connie leapt on Belle's bed, showing her the doll from Mrs Driscoll that was larger and more grand than Betsy. There was a dress for the doll from Amelia and Boy. There was a book on Africa from Belle and Walter. There were oranges and nuts, and a handkerchief from Binnie and Dora, a mouth-organ from Sandy.

'Don't play it,' warned Belle quickly, looking towards the dressing-room. He had to give his sermon. Nothing must upset him.

They ate breakfast in the kitchen, all of them, squashed against one another, giggling and laughing whilst Joseph lay quietly in the pram. Later they took their places in the front pew whilst Walter greeted the congregation. The men from the mission attended. The neighbours were there and the gang. They waved and whispered and eyed the Christmas parcels whilst Belle smiled until her face ached.

They sang carols without music. Belle still smiled. They mouthed prayers, they kneeled, they stood, and finally they sat as Walter mounted the pulpit. He looked at Belle, his face pale. She rose, walked into the vestry, then carried out, with Matt, the nativity scene he had carved. They set it on the table they had erected in front of the altar.

Each figure was one foot high. Each figure was brown and the lights picked up their colour. The congregation murmured, turning to one another, their faces angry.

Walter began to speak. 'God is not an Englishman. Christ was not an Englishman. Christ lived in a land where there is a need for protection from the sun. God provided extra pigment in the skin. God works in a wonderful way. He creates with such sensitivity, and with such common sense. In a garden there are red flowers with little scent, but which delight the eye. There are white flowers which fill the air with fragrance. God designed them so, to attract the right insects to pollinate each one, in its own way. So God has designed us.

'He chose that Christ should come amongst us as a man whose colour is that of an Arab, one who is a mixture of black and white. We love him, we accept him as that. We have here today in our street, a beloved child called Joseph. We have just fought a war founded on fear and suspicion. We have all lost loved ones. We are all damaged in some way, perhaps for ever. Can we allow fear and suspicion to rise again, even for a moment, and amongst ourselves, especially on this most wonderful of days?

'May the glory of God, and the fellowship of the Holy Ghost be with us all, and remain with us. Amen.'

They ate lunch in the hall with the men. Belle sat with Mary and this time the smile on her face came from her heart as she looked at Walter, because how could a man with no love for his wife, or God, have spoken as he had? It had been from his very soul, and too full of feeling to be merely for the sake of the exchange scheme.

She pulled the paper hat more firmly on her head and pulled the cracker with Mary. Sandy, Martin and Frank brought out the chickens from the kitchen whilst Walter poured the beer.

Belle held up her glass. 'Here's to the cooks, and Matt's Nativity figures.'

'He's carving the chickens as well,' Sandy shouted above the cheers. They all laughed. Belle hugged Mary. 'Merry Christmas, my dear.'

Mary stood up then, putting up her hands for silence, before turning to look at Belle. 'We know how hard you work for us and the bairns. We know it's because you love us and how can anyone repay love? We can't, bonny lass, but we can show you that we, in return, love you.'

Charlie, the plumber, went to the second alcove and brought from it a bird table. 'So you can have birds as well as flowers in your garden.'

Belle looked across the table at Walter whose eyes were dark, and whose hands trembled. 'We should all be thanking Walter really, for the sermon he gave.'

He shook his head. 'I wouldn't have made it without you to guide me.'

Love flooded over her; could he see it – would it repel him? He held her gaze and there was something in his eyes and smile that made her want to go to him. But no, she would be careful, gentle. She would wait until tonight.

As they ate the food the men had cooked Belle said to Mary, 'Joseph has put on just the right amount of weight; it's wonderful to see him so strong, so happy, and he does seem to love Connie.'

Mary said, 'She's very easy to love.'

Belle looked across at her daughter who was feeding her new doll. She called across to Jim, the tailor, 'How about making doll's clothes, Jim? I think we could sell them.'

Mary groaned and Claire said, 'Stop working, just for a few hours.'

Everyone smiled but Binnie.

They ate the Christmas pudding and made wishes on the threepenny bits as Joseph began to cry. Mary rose, but Sandy was quicker, picking up the child and holding him in his arms, walking, soothing him. 'Finish your pudding, pet,' he said to Mary, who blushed and looked at Belle.

That evening Mrs Gribble brought a tiny piece of Flemish lace for Joseph's christening robe and Belle sang to herself as she climbed the stairs, bathed, stood in front of the mirror, brushing her hair, her nightdress clinging to her body. Walter would be there, in their bed, and though they may only speak kindly to one another, at least their lives would begin again tonight, and her distaste for Binnie disappeared as though it had never been. Oh, my love.

She pushed open the bedroom door and moved towards him in the darkness, feeling for him. 'I love you, Walter,' she whispered.

But the bed was empty and Belle couldn't understand the cruelty of the man she had married so long ago.

8

Easter 1921 had been and gone, and all that was left of Joseph's christening tea were the crumbs Belle was putting on the bird table. She checked Claire's baby, Josie, rocking the pram gently. Not even Mrs Ellis had come to the christening tea, though the gang had.

'I don't see you at Sunday School any more. In fact hardly anyone comes, and it's been going such a short while. Are you too busy?' she had asked as they ate the cake they had helped her to make.

They had shaken their heads and looked at Connie. Connie had said, 'It's no fun. They can't make a noise. At other Sunday Schools they have sing-songs, sometimes games, as well as a Christmas tea. That's why people don't come to church any more either. It's all so miserable.'

Belle bent over Josie and smoothed her hair, touched her soft skin. She had had such hopes on Christmas Day that they were about to start afresh but not only had he not come to her bed, he had turned from the congregation, from the parish, isolating himself in his study, making plans for the exchange visits, leaving only to teach Binnie.

She drew the blankets up around Josie's head. 'You can come when I take the Sunday School to the sea in July, and to Town Moor sooner than that,' she crooned. 'But best of all, you can come to the party and listen to the piano.'

Because at Joseph's christening she had decided that there would be singing, laughter and joy in their lives again. This could not go on a moment longer. She would repair the harmonium and there would be music in the church at last. She would organize a party and invite the neighbours, the congregation, the children who had drifted from Sunday School, and Walter must come.

'You realize that church music and a party would amount to shock tactics?' Sandy had said when they had discussed the situation. 'But what else is left?'

Mary and Sandy came out into the garden, Sandy carrying Joseph, his other arm around Mary.

'Has he agreed to the party? Have you told him about the repair of the harmonium?' Mary asked, wheeling Josie into the wash-house, lifting her from the pram, humming to her.

Belle shook her head. 'I haven't mentioned it yet; I can't get him alone.' Her eyes met Mary's. They walked through to the kitchen. Binnie was there, sitting 'at the feet' of Walter. Belle dug her hands into her apron, listening to the gentle tone of his voice as he talked to the woman of the work Sir Arthur Evans was doing at Knossos, and the Minoan civilization. 'I will explain it to you more fully next week.'

Would the party change this? It had to.

Sandy said, 'It's your shift, Binnie.'

Binnie looked up at the clock and smiled sweetly at Belle. 'Another five minutes to go. I'm learning so much.'

Belle wanted to push her from the chair, and Walter too, but she was wrong. He was communicating, he was taking time to talk to someone, to reach out to another person – but she wanted that someone to be her.

She followed Sandy and Mary through to the girls' sitting-room and watched Sandy put Joseph into one of the cribs that stood against the wall.

'I'll do the child-care class,' Mary said gently. 'You look tired.'

'I am,' Belle said quietly. 'Too tired to be facing Walter, but what else can I do? Dr Scott can think of nothing either.' Instead of confrontation she wanted to talk to Walter of the love which was suffocating her.

She wanted to ask him again why he had not come to her on Christmas night, why he had withdrawn from them all on Boxing Day.

Sandy moved past her, touched her arm, then led her into the passage. 'I've been checking the stores. They're going down fast again.' He drew out a piece of paper from his pocket. 'Look at this. We'll be out of eggs, flour, sugar, cocoa before the end of the week and we're almost out of money even with the extra we make from the doll's clothes. Has Amelia written back about that friend of hers in London with the shop, by the way? Will he take some?'

Belle shrugged. 'Not yet, I'm waiting. Look, we've got to make the stores last until the end of the week, we've just got to.'

Sandy said, 'It's that Binnie, I know it is. She's flogging it cheap.'

Belle looked at him, hearing Josie crying. 'You tackle Walter over that, Sandy. I don't seem to be able to get through and I've got the party to handle.'

Sandy shook his head. 'It's up to you, Belle. She's your pigeon, and what's more, she's getting too close to the nest. She's still in there and her five minutes are more than up. She's in no hurry to get to her shift on time because Walter's on mornings, isn't he?'

She watched him walk down the passage and wanted to scream after him, All right, so you've noticed too, but what does he feel for her, what is going on?

She approached the kitchen and drew a deep breath as she always did now, feeling the door-handle cold beneath her touch. She turned it, hardly able to look towards the table. When she did, she saw Walter's hand guiding Binnie's as she traced the lines of Knossos. She felt sick with pain. Then anger overcame the pain and her voice was raw as she said, 'Binnie, there appear to be stores going missing. You have a key.'

Walter looked up at her. She ignored him and stared at Binnie who straightened, narrowing her eyes. 'Are you saying I'm a thief? Or is it that Sandy? He and that Mary are up to no good; she'll have put him up to it. They're ganging up. Everyone has someone but me. It's not fair, I tell you.'

Belle put up her hand. 'I'm too tired for all this nonsense, Binnie. The stores are going down too fast. Why do you think that is?'

Walter was on his feet, his hand on Binnie's shoulder. Leave that woman alone, Belle wanted to scream, but she stayed silent as he said, 'Yes, I think that can be the only reasonable explanation for this, Belle. You must be tired, otherwise this is inexcusable. I told you it was a mistake to take in these girls – look at you, worn out, and even with our Christmas Day effort the neighbours are not exactly supporting us.'

'It is not the girls who make me tired; they look after themselves. It is everything else. Everything.' She knew she must stop, find control. She pressed her hand to her mouth.

Binnie had tears in her eyes as she said, 'It's not me. It's those men you say I have to have in the kitchen, "helping" me. They're not helping. They make mistakes, throw the food away, then lie about it. I've seen them. You come on into the kitchen.' Binnie threw her pencil down and rushed from the room.

Belle stared at Walter as he said, 'This is unforgivable after all we've done to that girl. Have you taken leave of your senses?'

Her hand was still at her mouth, she could feel it trembling, feel the whole of her body trembling. She dug her hands into her apron pockets, hiding them, bunching them into fists. 'We did not do anything to her Walter, you did. I am merely trying to fulfil your wishes, and address the problems as they arise.'

Walter shook his head, jabbing the air with his finger. 'You made those problems, taking in those girls – it's brought us into disrepute, it will affect the hostel. How will the exchange programme flourish in this atmosphere?

You promised me that if I spoke up at Christmas it would bring the neighbourhood together.'

'It has Walter; they say good morning, they gave us a present for Joseph, they just don't like coming here because it's so damn miserable. Open your eyes and look around. At least when we first came you cared a little for your parish, but now it is only I who traipse the streets. It is I who visit the Board, take calves-foot jelly to your parishioners, sit with them, try to find them food, shoes, while you ban the harmonium, ban singing in Sunday School, and shut yourself away in the study, writing letters, or are you just studying your navel?'

'I beg your pardon?'

'And so you damn well should. You don't even sit with the men any longer. You just talk to that woman about Greek civilization, or plan the exchange. Will it ever happen? What will they think of us when they come?' She leaned on the table, gripping the edge. 'You should be out there caring for your flock, being a father-figure to those girls, to your own child. You should be a husband to your wife. That's reality, not this world you are creating. You've got to wake up Walter, leave the past behind, take up the challenge.'

He stared at her.

She said, 'Now, I'm going to check the kitchen and then I must talk to you again.'

In the kitchen Binnie hurled eggs into the bins. Had they broken? Yes. She tipped some flour, the sugar, a bit of cocoa. Was it chocolate cake the men had cooked this afternoon? She stopped. Yes, she was sure it was. She dusted her hands. Quick, for God's sake. She shut the bin lid, leant back against the table, forcing herself to breathe quietly, slowly, as she waited.

Belle entered, checked the cupboards, showed Binnie how much flour they should have had.

Binnie crossed her arms. 'I told you, I've taken nothing. You should check the bins.' She looked down at her hands; there was flour round her nails. She put her hands behind her back and smiled at Belle. 'Go on, check the bins, then I need an apology, Mrs Symmonds.'

Belle lifted the lid and looked into the bins and saw the mess. She looked up at Binnie. It resolved nothing. Binnie had the key, she could have put it all in there. Why hadn't she followed immediately, damn it? Why were the woman's hands behind her back? She wanted to grab her, check her nails, but Binnie would only say it was from the earlier cooking. All she could do was smile and give the required apology, though it nearly choked her.

In the morning Belle showed Sandy. He shook his head. 'It's not the men.'

Belle agreed. 'But we must just watch and wait.' She waved through the hatch to the men, taking her tea and sitting with them, as Walter did not now do.

'How're the carvings coming along, Matt?' she asked. 'Have you sold any at the market?' He'd taken a suitcase along last week.

'Aye, lass. The seamen cleared me out.'

She sipped her tea. 'How would you feel about training some of the lads up? I've placed a few in jobs, but some have nothing to do and nowhere to go.'

He agreed and Belle set Sandy onto it, asking him first if the organ-mender had been in.

'Aye, came last night while Walter was at the Bishop's. You've told him then?'

Belle shook her head. 'But I will; this has all gone on too long and I can't stand any more.' Sandy put his arm around her shoulder and she drew away. 'Don't be kind to me; I shall break.'

Connie threw the slate, hopped along the square, jumping number six, returned, picking up the slate, watching as Sadie did the same. Along the next back alley men were playing pitch and toss and Nellie from the gang was earning a penny by keeping a watch for the policeman.

'So, why're we having this party then?' Sadie said, licking on the toffee they had made at Belle's on Saturday.

Connie said, 'Because Mam wants people to know that everything is all right with Da.'

'But it isn't; he's gone all quiet and a right misery-guts and he was no ray of sunshine before.'

It was Connie's turn again. She threw, jumped, then watched Sadie, calling to her, 'I know. It happened on Boxing Day. He just came down with a face all dark just when we thought everything was going to get better.'

'So why's your mother having the party?'

'Because she wants the children to come again, and the neighbours to smile in church as they did on Christmas Day, and the girls in the house to laugh, and the men too. If she can get the harmonium going and borrow a piano for the party and Sunday School she thinks it will change Da. Shock tactics, she calls it.'

'What does your Da say?'

Connie looked towards the house. 'She hasn't told him yet; that's why I'm out here.'

She turned to Dora and called, 'Stop yacking Dora, it's your turn.' Then looked towards the house. She wanted to be there with her mother but Belle had said no.

Belle knocked on Walter's study door. The room was empty. She checked in the kitchen. Mary was bringing coal through. 'Have you see Walter, Mary?' .

Mary shook her head. 'Have you told him? Frank's arranged to borrow the piano.'

'No, I'm on my way.'

Mary grimaced. 'I'll tell everyone to duck, shall I?' They both laughed but the sound was devoid of amusement and full of strain.

He wasn't in the hall either. She asked Sandy.

'He's in the church,' he said. 'Shall I come?'

'No, this is my job, just as accusing Binnie was.' Her voice was tense and Sandy dropped his eyes. 'I'm sorry.'

'It's all right. You were quite correct; she is my pigeon.'

In the church it seemed so quiet. Light streamed blue and red through the windows. She walked towards the altar, standing at the communion rail. The blossom was fading in the vases. Petals had dropped. She moved, picked them up, touched the brass of the vase. It was so cold. She stared up at the window. Motes danced. She turned and looked at the empty church. These pews needed to be filled, Walter's heart needed to be warmed, his parishioners' and family's too.

She heard him now, in the vestry. She looked towards the harmonium, set at the side and slightly behind the pillar in the right aisle and dropped the petals into her pocket before moving across. Shock tactics, Sandy had said. Well, perhaps they should begin now. The time for words seemed to be past.

She sat and held her hands above the keys, her feet in place. She played, loudly, 'Lead Kindly Light'. Her fingers were stiff with tension, her feet moved inaccurately. What would happen? The vestry door swung open. It slammed back against the wall.

Walter rushed into the church, his face distraught. 'Alec, Alec.'

She stopped playing, alarmed at the hope which blazed from her husband's face. What had she done? She called, 'No, it's not Alec, it's Belle, your wife. But why did you call Alec? Tell me. You must tell me.'

He stopped, the hope gone. His shoulders dropped; he covered his eyes, shaking his head. He slumped onto the pew.

Belle said again, gently, 'Tell me about Alec. Let me help.'

Walter looked up. 'Come away from there!' he cried. 'I can tell you nothing. There is nothing.'

She played note after note. 'Tell me about Alec!' she shouted in desperation.

She watched him rushing towards her. She didn't stop because this was all that was left. She said again, 'Tell me about Alec.'

She felt his hands on her, pulling at her, dragging her off the stool. She fought, brought her hand down on the keys. 'Tell me about Alec.'

He dragged her off the stool. 'I hate you, I hate you,' he screamed at her. 'How dare you?'

He pushed her away and she clutched the pillar. Her dress was torn. 'Tell me about Alec.' Her heart was beating so hard and so fast she could hardly breathe.

He was panting, his face was contorted. 'I hate you. Keep away from me and from my life. Keep away,' he gasped, his arm up before his face, as though to ward her off.

She grew cold and calm and stood upright. His hair was ruffled; the light from the window fell on his face. He looked so tired. She spoke quietly, deliberately choosing her words, 'For Christ's sake, I am your wife, you stupid bugger.'

He reached out, grabbed her arms, shook her until her hair loosened and fell to her shoulders and pins scattered on the stone floor. 'You blaspheme in here, are you mad?' He pushed her from him again.

She said, 'But there's no God; there's no Alec. I can see neither of them. You deny one, you refuse to discuss the other. You keep them locked inside your head, cherishing the nightmares, denying your God, just like you deny me and Connie. There is no life outside your head, your pen, your ideas, your Binnie.'

He was walking away. She called, 'Tell me, Walter, where has all the love gone, all the life we should be having? We survived, after all.'

He stopped. 'Is this survival?'

He walked away, and now she ran at him, grabbing him, hitting him, pulling him back. 'Don't you dare say that when you brought us here, when we have worked to make your life worth something. Don't you dare ignore me, or Connie, or your life any more. Don't you dare ignore your God, whom you defend to me. He's alive in you, just as I am. Aren't I, Walter? Or is it Alec who is – is he more important, and the image you have of him, whatever it may be? What do you think you did to Alec? What do you think you are doing to all of us? Think of that, not of the past. That is over and done. We are not. We can dance in the heat of evening again, we can laugh, and love.'

He wrenched free of her. She ran after him again. 'I'm playing the piano at a party we're having in two weeks' time. This parish is going to put the war behind it. You are going to come alive. You are going to let me into your life. This is going to be the turning-point.'

He tried to shake her off but she clung to him. He shouted at her, 'Do not defy me. There will be no music. There is no need for any. Leave me in peace.' He thrust her away from him.

Belle lost her footing, tried to hold on to his arm. He walked away. It was all happening too quickly; she tried to call but she was falling, falling. She knocked her head on a pillar and crashed onto the stone floor. It was so quiet suddenly.

She looked at Walter who had stopped. He turned. 'Help me,' she said because she could see blood on the pillar, she could feel it warm on her forehead.

He stared at her, seeing Alec, seeing the broken doll, and he ran out into the street, slamming the door, not hearing her whispered 'Walter.'

Belle staggered to her feet. She pulled her hair back into its bun, using two pins – all that were left. She wiped her forehead with her hand. The blood ran down her wrist. She spat on her handkerchief, wiping her skin again with it, then holding it to her forehead.

She was shaking but there was no pain; there was nothing. She walked, hunched over, and her legs felt as though they didn't belong. She reached the door to the hall, straightened. She lifted her head and forced herself to open the door and walk through the hall in the silence that fell, looking neither to left nor right, waving aside those who came to help.

She went to Mary's room and waited. Mary came, running in. 'Oh hinny, Sandy told me something had happened. Did he do this to you? Oh God, I can't believe it.' She pushed Belle into a chair and tore up one of Joseph's sheets to staunch the blood.

Belle whispered, 'Get Connie. Pack some of her clothes, some of mine. We can't stay here. I must go. I really must go now, this minute.'

Sandy took her to the station in a cart he'd borrowed, his arm round Connie who held her mother's hand and said nothing. He lifted Connie down, then Belle, holding her close, and now she almost cried. But she wouldn't, she mustn't, not over Walter, not any more, because it was over.

'Come back,' Sandy breathed into her ear. 'Come back, he needs you. That wasn't him, it was the war.'

She said nothing.

Connie said, 'Where are we going, Mam?'

'To Rempton.'

9

In the Rempton vicarage Belle couldn't sleep. She lay in the high double bed, her head aching but not as much as her heart. She listened to the owl's hooting, the bullocks coughing and Connie's murmurings as she lay beside her. And as dawn came up, the cockerels.

In the dining-room they ate boiled eggs and crisp toast. Boy said, 'I painted faces on eggs for Easter, didn't I, Grandma?'

Helen Driscoll smiled at him. 'You did indeed, young man, and we've saved one for Connie, haven't we? We were going to send it so it is a wonderful surprise to be able to give it to you instead, Connie.'

Connie put her hand on her mother's thigh. 'Does it hurt, Mam?'

Belle smiled. 'Very little now. How silly of me; I was just like Humpty Dumpty, Boy, only I crashed off a pew, not a wall. So clumsy of me; I was trying to catch a butterfly and set it free in the street.'

Boy grinned, then flicked his black hair off his face. It shone almost blue. 'I'm glad you did, because it made you come here. How're the gang, Connie? Come and chalk some hopscotch like we did last year in the alley, then show me how to pitch and toss.'

Helen Driscoll laughed. 'No pitch and toss here, young man, or you'll have the village policeman round. Off you go, you two.'

Connie looked at her mother. 'Are you all right?'

'Absolutely, now go along and make the most of this time with Boy. He has to go back to Amelia in a few days.'

Connie grinned and rushed from the table, coming back when Helen called, pushing in her chair then chasing Boy down the hall, through the lobby, past the boots and James Driscoll's walking-stick and out into the fresh cold of the garden.

Boy called, 'The chalk's in the shed. Grandma said we could draw it out on the terrace and there's slate there too. Race you.'

He ran ahead and Connie jogged behind, letting him stay in front. She looked up at the trees, still leafless but with buds. She looked across the fields to Longdale where the slag buckets groaned as they swayed up the heap.

She was glad they were here, glad to be away from Da because she knew he'd hurt her mother somehow. Had he pushed her? She shook her head at the thought. She'd like to kill him if he had. Had he shouted at her? What had he done? Why were they here? What was going to happen to them? Would she see Joseph again? Would she see the gang?

Yes, she was glad to be here but she missed the back alley, the babies, the women, the men. But not him, not her Da. Oh Mam, what has happened?

Boy was in the shed but she didn't go in yet. She ran round and round the garden as fast as she could, pumping her arms and legs, feeling the cold rasping in her throat and chest, running and running until she couldn't think any more.

Belle and Helen Driscoll watched her from the window.

Belle said, 'She's ten years old and knows that something is wrong, but I don't know what to tell her, so I've said nothing.'

Helen put her arm around Belle. 'Let her play for now. We'll take them out to the beck later. It's cold but sunny and we shall have a picnic and then when you know what you think, you will know what to tell her. Until then, talk to me if you wish, or just recover.

I shall ask no questions, but you know you are surrounded by those who love you.'

Helen rang the bell. 'Now, we'll let Maud clear away these things while we sort out the next round of food, then pick up the Greens' pony and trap. They are kind enough to allow us to borrow it whenever we wish, though that is really only in the holidays when Boy is with us.'

At eleven o'clock they all walked through the village and at each house they stopped and talked to the women who came to kiss Belle, hug her, tell her they missed her and Connie, and to ask after Walter.

'Busy, but well,' she replied to them all as the sun melted the last of the night's frost from the slates of the houses. Connie talked to the children, telling them of the money she earned keeping watch for the pitch and toss games. 'But don't tell Mam.'

They told her of the new headmaster and the drip he always had on his nose. 'Bye, you'd 'a' thought he'd have an icicle this winter.' They laughed. 'Come and play hopscotch when you're back from the beck.'

At the post office Connie and Boy bought liquorice and toffee. Connie said, 'I wonder if the gang have any toffee left? Will they wonder where I am?'

Boy said, 'Your Da will tell them.'

She couldn't even smile.

As they passed the butcher's Belle rubbed her forehead. 'Who'll do the shopping at the hall? I haven't left instructions. Is Josie well? Is Joseph over his cold? Is Walter—?' She fell silent.

Mrs Driscoll said, 'Everything will be all right.'

Heavy horses were hauling kegs on the drays; the Co-op was just the same. Mr Evans waved to her. The sweet smell of bread wafted from the baker's and in the window Mr Green puffed flour from his clothes as he signalled for them to go into the yard. Connie and Boy ran round, under the arch. 'Don't slip on the cobbles,' Belle called.

The smell of dough and yeast was strong, caught as it

was between the walls. The sun struck the grey stone. The pony whinnied, tugging at the rope which tethered it to the post. Connie and Boy soothed it while Belle smiled and felt its warm breath on her hand.

Mrs Green came out to them then, her face round and red, her apron as floury as Mr Green's had been. She took Belle's hands in hers, tutting at the cut on her forehead, at the tiredness beneath her eyes.

'Bye, looks like this lass needs a good feed-up,' she wheezed to Helen. 'I'll just pop some stotty cake in the basket as well.'

She called to her youngest son. 'You put four shives into that basket I made up, pet. Good ones, mind.'

Helen Driscoll said, 'You shouldn't but how very kind.'

Mrs Green smiled, kissed Belle's cheek. 'Not every day we have the vicar's wife back. We miss you, hinny. You're working too hard; you fall and slip when you're tired, mind.'

Belle looked at Alec's brother, John, as he lugged out the basket which was almost as big as himself. He was practically a replica of the young wicket-keeper who had gone with Walter.

'Was Alec musical, Mrs Green?' Her voice was quiet. She saw the shock on the woman's face, then the great wash of grief and wondered how she could have said such a thing, out of the blue. Had she become as cruel as Walter? 'I'm so sorry. Forgive me. I don't know what I'm thinking of. Yes, I'm rather tired.'

Mrs Green shook her head. 'Not to worry, and no, he wasn't. He lived for his cricket.' No-one spoke or moved as the war fell between them and around them – the long years of casualty lists, of grief, of sewing-circles, of children growing up without fathers.

At last Helen Driscoll said, her voice subdued, 'Come along, or we'll get there just in time to come home.'

They bowled along the lane, past the deserted school. 'Do you remember the concerts we gave to raise funds for the Red Cross?' Helen Driscoll asked. Belle nodded but she didn't want to think of the war any more.

She looked at the rooks' nests high in the elms, at the sheep grazing on the hills. 'Soon there will be lambs. Joseph must see them.'

But no, she didn't want to think about Newcastle.

She shook out the reins, feeling the jarring of the wheels on the ruts, forcing herself to listen to the children, to Helen, but all the time wondering why Walter had called Alec's name.

At the beck they stood on the stepping-stones looking down into the ice-cold water as it nudged their boots. It was so clean and clear. They ate cold chicken, soft broken stotty cake, and Connie rolled her hard-boiled Easter egg from the top of the hill, and only then would she eat it.

Belle took the two children back up the hill with the trays. 'Come along, sit on them,' Belle said. They slid to the bottom as they used to do.

All day she was busy and in the early evening she embroidered, pushing in her needle, pulling it through, smoothing the pink silk, counting the stitches, counting the strokes of the clock, trying to push Walter from her, trying to push the pain away.

'Teach me "Chopsticks",' she asked James, and sat at the piano with him while the children threw up the jack ball and grabbed the pebbles.

She made mistakes. James said, 'You are worse than ever; let me rescue these poor old keys.'

James played the 'Moonlight Sonata' while Helen Driscoll nodded in time to the music, her gnarled hands moving slowly with the knitting needles, and the tension eased in Belle as she sank into this other world which was Rempton and at last smiled from the heart, easing for a moment the knot of grief and despair at the death of her marriage.

She read to the children, then chased them up the stairs before bathing and drying them in huge soft towels. She and Connie tucked Boy into bed, feeling his arms around her neck, his lips on her cheek.

'I love you, Belle,' he said.

'I love you, Mam,' Connie said, after she'd clambered into the high double bed in the spare room. Belle closed the door gently, the scent of the children still with her, the peace of their mutual love warming her.

She sat with Helen and James and the only sounds were the crackling fire and the ticking clock until the doorbell rang.

'Mrs Green, madam,' Maud said as she ushered her through. Mrs Green's cheeks were still red, though there was no hint of flour, or of the sadness that had sprung up in the yard.

She stood, shaking her head at the chair, wanting to be quick. 'We'll be up early in the morning, you see. Now, Belle, I've been reading our Alec's letters, and the one Walter wrote when he was killed. He didn't play anything you know, but he looked after your man's harmonium. Your Walter thought it would keep him away from danger. He was looking after it when he died. Up till then, he was the only one of the team, apart from the schoolteacher, left alive.'

That night Belle lay in the bed, her daughter's body against hers, her breathing slow and light. She looked out of the window at the wind-driven clouds and at the mirror near the wardrobe.

James Driscoll had withdrawn when his son was killed, finally losing his mind when Philip's uniform had been sent to them. He had come here, to this room and dressed in his son's uniform which was still blood- and mud-drenched. He had held his son's photograph and stood before the mirror. 'Take me, instead of my son, God,' he'd prayed. 'Take me, and let him come home. Swap us, just swap us over.'

Belle could still smell the odour of death as she had stood before him, breaking the mirror image, coming between him and his pain, talking, returning every time he pushed her to one side, his voice cracking with madness. She had brought him back to them at the end of that long night.

But it was a different James who came back. He was kind, tolerant and he gave Helen the love he had always felt, but never acknowledged, even to himself.

She looked towards the window now, hearing Walter's cry. 'Alec, Alec.'

She should go to Walter, stand again between him and his pain. She should fight for his life, for hers and Connie's but all she could see were his eyes looking at her as she lay on the floor, and then the sound of his feet running from her.

Yes, she should go back. But could she?

Binnie leaned over Dora. She poked her. Dora stirred but that was all. She was asleep. Binnie checked the clock. Midnight. Mary would be in bed, the other girls too, though Walter wasn't. He was in his study where he had been since he had stumbled back at eight this evening. He had eaten nothing; he had not spoken. He had looked at her and Mary.

Mary had said, 'She's gone.'

Binnie smiled now, licking her finger then smoothing her eyebrows. She brushed her hair again, leaving it loose on her shoulders. Red hair looks good against green, she thought, tying the shawl loosely round her dress. She undid three buttons then a fourth. She ran her hands over her breasts. She wore nothing underneath. She caressed her nipples. They hardened. She felt her mouth slacken. There had been no-one for so long. You couldn't count the odd bit against the wall in the back alley.

She shut the door quietly behind her, walking down the stairs – they creaked. No doors opened. The landing was dark but she knew her way. Soon she wouldn't have to creep, soon all this would be hers, and these rooms would be empty. And that Sandy would go too. The men could get out. She, Dora and Walter would move to Jesmond and she'd have it all, as she deserved.

Walter stared at the embers of the fire. There was barely any heat left in them but he didn't feel cold – all he felt was bereft. How could he live without her? Didn't she know he needed her? How could he run the hall? How could she leave the women and their babies? How could she play the harmonium, and then fall? How could she do that to him, bringing Alec back, the war back and all the pain he had shut away – then leave?

He looked at his hands on the arms of the chair. They were white. She had been white as she'd cried out. He dug the nails of one hand into the skin of the other. Think of that, not her, not Alec, not the dark yawning future without her.

He heard the knock on the door.

'Belle?'

It was Binnie, holding an enamel mug in her hand; there was steam rising, there were dark trails from the rim to the base. He dug his nails back into his hand. It wasn't Belle.

Binnie said, 'I was making myself a drink and thought you would like one.'

Walter smiled. 'I haven't played chess with you tonight. I've been – busy.' How normal his voice sounded.

Binnie placed the mug on his blotting-pad. The brown trails were cocoa, of course; how stupid of him. They were staining the blotting-paper, growing larger and larger. He picked the mug up with both hands. There was a circle on the blotting-paper, a dark brown circle. He drank the cocoa.

Binnie said, 'You need some more coal on your fire.' He looked at her as she stood there, so still.

'It doesn't matter.'

She leaned forward, over the desk, her shawl-ends brushing the cocoa stain. She touched his face. 'It does.'

He didn't mind her near him, as he minded Belle,

because Binnie was easy, she didn't move him, touch his soul, demand feelings beyond pity and remorse. He put down the mug, nudging it this way and that, until it fitted the stain. It had to fit. He stared at the bubbles. It wasn't sweet like the cocoa Belle made, the cocoa she brought him every night, in a cup. She would sit by the fire in the kitchen, the light catching her hair, her eyes, her beautiful mouth, her forehead.

Oh Belle – how often he had wanted to reach across and touch her, hold her, feel the joy they had once shared, the laughter, the love. But if he allowed himself to feel love, he would also be able to feel pain and anger at the loss of his men, and perhaps the sounds would come back. And how could he be expected to cope with that? Today had been bad enough. He had work to do, valuable work that was restoring men's minds, couldn't she see that? Oh Belle.

He saw the blood as she had lain there, he heard her voice. 'Help me.' The pain he had felt then sliced through him, so that he couldn't breathe, he couldn't move. It was too much, on top of the pain of Alec, of the team, of the war.

He heard his own sobs. He bunched hands against his mouth but still they came, and then there were arms around him, holding him, rocking him, and there was a voice that soothed, hands that stroked his hair, lips that kissed his forehead.

It was Binnie, holding him to her, swaying with him, crooning to him, warming him. He had been cold, he hadn't realized, but she wasn't warming him inside. Who could do that? Why couldn't he get warm, why couldn't anyone stop that terrible noise of crying?

'Stop this noise,' he gasped. 'Someone stop this noise.'

He gripped the arms, holding them, clinging to them, then there was a softness against his face, pressing into his nose, his mouth, and the noise was stopping, and the smell and taste of soft skin was there. He could bury his face in it, pressing in further, and still the arms held him, stroked him, and now his body was still; there were no racking sobs, there was peace against the soft breast.

There was warmth too, rising from his groin, into his belly, his chest, his throat, his tongue, and there was warmth in the voice which still crooned, and it was so long since he had felt warm. Now there was a nipple, hard, urgent, against his tongue. It was in his mouth, there were hands pushing, pulling his head in and out, and the nipple slid along his tongue, then away, then in his mouth again and the warmth was greater.

Someone raised his head, there was a tongue in his mouth, probing and he couldn't breathe, he couldn't think, he could only groan as the heat roared into his brain and the nipple was back, sliding in and out, in and out.

There was the smell of naked skin, and he was sinking into it, into the boiling heat. There were hands on his belly, tearing at his trousers, and then they were stroking him, gripping him, stirring the heat until he wanted to explode.

'Take me, Walter,' Binnie groaned, her mouth against his, pulling him from the chair.

The voice burst into his mind, drenching him. He reeled from her, struggling, seeing Binnie, her dress undone to the waist, her red hair on her pale shoulders, her lips slack, her eyes glazed, his saliva still on her breasts, her hand wet from his semen.

'Oh God, oh God.' He wrenched away, pushing her from him, stumbling past the chair. It fell. He reached towards her, not wanting to touch her, knowing he must. Oh God. 'Forgive me. Stand up.' He fastened his trousers, picked up her green shawl which had fallen on the floor, handed it to her, turning away from her nakedness. 'Binnie, forgive me. I was mad. I was insane, I wasn't here. I was in my head, not here, not in my body. Oh God.'

Binnie's rage grew until she thought she would scream, 'You're not mad. She's left you. I know you like me. You sat with me when you wouldn't sit with her; your hands touched mine. You talked to me when you wouldn't talk to her. I know you love me.' She dragged herself up and gripped his arms. 'Look at me, I know you want me. Look at my hands; this is you.'

She bared her breasts again, wiping her hands on them. 'Look at me. I have you on me. See it.'

He did, then draped the shawl around her shoulders. What had he done to this poor girl? It was all his fault. She was right; he had touched her, he had taught her, but only because she meant nothing to him. It was Belle who meant everything. It was Belle whom he had longed for, but could not risk being near. It was Belle's touch which had fired him, and from which he had withdrawn, because it was too much.

He was panting. His legs trembled. He could still feel Binnie's hands on him and he wanted to vomit, to rush from the room, wash her from him. Oh God, what had he done?

He walked towards her. She backed away. 'Forgive me,' he said again, forcing his voice to sound calm. 'I have misled you. I care for you, Binnie, but I love my wife. I have been insane and I don't understand myself.'

He straightened his hair, trying to think how he had come to undo her buttons, to kiss skin that he had no right to be near, and no wish to be near. He reached out. Binnie shook her head. He looked at the fire, at the window. He saw his image in the glass, saw Binnie.

He said, 'I am appalled at myself. This will never happen again, I swear.'

Binnie tied the shawl, and redid her buttons, her fingers trembling, her rage silencing her. For Christ's sake, was it going to end like this, all that she had been working for? She forced tears to come. 'But Mrs Symmonds has gone. You need someone.'

He came to her then, taking her hands, leading her to the chair, righting it, sitting her down, then standing at the end of the desk. 'She'll come back. I know she will. When she does I'll tell her of this, of how I abused your trust, made use of your body.'

He could hardly bring himself to use the word. He still felt her breast in his mouth, her hands on his penis. 'You are a kind woman, Binnie, and there will be a far better man for you one day.'

Binnie sobbed, and they were real tears now, but tears of anger, because not only had he taken Jesmond from her, he had taken blackmail as well, the stupid bugger.

Belle did not reply to Walter's letter which begged her to return. She was too tired, and she had no answer to give him. *'Please forgive me, and come home. I beg you.'* Instead she walked and read and slept, that day, the next day, and the next. She talked to Helen, she listened, and slowly she noticed that the birds were singing, that the wheat was being sown, that lambs were being born, that hymns were being sung in the church.

She walked to Brenan's Hill with Connie and stood beneath the racing clouds, and above the fields, seeing the pond, the houses, the gardens.

'It all looks so small, Mam,' Connie said.

'Yes, we're all so tiny in the huge scheme of things, aren't we?' Belle murmured.

That afternoon, she learned to laugh again, to run with Connie and Boy, to roll with them down the hill slopes as they did, seeing the sky, then the ground, then the sky again. She learned that joy still existed.

That evening she thought of the girls and their babies, of the men, and knew that they needed her. She thought of Binnie, and knew that she must be dealt with. She thought of Alec, and finally, more than a week after she and Connie had arrived, she thought of Walter.

'We're going home,' she said to Connie on Friday evening. 'We'll need to put the seeds in their trays, we'll need to bring the piano round for the party, and arrange a trip to the seaside for Sunday School, and the street. And you, madam, can keep watch with your gang for the pitch and toss.'

Connie gasped.

'Yes, there's a great deal a mother knows, you know. We're seldom surprised,' Belle grinned.

In the evening Walter waited for her in the kitchen, knowing she would come in through the garden. Mary and the girls had polished everything, the men had cleaned the hall. The babies were being bathed, Binnie was upstairs, putting Dora to bed. There would be no-one to disturb them.

He saw his family open the gate and walk down the cinder path. They came through the wash-house, the scullery, and finally into the kitchen. Belle put her case on the floor.

'Hello Walter, we've come home,' Belle said. Her wound was healing, the bruising had almost gone, but he would never forget what had happened, any of it.

Belle waited, feeling Connie's hand in hers. Walter said nothing for a moment, then looked at Connie. 'Was Boy well? Did you play hopscotch?'

Connie felt a shock of surprise because her father was smiling. 'He was grand. He's gone home to London now, to Amelia.'

He still looked at Connie, not at Belle. 'The gang have been calling for you. I promised them some toffee when you and your mother returned.' Now he looked at Belle and there was pain in his eyes, but there was love also.

She moved towards him, but he turned away, walking to the door, opening it, and her heart failed her. She shouldn't have come back. How could she fight for him as she would need to?

He said, 'Please, both of you, come with me.' They followed him down the passage, into the hall. There were decorations along the walls, and a piano near the door to the church.

Belle knew she mustn't cry, she simply mustn't, not with the men standing there, and Sandy grinning, but she could taste the tears which were running as though they'd never stop. She felt the touch of Walter's hand.

He led her to his study, saying, 'Sandy will take Connie to Mary. I have to talk to you now.'

A fire was burning in the grate, and love flowed through Belle as the tears ceased and she stood feeling the warmth of his hand, seeing the soft shadows of the room. There were photos of her on the desk. There was one of Connie on the wall. There was one of the cricket team over the fireplace. She walked across and touched it.

'I know about Alec,' she said, turning to face him.

'Belle, that is all over with. I have faced it; I have faced more than that and the shock of doing so has made me see myself and my life. I love you more than anything on this earth. I always have.' Walter held out his hand. 'But I have nearly drowned in self-pity, in selfishness, in fear, and have struck out blindly, cruelly, not allowing you to help, denying both of us the comfort and passion of our love. I have rejected you, turned from you when you touched me, though I longed to take you in my arms. I turned from you on Christmas night, when all I wanted was to adore you, thank you, worship you. It was out of fear, and selfishness. I have mistreated you, and Connie, throughout all that time. I have mistreated you again, more badly, more painfully, in this last week.'

Belle came close to him, put her arms around him, wanting his round her. Walter gently pushed her from him but held her hands as he told her what it was that he had done.

Belle heard the words, felt his hands on hers. She saw his lips as they moved again. 'I was appalled at myself. I was out of my mind. It was all my fault, I misled Binnie.' He shook her. 'Belle, she means nothing to me; that's why I allowed her to come close. I was insane. I didn't know what was happening. I just wanted to be warm. I don't remember how it happened.'

She was pulling away, wanting to be free of his hands, wanting to stop the sound of his voice but he held her and he wouldn't stop speaking.

'When we came to the mission I knew I loved you, and

only you, but I feared that if I allowed myself to feel love, to allow myself joy, I would be betraying the dead. But more than that, I feared the pain that any feeling would bring, ignoring entirely the pain I was inflicting on you.'

Belle looked down at the carpet. She had never noticed the pattern before, the threadbare patch, the scorch marks. He dropped her hands. She gripped the mantelpiece.

'I've never noticed the chips in the tiles of the fireplace, the cracks.' The fire-irons glinted. She must watch the flames, she must follow the sparks, watching them cling to the soot but she couldn't because now the agony erupted. She couldn't bear it, any of it. She couldn't bear the thought of him and Binnie, she couldn't bear the echoes of his words of love. Were they true, or a scramble of desperation to keep her at the mission now that he had known another woman? She was rocking backwards and forwards, she must stop. She couldn't.

'I can't bear it,' she screamed at him. 'I can't bear the pain, the thought of you and her after everything. I can't bear the lies you have told me. Love? What love?'

He grabbed her. 'Our love. It's true, I love you, all of that is true. Please, believe me. I told you everything because I know I must never hide anything from you again. I love you. I remember how we would dance and sing. I remember the feathers floating in the air. I remember holding you, loving you, kissing you.'

She tore from him, shaking her head, the images of their love being drowned by images of Binnie and he together at the table, his voice so patient and gentle, but so abrupt with her.

'Believe me,' he pleaded. 'It is you I love. I don't know what happened, suddenly she was there.'

'Suddenly your arms were round her, your lips were on hers. Suddenly! Suddenly! This is our life that has suddenly been destroyed. This, after everything else.' How could her voice be heard against the roaring agony?

He reached out again, and she wanted to weep in his arms at the pain she felt. She wanted him to soothe her and comfort her, but how could he, when it was he who had inflicted the ultimate betrayal? She pushed him away and he grew more pale and drawn. His mouth was working; he was weeping. Good, he must suffer.

He said, 'No, it wasn't like that. She brought me cocoa, and somehow she was just there, her bare skin pressed against me.'

Belle laughed then, an ugly harsh sound. She wrenched at her own dress, tearing the buttons open. Her bodice was beneath.

She wrenched at that, trying to tear it. He tried to stop her. She turned to the desk, picking up the scissors, hacking the bodice because the material was too strong, and then she stopped, wept, throwing the scissors to the ground. 'She was just there, was she? Oh Walter. What have you done to us?'

His arms were round her, gripping her, rocking her, kissing her hair, not letting her go until at last the roaring in her head was gone but not the exhausted anguish, because this man could never again bring her comfort.

She tried to push him away, but he wouldn't allow it. He made her listen as he told her exactly what had happened in the war, in his mind, then and on his return, and he told her the depths of misery to which he had sunk and things that no man would normally admit to. And the truth was in his voice and eyes, and at last she recognized it. He explained again that Binnie had been so easy to be with. He explained his deep love for Belle, his fears of the consequences if he acknowledged it.

She made herself listen calmly to the stumbling bewilderment of her husband as he recounted the episode with Binnie, and finally he was finished. Silence hung between them. She looked down at the scissors. It was now that she understood fully the woman they had taken under their roof.

It was she who held him, now. It was she who stopped his mouth with her kisses, holding his face as she told him that Binnie could not have worn any clothes beneath her dress. That she had come intent on seduction, on destruction – and they must not be destroyed.

She said, 'Mrs Driscoll has discovered that she was thrown out of her home when her seaman found her with another man. She was only in the workhouse for two months. She has taught her daughter to lie about her past too. In my heart I know that you are not a liar. I know that if you say you love me, you do, and those are words I've longed to hear.'

He took her upstairs then and looked at her in the light from the moon, kissing her wound, the corner of her mouth, the nape of her neck, her shoulder, her breast. She put her hands either side of his head but for a moment she saw his lips on Binnie and wanted to push him from her.

He sensed her stiffen and kissed the inside of her wrist, holding her tightly. 'I love only you. I will always love you. The past is behind. It took that dreadful day to show me that.'

His voice was strong again, his hands certain as they removed her clothes, then his own. He held her against him.

'I love only you.' His mouth found hers and now desire gripped her and her kisses were as fierce as his, and her hands and mouth were eager as she explored his body and came to remember the inside of his thighs, the smoothness of his belly, the strength of him as he dragged her down to the bed, lying alongside, then on top, then beneath.

All the time they kissed, whispered, groaned, and it was as though they were wiping the past from their lives, and then he was inside her, moving gently, wanting to merge with her, wanting always to be part of her.

'I adore you. I have wasted too much of our time. I want to live each second of my life from now on,' he murmured against her mouth, and at last she said, 'I love you, I will never leave you again.'

When they lay at last in bed, Belle breathed in the scent of his skin, listening to his breathing, kissing his neck, feeling him stir. She kissed him again and felt the rekindling of her desire.

She ran her tongue along his lips and his mouth opened, his lips met hers and there was soft laughter between them, and joy and familiarity in the body which stirred against hers and the hand that found her breast and the leg that moved across her. Tonight was theirs – tomorrow she must see Binnie.

Belle sat in Binnie's flat, smelling the stale smoke of her Woodbines, pushing the plate of dog-ends away from her.

She repeated, 'It's important that we understand one another, Binnie, understand one another absolutely. So, I'll say once more, that I know what happened while I was away and I know your past. The question we have to consider is, what about your future?'

Belle looked at Binnie who was tracing lines in the ash which had dropped off the end of her cigarette onto the table, feeling the hatred surge, the anger. She wanted to push this woman from the flat, from her house, not caring what happened to her, but there was Dora and how could you toss a child aside because of something the mother had done?

She continued, 'You have a daughter, so for that reason I am giving you a choice. You may remain with us, because Dora sees this as her home, or we could find you another position, one which will welcome Dora too.

'If you stay, you work as you have been, with the girls and the mission, but there will be firm rules. You will treat all the babies with kindness, and equal consideration. Joseph too. You will not try and spend time with Walter. You must return the key to the kitchen cupboards and larder to Sandy at the end of every day, and account for all goods used. At this mission we must all work together.'

Belle paused, wanting to wave away the cigarette smoke which was wafting towards her, but not doing so, because this was Binnie's home, for now. 'Or, as I say, we shall find you a new position elsewhere.'

She waited, looking straight at Binnie, willing her to choose a new position, but where? And how could she and Walter write a reference?

Binnie stubbed out her cigarette, then rubbed the finger which was black from the ash. 'I want to stay because you're right, it's Dora's home and it's mine too. But as well I want to say I'm sorry, I was stupid with Walter. I just wanted someone to love. And I've been stupid about other things.'

Belle fought to keep her features still. She must not show her disappointment – she had given the woman a choice, she must abide by it.

Binnie lifted her head and there were dark smudges beneath her eyes that Belle had not noticed before. She waited.

Binnie said, 'I want you to know that I've been taking food and selling it.'

Belle jerked in surprise. 'You're confessing?'

'Yes. I even tried to blame the men, like I tried to blame Rachel back in the village. I know I've done wrong all along and I want to say sorry, and I want to say it'll stop.'

Belle knew that she should go to the woman who was crying now with great racking sobs. She should hold her, she should remember that young girl who had been drummed out by Walter from the village, remember how she had none nothing to truly stop it. But still she didn't move, because she also remembered the woman who had seduced her husband, the woman who had trained her daughter in a lie.

Belle said, 'It will be all right, it's all over; this is a fresh start for us all.' But was it? She wanted to feel certain of Binnie's honesty but she knew it would take more than these few words, these tears. She left the flat and walked back down the stairs.

Later that day Binnie finished her shift in the kitchen,

standing quietly while Sandy checked the food, smiling as he locked up, then she climbed the stairs, sipped her cocoa in the flat, hearing the cries of the new baby in Room 4, sucking deeply on the last of her cigarette, stubbing it out.

Oh no, my fine Lady Symmonds, I'm not going anywhere. Turn me down, would he? I might have lost his body, and his money, but as long as I stick it here, you'll go on paying us one way or another, I'll see you do; and when you go, which one day you will, they'll want someone who's been here the longest, and that'll be me.

10

On the way back from the market Belle saw the notices in the shops. *No credit given.* She checked her purse. Only sixpence left. It was 1926 and there was no work, no money, no hope for all these people, and at the mission they only had coal for another week.

She sat with Walter that night, poring over the figures, their hands touching.

'Connie needs another skirt for grammar school. I can make one, but I still need to buy the material.'

Walter pursed his lips. 'I'm still trying to get through to Dora about working hard if she wants to get a scholarship too. I sometimes wonder if it's worth it.'

Belle kissed his cheek. 'We promised ourselves we'd do for Dora what we do for Connie. If she doesn't make the most of it, then that is her fault, not ours.'

They sat listening to the sounds of the house, the crying of the babies, the laughter of the mothers.

'This won't get us coal for the rest of the month.' Walter kissed the inside of her wrist. They ran over the figures again.

'Can we sell any more Nativity figures?' Belle pondered.

'Let's try.'

'More stotty cake from the front-room shop, and toffee?'

'Let's give it a go.'

In the morning Mary came into the kitchen with her coat on. She handed Belle hers. 'Come on, my girl, we're off to the slacks.'

They walked through the streets where men were grouped, talking about work which wouldn't come. The fog swirled around them all. They passed pawn shops, the lamps of which were lit long into the evenings these days.

Along the slack bank the winds snatched at their hats, their coats, and the foghorns wailed. There was no sun to shine on the high tide, on the flotsam, the pieces of wood, boxes, the sleepers.

'When I was a bairn we'd come here at night and haul out the best bits. We'd drag them sleepers with tar home, Belle. They were best.' She went on to mimic Mrs Gribble. 'Bye, don't you worry about coal, bonny lass, this'll do us just grand.' She slapped her hands on her arms. 'If this fog holds it'll really help.'

That night, with Walter and Sandy, they dragged home two sleepers on a handcart for what seemed like miles. The men sawed them. 'And a man of God too?' Mary joked as she and Belle brought the logs in, setting them up round the kitchen fire to dry.

'A man of the people,' Belle whispered to Walter and kissed the back of his neck gently while he continued to saw, because she had seen the rigidity of his body at Mary's words.

He leant his head against hers. 'I love you. I am truly happy,' he said.

'I have never been happier,' Belle replied.

She called the men through from the mission to carry some to their stove and to the girls' sitting-room, and listened while they talked of the rota they would set up, taking it in turns to collect what they could.

Connie looked up from Dora's homework, her hand pointing out the algebra error. 'I'll make tea.'

'You'll get on with your work,' Belle said, panting, her gloves soaked as she stacked another arm-load by the fire.

'My mam says it's stealing to do what you've done,' Dora said, patting her reddish curls, opening her blue eyes wide.

Belle laughed at Dora. 'Your mam is quite right, but it's there for the picking and will just go to waste. I prefer to call it "taking advantage of the situation".' She wanted to add, 'And your mam will know all about that.' She didn't.

The next day, after school, Connie grabbed Sadie and the gang, taking them out to the tram sheds. They carried sacks and followed the tracks, picking up coal which had been dropped by the coal carts as they went over the links. They pulled boxes and planks from the slacks. Dora hadn't come. 'I must work,' she'd said.

'First time ever,' Sadie grunted, wiping her hands down the hessian they had tied around their waists. 'Don't know why you put up with her, or that mother of hers. She's in the betting shop, pet, every night.'

Connie wondered why they did too, but her mother had just said, 'We need to think of Dora. She had a poor start. We owe it to her.'

In the morning they called in at the baker's for yesterday's bread, sharing it out between them. Connie took hers back to Belle, dumping it on the table. Belle smiled. 'That new skirt will be ready for you next week.'

'You look tired, Mam.'

'We all look tired but at least we're warm and happy, which is more than you can say for most of them round here.'

In the summer of 1928 Sandy returned from an exchange trip to Germany, and Mary cried for joy.

Belle said, 'You should be married.'

'We have nowhere to live,' Mary said.

Belle talked to Walter about the attic rooms which abutted onto Binnie's flat.

He shook his head. 'They wouldn't be big enough, my darling.'

'They would, if we took a few feet from Binnie's sitting-room. The walls are only wood.'

She asked Binnie if she would mind. 'Why do they need that much space?' Binnie asked.

'Because there are three of them. I will, of course, increase your wages to make up for the inconvenience.'

Binnie's eyes narrowed.

'I'll just have to then, won't I?'

'No, you don't have to. You can object and then, of course, we shan't continue.' Belle wanted to add as she had objected to Dora helping to collect coal and bread, but as she hadn't objected to burning the coal or eating the bread.

'How much more money?'

Mary and Sandy were married in the church, with Walter officiating. Dr and Mrs Scott brought a table-cloth, Helen Driscoll brought rose petals, and a ham from the squire. Belle wrote to thank him, telling him how hams were always needed at the mission, and in the neighbourhood.

After that he sent one every month, and eggs, and cheeses, and apples. His wife sent a clothes parcel too, in September.

Belle took the best of the clothes to the market, taking Mary and Joseph, drinking tea in the café as they always did, waiting until the day's shopping was almost over, then she bargained for end-cuts, for broth bones, for cabbages, potatoes, anything. She took the squire's old hunting jacket, Lady Smythe's cocktail dress, her evening bag, to Janet's, the second-hand clothes dealer.

'This is a better lot than usual, Mrs Symmonds,' Janet said. 'Is the mission going up in the world?'

Belle shook her head, the breath catching in her chest. She made herself speak. 'What do you mean, Janet – better than normal?' Though she knew; she'd always known, she realized now.

'That Binnie, brings it along regular. Says it comes from some vicarage, Rempton way.'

Belle haggled over the price of the hunting jacket and pocketed the money, not looking at Mary or Joseph, feeling the vegetable bags cutting into her hand, looking at Joseph's threadbare coat, her own, Mary's.

They passed the betting shop as they returned and Belle gripped the handles of her bags. She and Mary put away the vegetables, the bones, the end-cuts. She climbed the stairs to Binnie's flat, knocked, entered.

Binnie was sitting with her feet up on the fire-guard. Belle said, 'Go down and let Walter check your home-work, Dora. This first year at grammar school is very important.' She stood beside Binnie, her arms folded, while Dora left.

She told her that there would be no more clothes to sell at the market, then looked at the woman, her blotched face, her sagging jowls. 'How could you sell the clothes Mrs Driscoll sends, Binnie, when we are so hard pressed?'

'You put that bloody family next to me. You took my space and only gave me three extra shillings a week. Why should she have a husband? It's not fair. I'm alone; no-one cares about that so I've got to look after myself and my bairn.'

Belle left. What was the point of arguing or giving in to anger? Binnie must have been selling clothes for years but she'd never change and at least now Belle knew that for certain and could take steps to contain this foul woman. But there was still Dora. They must somehow show her another way.

Binnie pulled out the beer bottle from the side of the chair. The stupid cow hadn't even torn her off a strip, had she? What did they think she'd do after they pushed her out of the way for that Mary and her by-blow. Why should they take her space? Bloody hell, three shillings was nothing. Belle knew that because she'd just walked away, hadn't she?

Just give it time and she'd be on top because, from the look of him, Walter wouldn't last long. When he went, there'd be a new man in and that Belle would be out, back to her bloody Rempton. Then that lot next door would be out quicker than a dose of salts, and she'd have the keys for all the cupboards.

In 1929 the postman brought news of Connie's success with her Senior Cambridge exams, and therefore her admission to teachers' training college.

Belle and Mary possed in the wash-house, grinning at

one another, forgetting for a moment the huge heap of clothes from the visiting German and French ex-soldiers.

'You know what this news will mean, don't you?' panted Mary.

'Don't ruin my day, Mary,' Belle laughed, knowing that now Dora would expect training college also. 'I've told Dora that she will only go if she works hard and gets a bursary too. She's brighter than Connie in a lot of ways, but she wants something for nothing and I can't bear to see Walter working so hard with her, night after night, when she's barely listening.'

'Just like her mother,' Mary said, sweat staining her dress.

Belle didn't want to think of Binnie, not today, not ever. 'There's too much to worry about to spend any more energy on that woman.' The anxiety which was always there caught at her chest.

She looked up. The windows were too steamed up to see through.

She rested the poss-stick. 'I'm just going to check Walter.'

Mary nodded. 'I thought he was looking a little better.'

Belle didn't answer; she just wiped her hands and wouldn't think of how pale her husband was, how ill he had been when the scarlet fever had burned up his body, weakening his heart so dreadfully.

She walked out into the warm summer air, and crouched by Walter's chair, kissing his cheek, watching as Joseph rocked a new baby in the pram.

'I can't believe he's nine,' Walter said. 'What a lot of very good years I've had.'

Belle held his hand to her face. 'And will go on having, my love. We need you to keep us stable and stop us from panicking when there seems no way forward.'

Walter shook his head. 'No, it is you who do that, it is you who are the heart of all of this.' He waved his hand at the building, at Joseph.

His skin was almost transparent; the blue veins stood

out on the slender bones of his hands and Belle wanted to hold him to her and breathe her life into him, for she knew that his was ebbing.

'You'll be so proud when Connie goes to college, and then when Dora makes it, but it's time you did less with her. Why not work every other night, my love, and leave me to do some? Now, I shall get some lemon barley, how would you like that? Dr Scott will be here soon.'

She rose, feeling the pain in her joints. 'Good heavens, I'm getting old.'

'Forty isn't old,' he murmured.

'Neither is forty-five, so you take good care of yourself. I'll fetch that drink.' She brushed off her skirt, smelling the roses, hearing the clinker beneath her feet, and then his voice, saying words which seemed to stop her heart.

'I think I'd like to go to Rempton.'

She walked on, poured water into a jug, made lemon barley, stirred it again and again, her heart aching, because she knew what this meant.

They arrived at Longdale in bright sunshine. 'I thought you could go in the wing. The tenants left at Christmas,' Helen Driscoll said, flicking the reins of the trap. 'I didn't want you to know, or you would have become ridiculous and not accepted our financial support.'

Walter smiled. 'You don't know our Belle; she would still have taken it, and asked for more.'

Belle stroked his cheek and Connie watched them both. Belle's hair was grey, her face was thin. She was too tired. Her father was so white – his hair, his skin. Connie wanted to hold them both to her, keep them safe.

She looked at the hawthorn hedge, the church tower, the elm trees and the darkness of the yew, then back at her father. Oh Da, I love you, she thought, and I think I know why you've come back, and I can't bear it, and I don't know how Mam will.

Helen stopped the trap at the gate of the wing. James steadied Walter, chuckling as he said, 'One old fogey helping another, eh? But soon you'll be spry again, and lend your arm to me.'

Connie walked behind her parents as they approached the house. There were snapdragons, roses and stocks either side of the path, there were delphiniums and hollyhocks against the house, and honeysuckle over the door.

'I grew that for you, my love,' Belle said.

Walter stopped and touched the flowers. 'I'm glad I'm back at last,' he said.

That night he and Belle lay in one another's arms, and there were the sounds of the bullocks, of dogs barking, cats fighting. There were no foghorns, no babies crying, there was no shouting in the streets. Belle lay listening to his breathing, feeling the weight of his arm on her body, willing her strength to flow into him.

Walter watched the dawn break, saw the light seep into the room. He rose, shaking his head at Belle. 'No, I have things to do, alone.'

He dressed, opened the door, then walked through the village and along the lanes where his cricket team had played, hearing their voices, their laughter. He stopped at the school they had attended, and where Archie had taught. Would Dora be a teacher like her father? The mission seemed so distant now, not part of his life, and the sound of the team was louder, joyous, welcoming.

He rubbed the lichen on the wall, he felt the early sun on his hands, bringing him strength, bringing life. He returned to the wing and ate breakfast – the egg was rich and runny, the bread was soft and warm. He sat with Belle in the garden. Connie brought them hats.

'You'll need these, the sun's strong,' she said. Soon the church bells rang and he and Belle walked hand in hand down the nave to the sound of the harmonium, to the handshake of the Longdale vicar, to the smiles of the congregation who stood in welcome.

Mr and Mrs Green came to him. Billy's mother, Fred's, Frank's. They all came.

Walter listened while hymns were sung, and prayers

were said, seeing the stained glass window, the flowers in the vases. He listened as the vicar gave the blessing and then paused. 'Walter, would you give the sermon, though I know you are unprepared?'

Belle shook her head, holding his arm. 'No, you're too weak.'

Walter bent and kissed her forehead. 'No, not any more.'

He had colour in his cheeks, and light in his eyes, and his tread was firm as he bowed before the altar and climbed the steps to the pulpit.

Belle grasped Connie's hands and they sat as the light streamed through the windows and Walter spoke of the last time he had been here, of the years of the war, of the years since.

'I have battled with myself, we have all battled to set up the mission, and to care for the girls and their babies. My daughter Connie has picked up coals from the coal carts, Belle has haggled in the market.'

He leaned forward and smiled at Belle. 'Our first mission baby was Joseph; he is now greatly loved by everyone. He was a gift from God.'

Belle looked up at him, breathing in every inch of him, every sound as he said, 'I lost my way; I turned from God but as I sat this week in the garden that Belle created, watching Joseph rocking a newborn baby, I said, "Thank you, Lord, for my life," because I knew then, with absolute certainty, that God exists. How could he not with the blessings I have received?'

She met him as he stepped down from the pulpit, and together they returned to their seats. She held his hand and stared at his fingers, at the veins, the skin, at the cuff which was as white as his face, and knew that there was very little time left.

They left the church at the end of the service side by side, Connie with them. Belle knew they would not go to the wing, but to the cricket field. She didn't speak, neither did he; there was no need.

They passed the cottages and walked slowly along the lane where loosestrife and meadowsweet grew. The cricket pitch had been newly mown for hay, the scent of grass was thick in the air, the pavilion was white against the blue of the sky and the black of Longdale's slag-heap.

Walter sat on the bench erected in memory of his friend Philip Driscoll. He held Belle's hand, and Connie's, and gazed at the young oaks which had been planted, one for each member of the team.

He said gently, 'In the war I found such solace in the Psalms. Their anguish reflected so much of my own condition.' He sat quite still, then said, 'Since the war you, my family, have been my salvation, and so too has my God, though I have only just understood that.'

Belle said, 'I love you, my darling.' Her voice was quite quiet and calm.

Connie kissed her father's hand and they sat as he heard the sound of leather on willow, as he felt the heat of the sun on his back, as he stepped forward to take the ball. He turned, and Belle's hair was fair again, her face unlined. She sat with a young Connie on her knee.

He heard the team calling to him. 'Come on then, Walter. It's your turn.'

He smiled, lifted his head. 'I'm coming,' he said.

James Driscoll conducted the funeral. The following week Belle could hardly bear to leave Rempton, and Walter. Mrs Driscoll pleaded with her to stay. 'James is so frail, I need your support.' Using any device to try to keep her.

Belle returned to the mission though. She smiled and functioned, held new babies, and tried not to hate Binnie who had been the only one not to travel to Rempton for the funeral. 'I knew I wouldn't be welcome,' she said. 'Not after you and Walter threw me out of the village.'

In September the new minister arrived.

'Please help me appoint my team,' he asked. 'You will be staying on, I hope?'

Connie looked at her mother and smiled as Belle shook her head. 'No, I'm needed at Rempton and it's time Sandy and Mary were given that responsibility.'

For Walter and she had decided when Binnie cheated on the clothes that she must never have a position of authority. It would be irresponsible of them. She explained now, to the Revd Philips about Binnie, her history, her dishonesty, her disloyalty and about the debt they owed her.

'If you feel you can't keep her on, I could take her back to Rempton with me,' she said.

Connie leaned across the table. 'You will not. You have done enough.' Because Mrs Driscoll had told her of Binnie's reason for leaving the village, of the thieving of the clothes, the food. She repeated, 'You have done enough, your debt has been more than repaid.'

Connie then looked at the young minister. 'Please keep her. We will warn her to behave; Mary and Sandy will keep an eye on her. My mother has done enough.' Her voice was strong; after all her mother needed her support.

The vicar agreed, smiling at Connie. 'You'll be a Tartar in the classroom.'

Connie smiled in return. 'You'll wish that you were in that classroom when you break the news to Binnie that she's not in control.'

Belle smiled wryly. 'We can't leave that to a young innocent. I will explain to her.'

She climbed the stairs for the last time and as Binnie sat with her feet on the fire-guard Belle told her that Sandy and Mary would be in charge, but that she was assured of a job and home as long as she wished.

Binnie sat upright as Belle continued, 'But, Binnie, if you steal, lie or cause mischief, the minister will have no compunction in dismissing you.'

'But that's not fair. I've been here longest. I know everything. That's not fair, it's not right. It's mine. You should give it to me.' She pushed herself to her feet and paced backwards and forwards. The ash from her cigarette fell to the floor. She gripped her elbows. She must cry, that's what she must do. She hung her head, putting her hand to her mouth, sobbing.

Belle just looked at her. 'I'm sorry, Binnie, but you lost that right when you stole the clothes. It was the last chance, can't you see that?'

Binnie snatched her hand from her mouth. 'All I can see is you throwing us out of the village, to this bloody city, and leaving us. That job was mine. It was my right. It's not fair. We're here because of you. You're going back to my home.'

Belle shook her head. 'No, you could have come when Walter died. You wouldn't.'

'I wouldn't have been welcome.'

'Binnie, don't be silly. At funerals all is forgiven. But even if you had come, I wouldn't have left you in charge of the mission and the girls. You are too dishonest, and that is that.'

Binnie stubbed out her cigarette, lit another, threw the packet back on the table, her head up, all thoughts of tears forgotten.

'What about my Dora? She's a headmaster's daughter. She's got her exams to do.' Binnie gripped Belle's arm, wanting to hurt her, push her against the wall. What did it matter if Dora was a seaman's kid, this bitch wasn't to know that.

How dare she put her under the control of a woman who'd slept with a nigger? How bloody dare she? That job was hers. Now everyone would see that she was just a hired help, when before she'd been different, she'd been special.

'What about my Dora's uniform? What about her feelings? How'll she feel being under a woman with a nigger for a son?'

Belle pulled from Binnie's grasp, shouting, 'You don't deserve any sort of a job, Binnie. You are such a foul woman and I can't bear to be near you any more.'

Binnie breathed smoke in her face. Belle waved it away, her voice cold and tight as she said, 'Since Dora only gained a half scholarship Walter has provided in his will for Dora's education until she leaves grammar school. Then it is up to her. If she works hard she'll get her Senior Cambridge and perhaps a bursary – she knows that, she's more than capable. I have done all I can for you. Walter did his utmost also. It is at an end, Binnie – you have sucked us dry, and you deserve nothing more. Connie was right. The debt is paid in full.'

Belle left. Downstairs she picked up her bags, hugged Sandy, Mary, Joseph, then walked out through the garden, holding on to Connie's arm.

Binnie watched them go from the top window. 'Connie said that to you, did she?' she said, looking down at Connie. 'Well, I've got a daughter too, you know, and she expected to be queen of all this. Oh no, we haven't finished with you yet. I'll work on that vicar and get Madam Mary out, just see if I don't.'

BOOK TWO

11

Belle called up the stairs to Connie, 'Make sure you don't fall out of that window looking for Boy.'

'For heaven's sake, Mam, you'd think I was still a child. I'm twenty-two and more than capable of staying the right side of a window; calm down, will you?' They both laughed.

Connie looked out of her bedroom window, towards the village, then down onto the vicarage garden where the flowers were wilting in the heat. How the years had passed since they'd moved back here after her father's death, but somehow season after season the village looked just the same. It constantly made her marvel.

She had a quick look in the mirror. She certainly wasn't the same and she was grateful for that. Her face had thinned, her hair was coiled up into a bun, like her mother's. She was a woman, where before she had been a mere girl.

The years at college had been wonderful. She had lived in a hall of residence, and travelled home for the holidays, revelling in Rempton, in Boy, glad to be free of Binnie and Dora. She had felt guilt at her relief, but pushed it aside as her mother had become full of life again, laughing, joking, playing cards with Mrs Driscoll, arranging harvest suppers and carol services.

Belle still visited the mission, but only once a month. Connie smiled at the memory of the party her mother had thrown when 'her one and only daughter' had been given the village schoolteacher's job. Good heavens, her headache had lasted days.

She hurried back to the window now, still smiling.

She could hear the clink of the hoe on stone but James Driscoll was really waiting and looking as she was. When would Boy come? She laughed to herself. How long could they go on calling him Boy – he was eighteen. But Philip sounded too strange.

She looked towards the school, her school. For a moment she could smell the chalk, hear the laughter, the clatter of boots on the playground, the classroom floor – how could she bear to leave it? She looked at the letter again, crushing it to her with excitement, and fear. India.

'Come on, Boy, I need to talk to you,' she said aloud.

The hoeing had stopped. She leaned out of the window as James Driscoll straightened and waved his hat at the fine-boned, black-haired young man who was walking along the lane, his bag slung over his shoulder, whistling as always. Now he was entering the drive, the gravel crunching beneath his boots.

'Grandpa!' he called, then ran towards the old man, throwing his bag to the ground, pumping his hand, then holding him in his arms.

Connie said nothing because she knew he'd look up, he always did, and there – he was lifting his head, grinning. She thrust the letter into her pocket and rushed down the stairs.

'He's here,' she shouted to her mother as she ran out of the front door.

Belle came from the kitchen, wiping her hands. 'I don't know, twenty-two and rushing about like a five-year-old.'

She watched her daughter running through the gap in the hedge and into Boy's arms – no real brother and sister could be closer. She followed now, waving at Helen as she came out also, pushing past the hollyhocks and through the gap in the hedge. She must stake those more firmly next year.

Boy's kiss was warm on her cheeks, his arm strong as he hugged her to him, then Helen.

'There's champagne on ice. We must celebrate,' Helen insisted, leading the way through the house, onto the terrace. 'It's not every day our grandson is accepted for university.'

Connie caught her eye and knew that Helen was also celebrating India. She touched the letter, feeling Boy's arm around her, and again she felt the excitement and also the fear. How could she leave them all? How could she tell her mother? Boy would find some way, but first she had to tell him.

They drank champagne on the patio. Would she need a parasol in India?

They ate salad, home-cured ham and pickles in the dining-room. Would she have to eat curry in India?

They drank coffee after lunch on the terrace. Would she have to drink tea in India?

The wicker chair creaked and she pulled up the cushion behind her, shading her eyes from the glare, peering at the croquet hoops and the shadows they were casting and at the mallets which were propped against the shed.

'Give you a game,' Boy challenged, leaning forward, his grin wide. He grabbed her hand. 'Come on.'

She shook her head. 'I'd rather go for a walk.' You could talk out in the meadows.

Boy sat back. There was something in her voice, in the set of her mouth, the way she held her head. God, he'd missed Rempton; he'd missed her. He grabbed her hand again. 'Come on then, race you to Lowe's Meadow.'

They ran down the drive, the laughter jogging in their throats, and Connie didn't have to pretend to let him take the lead now. They were into the lane, running through the village, dodging Mrs Green, weaving between the butcher's boy and the letter-box, and he was still ahead of her.

They passed the school. What would her children think if they saw her? She didn't care – Boy was here for what was left of the summer holidays. Her hat fell off. She stopped, panting for breath. He called her on, leaping the stile into the meadow. She followed. 'Wait for me, you little devil.'

He didn't. He ran through the long grass and there was pollen on his trousers, and on her skirt as she followed. There were poppies, cornflowers. There were swifts, skylarks.

'First to the haystack,' he called, looking back over his shoulder, slowing his pace, letting her catch up as she had always done when he was a child. But he was a child no longer. He was going to university; he might teach as she did, he might write. It didn't matter. At least he was adult like her, and they had years now, to spend together. He felt as though he had caught her up, as though they were both equal.

He heard her breath as she drew level. They were running more easily over the newly mown section and reached the haystack together, leaning against it, the breath rasping in their throats. They slid to the ground, giggling and gulping. Boy looked up at the sky. It was so blue, so hot, so empty. No clouds. Perhaps he'd be a poet?

'Come on,' she said, standing up, stretching out her hand to him, pulling him to his feet.

They ambled along the path at the edge of a cornfield where stooks stood, towards another field, then on down the lane which led to the beck. He looked up at the branches which linked arms above them, shielding them from the sun, holding them as though caught in time. He liked that. Yes, perhaps he'd be a poet.

'Dora failed to get a bursary for college,' Connie said, picking a blackberry, eating it.

'Give me one,' Boy said.

'Pick your own, little Boy.'

He laughed, pushing his hands into his pockets. 'Come on, I'm the blue-eyed one today. I'm celebrating, remember.'

Connie looked into his eyes. 'Those will never be blue. They're more like the coal that's dug up at Longdale.'

She tossed him a blackberry. He was too slow to catch it. She picked another and pushed it into his mouth. He felt the touch of her fingers on his tongue, and it was as though he had been speared through his heart. She was walking on. He felt the trembling in his legs, the shaking in his hands, and he wanted to call her back, he wanted her to reach up and touch his mouth again. Why?

He called out to her, running to catch up, 'Why?' He heard his own voice and wanted to grab the word back. He was going mad.

Connie turned round. 'Because she didn't work. We kept going across to help, but she was never in.'

Boy shook his head, trying to clear it, not knowing what was happening to him. 'Who wasn't in?'

'Dora, you idiot. She's failed and now she wants us to pay for teachers' training college. I wrote back this morning and said no – we've done enough. I can't leave Mam with that problem.'

They were through the lane now, out into the pasture that led to the beck.

Boy caught her, held her arm. 'What do you mean – you can't *leave* your mam with that problem?'

Connie pulled away, startled at his strength, at his voice which was hard. She walked on towards the beck, crossing on the large stones, pulling her skirt around her and squatting on the last rock, looking down into the clear water as it ran over the pebbles. Boy was with her now, his shadow darkening the water. He trailed his hand in the water.

'What's going on, Connie?' His voice was gentle again; his smile lit up his eyes, his dark, dark eyes.

She watched the water dripping from his hand as he withdrew it.

'I'm going to India in February. Helen has written to a friend and has arranged for me to teach in a Church of England Mission School in the Punjab and I don't know how to tell Mam. I know you'll help.'

She looked back at the water, seeing the sunlight where

his shadow had been. She watched him reach the bank, walk past the blackberry bush, and the elder tree, tearing leaves from it, throwing them onto the water so that they floated away from him, from her.

'Help me, Boy,' she whispered, knowing that to leave him, her mother, her school, her village would hurt like nothing else had done, but knowing that she wanted to go. Knowing that she had blurted out too harshly the news of her going to him, and now she regretted it and wanted to take back the words.

Boy looked at the leaves as they floated away. He couldn't believe the pain and wanted it to go, as the leaves were going, as she was going. No, not that. How could she leave?

'How could you?' he shouted at her, feeling four years of age again, watching her leave the village for Newcastle. 'How could you, again?'

Connie stood, wiping her hands on her skirt, hearing the words he had said to her so long ago. Then, all those years ago, she had shouted back at him, 'I can't help it.'

This time, though, it was her decision.

She joined him on the bank, slipping her arm through his. 'I've always wanted to travel, ever since Da took me to the docks and I saw those seamen. My contract is up with the village school in December. It seems the right time.'

'But—'

'No, it is the right time. I would have to find another job here, in England. If I did, Mam would come too. She would feel I needed her.' Connie leant her head on his arm, watching the water bubbling over the rocks. 'If I go to India she can't come. She can stay here, with Helen, in peace. That is why I have to go, and that is why I had to write to Binnie and Dora.'

Boy asked, 'When do you go?'

'The Revd Williams needs me in March next year – 1934. I leave in February. How do I tell her?'

Boy looked down at her. 'As you told me; there's no other way. You use words.' Words aren't supposed to hurt, he thought, but they do – they cut and slash but there's no blood, though there should be, somehow there should be. He said, 'How long will you be gone?'

'Two years. I'll be twenty-four. An old woman. You'll have a girlfriend; you'll almost have your degree. You won't have me to nag you, play older sister.'

'You'll never be old. I'll always think of you running in the garden, letting me win,' Boy said. Yes. It didn't sound too long. Yes, he would have girlfriends. But for twenty-four months Connie wouldn't be here.

Binnie received the letter the next day. She shook it in Dora's face. 'You stupid little cow. Why didn't you work?' She whipped the back of her hand across Dora's face.

Dora reeled, her lipstick smeared. It was streaked on her mother's hand. 'For God's sake, Mam. I've told you, I don't want to teach at a poky village school like Madam High-and-Mighty. I want a bit of life. Sadie's gone into nursing, married a doctor. That's what I want, not a load of snotty-nosed bairns yelling out their bliddy tables.'

Binnie tore up the letter, throwing it on the floor. 'We could have got some money out of them if you'd tried. They'd have given you something extra. We've lost out now. Thought I'd have got rid of that Mary by now, but no chance, and now that great dollop of a minister has decided to get married, so I won't get anywhere with him.'

Dora looked at her. 'Don't go on – we can still get something out of them. There's the nurse's uniform. We'll just make out it's more than it is; we can sort it out. There'll be lots of opportunities, I know there will, especially with that Connie going.'

In November Connie ran on the spot in her gym tunic, seeing her breath in the cold. 'Come on, girls and boys, higher.' The children groaned. 'Come on, or there's no trip to the squire's dairy.' She grinned as they brought their legs up. There would be scones and jam at the squire's.

She stopped, waving at them to keep on, feeling the stitch in her side. Mam would be at the dairy, cutting open the scones, pouring milk. The image caught at her as she remembered how Belle had paled when she had told her of India but then smiled, saying, 'Of course, it is the obvious thing to do.'

Belle had shaken her head when Helen told her that she had helped. 'I should be angry, but I'm not. She was always going to travel. It'll be good for her.'

Connie straightened now, her hands on her hips. Her mother had never spoken of the distress the separation would bring, but it was in her eyes, her every gesture, as it was in her own. She looked over the heads of the children to the rooks cawing above the leafless oaks. Just three months to go.

At the end of November they began rehearsals for the nativity play. Belle, Helen Driscoll and Mrs Green helped to coach the children. They measured them for costumes, then sewed with Connie into the late evenings.

Each day, Connie played the piano for carol rehearsals, lining up the children, listening, clapping her hands to stop them, beating out the time with her arm. How could she go and leave them?

She wrote to Boy, asking if his English tutor had moved on from Chaucer, asking if there were parties every night, wanting him here with her, because February was drawing closer.

They arranged the dress rehearsal for Friday. Belle and Helen Driscoll laughed as the vicar of Longdale reminded them of the concert they had held in 1917 in aid of the Red Cross. He said, 'It was Connie's dance that brought the house down.'

'I remember it all too well, and it wasn't only the house that was brought down,' Belle said, taking the pins from her mouth, making Elsie turn around, sending her off for a drink of lemon barley. 'Boy was the scarecrow.'

They were all laughing now as they thought of the straw which had been stuck up his sleeves.

'It itched,' Connie said. 'That's why he pulled it out and threw it to the floor.' They laughed again as they pictured the robins slipping and falling.

Belle said, 'All we could see were broken beaks and thrashing legs.'

'No robins this time, my pet,' Mrs Green said to Connie.

'No scarecrow,' Connie murmured.

Belle looked at her and suddenly her eyes filled with tears. Connie came to her. 'I can't leave you, Mam. I can't leave Rempton.'

Belle had longed to hear these words but now she hugged her daughter and stroked her hair. 'Nonsense. You can and you must. India is waiting. There you can teach, explore – not just the country, but yourself. You will come back. We will still be here. It's only two years after all.' With that, Connie knew the depth of her mother's love.

The nativity play was a success and Connie's heart swelled with pride as she saw the faces of the parents and the smiles of the children. She gestured at them, mouthed, 'Come off now.'

They didn't move but looked towards the headmaster who stepped forward, putting up his hands for silence. 'We have to say goodbye to Miss Symmonds, though with great regret.'

The children handed her paintings they had done of the church, the vicarage and the school. Mrs Green brought forward a topee the villagers had sent for from Harrods.

On Christmas Day Helen and James Driscoll gave her a deckchair. 'For the voyage, and the veranda. I hear all bungalows have these,' James said, his voice that of the old man he now was. Would he still be here in two years? He had to be.

Amelia and her new husband Tim gave her a bedding-roll. She undid the heavy straps, saw the sheets and pillows, together with a mattress filled with kapok. She looked up at Amelia. February seemed too close.

Her mother gave her an enamel basin with a top cover made of leather and straps running underneath. 'With the *bistra*, or bedding-roll, and the basin you can travel the length and breadth of India.'

There were handkerchiefs from Boy. Plain white ones that could be bought anywhere, with the minimum of effort. Connie smiled at him. 'Thank you, Boy.' She read his Christmas card. *'To Connie, from Boy.'* That was all. Her smile faltered.

Throughout dinner he talked of Fiona, a Scottish girl he had met. She was fun, she was young, she sang like an angel.

Amelia cut across him, her voice icy, smiling at Connie and talking of the Punjab, and the irrigation scheme that the British had initiated to transform the plain. 'My dear, they grow everything, so much wheat. It will be like being at home.'

Connie cut her beef. No, not like being at home. These people wouldn't be there.

The pudding was brought in, flaming. Boy talked of Fiona's dancing, her intelligence, her humour. Connie found a sixpence.

'You must wish,' her mother said gently.

Connie looked at the fire; she heard it crackling, she heard Boy, and wanted to wish for his silence and for a Christmas card that said 'with love', as it always had before. Why was he like this? Why had she no place in his life because he had found a girlfriend? It was as though she was already gone from his life. It was as though their years together meant nothing. There had always been room for Boy in hers, even when she had longed for her boyfriends' kisses.

'Come on, my love, have a wish,' her mother said.

She looked up at Boy who was pushing his Christmas

pudding around the plate. The light was on his hair, on his cheek-bones, on his long, fine hands. She wished that everyone would be here, around the table, in two years' time when she came home and that Boy would have missed her, and made space for her.

In February she boarded the train at Newcastle, lowering the window, securing the leather strap, glad that her mother was coming to London with her. She clutched Helen's hand. 'Look after James. Keep him well. I've dug the beds for next year's beans. All he has to do is a little hoeing.' .

Helen shook her head. 'I'll do that, and your mother will help. Just write to us, Connie.' Her voice was breaking; porters were rushing, passengers were boarding.

Sadie stood on her toes, kissing Connie. 'You look after yourself, bonny lass.'

Connie hugged her and whispered, 'Keep Dora and Binnie away from Mam if you can.'

'Aye, I will, and I'll keep Dora at arm's length from meself, though she's running so hard after the doctors she's no time to see me.'

Connie laughed.

The smell of sulphur was strong, the hissing was loud. A whistle blew. She looked along the platform. Boy hadn't come. He hadn't even written.

She and Belle slept sitting up. They talked of Walter, of the village, of the back alley, of Dora and Binnie. 'It's over, Mam. You've done enough.'

'Yes, I think I have, more or less, and it seems that Dora really wants to nurse. I'm glad she has a vocation and is happy; it makes Walter's efforts seem worthwhile.'

She told Connie then that Binnie had confessed to Mary when she was drunk one night that Archie could not have been Dora's father – that after everything it could well have been Rogers. But she did not tell her of Binnie's nakedness, of Walter's mouth on her flesh. There was no point. The train was rattling and clanging.

'You owe them nothing more now, Mam. Remember that.'

In London they took a taxi to a boarding-house.

'Are there any messages?' Connie asked.

The receptionist smiled and handed her a telegram. Boy, at last. She ripped it open. *'Bon voyage – we love you. Mary, Sandy and Joseph.'*

She showed it to her mother who said, 'He's hurt; that's why he's been as he has. He's grown up with you, he never thought of life without you. You have always looked after him, bathed him as a baby – remember?'

Connie snapped, 'Well, he's still behaving like a baby.'

Belle led her to the lift. 'Write to him from India, he'll appreciate that.'

India. Connie couldn't sleep.

They took the taxi to Liverpool Street and followed the porter to the Tilbury train. Connie barely noticed the crowds, the noise, the trolleys. She clung to Belle. 'I don't want to go. I can't go.'

'Nonsense.'

They tipped the porter and stood on the platform, the bitter wind whipping their coats.

'It'll be warm there,' her mother said, straightening Connie's hat. 'Though it's still just the cool season. March will be much hotter.'

Connie shivered, pulling at her gloves. Why were they talking of the weather when she was leaving this woman for two years? She threw her arms around her mother. 'Oh Mam, I'll miss you. I love you.'

They held one another so tight that their buttons dug in, then she heard, 'Connie, Connie.'

It was Boy; he was running towards her, forcing himself between porters, past relations, past piles of newspapers. She held out her arms. 'Boy, oh Boy, you came.'

The whistle was blowing, the engine was getting up steam. He leapt a carton of eggs, then he was there, standing close to her, the breath heaving in his chest.

'I couldn't let you go without saying goodbye,' he said.

He thrust a small parcel into her hands. 'I've behaved so badly. I can't think what it will be like to know you aren't here any more. God be with you, my Connie.'

He looked so young, so unhappy, and the guard shouted, 'Mind the doors.'

Belle called, 'Come on, Connie, you must get on the train. You'll miss the ship.'

She wanted to miss it, to stay here with both of them. She couldn't go. His arms were round her, and hers were round him. His cheek was rough, not like the child he'd been. His lips were hard on her cheek. 'Come home again, for the love of God,' he whispered.

He was pushing her onto the train, slamming the door. Belle was reaching up. Connie leant out of the window, kissing her mother, hanging on to Boy's hand. The train began to move and Boy ran along the platform still holding her hand. The train increased in speed; he ran faster, faster, then his grip loosened. 'Oh Connie,' he called, as he let go.

She opened the present as they neared Tilbury. It was his most treasured possession, left to him by his father. She ran her fingers over the embossed brass box which had been sent to the troops in the trenches by the Royal family, for Christmas 1914. She opened it. Boy had filled it with needles, thread, scissors and a thimble. There was a note.

Forgive me. Enjoy India. Come home.
With my love, Boy.

12

Helen Driscoll had bought a first-class ticket for her, insisting that she take it. 'It'll make sure you start off on the right foot and travel POSH – port-side out, starboard-side home. That way you'll avoid the worst of the sun.'

The band played as the ship sailed and Connie hugged her coat around her, wondering why she was here, wishing she had never seen those Dutch seamen so many years ago, wishing she hadn't listened to her father talk of Egypt, of Knossos on Crete. Wishing that she had never become a teacher, then there wouldn't have been a job for her. But all the time there was excitement tearing at her too.

She stayed in her cabin when they passed through the Bay of Biscay with its raging seas, and there was no excitement left, just misery and sickness. 'Oh Mam,' she whispered. 'I want to come home.'

There was a banging at her door. 'Get up and dress, or we'll come in and help you.' It was Mrs Lewis who sat at her dining-table. 'Come along. Be up on deck in thirty minutes.'

'I can't,' called Connie, her hand to her forehead.

'No such word as "can't".'

Connie staggered on deck an hour later. She played deck-cricket as a fielder and wanted to die as her legs trembled, her stomach rebelled. She picked up a ball, staggered. A young man steadied her. 'Keep going, you're doing splendidly.'

She couldn't smile or talk. She mustn't open her mouth. But by lunch-time she was cured and sat with Mrs Lewis, eating a light meal, drinking lime water, laughing, smiling, the excitement back, the homesickness lessened.

'Exercise works every time,' Mrs Lewis said. 'You need to keep your eye on that boy, James – quite a catch. He's a "heaven born".'

Connie patted her mouth with her napkin. ' "Heaven born"?'

'Indian Civil Service; quite the best catch for a girl, or are you already betrothed?'

The steward refilled her glass. She drank the iced lime. 'No, I'm to teach at a mission school.'

Mrs Lewis's face changed – her smile was less warm, her eyes less interested. 'I see. Well, of course, you wouldn't do at all.'

There were so few passengers that the first-class dining-room was half-empty and their deck-dances so dull that the second-class passengers were invited to share the band. Connie wore a beige silk dress that floated in the breeze then clung to her body. She danced with James, looking at the rope which was strung across the deck. It hadn't been there the evening before.

'Why?' she asked.

'To divide us from the second-class passengers,' he said, humming to the music of the band.

They drank Pimm's and he talked of his home, his horses. She danced with his friends, laughed with them, loudly when she passed Mrs Lewis, who smiled at her more warmly now. Connie felt lonely, an outsider, and angry at the rope.

At Port Said the bum-boat men came alongside. She pulled up a basket, put her money in, lowered it for oranges. She watched as boys dived for pennies. She watched the gully-gully man's magic tricks, laughing as James said he reminded him of his nanny producing yet more rice pudding. His voice was quieter now, his laugh less strident, his body less rigid.

As they passed through the Suez Canal he told her of his fiancée who would be coming out in time for the cool season. She didn't tell Mrs Lewis this, but she did tell him of Mrs Lewis, and so he smiled and held her closer when they danced, and laughed more when Mrs Lewis' smile grew wider. 'I should really be in second-class,' Connie said.

'My fiancée once thought of teaching too. Take no notice, have faith in yourself. It's this hierarchical thing in India – missionaries are outsiders; we don't know quite where to slot you.'

After Aden they watched the sharks, the flying fish, the ships that passed in the distance. The heat increased. She stayed on deck until late at night, feeling the breeze, reluctant to return to the cabin, watching the stars, waiting for India, writing to Belle and Boy, talking to Mrs Lewis and Mrs Norton, listening as they spoke of the eight-year-old children they had just left at boarding-school.

'I can't bear the thought of not seeing them for four years.'

Connie put down her pen and stared out to sea. Four years?

'Why so long?' she asked.

'Tea planters are not made of money so their wives have to make a choice. Leave India to be with the children, or send the children to school and see them when home leave is due – every four years.'

Connie put this in her letter, adding, *'I'm so glad I'm going home in two years. How can one have children and then send them away?'* She put down her pen. 'Couldn't they stay in India?'

Mrs Lewis shook her head. 'You'll find, if you land young James, that it isn't the done thing – and one's children are English after all – they should be familiar with their motherland.'

Suddenly England seemed very far away. It seemed further and further as the next week passed and the land grew near. The flying fish soared; droplets of water fell from them onto the smooth sea. There was a difference in the air, or was it in the heat, in the breeze? Dusk fell rapidly. Mrs Lewis and Mrs Norton seemed to want to suck every moment of leisure from the days, every fragment of conversation that they could, falling silent as they finally saw the distant towers and domes of Bombay.

They stood at the rail with Connie, stiffer, quieter. Then Mrs Lewis said, 'I do hope that wretched little man Gandhi and his Congress have stopped stirring up trouble – it's so very tedious.'

Mrs Norton agreed. 'All this nonsense about freedom. They've a voice in local government, what more do they want? They're just not capable of conducting foreign policy, or policing themselves, let alone ruling. My mother can remember when they knew their place and when Congress was a polite debating society, not this unruly mass party.'

James said, his voice cold, his eyes distant, 'My superior says it all goes back to that fuss and nonsense they made about Dyer, but what did they expect? After all, what do you do with children except give them the strap if they get out of hand? What do you say, Connie?'

Connie looked from the land to James who was neat, erect, different to the boy who had laughed and danced. 'I don't give the strap; I listen to the children.'

They looked at her, then away, and it was as though they had never dined together, danced together. They were strangers again.

She turned back to India. She would travel second-class for the return journey and be with her own sort.

At Bombay's red-arched Victoria Station she followed the bearer, feeling the heat, smelling the spices and urine, passing men in dhotis, and women in saris whose bare arms and feet jangled with gold bracelets. She passed Sikh soldiers, children, beggars thrusting out their limbs for baksheesh. She climbed into her Ladies Only carriage. It smelt of disinfectant. She reeled from it all.

She watched the bearer stow her luggage below the bunk. She heard *'Hindi pani, Mussulman pani,'* from the water-carriers. She checked in her notebook. Yes, separate water for Muslims and Hindus. She listened again, trying to memorize the sound, writing it down phonetically, keeping busy because she was remembering Liverpool Street, Belle and Boy.

She travelled for four days, lifting first the gauze then the venetian blinds and looking out on mile after mile of huddled mud villages, buffaloes wallowing, men, women and children working. They passed through stations where people waited with bundles or slept on the platform. They passed dried-out nullahs and rocky outcrops. She watched the blurred horizon where the colourless sky and the earth merged.

She felt the heat, looked at the fan, sank into the leather upholstery, listened to the rattling, the drumming of the train. Oh Mam, Boy. I want to come home; but there was the excitement too, always there was that.

She arrived at Amritsar as dawn broke. It was the middle of March. She took a rickshaw through the streets to the Golden Temple, removed her shoes and descended the steps. The temple gleamed in the centre of the water, the Sikhs walked along its black and white marble walkway, pilgrims bathed their feet in the healing water.

She took the car which the Revd Williams had arranged for her, bumping and jolting through the flat green landscape of unripe wheat and clover, past more low mud houses, watching the huge sun rising ever higher. The heat haze danced, the sweat bathed her body. Would they never arrive?

Darkness came; they drove along pitch-black tree-lined roads, through a town, then a village, then down a rutted cart track and through the open gateway of a compound. The car stopped at the steps of the bungalow. The Revd Williams was waiting.

He took her into the house lit by hurricane-lamps. He showed her the bathroom. 'Then we will eat.' He was tall, his cheeks thin, his skin yellow from the ravages of malaria.

She looked first at the thunder-box, then at the tap, the bucket, the copper scoop, the cemented floor, the slimy runnel for taking the water out through the hole in the wall. She wouldn't think of or look at the lizards, or listen to the chopping squawks, or the buzzing mosquitoes, or the croaking frogs – how could they be so loud? She stripped, sluiced herself. A gong sounded. 'Dinner,' called the Revd Williams.

She ate mutton curry. It was so hot it stuck in her throat. She smiled at Mrs Williams, Revd Williams's mother. She didn't smile back, just chewed and swallowed.

Revd Williams said, 'My mother is very old, not quite the same as she used to be, but a chaperon for you, of course.'

'Of course,' Connie said. 'Do I start tomorrow?'

Revd Williams shook his head, nodding to the bearer to remove their plates. 'No, Mr Peter Paul Brannbi, a convert, is not back with us yet. He is our present teacher, but we share him with a mission school well beyond Amritsar. The children do not arrive for two days. After that we shall make good use of your services, Miss Symmonds. We do need stability and with Mr Brannbi's comings and goings it has to be said that has been lacking. I just hope you can cope when it becomes really hot. If not, then we must arrange for a transfer to a hill station school.'

'Please, call me Connie,' she smiled.

He shook his head. 'I think it is best that we retain as much formality as is expected. It is the way of it.'

That night she lay beneath the mosquito-net, hearing them buzzing, the geckos clicking, hearing Mrs Lewis's voice, James's, Boy's, and Belle's. Oh Mam.

She woke at dawn. On the teapoy was a tea-tray with bananas, bread and butter. She opened the mosquito-net, remembering her da's tales of scorpions. She tapped her slippers, then ate a banana, drank tea, washed, walked out into the compound and across to the gate, looking over the flat misty fields to the shisham trees. A Sikh recited morning prayers in the distant village. She listened, watching the orange on the horizon turn into the sun, feeling the heat as it emerged, seeing the mist disappear.

She helped Revd Williams pack up his car. 'I am a doctor and run a clinic. I try to encourage the women to come to me instead of the local *dai*,' he paused. 'The midwife.'

Flies crawled on her face, her arms. She brushed them away; they came again.

'Come inside,' he said, mounting the steps. The punkah wallah pulled the fan with string attached to his toe. They packed small bottles of iodine and other medicines in long boxes. He left, calling, 'Sleep for today. Young Mr Brannbi is back tomorrow.'

She walked out along the lane, twisting her ankle in a rut. Cattle grazed, women collected cow-pats – fuel, she read in her notebook. She walked alongside the unripe wheat. There was vetch at the roadside, mallow; the air was full of birds, larks, rollers, bee-eaters. It could be England if you looked just at those, not at the huge expanse and the mud huts, and didn't breathe in the smell of ordure.

She walked back and lay on her bed. Think of the vetch, of the larks, the mallow, she told herself, trying to shut out the noises of India. She wrote to Boy and Belle but it didn't assuage her loneliness. She slept.

In the morning the Revd Williams led her across the compound to the mud schoolroom, with its corrugated-iron roof. He stopped outside, pointing to a fire at the side of which a woman crouched. He said, 'Though we are committed to educating our dark brethren in Christ, too few seek us, so I have introduced chapattis at lunch-time. It brings some in. The teaching of English brings others. There is a wish to serve in the Civil Service and for that they need English. It is the language we use in the school.'

She warmed to him, thinking of James, of Mrs Lewis. Yes, she would be happier travelling second-class with people like Revd Williams who did not sneer at others, but made their dignity possible.

'We also have children from the orphanage – over there

to the west.' He pointed. 'It is Christian, so we do not lose them at the times of the Hindu or Muslim festivals.'

She entered the schoolroom. Children sat on benches and as they saw her they rose. 'Welcome Miss Symmonds-mem,' they chanted.

She stood there, surprised, not knowing what to say, wanting to reach for her notebook, trying to marshal some Hindi, or Urdu, and remembering none.

'I am pleased to be here,' she said in English, angry with herself.

Revd Williams gestured to a young Indian. 'Mr Brannbi, may I introduce Miss Symmonds.'

Mr Brannbi was standing on the dais in front of the children, his white shirt pristine against his skin, his tie as dark as his suit, a chair and a blackboard next to him. The light caught his blue-black hair, his thin face, his hands and for a moment she felt she knew him, but then it was gone and a stranger remained.

Revd Williams said, 'I have to leave. Mr Brannbi will explain the structure of the school day, Miss Symmonds. I believe his task is to educate the children in history today – Queen Victoria's reign perhaps?'

He left and she held out her hand to Mr Brannbi. He looked from it to her, with suspicion, then took it briefly. 'How do you do, Miss Symmonds-mem.' His voice was almost Welsh; lilting, sing-song.

'Tell me what you wish me to do?' she said because his eyes were cold. Was it because he thought of her as an interloper? 'Tell me, I'm here to help.'

They sang a hymn first. 'All things bright and beautiful' and it reminded her of England. Were Mrs Lewis's children singing it now on a frosty morning? Were her own schoolchildren in Rempton?

She gathered the girls at one end of the long room, bringing her chair down from the dais, sitting at the children's level, speaking in halting Urdu. 'Tumara nam kya hai?' The girls just looked at her, then at one another, then giggled.

She repeated in English, 'What is your name?'

They told her, only she couldn't remember the Indian names, only Ruth, Sarah, Mary, from the Christian orphanage.

She looked at Mr Brannbi. Peter Paul – it didn't suit him somehow and how could he wear his jacket in this heat? He had drawn two figures on the board, and was telling them of Shiva, of Mohammed, of the need to understand both in order to have peace.

She was soothed by the lilt of his voice, by the English words. He looked up and saw her watching. She smiled then paled as a look of disdain flashed across his face, but then he also smiled.

She looked at the girls, then back at Mr Brannbi. His voice was gentle; he was talking of Queen Victoria and she knew she had imagined it.

She took her girls out into the compound, pulling a ball from her pocket. 'You have to call your names when I throw the ball to you,' she said.

She threw it to Ruth, who dropped it, giggled and bent to pick it up. She looked at Connie, threw it. It veered to the left. Connie ran after it, looked up and saw Mr Brannbi watching from the doorway.

He said, 'I thought you were going to measure the windows and teach them some maths.'

'I can't teach them anything until I know them, and they know me.' Her voice was firm. He shrugged and returned to the blackboard, then came back to the doorway, saying, 'These girls do not know how to play; they are taught only how to survive. This is India, not the Home Counties.'

She threw the ball again as he returned to the blackboard. The girls learned to catch and throw, and she gloried in their success, in the strength of their throws, and their voices, and tried to forget Mr Brannbi.

Only when the names were fixed in her mind did she lead them to the classroom and measure the window, calling each girl by her name, not looking at Peter Paul, but hoping he was watching. She smelt the cow-dung fires through the windows and door, she heard the chatter of the women as they cooked the chapattis.

At lunch-time the children ate them, sitting in the shade of the banyan tree, then walked home carrying their canvas bags. She watched them until there was no longer even the puff of dust. The sun was on her back, the sweat dripped from her body. She walked into the classroom. Peter Paul had gone.

She slept all afternoon, then ate chicken pulao in the evening with Revd Williams and his mother.

'We are indeed fortunate to have Mr Brannbi with us. He felt driven to sacrifice an academic post at a Government Training College for work with the mission schools. It is because he has an uncle in the town that he comes to us for some of the year but you can see why I needed you.'

She carried a hurricane-lamp across the compound after they had eaten, hearing the frogs. She would teach the girls to sew their names on the treasure pockets they would make this week. She cut the material in the schoolroom as moths banged against the lamp. She counted out the needles in Boy's metal box. Two short. She hurried to her room, hunting through her travelling-bag, finding another half-dozen, wanting to hold her hands to her ears to shut out the croaking of the frogs as she returned. Did they never stop? She stopped short at the sight of Mr Brannbi at her desk. He was holding her box. The light caught his cheek-bones, his eyelashes, his hands. Now she knew why he was familiar – he was like Boy, and she felt a flood of warmth for him.

He spun round, his face watchful, distant.

She said, 'I thought I'd teach the girls to sew. Do you think it is a good idea?'

'It would be a better one to teach them enough to attend Government Higher Schools or at least the orphanage girls who have little hope of marriage.' His chin was up, his eyes were hard.

'They can learn both but where do they go from there?'

'That is absolutely the problem, is it not, Miss Symmonds-mem. Where do they or the boys go? Perhaps medicine, or teaching.'

'Or the Civil Service?' Connie was watching the moths storm the lamp.

'Oh yes, indeed, if they want to work in Telegraphs, the Post Office, the bottom of the pyramid. I prefer to steer these children to where their talents lie. I have a boy I think will be an engineer. We'll need them when—' He stopped, then picked up the box again.

'When what?' she prompted, puzzled at the look on his face, sorry that it had closed as it had, wanting to reach out to this man and reassure him that she was not an outsider coming into his school, to take over his territory. She wished now she had not moved her chair from the dais. Perhaps it looked too much like a statement.

He looked at her, then at the box. 'This is interesting?'

She reached forward and touched it. 'It's Boy's; my sort of younger brother. His father left it to him. It was a royal gift to the troops; there were cigarettes, pipes, tobacco, all sorts in it. His father was killed outside Ypres, just after the Christmas Truce.'

She fell silent, thinking of the men in the mission, then said slowly, 'The war hurt so many people. My father tried to help, to talk to all nationalities, and to arrange joint ventures to remove fear, prejudice.'

She thought again that Mrs Lewis could have done with a dollop of her father. 'He set up a mission to feed ex-soldiers and give them a roof over their heads. It sort of escalated and we ended up helping unmarried mothers, the poor, the needy.' She was thinking aloud, conjuring up the past, wanting to hold it close to her.

He put down the box. 'So, someone who admits that the whites know poverty and despair; how strange.'

'I beg your pardon?' she asked, confused.

He ignored her. 'My father also had one of these tins.

It contained sugar candy and spices. He, like your Boy's father, is dead.'

Peter Paul Brannbi was standing quite still, gazing at the box.

Connie said, 'My father said Indians were in the trenches and even though it was freezing they never complained. He said you seemed so proud to be there, fighting for us.'

Peter Paul's laugh shocked her. It was so loud, so bitter. 'Oh yes, they must have been very proud, mustn't they? My father was sent to Mesopotamia after a year. It was a warmer place to die.'

Connie picked up the box, feeling the anger in the air, remembering her father's torment. It seemed to be shared by this young man. 'So that's where he died?'

'Oh no, he died at a place called Amritsar, after a visit from your General Dyer.'

He left abruptly, walking out into the night without another word, but she saw him briefly in the light from the lamp before he turned away, and all the bitterness and rage of her own father was in his face.

13

Belle sewed in the morning light, laughing as she tried to thread the needle. Good heavens, how small the eye was getting these days, or was it something to do with her forty-five years? 'Perhaps I need spectacles?' she said to Helen Driscoll who was reading the newspaper.

Helen smiled. 'Most probably but it's just eye strain. Think of all those letters you've written to Connie. It's only the end of March, she's been gone a mere few weeks, but she'll still have a sackful descending on the school.'

They laughed, hearing the chiming of the clock, the knock at the door. Maud showed in the doctor. 'How's the patient today?' he asked, rubbing his hands in front of the fire, his vast stomach straining beneath his waistcoat.

Helen said, 'He had another restless night, but no more discomfort.'

Dr Seaton smiled gently. 'Well, that heart of his is very tired; it's been ticking for well over eighty years.'

'Don't be patronizing, young man,' Helen snapped. 'Do you think I don't know that?'

Dr Seaton shook his head. 'Now don't go getting grumpy, Helen, just because you haven't had a letter from Connie, but thanks for the "young man". I retire in two years. Now just show me up, there's a good young thing.'

Helen tucked her newspaper behind her, using her walking-stick to lever herself up, shaking off Dr Seaton's hand, looking at Belle. 'Don't know what the young of today are coming to.' She grumbled her way out of the room as Belle laughed and checked the clock.

Boy had rushed back when they had telegraphed him

about James's heart attack, and had only left half an hour ago. Had Helen noticed how the light had gone from his eyes when Connie left, and how it was still absent?

Belle stared into the garden. Did he think of Connie as a woman, not a sister? But that was nonsense – he was so young, he had his life before him – there was Fiona, all the other girls. She shrugged, sighing, looking at Binnie's letter, knowing she must send more money for Dora's uniform – what did the girl do with her clothes? But instead she wrote another letter to Connie; it eased the pain of her loss, but only fractionally, and as her pen slid over the page she knew that she must find something to do with her days, if the two-year wait was to be endurable.

Connie woke, lifted the mosquito-net, tapped her slippers, put them on, ate her chota hazra, but only half the banana. She helped Revd Williams pack his medicine box, handing him the iodine, the bandages, the box containing the syringe, the stethoscope. She helped him carry them to the car in the silence of early morning. The shadows were long; there was a faint breeze.

She looked towards the schoolroom, then climbed the steps onto the veranda.

'Tea is poured, Miss Symmonds,' called Mrs Williams.

Connie was surprised. She had not heard the old woman speak before. It was dark in the dining-room. She sipped her tea, ate toast and Olde English marmalade. Would Belle have finished breakfast? Would she have received any of her letters yet?

'When does the mail come?' she asked.

'Monday of every week,' Revd Williams replied.

Connie asked. 'Where did you live when you were in England?'

Mrs Williams did not reply.

Revd Symmonds said, 'She's so very old she only joins us, as it were, in fleeting moments. She came from Suffolk originally but worked in India with my father on a similar mission. India is her home; it gets under your skin and somehow one becomes unable to leave.'

Connie looked out into the compound. How could anyone not want to go home? How could anyone turn their back on a village like Rempton?

She walked with Revd Williams to the car. The heat was beginning; she felt the sun on her hands, her face. The handle was hot when she opened the door for him.

'Would you tell me about General Dyer and Amritsar?' she asked, watching the sweeper, a young girl of twelve, walk to the back of the bungalow.

'Where is that fellow?' Revd Williams stared down the lane to the village. Mr Pradesh, the clinical assistant, was late. 'I could always collect him I suppose, but it's the discipline – one must have discipline or these orderlies take advantage.'

He looked at her. 'Why are you asking about Amritsar?'

'A Mrs Lewis was talking about it on the ship.'

'Well, it all gets back to discipline you see.' He looked back at the lane again, tutting, tapping the steering-wheel – sweat smudged the leather. 'Come on, come on, damn fellow.'

He looked up at her. 'Amritsar was a long time ago now; 1919. There was unrest, as there always is with these heathens; more so since the war. That Gandhi fellow's the worst, prating about non-violence but his demonstrations always end in death. He's got them all agitated and they just don't understand that they're not ready to rule themselves; these things take time.'

Come on, come on, Connie echoed in her mind, impatient now, anxious that Mr Pradesh would come too soon and she would not know why Mr Brannbi was as he was.

Revd Williams continued. 'In Amritsar a mob ran wild, killing three Englishmen, violently assaulting two Englishwomen, burning shops, banks, and looting. This sort of thing grows, you know; the natives get carried along by it so of course trouble began in other parts of the town. It all had to be stopped before it became any worse. I mean it wasn't as though General Dyer acted without warning. He read a proclamation in Urdu and Punjabi that any gatherings would be dispersed by force. No-one took any notice. It comes down to discipline as I've just said.' He turned again, looking down the lane. Mr Pradesh was coming. Revd Williams hooted his horn.

'And?' Connie prompted as the assistant entered the compound, panting across to them. He bent down and turned the starting-handle. The engine caught, fired. The Revd Williams shut the door and wound down the window. 'He ordered his men to fire into a crowd that had gathered. He had to show them that we meant business and he probably saved countless lives. Just think if that mob had grown, gone on the rampage, killed more people, assaulted more women. They're animals when their blood is up. Could have set the whole continent ablaze, not just hurting the British, but setting the Muslims on the Hindus, the Hindus on the Muslims, then there are the Sikhs . . .'

The car was moving forward. She stepped back, tasting the dust in her mouth as the wheels turned on the baked earth. She remembered the hatred on Mr Brannbi's face. Had his father been a murderer, a molester of women? Did Revd Williams know that the man who taught his children spoke with great bitterness of that day? Was Mr Brannbi a rioter? But whoever he was, how dare he take out his anger on her?

She strode to the schoolroom as the children began to arrive from the village and the orphanage, her arms folded. She thought of his eyes, his hair, his hands, his kindness with the children. But the disdain too. She must talk to him, she must find out the truth if she was to work with him, if she was to like him as she knew she could.

As she wiped the blackboard a chit arrived.

Miss Symmonds-mem,
   I have been called to Revd Seaforth's mission. I
will not be back until 14 April.
   P.P. Brannbi.

She looked at the writing – black ink, thick nib, a strong
hand and felt a deep disappointment grip her.

She taught the children until the chapattis were cooked,
then lay on her bed, tossing and turning, thinking of his
face, his voice, the anger, the bitterness, the sensitivity
with the children.

She rose, walked out to the gates of the compound,
staring across the flat wide Punjabi plain, hearing and
seeing the wheeling, cawing crows. She felt crushed by
the space, by the weight of the sky, by the distance
from Rempton, by the thought of a young man whose
father had run amok, by the thought of a young man
who enthusiastically taught children, and whose eyelashes
were long and thick, and whose eyes were like dark
pools.

The heat was increasing, the shadows were sharp
black, the breeze was dropping. She walked back into
the schoolroom. It was so quiet, so dark. She leaned
against the desk, feeling the sweat running down her
back, wanting to be home. How could this place get
under your skin? How could anyone not want to take
the first ship home?

'I could go. I could tell Revd Williams I want to leave.
I could telegraph Rempton. Boy would meet me.'

She picked up the chalk and drew Rempton vicarage
on the board – the honeysuckle, the phlox, the mullioned
windows, her bedroom. She dropped the chalk. It broke,
so white against the mud floor. She looked up at the walls.
What a fool she would seem if she arrived home.

She felt trapped by the room, oppressed by the space
outside, by the wheeling crows, and by the darkness in
this drab schoolroom. Had her mother felt like this when
she left Rempton for the mission? She knew she had.

She remembered the dirty green paint, her mother's eyes, so sad, so determined. She remembered the smell of the paint, Sandy's laugh, the way the men had helped, how it had brought them all together.

She moved out into the searing heat and found the old store at the back of the bungalow. It smelt of Helen Driscoll's shed. She lifted old sacking, peering into old teachests, searching until she found whitewash which she had known must exist because the walls of the bungalow were white.

She lugged it across the compound. Her hands were slippery with sweat and she dropped a brush. She dumped the paint on the schoolroom floor and retrieved the brush, dusting it on her hand, running back to the bungalow for an apron, picking up her topee, walking slowly back, her head aching now.

Mr Brannbi had said he wasn't going to be there for two weeks so let him stay away, but when he came back they would talk. They had to, because no-one could work with a person who looked as he did at her, and one of them must go if it couldn't be resolved, and she had just decided it wouldn't be her. If her mother could stay at Back Dock Mission, she could stay here.

She whitewashed the inside of the schoolroom, and the anteroom which held pots and pans, and under sacking she found an old tarpaulin, and under that an old printing-press. She heaped the pans on top of it and covered them all with the sheeting, making more room for storing the paintings that the children would do.

Joseph came as the day ended, standing in the doorway, shaking his head. At dinner Revd Williams told her that it was Joseph's job to paint, not that of memsahib.

She apologized to Joseph, saying it was now finished. It wasn't, and it was up to her to do it. She rose at 2 a.m., stepping over the *chaukidar*, the night-watchman, on the veranda, lighting the hurricane-lamp, feeling the coolness in the air as she crept across the compound, hearing the moths battering the hurricane-lamp after she had lit it, painting the last wall, ignoring the mosquitoes, then returning to bed smiling. Now she was ready to begin her life in India.

She took the children to the river, leading them in a crocodile, balancing on the narrow earth bunds that divided the plots, hearing the wheat crack, keeping in her mind Joseph's directions, talking to the children in faltering Urdu and Hindi, listening to their hesitant English. She carried paper and pencils, leading them to the left then the right until at last they were there.

It was so large, so slow. She smiled as she thought of the beck. Here, there were basking turtles lining the sandbanks, egrets strutting in the shallows. It was so quiet. She gestured to the children to sit on the ruins that were to her right. There was bougainvillaea and jasmine climbing the higher walls, there were lizards, flies, always the flies.

'Draw the turtles,' she told them. 'Then watch, and later we will write about what you see, what you think when you look at them. Would you like to be a turtle?'

They giggled. 'Ruth, here's your pencil and paper.' She handed out magazines for them to rest on and looked over their heads at the sky. I'm glad you're not here, Mr Brannbi, she thought. I don't need your bitterness; all I need are the children.

The next week they made treasure pockets and she read the ten letters which had arrived from Belle, and the three from Mrs Driscoll, but there were none from Boy.

She talked to Revd Williams about educating the brighter children to Government Higher School standard.

'Nonsense, these are village children, and none of the families could afford the lodgings, even if you could persuade them.'

'I was thinking of John from the orphanage as well.'

He rustled his newspaper. 'That's even more ridiculous. There is barely enough money to keep the children fed and clothed.'

She looked at his mother who was knitting. How could those arthritic hands move so quickly? The moths were battering the lamp, the frogs were croaking, the lizards were clicking. She clasped her hands tightly together. Mr Brannbi would be back in a week. She had to get Revd Williams's permission before then.

Why? she asked herself. She didn't know; all she knew was that anger had been growing with each day, because she had come so far to teach, and had been met with an anger she had done nothing to provoke.

Connie took a deep breath. 'Think of the prestige if we raised the school to that sort of level. You have done a wonderful job bringing in the pupils with the chapattis, and now we can build on that. The British in the town would be impressed.'

He said nothing, just continued to read his newspaper. She waited, knowing that this man felt an outsider, knowing that he was treated as one, by those like Mrs Lewis.

She returned to her letter to Boy, telling him of the turtles, of the child who had said she would like to be one because she would have her house on her back and wouldn't then have to live in an orphanage.

Revd Williams did not refer to her plan all evening but as they were loading the car in the morning he gave her permission to approach the mission for money.

'I shall write home to my mother to see if they can help, though the times are worse than ever in England,' Connie said with a smile.

'Do as you wish. We can only wait and see what God will provide.'

She wrote to Belle that day, and to Sandy and Mary at the mission, telling them of her scheme, telling them of Ruth, who would like to be a turtle, explaining that it was necessary to help these children achieve their full potential. But not telling them of the problems of caste, which made it almost impossible for the Hindus to break out of their given roles. Perhaps when Mr Brannbi came back, he could advise her. She grinned wryly – perhaps when Mr Brannbi came back he would simply pour scorn as well as bitterness on her.

On 14 April he was in the schoolroom when she entered. He looked up from the desk where he was working, his dark suit spotless, his white shirt as pristine as it had been on that first day. There was a bandage on his right wrist; his cuff was undone because of it.

He said, 'I thought you'd have run to the hills by now.' His eyes were lowered, his voice flat.

She felt anger flare, then she moved on down to her end. He had turned the boys' chairs back to face him.

'I've been too busy sorting this place out.'

'I noticed the white walls. My word, yes, you have been busy standing over Joseph.'

She dropped her books on her desk. 'I did it myself.'

'Goodness me, only here two weeks, and upsetting the servants.'

She turned her back on him. 'I've been taking your boys to the river with the girls. It's a new regime I've begun in your absence. Today I will leave them to your tender mercies.'

She swept out, then called back, 'I've also begun raising funds for a lodging bursary and am sorting out a curriculum for the more able children to improve their chances of entering Higher School. We need to encourage their parents. That's your job, or won't you get involved because I am?'

She didn't turn, she just stood there.

He called, 'The girls will leave when they're ten. They're only here to improve their marriage prospects with a bit of education, a bit of English.'

She turned now, dismayed. 'But you said I should be thinking of their futures.'

He didn't look up at her. 'You shouldn't be so hasty.'

She felt her face flush with rage and wanted to walk back into the room, stand by his desk, force his head up and make him tell her why she must suffer just because his father was a hooligan. She didn't; she walked to the banyan tree and waited for the girls, then took them to the river, stopping to look at the ripe wheat which was the colour of the mud walls of the village, picking some, showing them the chaff.

The village girls already knew, but the orphans did not. The orphans did not know so many things of everyday life and they should, damn it.

She talked slowly in English of the harvest in England. 'I look forward to seeing your harvest,' she said. 'I will write of it to my mother. I will ask her to write to you of ours. I will ask the children in our village to write to you.'

They returned at eleven and wrote of the egrets. She could smell the chapattis cooking, she could see Mr Brannbi, though she pretended she did not know he existed.

The children ate their lunch under the banyan tree. She sat with them on the rug, watching them scoop dal from the bowl, grinning, laughing, before they walked home.

She entered the schoolroom. It was empty as she had known it would be. She lay on the bed in the afternoon, tossing, turning, moving from wet patch to wet patch, longing for coolness, for ice clinking in a glass, for snow chilling her feet and hands. She ate curry that evening and then she walked to the schoolroom. Would he be there?

He was. He had hauled the old typewriter from the storeroom and was sitting at it, the hurricane-lamp casting light on the machine, on his face, his eyelashes. She stood in the doorway and saw him wince as he used his right hand. He stopped, supported it with his left, then continued – tap, tap, tap. Those hands were so like Boy's.

She moved towards him. He looked up, startled, wrenching the paper from the machine.

'I was just catching up on correspondence, but keep making mistakes,' he said, folding the paper, leaning back, looking at her, then at the doorway as though he wanted to escape.

She looked from him to the balls of paper on the floor. She picked one up. He started towards her, his hands out to take the paper, but the pain of his wrist caught at him. He winced; she moved back. He dropped his hands to his lap.

She smoothed out the paper and read.

> While the teacher remains, there is a semblance of unity, but when the teacher goes, as he must, that unity must be preserved and enhanced or disaster will result. After all, children grow up, don't they, and if the parents or tutors refuse to let them go, they break the bonds. Is the British government listening to its children?
>
> They can hear us, but they ignore us. It is not enough to burst from our bonds; we must live on, in unity, in peace. We must put aside our differences once those who repress us remove themselves, we must look within our hearts, or we remoooov

Connie went cold with fear. She had read of the freedom movement before she left England and of the drive for Home Rule. She knew of the deaths that occurred every year when rioters ran amok. Mr Brannbi was sitting very still. She backed away, then looked again at his hands, those fine hands. She swallowed, gripped the paper. He didn't move.

His bandage was pale against his skin. She stood quite still, afraid to leave, not knowing what to do. 'So like your father, aren't you? Is there going to be a riot here – have you strained your wrist heaving your stick onto someone's head – are you going to assault me, kill Revd Williams, the children?' She cursed herself for the words which had burst from her. He rose. She flinched, trying to scream, but no sound came.

The disdain was back in his face, and such anger. He stared at her, came round the desk, took the paper from her. She could hardly breathe. He picked up the other balls of paper from the floor. She watched him. She must run. But she couldn't move. He was between her and the door.

He shoved the paper into his pockets. 'Now you have no proof, not even of the mistakes I have made this evening.'

Her eyes never left his face.

'And no,' he said. 'I would not assault you; why should I? I am a teacher, not a rioter, and you are a good woman.'

He left then, walking silently from the compound and now she began to tremble. She should tell Revd Williams, she should run across, shout for help, but Mr Brannbi had smiled, and it was as though she had been with Boy, for that moment, and Boy would hurt no-one. But she should tell Revd Williams.

14

Belle took the register in the classroom, smelling the damp socks which had been draped over the hot-water pipes, and the boots which were in neat rows in front of the fire-guard. She had been nervous when she had applied for a teaching post, but the headmaster had been grateful.

'Connie could have stayed on after all; our Mr Smith let us down at the last moment,' he had said.

Belle ticked the names, smiling at each child, seeing their threadbare clothes, knowing the cardboard in their boots would be sodden from the rain.

When she had finished the register she folded her hands on the desk.

'I've had another letter from Miss Symmonds this morning. She tells me that she has almost arrived in India so it has taken some weeks to reach us.' Belle pulled out the letter. 'Now let me see. She also says that when she begins at her new school she hopes the pupils will write to you about their lives. Now, who can show me on the globe where India is?'

The morning proceeded and during the lunch-break she hurried to the vicarage. She walked straight through to the sitting-room. 'How is he?' she asked Helen Driscoll.

James had had another heart attack in the night.

'Dr Seaton says that it was only slight and from where I'm sitting, my dear Belle, it looks far more likely that the next one will be yours, rushing around like this. Sit down at once.'

Helen rang for another cup for the tea-tray.

'You're so calm,' Belle said, kissing Helen.

'You're so cold.' Helen poured the tea and handed it

to Belle. 'Now, have we decided on a fête, or a concert?'

Belle stirred her tea. 'You can't feel like thinking of this at the moment – let's wait until we know how James is. Has he agreed to hospital yet?'

Helen shook her head, looking at the clock. 'No, he won't go to hospital and I can't say that I blame him; nasty tiled places. And no, we won't wait until we know how he is. This fête is important for the village, it's important for Mary and Sandy, and my dear Belle, there is always a good reason for putting things off, but life must go on. And besides, it is James's wish and Dr Seaton expects a full recovery.'

Belle put down her cup. 'Well, if you're quite sure. The villagers will be pleased, and Mary and Sandy really wanted a day out for the mission. It should raise funds for both.'

Belle spent the rest of the lunch-hour with Helen, deciding on the stalls and the dance display. She then spent an hour after lunch helping the children to cut out fresh cardboard for the inside of their boots, and telling them of the dance they would have to learn for the fête. 'Yes, you boys too,' she said sternly, then smiled as they grizzled.

She wrote to Mary that night, giving her the date of the fête, telling her that the squire would send a tractor with a trailer to pick them all up from the station.

'Not very smart but try and get as many men as you can, and of course all the girls and their babies. What about Sadie? She wrote and said she might be able to come. We should ask Binnie and Dora, I suppose. I'll write to them myself.'

She sat with James for half an hour. His breathing was surprisingly even. He smiled at her. 'Have you organized the stalls?' he said.

'Not yet, but we will,' she replied.

'You must write and tell Connie all about it, and send her my love.'

Later she sat at her window looking out across the

village. Teaching made her feel closer to her daughter, and it made her feel as though she was contributing something in an area where unemployment was biting even deeper. Tomorrow the squire would be sending vegetables to the Newcastle Mission for the soup which they now made for all those men without jobs, and no hope of jobs.

'Oh Connie,' she said. 'I miss you, my darling, but I'm glad you're extending your life.'

Connie was lying awake under the mosquito-net. She had not slept all night because of the words Mr Brannbi had typed, and about which she had said nothing at dinner; but at breakfast she must.

She heard a light knocking on the shutters and pushed aside the mosquito-net, feeling for her slippers, forgetting to tap them. She walked quietly to the window and peered out. It was Mr Brannbi. She pulled her dressing-gown around her, stepping back. He put up his hands.

'Look, no weapons.' His voice was gentle. 'Perhaps as you care for the river so much, you would walk with me before the heat of the day.' He was whispering, looking around him.

'Why?' She was frightened, but moved forward, looking into his eyes.

'Because I need to talk to you of myself, of Amritsar, of my work which you saw last night.'

'You are a teacher; that is your work, isn't it?' she challenged.

He put his finger to his lips. 'Shh, you will wake the *chaukidar* or Joseph. Please come. I will wait at the edge of the field.'

She closed the shutters. Of course she mustn't go, it was sheer lunacy to even think of it. But she dressed and slipped from the bungalow because his eyes had met hers and there was no disdain or bitterness.

They walked silently along the edge of the fields. She could smell the wheat and see to the horizon as there was no mist. Were there really mountains on or beyond the horizon? Could there really be a cool place?

They reached the river and neither had spoken. Connie walked silently behind him, wanting to see him at all times, feeling nervous, vulnerable. He walked faster now, across to the ruins, sitting down, gesturing to the other side.

'Where I can't reach you,' he said.

She sat and waited, looking at him. He put his hand into his pocket and she tensed. He drew out an embossed box like Boy's. He passed it to her. 'You see, I do not lie. I have a box and neither do I assault people.'

She returned it. 'But your father was at Amritsar and three Englishmen were killed. Dyer shot the rioters. The Revd Williams told me all about it.'

Mr Brannbi looked down at the box in his hand and rubbed it gently. 'Dyer did not just shoot the rioters; he shot and wounded or killed hundreds and hundreds of Indians who could not escape. Somewhat like your grouse-shooting, I feel.'

'But Revd Williams said—'

Mr Brannbi put up his hand. 'Please, let me talk. Let me tell you what happened at Amritsar, from our point of view. Then you may still fear me if you wish.'

Connie showed her surprise. He said, 'Oh yes, I know the smell of fear, for I have felt it many times. But I digress.' He held up the box. 'My father was proud to receive this; your father was quite right. India sent and paid for, and fed, a million Indian soldiers to aid the Empire. They went willingly because they felt sure that they would be given their independence when the war was over. Indeed, it seemed in 1917 that your government said as much.'

He returned the box to his pocket. 'In 1919, to our delight, a scheme was developed. In each province of India the Governor was to have two roles. He would be the old-fashioned Governor where policing and finance were concerned, but in respect of other subjects, like

189

education, health, agriculture, he was bound to accept the advice of elected Indian ministers.'

'What has this to do with Amritsar?' Connie asked watching the sun creeping over the horizon.

'A great deal. I am sorry to keep you from your chota hazra.' His voice was edgy, angry again. He rubbed his forehead. 'I'm sorry, Miss Symmonds, anger becomes a way of life. Please allow me to go on. My father and his friends, and Gandhi and the others thought it was a step to independence, even though you still kept policing in your hands. They trusted you all. Then Amritsar happened.

'There had been some demonstrations against the British and some repressive laws were brought in to control us. We felt suspicious – what did this mean? We were to govern ourselves soon, weren't we?

'In Amritsar a mob ran wild, killing, as you say, three Englishmen, assaulting two Englishwomen, and on and on. There was no way this should be condoned and it is true that there was further violence. But General Dyer committed a greater crime.

'On the third or fourth day of violence, I forget which, he toured Amritsar for two hours accompanied by a town crier and drummer. This town crier read a proclamation in Urdu and Punjabi that any processions or gatherings of at least four men would be treated as an unlawful assembly and dispersed by force of arms if necessary.

'But he did not read it out anywhere near the Jallianwala Bagh, where Dyer knew there was to be a meeting held that afternoon.'

Mr Brannbi was walking up and down now, his eyes on the ground, his left hand supporting his right.

'The crowd in Jallianwala Bagh were also there for the start of a religious festival that attracted many Sikhs. Others had come for the horse and cattle fairs. My father was one of them, lying wrapped in his blanket near the well. There were thousands and thousands of people.

'General Dyer marched his fifty or so riflemen to a

raised bank, gave the order to kneel and fire. They did so, for six minutes, loading, firing, reloading. The three lanes out of the Bagh were made impassable by the bodies which mounted and mounted. My father was shot where he lay, near the well. I can still smell his blood, hear the flies, the vultures, because you see, Miss Symmonds, I was there too. My mother also.

'No relatives came to help until nightfall, or in my case, until the coming of dawn. There was curfew, they were frightened. The vultures clawed and beat their wings and I thought they would take me. My uncle didn't know we were there. It took him that long to realize.

'Mother and Father were dead. My uncle brought me here, to the town where we both now live, but Indians have not trusted the British again.'

Connie was silent, watching the blood-red sun rise, thinking of a small child and the clawing of vultures. He was still pacing and now she said, 'But you can't blame all of us for what happened. That was just one foolish cruel man.'

He looked at her. 'You are so very right that we shouldn't judge you all by just one man. But you see, Miss Symmonds, we don't. We judge you by what happened next.

'Dyer was made to resign his command and he returned to England. When his ship left, he was cheered as a hero by hundreds of you. One of your English newspapers raised more than twenty-six thousand pounds for 'The Man Who Saved India'. From this we learned of the depths of your contempt for us, of your determination to stay, of the struggle that lay ahead for our independence. Gandhi and Congress led us in our new awareness.'

Connie said, 'And this appeal for unity you were typing up?'

'India is a land of many religions. The majority are Hindus; there are Muslims, Sikhs, others. They are fearful of one another. Fear breeds violence. Differences breed hatred. I and others like me are campaigning for peace once independence is achieved. I write a column to that effect, I walk the Punjab, talking to that effect. It is what keeps me awake at night.'

'Is that why you teach the schoolchildren about the different cultures?'

'You noticed?' He was wary again.

She smiled. 'I have continued to do the same, in your absence.'

Connie was walking beside him now, up and down. 'But I don't understand your fears about unrest. You have all lived together so long. It's too confusing.'

He smiled at her. 'I know, even we find it so. But soon I will take you to the village; it is easier there where you can see the divisions. If you wish me to stay, that is? Or will you tell Revd Williams of my activities?'

She stood still. She had forgotten she should be afraid of him. 'How did you hurt your wrist?'

He shook his head sadly. 'I fell off my bicycle on my way from one village to another. All so very humiliating, but no doubt it is good for the soul.' He laughed now, and his face was alive, young. She put her hand on his arm. His laughter stopped. He looked at her hand on his skin, then back at her face. There was confusion in his eyes.

'White women do not touch Indians, neither do they shake our hands, as you did that first day.' he said gravely.

She looked down at her hand, then she told him of Joseph at the Newcastle Mission, and of her father and his views, of her mother. 'There is no room in my life for differences like that,' she said. 'Now, we must get back for school. I will say nothing until we have visited the village. Then I will make up my mind.'

They walked into the village that afternoon. The heat was beating up from the ground, down from the sky. She told him that she had hopes for two boys, John and Aja. 'They are bright, eager. What's more, they are friends. I have written to the mission authorities for funding but have heard nothing yet. Will you speak to Aja's parents, if I speak to the orphanage?'

'Let us see about funding first. Neither of us have the energy in this heat to chase dreams until we know we have a chance.'

He had said 'we'. She thought of the dark bungalow, the huge flat plain, the miles that lay between her and Rempton. Oh yes, she longed to be friends with this man who was so like the boy she missed.

They were entering the village, passing between its beige mud walls. There were buffaloes chewing in the yards, men squatting in groups under the banyan and pipal trees, women in open doorways, children peering past them.

'They know who you are, of course,' Mr Brannbi said, quietly. 'You should smile as though you were in your own village. Be yourself.'

She was, smiling, waving at the children she recognized as he gestured to the fields, to the houses.

'As in English villages, or so my uncle tells me from his time in your country, everything is used here. The mud from the land for building and plastering, timber and cow-pats for fuel, hemp for charpoys, thatch grass for ceilings, fodder for the milch animals, cotton for the clothes and bedding.'

A woman was spinning cotton; her daughters were watching.

'Gandhi wishes us to spin and weave our own *khadi* or cloth. It saves us from being dependent on material brought into the country. It makes us feel more independent. Perhaps that is how you felt when you painted the walls?'

She was beginning to understand.

She looked at the woman and remembered Ruth. 'The children of the orphanage should be taught these things. They have no mother to stand next to, no patterns to copy, so how can they teach their own children?' She wasn't feeling the heat any more, she was looking, listening, learning. They walked on. 'Could we bring them to this village? Would they allow our children to watch?'

'It will be difficult to arrange. There is the matter of caste but I will talk. It might take time but you are right.'

He now turned to her, a question in his face. 'Could you also teach your girls about hygiene?' He pointed to the left of the house in front of them. 'As Gandhi says, we try to teach the villagers to find a safe location for their wells and the communal latrines, if there are any. We show them how to filter the water with charcoal and sand.'

They were moving across a path which seemed to divide the village. Connie looked behind, then ahead.

'Why this path?'

He smiled. 'India is, as I said this morning, a nation divided. This is the Muslim section of the village. Sometimes they mix socially, sharing one another's feasts, sharing the implements with which they work, but over there is the Muslim well. We passed the Hindu well some time ago.

'Before the mission came, the Hindu children would learn from a *pandit*; the Muslims still learn from the sheikh, over there.' He pointed. 'Always there is a smouldering fire between them which can be fanned, or damped. Some of us are trying to damp it.'

The earth and sky were pale with heat. She put her hand on the mud wall, then snatched it away. It was too hot. She looked around. 'It is so peaceful, how could it alter? Surely when independence comes, there will just be rejoicing?'

He nodded towards the Hindu and Sikh houses, and then to the Muslim sector. 'In India, there are well over double the number of Hindus to Muslims. If independence brings a proper democracy the Muslims fear that they will be submerged, which they will. This frightens them. In some areas the Muslims are the majority. The Hindus feel fear. With fear comes hatred, death, a fight for survival.'

They were walking back through the village now.

Connie said, 'But what can you do? Are words enough? Is it wise to remove the British?'

He shrugged. 'People have a need to determine their own lives. I just pray that our Congress leaders will agree that there must be a certain number of reserved seats for Muslims in any legislature or council, so that there can be no reason for carnage.'

They were almost back through the Hindu section now and a woman approached, holding a plate, gesturing towards the shade of a tree. Connie smiled uncertainly.

Mr Brannbi said, 'Please, you must sit down, and accept their hospitality.'

Chairs were brought for them. Connie lifted the napkin and saw too many chapattis. A bowl of dal was presented. 'I can't, I simply can't, not all of them,' she said.

'But you must, you simply must, or you will insult them. It is a custom.' He was laughing.

He was also given a plate.

'All of them, Mr Brannbi,' Connie whispered. 'You simply, simply must.'

They ate then, one, two, three, whilst the women looked and smiled, and chatted amongst themselves.

They brought her a drink. Was the water clean?

Mr Brannbi said quietly, 'In this village they have charcoal filters, as you do in the schoolhouse.'

She laughed and drank. It cooled her; she drank more. She thanked the villagers and rose when Mr Brannbi did, thanking them in Punjabi.

Mr Brannbi looked surprised and she laughed again as they walked away from the village, towards the compound. 'I haven't been idle while you have been away, but I warn you, I'm only just beginning.'

The dust was kicking up from their feet, it was all around them. She turned and looked at the village, remembering the division, remembering Mrs Gribble and the efforts her mother had made, remembering the Germans her father had brought over, the unseen wounds that had been healed for the men.

'So, you really are pleading for peace and understanding?' she said quietly as they approached the gates, also remembering Mrs Lewis on the boat, and James. They had said that independence was inevitable, but that the natives were not, and never really would be, ready for it. This man walking beside her was one of the many trying to make them so.

'Yes, but, and now I warn you, I am also calling for independence, and I will write in my column to that effect.' His voice was determined. 'I have been imprisoned before so I am ready to be imprisoned again if you feel you must tell the Revd Williams.'

She could see the heat rising from the roof of the schoolroom, from the bungalow.

'You can't type with that wrist. I will do it for you,' she said, because this was a man of peace, like her parents.

15

Boy looked out over the vicarage garden. His grandfather would never plant and pick runner beans again; he and Connie would never see that old panama bobbing as he hoed the flower-beds. Behind him the voices were muted, as they had been in the church but he heard Belle say, 'I'm so glad he was buried next to Walter.'

Her voice was so like Connie's. Had the telegram reached India yet? He drank deeply from the glass; the whisky burnt his throat. Oh Connie, I wish you were here. He wanted her arm round him, her head close to his, her voice soothing away the hurt. She should be here, God damn it.

His mother touched his arm. 'Are you all right, Philip?'

No, he wasn't all right. They were calling him Philip, saying he was the head of the family now that his father and grandfather had gone. He wanted Connie, couldn't they see that?

Belle listened to Amelia. She couldn't think of Boy as Philip. Could Helen? Helen was talking to Dr Seaton, her eyes shadowed, her hands trembling as they rested on the walking-stick, and Belle knew that she must find something for Helen to do, once the fête, which now had extra stalls to raise money for Connie's star pupils, was over – it might help her in her loneliness. Perhaps she could write round to her friends for money for Connie's mission. It seemed like a good idea but would that be enough?

In Jesmond, Binnie took round the leaflets explaining about the mission school in India, and the mission in Back Dock Street. She smiled as householders gave her money, putting it in the box, listening as they said, 'We're so glad to hear that the mission continues, even without the Revd and Mrs Symmonds. And now their daughter is doing similar in our Empire. So stirring.'

Up and down the bliddy drives, smiling, nodding, thanking them. She finished at five and caught the tram home, handing the tin to the vicar, not to Mary. 'They gave all they could,' she said. 'But times is hard.'

The vicar put his hand on her arm. 'You are very kind, Binnie. Perhaps my wife can make you a cup of tea?'

She shook her head.

'Take your coat off at least, and warm yourself.'

'I must get upstairs and changed for the evening shift,' she minced, smiling at Mrs Philips, wanting to smash her face for stepping between her and this vicar, who would have been putty in her hands if only she'd had the chance.

She walked carefully, her hand still deep in her pocket. She climbed the stairs slowly, and it was only when she was in her room that she brought her hand from her pocket and laughed, hearing the clink of the money she had taken from the box, counting it, drinking beer, smoking her cigarette.

It made her feel good to take something from them all. She drew deeply on her cigarette before dropping it into the remains of her beer; it sizzled. She must get Dora to write to that Connie, make sure she kept in with her, just in case she could be useful. She'd be a soft touch too, that one, even though she'd written saying her mother could do no more. That would be Belle talking. No, that girl was just like her father – doing all those bloody good deeds. And out there, there'd be no Belle to get in the way.

Connie made up board games, asking Revd Williams's advice. She drew ladders down which the players would tap their seeds if they landed on children binding leaves on open cuts, or eating rice without vegetables, or fly-blown sweets from the bazaar. They went up if the children used filtered water, if they ate vegetables, if they used the ointments that medical clinics gave them.

She talked to the children about bridges, about buses, tractors, and Mr Brannbi shook his head. 'They are just repeating the words; they have no image. How can they know what a bus is, what a bridge is?'

She drew or cut pictures out of old newspapers, magazines and catalogues. Soon they were able to pinpoint that Aja had a sharp analytical mind.

'He should be a lawyer,' Mr Brannbi said.

John pored over pictures of bridges, drawing them, getting inside them, trying to see how they were built.

'He should be an engineer,' Connie said.

The next week they received a promise of some money from the mission authorities and now Mr Brannbi talked to the father of Aja, and Connie to the orphanage authorities. Each day she waited for a letter from her mother reporting on the fund-raising. Each evening she typed for Mr Brannbi, listening to his lilting voice as he dictated the words.

As the week ended she shook her head as he said, 'My wrist is better. I could type this.'

'No, I want to help – it's a good cause.'

'Remember that we must tell no-one of your part in this.'

Sweat was pouring down their faces. She could scarcely breathe in the heat, and drank the glass of Jal-jiri which he had taught her to make out of spices, lime and mint, satu and jaggery. It cooled her as the water had done in the village. She poured some for him.

'The Revd Williams would approve. Independence will come, he knows that. He's a man of God, he would appreciate your longing for peace.'

Mr Brannbi shook his head. 'Remember his interpretation of Dyer. Be careful, Miss Symmonds, say nothing, for both our sakes.'

Later she slept beneath the mosquito-net, wanting to cast it aside, needing to feel a breeze. There was none though. She moved from damp patch to damp patch. She should tell Revd Williams. She turned over feeling guilty. She hung her feet over the bed. But Mr Brannbi was right, for now. She spread her legs wide, her arms too. She remembered Revd Williams' face when he talked of Dyer. Yes, she must say nothing.

The next day Mr Brannbi arrived, towing a bale of straw behind his bicycle. He hauled it to the entrance of the schoolroom and poured water over it, and at last there was something of a cool breeze as she taught the girls to spin, her hands slippery with sweat, her face covered with flies. An hour later more water was poured, then again. She could smell the chapattis, the cow dung. She sat with the children as they ate the chapattis in the shade of the tree, but the trunk was too hot to lean against.

Mr Brannbi came across. 'I have asked in the village and the headman says the children may observe the skills. They must not touch, or come close. It is a great concession.' His smile was bright, his pleasure was in every movement of his body.

Connie received the telegram that afternoon. It had been seriously delayed and she wept at the thought of James Driscoll and wanted to be there as May was breaking in England, and the trees were soft green, and she wanted to hold Boy who would need her.

That night she typed up Mr Brannbi's column, and then some leaflets, feeding the paper in, typing the same thing again and again. It was too hot; her fingers slipped on the keys. Poor James Driscoll, he would never again hoe the garden, he would never wear his panama amongst the beans. She put her head in her hands.

Mr Brannbi stopped checking his column and said, 'Lean into the heat, don't fight it. Be at one with it.' He poured water on the classroom towel and draped it over her shoulders; the cool drenched her and pushed back the image of runner beans, of familiarity, of family and friends.

She said, 'I can't keep calling you "Mr Brannbi". I need friendship in my life. I need to call you "Peter Paul". I need you to call me "Connie".' It wasn't a question, it was a statement.

He stared at her. 'Very well, Connie-mem.'

She laughed, and he did too. 'Just drop the "mem", and we'll be all right,' she said.

She typed another sheet, then showed him the printing-press out in the storeroom. 'Why not use it for the leaflets? We can show the children how to work it – it will be another skill. I can print off some tracts or medical leaflets for Revd Williams as well, then it is fair.'

The light from the lamp didn't reach them in there. She could hear his breathing, she could feel him close to her as silence fell. She wanted his hand on her arm, she needed his arms around her, as Boy had always needed hers. Who was looking after him now – Fiona, Belle? Someone must.

He said, 'You like to be fair, don't you, Connie? That is a wonderful trait. But don't be so fair that you tell him, please.'

He walked back into the light. She said, 'I find it hard to deceive.'

'Then we won't use it. I won't use this typewriter. I will try to find one elsewhere – maybe the next town. It will only be until next year when my uncle comes back from the South. He will bring his.'

She followed him. 'No, don't do that. I want to help. It is the right thing to do. I was brought up arguing for peace, for tolerance. It's just that I feel I should be able to tell the truth.'

He gripped her arm; she felt his warmth. 'Trust me, I know him much better than you.'

She agreed and he dropped his hand, but she still felt it, and it was of this she thought, not the deception.

The next week, the printer was in operation, and Connie insisted that the children should print up the

Revd Williams's health leaflets first. There was a broken 'o'. She carried the leaflets across to the bungalow. The mail had arrived. There was a letter from Boy.

She rushed to her room, slit it open, read it sitting on the bed, and the words broke her heart. She walked to the shuttered windows, and leant her head on the wood, feeling the heat. What was she doing here, in this appallingly hot land which was waiting for the rains to bring green to its seared earth, when Boy was bereft? She read it again. The light sheered through the shutter slits.

> Dear Connie,
> I can't believe he's not here. He was my father really. I'm the man, now, of the family but I don't feel ready. Ma calls me 'Philip', not 'Boy'. Grandmother too. I need you. Why did you go? I miss him so much. I miss you so much. Don't stop calling me 'Boy'.

She helped Peter Paul to set the print. She was too tired, too hot, the humidity was draining her. She drank and drank. Poor Boy, she should be there. She was always there for him. She must write to her mother, to Helen. They must not call him Philip.

There was ink on her fingers; the sweat was in her eyes. She wiped her face with the towel, she drank. The glass slipped. She watched it break on the mud floor, and the liquid soak in, disappear.

'Dear God, it's so hot.'

She sat down, wanting the green lanes, the beck, wanting her family, and now she wept, feeling the sweat on her arms, legs, body, holding her hands to her face, smelling the ink. She looked at Peter Paul. Hold me, she wanted to call out to him. Stop being Indian, be my friend.

He picked up the towel, wiped her face. 'You are covered in ink.'

The tears were still running down her cheeks. They wouldn't stop and now he drew her to her feet and held her, stroking her hair, murmuring to her as though she was a child. He was slight like Boy, but his voice wasn't Boy's, and these feelings which were rising were not those she had with Boy.

Her tears had stopped and now there was silence between them. But then she heard the night sounds, the jackals, the moths beating on the lamp, and felt his breath moving her hair; it was in time with her own, it was melting her and now she lifted her face, her lips opening, searching for his – finding them. His arms tightened; a heat was in her belly.

Then he pulled away, pushing himself from her, stumbling to the doorway, gripping the frame, looking out into the darkness. She followed, wanting to be with him, reaching for him.

'No,' he hissed. 'Go to your bed. It is late. Go.'

His face was mask, it showed nothing. She left, stumbling, not understanding, turning. He stared through her.

It was Saturday the next day; there was no school. She woke to a knocking on her shutters. She knew it was him. 'Get dressed, come with me,' he said, his voice curt.

'No.'

'Come with me, please,' he said. 'You want to see India. This morning I shall show you.'

She remembered his lips again.

She left a note for the Revd Williams. She mounted the bicycle he had brought and followed him, pedalling over the ruts of the lane, her cotton-gloved hands slipping on the rubbers. The sun rose and beat on her skin. It was easier on the metalled road.

The temple was at the edge of the town. He ignored her look. At the archway to the main gate she removed her shoes as he did. Peter Paul paid money to the temple servant. They entered. It was not quiet as a church would be. Men and women were squatting under the trees in the courtyard, chattering. There were Hindu gods in shrines around the walls of the courtyard.

'I have arranged that we make *puja* to the Lord Venkataswara.' His voice was gentle now, his eyes kind, his lips full, the lips which had been on hers. She nodded, unable to speak. He was drawing her into his world, drawing her closer, and it was where she longed to be.

They rang the bell to warn the god that they were there. 'Look as though you are praying,' Peter Paul said gently.

They were led through a dark passage then stopped outside a brightly lit room. Peter Paul pulled the rope, put his hands together in front of the idol with the black face and the gilt robes. She did the same and prayed for James. It was no pretence.

They entered.

The others who were there drew in their breath at the sight of her and she wanted to cover her whiteness. They all held their hands out to the priest – was it for the host? She had done this with her father in their church, so many times.

The priest poured what looked like water. She raised the liquid to her lips, the lips he had kissed. Peter Paul was drinking too. It was sour. It stung. She copied his hands, bringing hers to her lips, passing them over her head.

You see, Father, she thought. They are like us. Gestures, rituals, we all have need of them. Why couldn't Mrs Lewis see that, and Revd Williams?

The priest held a golden basin over their heads and intoned prayers. He replaced the basin on the tray. Round the tray there were little mounds of coloured powder and strings of flowers.

She felt the priest's finger as he marked her forehead with the powder; she saw him place the flowers round her neck.

Peter Paul said, 'You have now done *puja*.'

She smiled at him, touched his arm. He didn't smile back. Her hand dropped. What was going on? They left, walking back through the courtyard and the people, and then he pulled her roughly down another passage and they were walking past alcoves and there was blood and the stench of putrid flesh. She turned away, not wanting to see. He shook her, forcing her to stop, the smell was everywhere. Flies swarmed around scraps of flesh and blood.

'Oh my God,' she gagged.

'Sacrifices, Connie-mem,' he sneered. 'Not human, but still not what is found in your nice English churches, not romantic like these.' He stroked his garland.

She tried to pull away, appalled, confused, frightened. Where was the man who had kissed her, held her, wanted her, because he had.

'Why are you doing this?' she gasped.

'Look at India. Look at it and see me, ' he said, and his voice was no longer gentle, it was full of anger and bitterness again. 'Look at it. If you have kissed me, you have kissed this. Look at it, I say.'

She pushed from him, running to the entrance, grabbing her shoes, forcing her sweating feet into them, shielding her face from the glare of the sun and her nose from the smell of ordure.

He was there behind her as she reached her bike.

'Do your lips sting? Does your stomach rebel at the cow urine you have just drunk?' He was holding the saddle; she slapped at his hand. He wouldn't let go but said as people jostled all around them and the sun burnt her face, her stinging lips, 'This is me, Connie. What happened last night should never have happened. It happened out of your grief for your grandfather. Forget me. Forget it ever happened. I am Mr Brannbi again. You are Miss Symmonds.'

He let go of the saddle. She pushed with one leg then the other, gaining speed, leaving him behind feeling the bile rising in her throat, tasting the sourness, the urine. She stopped and vomited again and again. She remounted and cycled on, tearing at the garland round her neck, throwing it to the ground.

Peter Paul Brannbi cycled slowly behind. When he reached the flowers he picked them up, held them to his face, then followed her again, not wanting her to know that he was keeping her safe, not wanting her to know, ever, that he loved her.

On Monday there was a chit, as she knew there would be. He would be away for a week. She worked, dousing the straw bale with water, keeping the children in the schoolroom, even for their chapattis. She prayed for rain, prayed for his return, because she had thought of the body and blood of Christ, and knew each culture had its own validity.

She also knew that the lips she had kissed had been those of a man she was beginning to love, just as she was beginning to love his country, and she wouldn't believe he didn't feel the same, his kiss had told her that.

At the end of the week she sent a chit to his uncle's house. *'Meet me at the river in the morning.'*

She walked along the bunds looking back at the stone-breakers squatting by the roadside, hammering, always hammering. She wished she were one of them, with nothing else to do, no need to think, no need to feel. She smelt the river before she reached it. How stupid, of course they felt and thought. They had families, they had each day to get through.

She waited, sitting quite still in the shade of the tree, unable to believe she had ever once been cool. She waited as the sun rose, as the heat grew, as it pressed the air around her, above her, until she could feel its weight, the weight of the world, on her shoulders, her head. Her topee dug into her forehead. She took it off. The sun burnt her head. She replaced the hat. She waited, waited, leaning into the heat, knowing that she wouldn't change it for the green of Rempton.

He came at last, walking alongside the river, in his dhoti. She had known he would wear it.

He stood before her. She remained sitting. 'Have you taught more villagers where to dig their latrines?'

He nodded.

'Have you shown them where to dig their wells?'

He nodded.

'Have you asked another woman to drink urine? Was she shocked like me? Did she throw her flowers to the ground, then wish she hadn't? Did she lie on her bed and realize, as I did, that it is no worse than Christians symbolically taking Christ's body and blood? Did you try to shock any more stupid, silly women? Tell me, Peter Paul Brannbi.'

She was shouting and the birds rose from the banks of the river. 'You see, I am here. I shout and the birds fly up in the air. I am here, Mr Brannbi, in your country, in your land, and it is your lips I kissed, and it was yours that kissed me back. We are two people, and you make problems where there are none.' She was panting, waiting, longing.

He reached down, pulled her to her feet, kissed her, his arms going round her, holding her tightly, knowing that he shouldn't, that this was not the time, or the place, but he loved her.

She stroked his blue-black hair, his cheek-bones. She held his long fine hands, kissing each one, and then his lips again. 'I love you, Mr Brannbi,' she said.

'My family know me as Romesh,' he said into her mouth.

16

Belle checked the tables they had erected on the newly mown meadow. There were flowers in jam jars, sandwiches beneath napkins, apples and pears in bowls, jelly, cakes. At least today, in the face of the depression and the cut-backs at the Longdale mine, there was plenty of food for everyone at the fête. The bunting flapped in the breeze as she checked for clouds.

Helen laughed. 'If there were any, Belle, I doubt that even you could order them to flee, though it would be close, very close. July is always a risk. Perhaps we should have tried June?'

'We would never have sorted out the stalls in time this year, my dear,' Belle said. 'But you're right, you must put it to the committee for another time. Though there will be the King's Jubilee in May of next year.'

Helen looked into the distance. 'James would have enjoyed that. He admired the King.'

Belle put her arm through hers. What would her old friend do, now that the pressure of the fête was almost over? There would be so many long days to fill without her beloved James.

Villagers from Longdale and Rempton strolled in front and behind them, eating toffee apples that Belle had made. Sadie slipped up behind her. 'Bye, do you remember, Belle, when you taught our gang to make those? That was a grand day, and a grand spate by Walter.'

Belle threw her arms round Sadie. 'Oh, I'm so glad you've arrived.'

'Now, how could I miss it, especially with Mary giving me no peace until I agreed? Arthur couldn't come though;

he's on duty at the hospital, praying he hasn't Dora on his team.' Sadie gestured behind her. 'Mary's bringing the girls along but we've lost Sandy to the coconuts over there.'

Belle waved to Mary who was coming through the crowds, then turned back to Sadie. 'But he hates coconut.'

'Aye, well, that's men for you.'

Helen laughed. 'You're too newly married to be saying that.'

Mary hugged them both. 'The girls are straight off round the stalls; they're looking for their patchwork. Has any sold?'

Belle nodded, tucking her arm into Mary's. 'It's practically all gone.'

'Well, Connie should be pleased with that – it'll all go to the bursary.' Mary put her hands on her hips. 'Oh, my feet are sore with traipsing around the nobs with me bleeding tin.' She grinned. 'Who am I?'

'Binnie,' they all shouted, before collapsing with laughter as Mary stubbed out an imaginary Woodbine in the remains of a glass of beer. Sadie pursed her lips. 'Hiss, hiss,' she said.

Belle begged them to stop as Mrs Green pushed two large plates of scones on the table, saying, 'Well, you lot are having fun, and you deserve it after all this work. But you're needed on the tombola, Belle, and the dance display is about to start.'

The afternoon passed in a haze of heat and laughter, and just before the tombola was drawn, the squire stopped at the stall the school had set up which showed a Punjabi village, a school, a clinic. 'Going well is it?' he called across to Belle.

'The fête, the mission school, or Connie?' she called back.

He shrugged, laughing as he said, 'Let's try all of them.'

'Extremely well, Squire, but the fête could do just that bit better if someone bought these last few tickets. You need a lovely big marrow, don't you?'

'Since I sent it over, I doubt it, but here you are, you hard grasping woman.'

The tombola was drawn, Longdale Brass Band played 'God save the King' and Belle watched Boy taking a final photograph. He was covering the fête for the local *Mercury* where he was cubbing in his vacation.

'May I have copies for Connie?' she asked him.

'I thought I'd send them myself, Belle. Would you mind?'

She touched his arm. 'That's a far better idea. I'll just send her share of the money. She might just be pleased with that!' He started to walk away and she ran after him. 'Will you take some photographs of the German exchange team coming to the mission next month – it would be a good follow-up to the fête, since some of the money's going to that as well as the unemployed? You will be here, won't you?'

He looked down at her, his dark eyes gentle, his black hair falling over his forehead. 'Where else would I be, but it's not the same without her, is it?'

She watched him walk away, and looked around her. She'd been so busy she had hardly had time to breathe, but he was right. It wasn't the same without her. She looked up at the sky again; the clouds were still there, but the sun was shining. It was the monsoon season in India, Connie had written, and there had been such joy in her letter, such happiness, and so many references to Peter Paul, though she had not told Boy that.

Connie and Romesh looked out from the ruins. All was peace now, after the rain that had slashed the earth, the stones and the river, for days. Water lay on the soil which was green with blossoming life. The swelling river was green, the creepers on the ruins too. His arm was around her, his lips on her neck, her arm, her hand, and then her mouth and she was drowning in the weight, the scent, the feel of him.

She clung to him, kissing his eyes, his forehead, the

nape of his neck where his shirt was unbuttoned, pressing her body to him, feeling him along the length of her, wanting something more.

He pulled back, smiling at her. 'Enough, my Connie. Enough.'

She reached for his mouth again and kissed away his words and heard the rain begin again, not feeling the humidity, only Romesh as he held her tight, as his lips grew stronger, as his body moved against hers, as his hand found her breast, undid her button, touched her flesh and it was as though he had pierced her.

She moaned deep in her throat and his lips found her skin, and she held his head against her, pressing him to her, but then he broke away again, sweat breaking out on his forehead, his hands trembling. She drew them back but he re-buttoned her dress, held her hand, and together they looked out at the river, and the rain.

'The villagers will be sweeping the water away from the bottom of their walls in case they collapse,' he said, entwining his fingers with hers. His breathing was shallow; he pushed down his hunger for her, his love.

'Aja said the mud is still dripping from the ceiling in his home,' she said; her voice sounded strange, her skin still ached from the touch of him.

'I have spoken to his father. His opposition is less. In fact, he is close to agreement, if only he can overcome his reluctance to allow his son the possibility of breaking out of his caste.'

'It is so like our class system.' But still she ached.

'Yes, but more immutable, with each caste having hundreds of sub-castes. It will always hold India up. It is absurd.'

His voice was angry now and she put her hand to his mouth. 'Someone might hear us.' His lips moved against her fingers.

He kissed her. 'You are becoming wise.'

The rain had stopped. Connie looked at the river

again. 'Why are you here, at the mission? You are not a Christian, are you?'

'I was born a Christian, but I am nothing, or perhaps everything. There seems nothing of importance except the struggle to free ourselves, and to do that peacefully.'

'So why teach here and at the other schools you visit?' Why was she saying this? She would die if he left.

He stroked her fingers, one by one. 'To make sure that mission children know of their own nation's cultures and religions, to balance Christianity and the British view, make them aware of everything, and everyone, and so fear and ignorance is cut away. It is through this generation that we can start the process of unity. There are others like me, but sometimes it all seems such a tiny action.'

Connie bent to kiss his hand. 'Someone said that my parents' work was a drop in the ocean.'

He turned his hand palm up and cupped her face. 'What did they reply?'

She closed her eyes and thought of the back yard, the garden which bloomed where there had only been bleakness, seeing her mother saying to Binnie as she now said to Romesh, 'It is better than doing nothing.'

He stroked her hair, his voice was soft, lilting. 'Bhagavad Gita, the great Hindu religious poem which inspired Gandhi, says, "Do the work that you have to do, for work is better than inaction."'

'Well, there you are then, we are linked by your poem and my mother.'

He laughed softly, looked at her hand in his. 'Dear Connie.'

They stayed in the ruins for another thirty minutes, and then Connie tore herself away, came back, kissing him again. Hating every minute without him. 'I shall go now, but I will be here again tomorrow morning. Work on Aja's father.'

* * *

The cold weather came, and she lay at night beneath a quilt, glorying in the crisp mornings, the light frost. She wrote of this to Belle and Boy, but never of Romesh, though she wanted to tell them of her love for him, of his beauty, of his goodness.

She told them instead that Aja's family had given their consent, and they replied, telling her that the school had cheered, and the *Mercury* had written it up in the newspaper.

Each day she and Romesh took turns to work on the curriculum with John and Aja, drawing along the other children, appointing monitors to give them an experience of authority.

On Thursdays Romesh walked them in a crocodile to the village on 'craft day', past the growing wheat, the wild flowers. On Fridays Connie printed with them, holding up Revd Williams' leaflets for them to see, explaining that each clinic would receive some, and that because of their efforts, some children's lives would be saved.

'You see, it is an important drop in the ocean,' she said to Romesh.

Some evenings she helped Romesh with his typing or printing. Each night she lay planning the next day, thinking of him, waiting for the dawn when she slipped from the bungalow, walking to the ruins, feeling his arms around her, his lips on hers. She had never felt so alive, or so happy, and she dreaded a chit telling her that he was going away. How could she live through those hours and days without him?

On a Monday morning in December, a chit was brought to her in the schoolroom. As she took it from Joseph, she couldn't understand because Romesh was there, looking across at her. She read the chit and her hand began to shake. She looked up at him. He walked towards her as though he knew the words she had read, as though he could sense that they were tearing her heart out of her body.

He reached her, gripped her hand, read.

Miss Symonds,
I thought you would like to know, since you
appear to have chosen young Aja as your rising
star, that I was called to his house as I drove
through the village this morning. He died at
dawn. Asian Cholera, I think. Fortunately for
his father there are three other sons, which
is all that matters to these people. And who
knows, perhaps one of them has his talents and
can replace Aja in your scheme.
Revd Williams.

She looked out across the classsroom; the children were talking. Aja's house had a leaking roof. Had it leaked onto him, onto his bright eyes, high mouth which smiled, his hands which had wanted to write legal briefs? She looked at her own hands as she gripped Romesh.

'I didn't notice he wasn't here,' she said. 'I didn't even notice. Will his family? They have three other sons, but there isn't another Aja. No child can be replaced. How can they think like that? How can a man of God think like that?'

She ran out into the compound. The crispness had gone. She looked up at the sky. Of course the roof hadn't leaked; it only leaked and dripped mud when the monsoons came. Was she mad?

Romesh came after her, wanting to hold her but unable to do so out here in the compound. He led her back inside and gripped her arm there. 'This is India,' he said. 'Death comes out of nowhere; it is accepted. But Revd Williams is wrong. There will be great distress and a sense of loss. But there will also be comfort because Aja was Hindu; he will be reborn into a higher caste because he has earned that.'

She pulled from him, angry now. 'No, don't you see, he could have *made* himself a higher caste. It is all such nonsense and I can't bear it.'

She wanted him to hold her, press her to him, make this stop. The children looked at her, their eyes wide. Had she shouted?

Romesh told them in Punjabi to begin their work. John stood, then walked towards them.

'I will tell him,' Romesh said and now she heard the tremor in his voice and knew that for him too, Aja would not just be replaced.

'Surely we both should,' she replied and followed Romesh out into the bright sun, her hand on John's shoulder. She held him beneath the banyan tree as Romesh told him, smelling the cow-dung fires, seeing the endless sky, hearing his sobs.

'I won't go to that school now. How can I, without him?' John said.

That evening she couldn't eat. She pushed her plate away as Revd Williams talked of his day, but said nothing of Aja.

'I miss Aja,' she said, interrupting him, weeping as she spoke. 'He was a wonderful boy.' She wanted some acknowledgement of the child who had held a place in her heart.

Revd Williams looked at her aghast and waved the bearer out of the room. *'Angrezi-log kubi nai,'* he hissed at her. 'Listen to me, English people never cry. You must learn the rules, you simply must. We have a position to keep.'

In the morning Revd Williams left for his monthly trip around his more distant clinics. He would not be back for a week. Connie hadn't slept. She didn't go to the ruins but to the schoolroom where she kicked the desk, flipped through the magazines to be cut today, looked at Aja's chair, at his treasure pocket, at the walls.

Romesh came in. He had not gone to the ruins either because he had known she would be here.

She shouted, 'This room needs repainting. It is dark, gloomy.' She strode to the doorway.

'Where are you going?' Romesh barred her way.

'To get the paint.'

He pushed her back, shaking his head. 'No, do not damage your standing, your relationship with Joseph. This room is not where your anger should be directed.'

She flung his hand away. 'Then where?'

He stood in front of her, his arms at his side. 'Perhaps nowhere. Or perhaps it should be turned into action.'

She clasped her hands. 'Oh, I should fight in the streets, should I, like you and your friends? There's been yet another demonstration, another riot in the town. I should go there, should I?' Her anger was too great; the words rushed out. She wanted to see him flinch, see the world flinch.

He smiled. 'Our action is non-action, as you know. It is just that out of that tends to come violence towards us, or by others, and yes, why don't you go to a town, to Lahore? Why don't you take John, show him the school, make him want to go? Be like your mother, don't be defeated. Make a garden out of a wilderness as your mother did. And may I take Aja's treasure pocket to his family? They are distraught. As I said, acceptance does not deny great grief.'

The next day she travelled to Lahore with John, ignoring the stares as they entered the compartment hand in hand, continuing to hold his hand as they passed buffaloes grazing in mud villages, pointing out irrigation channels.

'You see, all this countryside is very much the same. There is so little difference, the people will be the same too. Mr Brannbi says that Lahore is a kind city, that there are so many different sorts of people, so much tolerance, so much learning, so many people who could become your friends.'

Lahore was very different to the village, though, and as they walked along the platform, stepping over the betel stains, the bundles, before joining the throng of people, John gripped her hand because he had never before seen so many people.

She remembered Bombay, the smell, the heat, the people. They walked out into the light, taking a rickshaw to the address of Romesh's friends. They passed Sikhs, Hindus, Muslims. They saw the ancient wall, then they were inside it and there was a seething mass of people. There were alleys, souks, temples, mosques, shrieks, smells, the clamour of the bazaars. She clutched John's hand.

'Don't be afraid; I am scared enough for both of us.' She grinned and at last he smiled.

'Do you really feel fear too? Do you feel lonely? With Aja I did not. I had a friend. Now I have no-one,' he said.

'You have me, you have Mr Brannbi and one day you will be able to build bridges, or walls like that which we have just come through.'

He sat back now, his hand still in hers, and looked up at the buildings. 'Some are falling down,' he said.

'One day, you will rebuild them.'

The wallah stopped. They dismounted, paid him. Connie threw annas to the children who were clamouring and pulling at her clothes. She knocked at the old dusty wooden door. It opened.

'Come in, out of the crowd.' The girl was in European dress, her skin was coffee-coloured, her voice was singsong like Romesh's.

They climbed the stairs to the apartment. 'My husband is at work, on the railway. He will be back much later, but now you must drink, eat, wash and sleep. Or at least you must, little John.'

After they had eaten Connie led him to the camp-bed in the room he would share with her and sat with him until he slept. She then joined Angelique, sitting alongside her on the sofa while the beautiful Eurasian talked of her white father, her Indian mother, and how she and her husband Eric, also half-caste, were accepted by neither Indian nor British.

'But one day, when independence comes, it will surely be different,' Angelique said.

John and Connie stayed for four days, travelling around Lahore, looking at the Government School, the College, the Aurangzeb's great mosque, its faiences still glistening, though they should be dull from all the dust. They looked at its ninety-nine names of God written on its cenotaph. They saw the fort, and the three hundred fountains of the Shalamar Gardens and heard their hissing.

They walked the Mall, passing cafés, shops, restaurants, theatres. John studied temples, buildings. On the last day he pulled her towards yet another street. 'Look at this one.'

It was ornate, old, crumbling. She saw the prostitutes and led him away, laughing, telling Angelique that evening.

Angelique said, 'Lahore is so rich; there is every sort of person here and such beauty. It is cosmopolitan, it is tolerant. The races mix, accept one another. It is how India will be one day, if those who think like Romesh can work their magic.' She studied her hands. 'I fear though, that it might not be like that, and wonder if one day the streets will be full of screaming men and running blood.'

Angelique was smoking a cigarette using a holder. She offered one to Connie who shook her head. Smoking reminded her of Binnie. 'Do you really feel that will happen?'

'I just don't know. There is much argument in Congress about the number of seats to be reserved for Muslims. Many in the All-India Congress Party feel we should have a proper democracy. A proper democracy will bring a Hindu landslide because of their vast numbers. If, at this stage, Congress is not generous to the Muslims, they will fear us, they will fight us, because they think Congress will rule them as the British have. They will rush to the Muslim League, demand their own land, or that is what we fear.'

'Would their own nation be so terrible, if it kept the peace?'

'It would be a tragedy. How do you divide a nation? Do you draw a line on a map? Do you cut a typewriter in half, an operating table, a village, an irrigation scheme? How do you move people whose heritage is in their piece of land, and retain calm? No, we must still strive for unity, for peace.'

Connie looked round the room, at the sideboard heavy with photographs of a white man, a Hindu wife. At the carpets hanging on the walls, the heavy cotton table-cloth, the newspaper folded by the chair.

She had seen no violence, only heard of it. She thought of the mosque and the temples, and the Sikhs, Hindus, Muslims who were clamouring, walking, jostling in the streets below them. 'Nothing like that will happen. It can't. Independence will come; the British will leave, but I will stay.'

'You love our nation so much?' Angelique murmured.

Connie nodded. 'And Romesh too.' Safe in the knowledge that Angelique was trusted by Romesh.

Angelique looked down at her hands and said nothing, though she thought, oh Romesh, what have you done?

Connie was tired from the journey when they arrived back at the orphanage. She touched John's hair, then smiled at Sister Teresa.

'He said he wants to go to school in Lahore. My friend there, Angelique, said that she would like him to board with her.'

John tugged at her skirt. 'She said I could sleep in the room where we slept. She said it would feel more like my own since I already knew it.' He ran into the building and Sister Teresa smiled, then followed, her habit dragging in the dust.

Connie walked back to the mission school. She washed, had dinner with Mrs Williams and told her of Lahore though the old woman didn't speak as usual.

'I must stretch my legs,' Connie said, rising when the meal was finished.

'To the river again?' Mrs Williams asked.

Connie stood quite still, alarm making her voice terse. 'Have you seen me there?' But how could that be, she never left the bungalow? Had someone else?

'No, but each time I can smell it on you. I liked to walk by the river in Cambridge. I liked to walk by the Ganges.'

Connie relaxed. 'It reminds me of the beck at home,' she said, walking out, down the steps, across the compound, out along the bunds, to the ruins, seeing him. She ran to him, felt his arms around her. It had been so long.

His mouth was on hers. 'Has it helped John?' he asked at last.

'Yes, he will go, stay with Angelique.' She was impatient and drew his head to hers. 'I've missed you so.'

He looked into her eyes. He had missed her more than he thought possible. She was all that she seemed – good, kind, honest, and now his mouth was on hers, and there was no more hesitation from either of them as his hands found her breasts, her thighs, and hers followed the contours of his back, his buttocks. His lips were on her face, his hands on her buttons; hers on his.

They sank to the ground; the frogs croaked, the wind sighed in the trees and the creepers. A jackal called as Romesh's mouth found her bare breasts, her bare navel, her thighs. She saw the gleam of light on his skin, his dark, dark skin, and sank beneath the passion that would show him, and India, her love.

17

Belle looked down the lines of tables set up in the back alley behind the mission. Joseph had painted a poster and it hung on the wall. *'Silver Jubilee, May 1935'*.

Instead of washing strung up overhead there was bunting, and there was also laughter, chatter, squeals, but nothing could take away the thinness of the children's faces, their worn clothes, or the haunted faces of their parents. When would work come?

Mary was organizing the drinks, leaning over the heads of the children, pouring lemonade into the mugs on the tables. Sandy passed round beer to the fathers and to the men from the mission, all of whom stood with their backs against the walls talking quietly.

Helen Driscoll who sat next to Belle at the head of the line of tables said, 'It's a great shame the Germans haven't been this year.'

Belle sipped the tea that one of Mary's girls had poured for her. 'I know.' Anxiety tightened the muscles of her neck. 'With that man Hitler walking into the Saar, I fear another war is almost inevitable, Helen. I'm just thankful that Walter is dead, and so won't see his worst fears realized.'

Helen smiled her thanks as Nancy Gribble, Mrs Gribble's granddaughter, offered her a scone. 'Just one, my dear.' She turned to Belle. 'Come along now, it's not as serious as that.'

'But the Germans have introduced conscription – where will it all end?' Belle rubbed her forehead, looking down the length of the tables. 'And look at these people. When will there be jobs? The whole world's going mad.'

Sandy bent over. 'Belle, stop shouting, this is a party. If you want your soapbox I'll set one up in the garden and you can talk to yourself.'

Belle leaned back on the stool, laughing, her headache easing. 'You're quite right. I bore myself so much sometimes that the thought of what I do to everyone else is alarming. Now, how is Joseph doing at the grammar school?'

She smiled as the vicar arrived with the huge cake that the Greens had sent from the village. He set it down, and as his wife cut the first slice to a round of applause, Sandy said, 'Joseph's doing grand, and he's on the cricket team.'

She thought of that first mission baby and could hardly believe that he was fifteen. She watched the vicar's wife laugh with her husband and saw herself and Walter as they had been. Oh Walter, Connie, I miss you.

The children were putting on the hats Helen had helped the village children to make. Belle turned to her. 'There you are, I told you the school couldn't manage without you.'

Sandy squatted beside them. 'Aye, Mary told me Helen had set up a library there too. Grand idea.'

Helen picked at the icing on her cake, eating it, saying, 'Don't tell the children that the harridan who reads to them every lunch-time eats her cake like this will you, Belle?'

'I certainly will. It's a disgusting habit and you should be ashamed of yourself. I'll tell Boy too, and he'll write it up in the *Mercury* when he comes at the end of term, then you will never be able to hold your head up again.'

Helen tutted. 'Oh, I forgot to tell you that I received a letter from him this morning. He's not coming to Rempton, he's travelling to Venice with a group of artists and writers. Fiona is one of them.'

They exchanged glances. Did this mean that Boy at last was filling the space left by Connie?

Sandy stood now, tapping Belle's shoulder, whispering, 'Stand by to repel boarders.'

Binnie came from the garden, her shawl around her shoulders. She had become fat; a Woodbine hung from her lip, beer was on her breath as she sat on the end of the bench, next to Belle.

'Grand to see you, Belle,' Binnie said, her Woodbine still in her mouth. 'Been hearing about young Joseph, have you? They want him to go on to college. Don't know how they'll afford that, do you?'

Belle met Sandy's eyes. He said, 'We've saved hard, Binnie.'

Binnie looked at Belle; anger was in her voice as she said, 'Oh yes?'

Belle asked, 'Is Dora still enjoying her nursing?'

Binnie took the cigarette from her mouth and threw it to the ground. 'Yes, but it's her shoes, you know, Belle. All that walking the poor bairn has to do, and she needs a new belt, and a better watch. She was late for her shift and that Sister's a bitch.'

The cigarette was still smouldering on the cobbles. Belle ground it beneath her shoe as she longed to grind Binnie's endless demands.

She looked along the table at the children who were now eating jelly, seeing Dora, her curls, her wide eyes when she had first come, the doll she had been given, the bigger one she had wanted. Poor child, how could she be otherwise with Binnie for a mother? She looked at Helen who shook her head slightly.

She looked back at Binnie. 'I'll send you something towards it, Binnie.'

Binnie smoothed her dress over her stomach and heaved herself up from the bench. 'That'll be grand, Belle. You are always there when anyone needs you.' The words were right, but the harsh voice wasn't.

Belle watched Binnie waddle back into the garden, her garden which Mary and the vicar's wife now tended.

'But why, Belle?' Helen said.

'Because of Dora. How can one turn one's back on the child of a woman like that? She wrote to me, you know, telling me of her happiness at caring for others.'

'And you believed her?' Helen's voice was sharp.

'I think I have to; why else would she stay? It is hard work, you know.'

Binnie sat in the vicar's kitchen, eating the biscuits she had pinched from the tin. Had Dora written to Belle as she'd told her to – saying all the right things? She'd be all right if she could land this doctor, if he dumped his wife, that is. But she'd need help if it didn't work, because the hospital would throw her out, you bliddy bet they would.

Connie sat at the typewriter, reading through Romesh's column, feeling the heat from his body as he leaned over her shoulder, his hand holding the edge of the paper. No mistakes. He kissed the top of her head, his hands travelling down over her breasts to her groin, then to her breasts again.

She arched her back, pressing her head into his chest, lifting her face. He kissed her, his tongue finding hers. He dragged the chair round, kneeling holding her face between his hands, kissing her gently. 'Thank you, my darling.'

He leaned against her and she stroked his hair, wondering how life could ever have existed before Romesh, before India. 'John is working so well now,' she murmured.

'We've done a good job.'

She kissed his hair. Yes, they were a team, they were two halves of a whole. She leant back in the chair and into the heat. The monsoon was late. It was June. She longed for it to begin, thundering down, cracking through this heavy blanket of heat.

When it came she would run out into the rain, letting it douse her, drown her, as Romesh's kisses drowned her, as his body, on and in her, drowned her.

She hugged him. 'I didn't know anyone could be so happy.'

They listened to the moths and insects against the hurricane-lamp, the jackals on the plain, neither wanting to leave the other, but Romesh finally stood, kissed her hands. He took the typewritten piece and collected up the leaflets he had printed off, putting them into his bag, slinging it over his shoulder.

'The ruins, tomorrow?' he whispered as he left on his bicycle.

The heat clung to her as she climbed the steps, turning to look round the compound, the schoolroom and out onto the lane where she could still see Romesh. She watched until she could see him no more, then moved into the house. Mrs Williams was knitting.

They sat together in the heat which seemed to ooze from the very walls – when would the monsoon break? She listened to the clicking of knitting needles, she heard the Revd Williams's car returning, then the slam of the door. There was a flash of lightning, the crack of thunder, and the rain, at last the rain.

Revd Williams ran up the steps and into the house, into the sitting-room, his hair wet, his face rigid with rage, a leaflet in his hand. He stood before her, shaking it in her face. Water dripped from it and from his hair, his clothes.

'What is the meaning of this?' His other fist was bunched; the paper almost touched her face.

She took it from him, knowing what she would see, trying to think. She was right; it was a leaflet that Romesh had set on the printer. Fear rose, the rain drummed, the thunder rolled. The Revd Williams was too close to her; she could smell the curry on his breath. He shouted over his shoulder, 'Get to bed, Mother.'

Connie heard the creaking of the old woman's chair. Revd Williams was still too close. 'I ask again, what is the meaning of this?' His spittle landed on her lips, in her eyes. He was too large, too fierce.

She forced herself to sound calm. 'It's an independence leaflet, but why are you asking me about it?' Her voice was too high; it shook.

He wheeled from her, strode to his desk, searching amongst his papers, scattering them to the floor, and still the rain drummed, and lightning lit the room. She eased herself from the chair, moving behind it, gripping the back, wanting something between them.

He turned, waving a medical leaflet, striding towards her, his face even thinner in the light from the lamp. 'The broken "o". You see, it's the same.' He held up the leaflet, pointing to the 'o'. 'It's that damned black. He's been using the printer. How dare he? I'll get on to the police. It's your fault, you found the damned machine in the first place.' He paced up and down, tearing the leaflet into shreds. 'Seditious bloody bastard, how will the mission carry on after this? I'll get him locked up for life – how bloody dare he?' He rushed out into the hall.

She ran after him, her fear not for herself now, but for Romesh. She caught him by the arm, making him stop. 'Then you'll have to have me locked up too, because I have been helping him, and if you look at the leaflet carefully, you will see that it is a call for peace.' The sweat felt cold on her forehead.

She held it up. The shock was on his face. He shook her, then slapped her. She reeled, caught at the wall, fell into the sitting-room, catching her head on the table. The pain exploded as the thunder cracked.

'You have been alone with a black, printing this? Are you mad?'

'No, not mad. I think he's right; all this needs saying. But I'm sorry I deceived you.' Her voice was still so high, so scared. She tasted the blood from her lip. She pushed herself up, steadying herself on the sideboard, shouting above the storm. 'We love one another. You must understand, surely. You treat his people, you like them, you have devoted your life to them. You must love them too.' She struggled for control.

He walked towards her, his eyes bright with hate. 'You have allowed yourself to be defiled? You have kissed a native?' He spat the words out.

Now fear was ebbing in Connie, and anger took its place. Her voice was strong as she said, 'He's a man, like you. How can you talk like this? Romesh might be an Indian but he's also a human being. He would bleed if you struck him, as you have me.' The thunder roared.

He stopped, confusion on his face. 'Romesh? Who is Romesh?'

'He is Peter Paul.'

She put her hands out to him, her voice softer. 'It sounds as though everything is a lie, but it's because it had to be; look how you are shouting. He's not wicked. Neither am I. We're pleading for peace and unity, as my father did. We should have told you. It was wro—'

He hit her hands away from him. 'Get out of here, you harlot – I will not have you in my house. You have jeopardized everything. What if the British in town hear that you, a white woman, have been contaminated by this – this black, under my roof? What will my standing be then? I was becoming less of an outsider, but now you have taken that from me.'

He advanced on her. She backed away again and the noise of the rain was everywhere. She groped for the doorway, found it, then ran down the hall, down the steps, out into the rain which drenched her and drowned his shouts, but not the fear and anger which deluged her.

She ran on down the lane, looking behind. Was he following? There was no-one. She ran and ran, past the village. Then she walked, tasting the dust in the rain, feeling her clothes clinging to her, the mud on her legs, her skirt, feeling the fear of leaving, along with the anger.

She would go to him. Now it must come into the open and there was no room for anything but joy because now she could be honest about her love and face the disdain of the British, knowing she was not alone.

For two hours she walked and then she saw the light of the town. Where was the house? She must remember what he had said. She pushed through the bazaar, her hair in her eyes, hearing nothing but the rain and Revd Williams's words.

She passed the Gardens. It was near here. What had he said? There was a tamarind tree at the entrance, a flagged courtyard. Was this it? She saw his bicycle. She ran across the courtyard; the baked earth was now mud. She ran up the veranda steps, beating on the door, hauling on the bell.

A middle-aged Indian opened it. He looked at her, removing his spectacles.

'Romesh?' she gasped, exhaustion overtaking her.

'Miss Symmonds, I presume. I am Romesh's uncle.' He called to a bearer, telling him to wake Romesh, beckoning her into the house.

She shook her head. 'No, I am too wet.' She was shaking, her legs were trembling.

The man called to the bearer, then led her to the chairs on the veranda. 'Then sit here with me while we wait.'

The bearer brought brandy. She shook her head but Romesh's uncle pressed it into her hand. 'Drink, for you have come a long way and there must be a reason.'

The brandy seared her throat. She coughed, wiped her mouth, tasted the mud on her hand. Her lips were swollen, the cut was tender, her head ached where she had banged it. She told him of Revd Williams's discovery, stumbling over the words, repeating her love for Romesh, for his work. His love for her.

The Indian replaced his spectacles and looked across the courtyard. Rain lay on the earth, creepers dripped water, lightning lit the statue, the palms; thunder rolled.

'I knew nothing of this,' he said and left her, walking into the house, his dhoti moving in the wind.

She waited, she drank, then clasped the glass. She drank again. The trembling wouldn't stop. The echoes of Revd

Williams' hate wouldn't stop. Where was Romesh? She needed him. Oh God, how she needed him.

Romesh came, the white of his dhoti startling against his skin, and she ran to him, clutching at him as he held her, but then he pushed her away. Her mud was on his clothes. She brushed at it. He took her hand; his face was a mask, his voice was flat. 'Why did you come here?'

She clung to him, wanting to be in his arms again. 'He discovered that we were printing together. He insulted you. I told him of my love for you. I don't care what people think; I want them to know I love you, I want to share your life. I don't mind if the whole world knows. What can they say that will diminish us? I can bear being ostracized if I am with you. We can carry on the fight together and when independence comes it won't matter. I don't want you to protect me any more; I want to proclaim my love for you, and your country.'

There was pain in his eyes and while the thunder rolled again he said nothing, but still he held her hands, his arms strong as he kept her from him.

'You misunderstand, Connie. I can't have you here, or in my life. The secrecy was for me too, because you are the enemy. How can I fight a cause if I live with you? My uncle now knows that I have broken all the rules, through love, Connie. But I can't give up this fight, my place in its struggle. It's much bigger than us. I would be more diminished by you, than you by me, my love.'

His hands still held hers and tears were running down his cheeks.

Her trembling began again. This isn't what he should say. He should praise her, welcome the sacrifice she was laying before him. He should draw her into his life, accept her statement of love.

'Please don't send me away,' she begged.

'I must, for both our sakes.'

'But where will I go?'

'Go home, Connie, to where you belong,' Romesh said.

'But you are my home,' she said, feeling him leading her from the veranda, hearing a car starting, seeing lights coming from the side of the house. The rain seemed a solid wall, like the wall that was between them.

'I can't go, I can't leave you,' she wept.

The car pulled up at the veranda steps. Romesh's uncle got out, opened an umbrella and waited. Romesh was pushing her now. She clung to him. 'I'll see you again? It can't end like this.'

He said, 'It has to. Forgive me, Connie, it should never have started.'

A bearer brought out an umbrella. Romesh took it, opened it, then guided her down the steps. She brushed against the shrubs which grew in pots. 'John?' she said, turning, stopping, hope surging. 'What about John? I can't leave because of John.'

Romesh tried to pull her but she wouldn't move, she couldn't. How could she leave him? He was her world, she was his. He turned to her, kissed her lips, then said, 'I love you, Connie, for your goodness, your purity. I shall look after John. I shall arrange for a suitable teacher to "arrive" who will carry on with the children. Now go. The police will come. I must leave.'

He pulled her on, and now they were walking to the car. How could her legs be holding the weight of her body? His uncle held open the door. She grasped Romesh's hand. It was wet from the rain. She said, 'The police won't come. I promise you that. I shall make sure that they don't. I don't know how, but I will.'

She climbed into the car. It seemed quiet suddenly. He leaned in and said quietly, 'Never ever tell anyone about us.'

She looked at her hands, then at his face, seeing his anxiety, and now the agony was there, searing through her. The car started to move; Romesh slammed the door shut. She wound down the window and leaned out.

'Why? In case it affects you? In case someone decides you are a defiled Indian?' Her voice was ugly with anger and pain.

He ran after the car, catching up with it as they left the courtyard, shouting at her, 'No, this time for your sake. Remember, Connie. Never tell anyone.'

He dropped back as the car turned onto the street. She wound up the window, listening to the whine of the wipers, gripping her thighs with her hands, trying to stop the shaking that racked her body, trying to grasp the suddenness of how her world had changed, wanting it to slow down, trying not to see the great looming darkness of a future without him. She felt rage surging and wanted to shout at him, at his uncle who drove this car which was taking her from a man she had bestowed her love upon, a man whose colour she had ignored, a man to whom she had granted her body.

She looked out onto the land which had been so parched, so burned by the heat, and was now being assaulted by the rain. She hated it, she hated him, them. She shook her head at the Indians they were passing. Bloody Romesh, how could he throw away the love of a white—

She dropped her head onto the window-pane and it was as though the world fell silent all around; it was as though the storm had fled, and there was just emptiness, because now she saw herself as she really was.

She remembered Mrs Lewis on the boat, she heard again Revd Williams and knew that she had patronized Romesh; she had given her body to him, as though it was an honour she was conferring. She had only thought in terms of her own need for protection, never his, and she wanted to hide her face in shame.

'But I love him,' she said.

Romesh's uncle murmured, 'He knows that, and he has loved you also. But it is over now.'

He left her outside the compound. She walked through the rain, climbed the veranda steps and went into the sitting-room. Revd Williams was sitting, watching the door.

'I knew you'd be back for your things. I will take you to the train in the morning and you can find a passage when you are in Bombay. Only then will I tell the police; when you are no longer here to be brought into this and heap shame on us.'

She stood in front of him. 'I have shamed myself, but not in the way that you feel – and I am not going to Bombay.' The trembling was gone. 'I am staying in India until independence occurs, because it must, and it will. If you approach the police I will tell them of my love affair. I will tell that you shoved me to the floor, and your standing will never recover. You will find me a job with another mission school. You will make sure that John continues with his studies.'

She left the room. In the bathroom she stripped the clothes from her body, the body that Romesh had said would never again be his. She doused herself with water, trying to wash away the pain of lost love and the knowledge of her arrogance. She dried herself, put on her nightdress.

She walked into her room and lay on her bed for hour after hour, and as dawn broke she knew that her love would never die. Romesh must feel her body again. She would stay to protect him, but also to be there when India became free because her love was real, and his had been, and both would endure. They had to.

18

Belle tended Binnie's grave, arranging the flowers as she had arranged Walter's, looking over to his headstone. Even in death they weren't to be free of her, but 'How can you refuse a dying wish?' Belle had asked Helen Driscoll. 'Easily, if it's Binnie,' Helen had snapped.

Belle called to Helen, 'I'll be over by the wall when you've finished.'

Helen looked up from the vase she was cleaning on James' grave. 'I won't be long.'

'Don't hurry.' Belle leaned on the wall. What was there to hurry for? Only war it seemed. She rubbed at the stone with her gloved hands. September 1938 and Europe seemed intent on destruction.

Helen came up behind her. 'Shall we check the gas-mask procedures again before tea so that we know exactly what to say to the children? I think the headmaster's right to want to weave it into a story before we become caught up in a drill.'

'No, let's leave it until tomorrow. I feel I need a nice warm fire, some crumpets and lots of jam,' Belle said, smiling.

Helen nodded. 'You always come up with an idea to top mine, you wretched woman. Come on, let's get home.' They walked along the lane to the vicarage, the gravel crunching as they approached the door.

'Dora should be there soon,' Helen said as they passed the hydrangea.

'Any day now,' Belle sighed. Connie hadn't returned after two years and now Dora was out there too. 'Did we do the right thing? Should we have kept her here longer?'

Helen pressed her arm. 'The alternative was to have her with us until the end of time, and she wanted to go, so yes. We did the right thing.'

Belle thought of Dora, so distraught at the end of her love affair. 'Who is the man?' Belle had asked, hugging the weeping girl at Binnie's funeral.

'A doctor. I thought he was going to marry me,' Dora had sobbed. 'I have to leave the hospital; I can't stay there, it's too painful, and now Mam is dead there's nowhere for me, but at least poor Mam knew I had passed my exams.'

Dora had stayed in the vicarage at Rempton, of course; what else could they do? Then Belle and Helen had lived from day to day, wondering if she would ever leave, if there would be the smell of cigarette smoke and lipstick-stained tissues discarded around the house for ever, if there would always be telephone bills which they could barely afford, if she would sit until the end of time in the sitting-room drinking coffee and never clearing away the cups.

'I would have felt happier if the friend who found her the job in the Government Hospital had had contacts in Africa.' Helen was jabbing the ground with her walking-stick. 'Look at the slugs, they've eaten the red chrysanthemum.'

'The hospital's down in the south, though, nowhere near Connie, and anyway, we must stop being so paranoid about Dora. It was Binnie who was the problem; Dora is a new generation. I just hope we didn't show that we wanted her gone.' Belle opened the front door.

The heat in the sitting-room was wonderful after the bitter cold. They sat in front of the fire.

'I'll make some tea in ten minutes but let's get warm first,' Belle suggested, missing Maud who had retired to Scotland. There was insufficient money to hire any staff, but at least they had a roof over their heads and for that they were grateful. They had shut up the wing, closed off the top floor, and shared the expenses of running the big house.

'Who knows, Connie might be glad to see her. You have told her, haven't you?'

'Yes, I wrote to her, but she said Madras was a world away, though she would write. She seemed strange again, Helen. I sense something is wrong, as it was when she moved on to that dreadful school. I still can't think what possessed her. Why leave the mission in the first place, and why didn't she come home after two years anyway?' Belle rubbed her hands in front of the fire. '*Come home,*' Belle had written. '*I know something is wrong, my love. Come home.*'

Connie had said she had too much to learn. Her letter had been abrupt, confused, but then, as time had passed, a calmness had grown in her writing, a sensitivity to the people and the country which had not been there before.

There had only been one reference to Peter Paul and that was when she wrote of his marriage, last month. How much had that hurt her daughter, Belle wondered, because she felt sure that there had been love once between these two?

She rubbed her arms with frustration. She wanted to be there with Connie, to see her, hold her, but she and Helen had used their savings for Dora's ticket. '*Come home,*' she had written again. '*You still have your return ticket.*'

Connie had not replied to her suggestion. She had merely talked again of the widows they took in, the orphans she taught, the frailty of Miss Anderson. The most recent letter had been cold, and there had been anger too.

'It makes me feel old,' Helen said, 'to think of all these children living so far away.'

Belle smiled, pushing her anxiety to one side. 'You are, after all, just a youngster of eighty-two and that can't possibly be anything to do with how you feel?'

Helen peered over the newspaper. 'Exactly. Now Belle,

tell me if there's anything from Boy in the paper. It'll save me wading through it all.'

'Page four. He's reporting from Munich.'

Helen read it. 'He's improving, doing very well. His father would have been so proud of him.' She put down the paper, steepling her hands beneath her chin, gazing into the fire. 'I just wish he had a companion,' she said slowly.

Belle said, 'He has plenty of companions.'

'You know what I mean.'

Belle did, but she didn't want to think of Boy and the look on his face whenever Connie was mentioned. She also knew that she was becoming a crabby old woman, but she couldn't help it.

'If only I had known there was something wrong before we gave the ticket money to Dora, I could have gone over,' Belle said.

Helen smiled gently. 'You suggested that before, and Connie said no. You must wait. You must allow her to live her life, however hard it is for you both.'

Dora settled herself into the wicker chair, looking around the common-room. Oh yes, the Punjab was far more suitable. Madras was too bloody hot, and she hadn't come all this way to wipe wogs' bums. She offered her cigarettes to Lucinda and Caroline, then lit them with her silver-plated lighter, dropping it back in her bag, listening to their voices, so cultured, so like her own now was.

She'd learned a great deal on the boat, but she should have been first-class, like Connie had been; it just wasn't bloody fair. All she ever had were the leavings from that family. Look at that doll they'd given her, smaller than Connie's.

'Didn't you like Madras then?' Lucinda asked, her gold bracelet jingling as she tapped the ash into the ashtray.

'I will not nurse wogs and Matron wouldn't move me from the hospital into the private wing. I asked to be sent here; they agreed.'

'Why here? We have Indian officers.'

'But no private wing absolutely packed full of the buggers.'

Lucinda said, 'I see your point.'

'Besides, it's further north so it's cooler. And let's face it, Lucinda, there are a few tasty morsels around this area.' Dora winked and the girls laughed.

She hadn't, in fact, requested the Punjab, she had simply said she must leave the hospital because the heat made her feel too ill. She had written to Connie; what else could she do? Connie had asked a doctor here if he would help and he had offered Dora her job. *'Come and see me when you're settled,'* Connie had written.

'So, Major Bailey is here for another two weeks?' she asked the girls, blowing out the smoke, tapping the ash into the heavy glass ashtray. The fans were whirring, the old oak panels of the room were restful, classy. Yes, this was so much better.

Caroline laughed. 'You're interested, are you?'

Dora shrugged. 'Nice face, nice body.'

'Nice rank,' finished Lucinda.

They all laughed. 'But what about that Captain French? I thought you'd paired up with him at the dance last week.'

Dora leaned forward. 'Yes, I was a bit too hasty there. I want to ditch him, he's in the way, but who can I offload him onto – what about you, Lucinda, you like stocky blokes?'

Lucinda stopped laughing. 'Come on, darling, are you trying to insult me? He's Service Corps. I am not interested in that. It's the Rifles or Gurkhas, or nothing.' Lucinda's face was hard, her voice brittle.

Dora altered her tone. 'I'm sorry, I'm new out here, remember? It was a stupid mistake and it won't happen again.'

Lucinda drew deeply on her cigarette and exchanged a glance with Caroline, then laughed again. 'Oh, what the hell. Come on, it's dinner-time anyway. We can go across to the club afterwards and see if we can find you a little Miss Nobody to take on your leftovers, someone even more inexperienced, Dora.'

That night, in her room, Dora paced up and down, up and down. 'Bloody superior bitch,' she ground out. She stopped by the dressing-table, tapping out a cigarette, lighting it, drawing deeply. But she must be careful, she must listen and learn and not make any more mistakes.

She looked out over the cantonment, relishing its wide avenues, looking across to the officers' bungalows.

One day she would live in one like that, one day she would be an officer's wife – that's why she was in India. She leaned back on the window-frame, cursing herself for fluttering her eyes at David French. How was she to know the Service Corps was the lowest of the low? Christ, perhaps she should try for a hospital near the Rifles but she wouldn't get another move so soon.

Who would be a sucker enough to take him off her hands while the Rifles were visiting? Her cigarette burned her fingers; she dropped it onto the floor, stubbing it out with her foot. The bearer could clear it up in the morning. Who was there? She looked across to the town.

Connie cycled past the bridge, the temple, down the narrow dirty streets, sick of the smell of the river, of the ordure, of the bazaar, sick of the heat. On she pedalled past the open shop fronts, not returning the waves of the Indians, keeping her head down, forging ahead. She hated them, hated Romesh. How could he have done this to her?

A bullock cart pulled out in front of her, she braked, stopped, leaned on her handlebars, looking at the front wheel, not at Chatterji who called, 'Good morning, Connie.'

Not at Tejbir Singh who also called a greeting. She wasn't one of them, was she? It had all been a game.

She rode past the gateway to the bazaar, sick of the smell of its fish, meat, vegetables, down through an alleyway lined with crumbling houses, bumping and rattling alongside the old open waterduct. Then through the gate of the school compound, feeling the heat on her hands.

She dismounted, creating a path between the children who clamoured around her and pulled at her skirt. They fell back in puzzled concern at her lack of interest. What did it matter? She strode on in to the office.

Miss Anderson looked up from the bills she was studying. 'Did you get it?'

Connie put the package on the desk. 'I smell of coffee now, but it's better than the stink of these damned streets.'

She sank into a chair, ignoring Miss Anderson's look of surprise. People didn't swear here, did they? They served, as those poor devils in the cemetery had served, only they had been in the pay of the Empire, whilst she had been in the grip of love.

Miss Anderson said, 'We have another widow, she's waiting in the dining-room. She's in a bad way, poor wee thing.'

Connie stretched out her legs. Her feet were dirty. God, this stinking country got everywhere. 'I suppose she's been treated like a household drudge? I suppose she's been neglected by everyone, just because he who is God is dead?' She knew she was shouting, but continued. 'Perhaps suttee should never have been outlawed, perhaps it is kinder that they burn with their husbands. After all it expunges both their sins so they can have years of bliss in heaven. Isn't that better than the life we can give them?'

She walked to the window. 'All we really do here is keep orphans and widows alive merely to exist, and what is the point?'

Miss Anderson called gently, 'There is a letter here, from your mother.'

'I don't want it, just throw it away.' Connie turned. 'Just tear it up and throw it away.' The old woman hesitated, then tore it into shreds, her frail hands straining with the effort. The pieces fluttered into the bin. There was silence.

At last Miss Anderson said, 'It is time you went home, Connie.'

'I can't. I don't want to see her.'

'Why, what has she done, to make you so angry, so hurt?'

Connie looked at the frail old woman, whose only emotions seemed to be kindness and compassion. How could someone as good as she understand?

'She brought me up in her image, to believe that we are all equal, to live a life of service. That's why I'm here, that's why I met Romesh. You don't know about him, do you? You don't know I loved an Indian. He's written to me to say he's married someone else, an Indian of course.'

There was shock and compassion on Mrs Anderson's face now.

Connie spoke again, slowly, clearly. 'If it wasn't for my mother, I would never have seen the man behind the skin, can't you see that? It's her fault, and my father's. They're wrong; we are all different. Romesh knew that; he's chosen his own kind and all the time I really thought he would come to know he loved me enough.

'I'm so stupid. I thought I could prove to him that I was worthy of him if I stayed, if I came to really love the land, if I protected him from Revd Williams's exposure. Miss Anderson, I don't know what I'm doing any more. I want to leave, but I don't want to go home and see her.'

Miss Anderson's arms were round her now.

'I hate them for what they've done to me. I want to be like everyone else, I want to belong.' Her voice was ugly, the heaving sobs were strident, raucous.

Miss Anderson led her to a chair, poured water onto

a clean towel and damped her face. 'You must go home. It is time.'

Connie shook her head, feeling the rage building again, preferring it to the pain. 'No, not to her.'

Miss Anderson ran her fingers down Connie's cheek. Connie caught her hand, held it. The skin was so thin, the veins blue and swollen. What was she thinking of, to speak to this woman as she had done? 'How can I leave you when there is too much to do here?'

'There are others. You have stayed much longer than most. I see why now. The love a woman holds for a man is very enduring. I think also that there is love for India.'

Connie shook her head. 'All that's over.' Her head was aching, bursting. Why had she ever written to him? What did it matter to her that Congress had refused to share the spoils of office with the Muslims after the 1937 elections? What did she care if it led to a hardening of feeling between the races, and a bloodbath?

These weren't her people. Why had she written that letter, why had she said she would wait for ever, that her love had only strengthened? Why had she told him that after her years here she respected, admired, felt at one with his country, that she was his, for the rest of her life?

How long had he been married to this other woman? For how many years had he lain with her, touching her, loving her, laughing at Connie's efforts to be worthy of him? 'She is my wife. You must make your life, Connie. You must leave me behind.' It was as though those words were scratched, raw and bleeding, on her heart.

'It hurts,' she moaned. 'I'm all alone and in such pain.'

Miss Anderson held her, rocked her, soothed her. 'You don't have to be; go to the dance that your friend invited you to. Go and find your own people – it is time. The *dirzi* shall make you a dress, the cobbler will make you shoes.

We shall wash your hair, pin it, and please remember, Connie, that as well as food and education, we give our orphans and widows love.'

On Saturday night Connie sat in the tonga as the horse trotted through the bazaar, smelling the oily spicy scent and the burning charcoal, then on through the streets where Indians jostled, chattered. She looked at Dora's invitation and wanted to go back to the mission.

She smoothed her dress, touched her hair. What if no-one liked her, what if she was too sunburnt, too much of an outsider? She clenched her hands together. Where would her life go then? Oh God, Mam. But no, not her mother, not now, not ever.

They trotted over the bridge to the cantonment. It was a bridge she had only passed by before. Now they were on metalled roads with khatcha edges; there were trees either side, there were no Indians streaming, clamouring, blocking the roads. It seemed so light, although the day was fading.

There were lime-washed stones marking the culvert crossings over the monsoon ditches. There were orderly white-shirted Indian clerks on bikes pedalling towards the town. There were military trucks. She'd never really noticed them in the town; they hadn't been part of her life. Romesh had been her life. But no, not that, not here.

She turned her head to look at the long straight roads that led off this one. There were neat identical bungalows either side. They turned left. There was a large building; the tonga stopped. She paid the driver and walked up the path to the Nurses Home, next to the Government Hospital. She walked in.

It was quiet, clean. There was the smell of disinfectant in the lobby. The floor was polished. There was no dirt. The walls were painted with gloss paint. They were clean. Dora was waiting, standing there, and Connie saw again the small child who had come to their home.

She saw Binnie, her mother and father, Boy, and the pain scythed through her. Oh God, where had her life gone?

Dora hugged her. 'Darling, you look divine.'

Connie smelt the perfume, heard the voice. It was so different. She grinned. 'I hope this is what you meant when you said I would need to dress?'

Dora led her into the common-room. It was darker in here. The chintz covers on the wicker chairs sucked in the light, the dark panelled walls too. 'As I said, you look divine; David French will love you. Now meet Lucinda and Caroline – Lucinda's boyfriend will pick us up and take us to the club, but just before we mingle, darling, a word in your ear.'

Dora took her to one side. 'I have told everyone that my father was a headmaster. I have mentioned nothing of the mission, of the workhouse. I assume I can rely on your discretion?'

Connie said, 'Naturally. I also have no wish to discuss the past.'

The club was throbbing with light, with music, laughter and English voices. Connie held her rum and lime, and marvelled at the ice which clinked in her glass. She stood by the window overlooking the swimming-pool. Lights hung from the trees. It was like Christmas.

'Darling, do meet Captain David French.' Dora was at her elbow. Connie shook hands and smiled. 'How do you do.' They talked, she saw the lift of his eyebrows over grey eyes, his light brown hair with its side parting. He swept his hand through it, then gestured with his short stubby fingers which were so unlike Romesh's.

All around were people who used their hands as he did, their faces too. It was easy, so easy. It was like coming home.

Captain French stopped a bearer, took another rum and lime for her. She sipped it, feeling her muscles loosening. She looked back at the swimming-pool.

'Do you ride?' he asked.

'I have little chance. I am a teacher at the mission in the town.' She waited for his face to change. It did not.

He asked, 'Would you like to?'

Dora passed, smiling at Connie. Her hand was linked with a major's.

'That would be nice.' Connie looked back at David. His eyes were following Dora and they were filled with pain. Connie moved out to the veranda pushing away the sweeping misery that deluged her. Romesh.

She heard the music in the background and swayed to it, relishing its familiar chords after years of dissonant Indian music, using it to push Romesh away. She walked along the veranda, smiling at the people she passed – her people. She looked over the tennis courts. She had played at college.

'This is where you are?' David said. 'I thought I'd lost you for a moment.' His hand was trembling and she wanted to reach out and comfort him because she had recognized his pain as her pain.

'Perhaps I could take you riding?' he said. 'Or would you prefer not to, I don't want to monopolize you.' He drew anxiously on his cigarette.

Connie wanted to protect him. 'I'd love to but I have no horse.'

'Oh, but I have two, not good ones of course, but enough to play a few chukkas. We're coming up to the high season now; there'll be tournaments, and a polo week. It's better than the hot season, when the horses slow down.'

She knew all about heat. He stubbed out his cigarette in the ashtray on the wicker table. 'Perhaps you would like to come to a match?'

'That would be nice.'

The music was louder now. David said, 'Perhaps you would care to dance?'

He led her through to the larger room. He held her and there was nothing familiar about his broad body, the

244

strong hand that held hers, though there was everything familiar about the way he moved, the tenor of his voice, his Englishness.

They passed Dora and her major. Their cheeks were close together. 'Are you from an army family?' Connie asked.

David shook his head. 'No, not like Ben.' He nodded towards Dora. 'We were at Sandhurst together. He was always destined for the Rifles; they're a crack regiment, you know. I'm just the Service Corps.'

Dora paused and called over, 'You know, darling, the Flying Grocer's, the Rice Corps.' She floated on.

David flushed, stiffened. Connie said, 'What do you mean, just the Service Corps? I know you have to pass out very well from Sandhurst to be taken by any branch of the Indian Army. I think that is excellent. Your family must be very proud of you.'

'Not as proud as Ben's.' His voice was hesitant.

'But think of the pressure on your friend. Imagine if he had not really wanted to join up – perhaps he would have preferred to be something else, but never saw an alternative. How do you go against a family tradition?' She stopped talking abruptly.

David glanced down at her. 'I've never thought of that.' They danced on, and on, and slowly she relaxed again.

They talked of England, of the crispness of autumn, of India and the start of the cold season. They both raised their eyebrows together and laughed. 'The cold season?' he murmured mockingly. They had both been thinking the same, they had both shown it in the same way.

They stopped dancing. She drank another rum and lime. She laughed and talked to the people they met of their homes, their families. She joked as she had not done since she had arrived in India. She was home, she was amongst her own kind – do you see this Romesh, Mother, Father?

They danced out of the room onto the veranda. David's friends were there. She talked to Captain Tom Masters and to Lt Philip Penwith. She joked with David, who said quietly, 'May I take you to the cinema tomorrow night?'

She wanted to lean into his strong wide white body. 'Yes.'

'I'll pick you up.'

'No.' She did not want him to see the mud compound, or smell the part of town where she lived. 'I'll meet you there. I passed it on my way in, it's opposite the Chinese restaurant, isn't it?'

Lt Philip Penwith roared with laughter. 'Good lord no, that's the one for the wogs. It'll only be hours of Ramayana and you won't hear a blind thing over the chattering and you'll get fleas into the bargain and there's the smell of sweat and heaven knows what.' He was holding his nose and pulling a chain.

It was as though cold water had been poured all over her, wiping the pleasure of the evening from her. This boy's face was like Mrs Lewis's. So Romesh had been right about the British, but she didn't want to know this about her own people. She wanted to belong. She looked around. Romesh, I'm sorry, you were right. But then she heard David's voice. It was crisp and cold.

'That is quite enough, Lt Penwith.'

Connie swung back. He was angry. Captain Masters echoed David's words. 'Quite enough. Perhaps you should have some air, young man.'

Dora and Ben approached. 'Darling, you seem to be enjoying yourself. Come to the powder-room with me.' Connie's smile was broad as David said, 'Don't be long.'

She scarcely listened to Dora. She wanted to dance through these crowds because Romesh had been wrong after all. These people were not like those who cheered Dyer. They were her people and they showed anger at prejudice, and she belonged with them, and she wouldn't let the pain of him tell her otherwise.

David watched her go, seeing the swell of her breasts as she swung round to talk to Dora. She was nice, she was fun, she didn't seem ashamed to be seen with a Grocer's Boy, and after seeing Dora with Ben, he knew that he had lost her.

19

For the next month, Connie saw David nearly every evening, and sometimes in the afternoon too when she watched him play polo, seeing his golden brown arm swinging through the air, hearing the click of the ball, the cheers, seeing his thighs as they clung to the sides of the horse, his back as he wheeled this way and that.

They danced every Saturday and she listened as he talked patiently to the elderly woman, who had travelled from England to visit her daughter, at him repeating his sentence again and again. He was a kind man, a strong man and she liked the feel of his arm round her when, in November after the Guy Fawkes celebrations, he took her to his bungalow which he shared with three fellow officers.

He touched his glass to hers. 'Cheers.'

Her rum and lime was strong and she tasted his gin when he kissed her. He took her glass from her hand and pulled her closer. She stroked the back of his neck, the short hair. He kissed her eyes, her mouth. His tongue stroked her lips. Her passion surged along with his. His hands stroked her breasts; her nipples hardened. His breathing was quick, shallow, as was hers.

Her eyes were closed; he kissed them again and she felt his fingers at her buttons. He kissed her mouth, and leant away to see her naked breasts. She looked down and saw his stubby hands where Romesh's long fine ones had been, and passion fled.

She pulled away, frantically doing up her buttons.

'No, it's too soon. No, David.' He reached for her. She wrenched from his grasp. 'No.'

He stood up. 'I wasn't trying to touch you again, just to do up your buttons. I understand, don't be frightened. Please Connie. I'm sorry.' His face was uncertain, his hands were trembling. 'It was unforgivable. I'll take you home. I won't see you again.'

He stood with his back to her, facing the fire-place. 'I'm so sorry.'

'I don't want to go home. I'm just not ready for this.' Her voice was gentle because this man was so kind, so unsure. They talked long into the night and he told her that he had loved Dora, or thought he had.

'I was lonely and wanted to meet someone I could marry. I thought I had when I met Dora but of course she prefers Ben.'

Connie put her hand on his, lifting it to her mouth, kissing the short stubby fingers, making herself like them because they were the opposite of Romesh's, making herself hold his hand to her breast. He looked at her. 'I thought I loved her. I don't. I think I've met someone much more important.' He kissed her.

The next day they played tennis. On the other court were two Indian officers. David waved to them. You see, Romesh, you were wrong, she thought, as she served. The British are changing, mixing; some are enlightened, this man especially.

That evening she had to be at the mission for Guides. She missed him, the brightness of the cantonment, the cleanness of it.

Miss Anderson called her into her study. 'I have a letter from a young teacher who wishes to join me.'

Connie said, 'I think David might ask me to marry him.'

Miss Anderson nodded her head. 'I thought that might happen. Will you? Do you love him?'

'He's nice, he's kind, he's unsure and he's lonely. I'm lonely.'

'But do you love him?'

'He's English, I recognize him. Can you understand what I mean?'

Miss Anderson nodded again. 'But take care, Connie, think carefully. Why not write to your mother tonight and discuss it with her?'

Connie didn't write to Belle and neither did she read the letter that had arrived. And neither did she think because she had done enough of that to last her a lifetime.

In the morning she took a tonga into the cantonment. There was a hush, as there was in Rempton at mid-morning. The horse clip-clopped into the peace. They reached a T-junction and turned right. The arcaded shops were familiar now. There were women in the arcades. Their cars were parked near by. She leaned forwards hearing the clink of the horse's medallions, smelling the driver's stale sweat. She noticed it here, where it was so light and clean.

'This will do, thank you.'

She dismounted, paid, walked into the arcade, looking in Singh's shop front. There were English goods. She entered. There were English women who smiled at her, asked her how she was, and talked of the Saturday dance, and the polo week that was looming.

'You will be coming?' Sally Masters asked.

'I hope so.'

Connie bought Pears soap for herself, then another bar for Miss Anderson. She bought perfume. Could David smell the mission on her as she had smelt the tonga wallah?

She met Dora for coffee at the coffee house. She was wearing slacks and made Connie feel dowdy. 'Darling, you simply must see this.' Dora held out her left hand. 'Ben has popped the question; I've got him. I thought I'd be left with—' She stopped, then laughed. '—a Grocer's Boy. How are you two getting on, by the way?' She spooned in sugar, stirring it, lifting the cup, her little finger crooked.

Connie looked down at the Pears soap and perfume. Poor David. She pushed her coffee to one side, wanting to spill it on those pristine slacks. How dare Dora?

'I must go. Felicitations, Dora. Binnie would have been proud at how the workhouse child has come on.' She watched the colour drain from Dora's face and stood up. 'I'm getting on very well with my Grocer's Boy, thank you. He's a good and kind man.'

She left, and that night she sat with David in the Red Dragon eating chopsuey while he drank too much beer and talked of the engagement of his friend Ben. She walked with him back to the chummery and steadied him as they entered the house. She asked the bearer for coffee. 'Black please, lots of it,' she called.

She eased him onto the sofa. 'It's not because of Ben's engagement,' he said. 'It's because I'm tired.'

She took the coffee from the bearer and made David drink, holding his hand, kissing his fingers. 'I'm so sorry,' he mumbled.

'I understand,' she said gently. Of course she did. She had also been rejected.

Tom Masters drove her back to the mission. 'He's a good man,' he said as the engine idled.

'I know that,' said Connie.

'But he's unsure. It makes him drink; bear it in mind.'

David bought her riding breeches for Christmas. 'I asked the *dirzi* to make up two pairs after Mrs Masters guessed your size. I hope she was right?'

Connie held them against her, smiling her pleasure. 'They're perfect.'

He grinned. 'Perhaps now you will ride with me?'

That night, after singing carols in the mission, she thought of the nativity play that Belle always set up, she thought of Mary, Helen, Joseph and Boy and realized that her anger had gone, that all feeling was subdued, calm, manageable, that somehow she had distanced herself from Romesh, from the past, from the pain, that she only looked ahead, not to either side. It was better that way.

She wrote to Belle, saying that she had been busy, that she hoped the sandalwood box had arrived safely, that she had been very tired, but was feeling better. She began to read the letters which arrived from England, but she never answered the questions Belle asked about her happiness.

In January David kissed her on the sofa at his chummery and this time she undid her buttons for him, guiding his hands. He looked down at her, uncertainty in his eyes. 'Are you sure?'

She smiled, closed her eyes in case he could see the lie. 'Yes, I'm sure.'

She felt hands which weren't Romesh's on her flesh, a mouth which wasn't his on hers. Romesh was gone; she would love David, this lonely Grocer's Boy, because he needed her, and she needed him. And she was glad they were his hands on her body. Yes, she was.

She stroked David's head, kissed his brown hair, and then his lips, again and again. 'You are a good and kind man,' she murmured against his mouth.

'Come riding with me tomorrow, Connie. I want everyone to see us together. They know no woman has ever ridden my horses.'

They rode out over the cool countryside and she loved the feel of the horse beneath her, the smell of it, the huffing and the coughs. She looked at him, and he at her. He held the leading rein. 'Let's try a trot?'

He kicked his own horse gently. As she rose and fell she remembered the horse she had ridden at college. They cantered and David shouted, 'One day we'll jump the nullahs together.'

The next day she could barely walk and stayed at the mission in the evening, sending a chit to him. He sent one back. *I miss you. If we were married you could soak in a bath here, and I could bring you aspirin, and love.*

'Write to your mother, talk to her,' Miss Anderson

begged. 'You cannot be sure that love will come, and marriage without it is interminable.'

Connie shook her head. 'Love is coming. I can feel it.' She went to her room because she didn't want to think. She just wanted to belong with this kind man, and with her own people.

Connie married David at the end of March. Captain and Mrs Masters displayed the presents on their veranda, and hosted the reception. There was cutlery, glass, tea- and coffee-sets. There was a table lamp from Dora and Ben.

'Of course, we will be married at the hill station; so much smarter,' Dora said. 'And what did your mother send?'

Connie said, 'Money, bless her. It's what we need more than anything.'

'Such a small wedding; such a shame she didn't come. Still, it saved your mother that little bit more and must have made the present a bit bigger?'

Dora's eyes were calculating, questioning. Connie saw David looking towards them and there was love in his eyes. She smiled, knowing her love was growing too.

She leaned forward saying quietly, 'I'm so sorry I said that in the coffee house – but for you I wouldn't have met David and I will never repeat anything of the past, I swear. I owe my happiness to you. I can't wait until we reach our houseboat in Kashmir. Will you be able to come to the buffet party I'm arranging on our return? I gather we're going straight to the hills.'

The colonel and his wife beckoned to Connie.

'You'll come, won't you, Dora, to the party, even if Ben has to return to his station?'

'If I'm not on duty, of course, darling. How could I bear to miss it?'

Connie kissed her, then called to Colonel Potter. 'Just on my way.'

Dora watched her go. Stupid bitch, doesn't she know she's supposed to have been insulted, doesn't she know I've by far the better catch? Oh yes, madam, my mother would have been proud of me, because I have come out on top, and if you don't know it yet, you soon will.

Connie and David took the mail train to Lahore, and arrived just before dawn. Connie didn't want to stop and see the place again and be reminded of Romesh.

'Let's go straight on to Kashmir, David,' she urged. 'I can't wait for you to show it all to me – and to be alone with you.'

They picked up the car. David drove and she looked neither to the left nor right until they were clear of the place and then she relaxed as dawn broke over a land which was stained green with young growth.

At Sialkot they pulled in at a dhak bungalow and David cooked bacon and eggs on the veranda, using the Primus stove he had brought.

'Breakfast, Mrs French.' He passed the tin plate to her, leaning over and kissing her cheek.

She was glad she was Mrs French – someone new, someone different. She would write to Belle from Kashmir and only then would she tell her of her marriage, for she had lied to Dora, to David, to everyone, because she had not wanted her mother there, she hadn't wanted even a letter from her.

She had wanted the ceremony to be performed, the die to be cast before she read a letter from her mother that voiced doubts. She had wanted this man who was kind and who would never hurt her as Romesh had because there was not that foolish sort of love between them; there was a deeper caring, a gentler liking, and it could be called love.

The day grew hotter and they were relieved when they reached Jammu – it meant they were in Kashmir. They passed the barracks which housed some of the Maharajah's Army and now they began to climb and wind along the road, and soon they were enclosed by hills. The air became crisp and fresh and it was as though she was drinking champagne.

'It's so wonderful,' she said.

'But surely you've been to the hills before?' He stopped the car and turned to look at her.

'No, I've been busy working.'

'Well, here's a little more for you to do; we need water.' He opened the door and fetched two cans of water from the boot, filling the radiators, then pointing to the stream gushing down the hill. 'First one there doesn't have to cook the meal at the dhak. Hey, wait for me.'

'Certainly not.' She ran down, hearing him coming after her, feeling the jolting in her body, the laughter bursting from her and suddenly she was back at the beck, running down the hill, rolling over and over with Boy, with Belle. 'I'm happy, Mam, truly I am,' she whispered as she dug the lip of the tin into the icy stream.

They slept at a dhak on their bedrolls alongside other travellers. David squeezed her hand in the dark and whispered, 'Soon we'll be alone.'

They drove between mile upon mile of paddy-fields threaded with willows and poplars. They passed a laden tonga, another car and then at last they parked near the shakira which waited on the river to take them to their houseboat.

They clambered in, and she sank back on the pillows, looking across at the snow-covered hills, her coat drawn against the chill. How glorious to feel the cold, to be sitting in the peace of a world where she could hear the drip of the icy water as it ran off her hand.

'We'll come again in June, one day, and pick the daisies, the pansies and verbena,' David said as they drew near the houseboat.

'I would like to stay here for the rest of my life.'

The houseboat was ornate, heavily carved. It creaked.

'The ceilings are made up of small blocks fitted together to form the designs. The floor has loose blocks so they can be lifted to store things underneath,' David said as they drank gin on the veranda. 'So tonight the creaks and groans won't be just us, it'll be the boat too.'

They looked at one another and burst out laughing.

The houseboy served chicken then fruit but she wasn't hungry as she watched David's hands on his apple, so big, so stubby, and she wanted to recapture the earlier laughter but he was quiet, his eyes didn't meet hers. He drank another gin, and then another.

'I must go to bed,' she said, rising, not looking at him.

She lay in the large bed, listening to the creaks, lying beneath the quilt, wondering when David would come, feeling the nervousness, the longing, the reluctance.

He came to her, at last, his breath heavy with gin, his hands clumsy, fumbling at her nightdress, his mouth searching for hers. He clutched her to him, his eyes tightly shut, pushing her nightdress up, rubbing his hands too harshly, too quickly over her skin, pushing her legs apart, climbing on her, thrusting, so quickly, panting his gin in her face, and all the time there was the creaking and groaning of the houseboat. It was finished, over. He rolled off her, onto his side, and slept.

She looked out at the crisp moon and wouldn't think of what had just happened. She would think of nothing; she would count each breath she drew in, each breath she pushed out, but first she rose, walked silently to the bathroom and sluiced him from her, rubbing her skin with the towel again and again, not looking at his still form snoring and slobbering.

She rose early and sat in her quilt on the veranda drinking tea, then she wrote to her mother of her happiness. '*The wedding was all such a rush because we more or less decided at the last moment. You'd like David, Mother. I shall send you a photograph. Dora was there, so at least the family was represented.*'

She wrote to thank those who had given presents. She wrote to Boy, seeing his fine-boned face, his long fingers, and now she couldn't go on because of the tears that

256

were streaming down her cheeks. And always there was the creaking and groaning of the houseboat.

David rose at noon, kissing her neck, ordering the shakira.

'I'm taking you on a surprise journey,' he said.

He took her to the native city. They passed under bridges.

'They take the Srinagar traffic,' David said.

They floated past modern houses jammed against filthy tumble-down hovels. 'Have a cigarette. It takes away the smell,' David said.

Did he think she wasn't used to smells? She shook her head. They disembarked. He showed her the silversmith called 'Suffering Moses'. She bought an embroidered tablecloth for Dora's wedding present.

He showed her the temples covered with flattened kerosene oil tins which glittered like silver and then pointed out the Maharajah's which was covered in gold leaf. She stood and thought of Romesh, and the love that had been in every movement of his hands on her body.

'I must go back,' she said. 'I must go back.' She walked blindly from him, her mind echoing the words and she knew it was to another time she wished to return.

He caught up with her, taking her arm. 'It's the long journey, you're tired. I should have thought. I'm sorry.'

They were silent in the shakira as they passed again beneath the bridges, and then she said, 'You must have been here before; you know so much.'

'Yes,' David said, then hesitated, looked down at those hands. 'Well, no.' He brought out a list. 'Ben wrote this for me, so I would sound less of an idiot.'

She took it from him, reading about the creaking and groaning, about 'Suffering Moses', about the bridges under which they had passed. David's hands were trembling again as he lit a cigarette and now she reached across.

He said, 'I'm sorry, I'm doing everything wrong. I wanted it all to be perfect for you.'

She said, 'So, we're discovering it together, and one another too. I prefer it that way, it makes *me* feel less ignorant.'

When they reached the houseboat she drew him into the bedroom and kissed him gently, searchingly. She held his hand against her cheek and looked into his eyes. 'You are a good man, David, and I'm so glad I married you. You are worth more than a dozen Bens put together.'

He carried her to the bed, stripped her of her clothes and then himself, drawing the quilt over them both. And now they made love, touching, kissing, coming together, moving away, and it was still clumsy and too quick, but not so rough, and this was David, her husband and he was a good man.

The next day they stayed on the houseboat, and the next, and each night he grew more and more gentle and each day more tender, and the cool breeze lulled them and the silence soothed them until there was only the two of them in the world.

20

'I can't bear it,' Belle wept.

Helen took the letter from her, read it. 'It is nothing to do with you. She is married. She says she is happy and you have to believe her, my dear. You have to let go.'

'But Dora said in her letter that it had been arranged for two months. Helen, Connie didn't want me to know. This man must be wrong for her; she is not in love with him. She is hurt and in pain. I know, because she called me "Mother".'

Helen put her finger to her lips. 'Dry your eyes, Boy is coming in from the garden. We have to tell him.'

They told Boy gently, showing him the letter. He pushed it away but said nothing, just stood, his eyes not on them, not on the letter, but they both saw the yawning agony. He left that afternoon, and enlisted in the RAF as a fighter pilot.

'Why?' Belle asked when he rang.

'Because there will be a war. Hitler has gone into Austria.' His voice was clipped, level.

'But why you? You could be a war correspondent, anything. Why the air force? You could be killed; you have so much to live for.'

'Have I?'

When Connie and David arrived at the hill station, she laughed. 'It's just the same as the plains cantonment, only higher, cooler. The bungalows are the same, the parade ground. There's just no *maidan*, no heat.'

She kissed David as he left for the barracks. 'Drop your cards round,' he called. 'And draw up the list for

259

the buffet party.' His boots rang on the tiled floor; the bearer salaamed. David was gone, she was alone.

She looked out at the Himalayas. Yes, the Hindus were right; the gods must live up there, and they must have woven their magic over the Kashmir lakes these last two weeks. She walked through the bungalow, touching the chairs, tables, the wedding presents which were all laid out. This was her home; she would one day have a child and she would belong here, with this man who was all that Romesh said the British weren't.

She dropped in her cards to the colonel's wife, and all the others. She looked at the huts and terraced fields which rose on the hill slopes, she smelt wood and dung fires. She walked through the bazaar, looking in at the open shop fronts, shaking her head at the offers of pan, soda water, chillis.

'Let Ahmed do the shopping,' David warned her. 'That is the way of it.'

The cuckoos were calling. She walked along the trail she found, finding wild balsam and lily of the valley. She breathed in the pine-scented breezes.

When she returned to the bungalow there was an invitation to coffee with the colonel's wife the next day. She showed it to David when he returned; he poured a large gin and sank into a chair.

He smiled, 'It helps me if they like you.'

She showed him the list for the buffet party. He stared at it, then looked at her, his smile gone. He shouted, 'You haven't sent out the invitations have you, for God's sake?'

'They're waiting to go. I thought I might have missed someone – so who shall I add?'

'You don't add any, you damn fool. What are you trying to do, ruin me?'

She sat quite still, looking at this man who had held her, kissed her, laughed with her, sat with his shirt undone on the veranda of the houseboat. His boots were spotless, his belt too. He leaned forward, his mouth ugly, gin on his breath.

He waved the list at her. 'For God's sake, I argued when they said that you were probably unsound after living with the natives. Were they right? Tell me that?'

She said quietly, 'I have no idea what you are talking about, David. What have I done?'

'You've asked the bloody wogs, that's what you've done.'

The colour drained from her face as she watched his finger stabbing at the list.

'You said invite the officers. That is what I've done.'

'Not the Indians, for God's sake.'

'But why not? They are your companions, you play tennis with them, they drink at the club.' She was still sitting motionless.

'Do you see their wives there? Of course not. We don't mix, we just have to have them. They know the rules; a quick drink, then home.'

'But David, you defended them, at that first party. You sent that young lieutenant out for being rude about Indians. Why are you being like this?'

David stared at her in amazement. 'He was talking about sweat and stink and fleas. That's why I sent him out.'

She gave the party. The salvers and tureens gleamed. 'The colonel's wife lent them to me,' she replied to David's look of enquiry. He preened himself and she looked away.

The bearers served cold consommé, pâté, chicken, turkey, ham, salmon, mayonnaise. Spun-sugar swans held fruits.

Dora and Ben came, Dora smelling of Chanel as she kissed Connie. 'My word, you look well, and so does dear David.' She kissed him, long and lingeringly. He flushed, then shook hands with Ben. 'When will war be declared?' he asked his friend, leading him to the bar.

'So, how is marriage treating David? I found him rather fumbling,' Dora said, her smile tight.

'Not fumbling in the least; perhaps it depends who

261

he is with.' Connie swept away, smiling stiffly at Sally Masters, talking to her of riding in the early morning, knowing that she would never belong and wanting to be somewhere else, but where? And did Dora mean she had slept with David? Oh God.

Mrs Mathers, the Lt Colonel's wife slipped her hand beneath Connie's arm. 'This is splendid, simply splendid. We did wonder whether you would be quite sound, with your background. It's so important, you know, that we all know our place, and that we recognize the place of others. It's the only way the Empire can work, but you obviously understand that now. I am delighted that David has made such a sensible match. By the way, did you know that dear John is taking over from Col Potter? The colonel's off to London, to what I fear will become the War Office.'

'Congratulations, and yes, I think I understand everything.' She feared she did.

Connie weaved in and out of her guests, smiling, talking because David was her husband, and before the party he had stood before her, his hands trembling, his voice cracking. 'I need a proper wife, Connie. I've had to struggle so hard to get here, and now I have to work even harder to keep up. Please, you must forget you worked amongst the natives. You are one of us now. Learn the rules; help me, please.'

She smiled at him now as he walked towards her, easing himself between Ben and Tom Masters. Tom slapped him on the back. 'Good party; well done, David.'

She met him, clinked her glass to his. 'Am I being sound?' she whispered before turning away. Mrs Potter, the retiring colonel's wife, put out her hand as she passed. 'Connie, my dear. I simply must talk to you because I know that you have worked in town.'

Connie saw the set of David's face.

Mrs Potter continued. 'I know that you have a Guide pack at the mission and expect you'll be keeping it on. I'm leaving as you know but I would like you to take over my pack too, if you have time.'

David's face relaxed.

'The thing is, I have been trying to build a bridge between us and them, as it were. It's an uphill struggle and all too late, but somehow I go on trying. There are so many unwritten rules, though, and we always have to think of our husbands' and their position.' She was talking quietly, but David was listening, his face puzzled, confused. 'So I struggle along with the children, and don't try to alter the club situation; it's simply not loyal.'

Connie looked at David, rage flaring. 'You have obviously heard that I was going to ask Lt Singh and Lt Monga?'

Mrs Potter laughed. 'No, rest assured, but I'm not a bit surprised and there are others like you. Sally Masters for one. She got her fingers burnt, so she will help you with the Bluebirds, which is what we have to call the Indian Brownies. We have been trying to improve the poor opinion these girls have of themselves.

'We have a Muslim pack and a Hindu pack. We have a Eurasian helper, but no whites, so perhaps you can see what you can do about that. The real *coup* would be to draw in the Mathers girl. She's a dreadful little snob and could do to have her eyes opened.'

Tom Masters was calling David, who left, shaking his head.

Connie said, 'I'll do it, if you talk to David about it, and the others. He's nervous.'

Mrs Potter smiled gently. 'I'll chat to him. We can do so very little, and what we do, we do for our own sakes, our own consciences. The Indians don't need us for anything, they just want to see that view of our backsides as we all get onto that ship. They'll kick us out soon and quite right too. Should have happened long ago. Of course, I don't know how they'll manage it, but they'll finally do it and God help them then, because a bloodbath will follow. But we'll have our own before then, or poor old England will.'

*   *   *

When the last guest had gone, Connie stood amongst the debris, smelling the cigarette smoke, the Chanel. David finished the last of his gin, throwing his head back, draining the glass.

'I'm sorry I shouted at you earlier. I didn't know that Mrs Potter felt the same as you, or that Sally Masters did too.'

'That makes it all right then, does it, if the colonel's lady approves?'

She went to bed and lay beneath his fumbling hands, his gin-soured breath and wanted to shut her eyes, her mind, and drift in a void and never return.

She saddled his horse in the early morning and rode along the paths, ducking beneath branches, smelling wood-smoke, seeing it rising into the sky, looking back down on the cantonment, seeing the terraces all around, the shacks, looking up and seeing the Himalayas, so huge, so immovable.

She stroked the horse, kicking it into a trot. She was here, married to David; the past was gone, the future had not arrived; she would live each moment, she would be loyal, but she would bring up the child she was sure she was having to throw off the shackles of the British in India.

'At least I can do that for you and India, and my parents, Romesh,' she shouted. But could she love her husband? She would try. Would she ask about Dora? No, what did it matter whether he had slept with Dora? It was in the past. Oh Romesh.

When war was declared David was recalled to the plains. 'Please God, let them use me in Europe,' he said, kissing her goodbye. They didn't. They sent others instead.

At the same time, the Indian provisional ministries resigned because they were not consulted before the viceroy declared war on India's behalf. And Romesh wrote to her at the hill station. She smoothed his letter and read it again and again.

*I was so glad to hear of your marriage. Yes, I
do hear of you, all the time. Does that worry you?
If it does, I shall stop. I know of the child you
are expecting. It brings me joy.*

*I know you will be distressed to hear that
we are insisting on a statement guaranteeing
independence now, for our co-operation in this
war. We feel that only a free country fights with
a will. We fear a repetition of all that has gone
before.*

*I wanted to tell you this, for I can guess at
your feelings – your concern for your country,
your exasperation at us. Forgive me, but I
must carry on the fight. There will be a civil
disobedience movement. I shall join it. I shall be
imprisoned but we shall not give up.*

He was right; she was exasperated. It was her country
which was in danger, her mother, Helen, Boy. Oh, Boy.
He was too young to fly planes, he was too young to
die. God damn the Indians. God damn the fact that she
understood their need.

She returned to the plains with the station and joined
the war-work committee. Plans were made to raise funds
for the war effort. Sweets were made and sent home.
Letters were written full of guilt at the lives they were
leading because the parties didn't stop; the dancing went
on until dawn.

Connie took a tonga to the mission, to open the first
Guides meeting but no-one came. There was only a chit
saying, '*We no longer come. You are the enemy.*'

She returned in the tonga, and now she noticed the
closed shop fronts, by order of the police. She saw the
looks, the scowls, the backs that were turned to her,
and she held her arms over her belly, hating herself for
the action, hating India and the world for what it had
become, and the confusion that was both outside and
within herself.

That night they heard that Dora and Ben had been married quickly, because Ben was being posted to Europe. David sat up drinking, and then came to bed, pawing her, trying to climb on her. 'The baby,' she gasped pushing him away from her. 'You're drunk.'

He grabbed her again, his mouth all over her face, her swollen breasts, pushing her on her side, forcing himself into her, thrusting. She fought him off. 'No, not like this, David.'

He pressed her down, and finished, withdrawing, turning away from her, lying still, heaving with tears. 'I'm sorry, but it's never me, is it?'

'Marrying Dora, do you mean, or going to the war?' Her voice was bitter.

'Going to the war, of course.'

Her daughter was born in December, while David was at Lahore. He sent a note. '*I will be there when I can be spared from this essential task.*' She knew he was drunk from his scrawl.

Dora wrote from Delhi. '*Can't come, but what good news, though I'm sure David would have preferred a son – son and heir, you know. Never mind. Better luck next time. I'm so busy here, so many troops to take care of. One must do these things, being a major's wife.*'

Romesh wrote. How did he know? She found it comforting that he did. She read.

> *Dearest Connie,*
> *Your beloved daughter will be the image of you. She will be good and kind and wise; you will give her the capacity to love, and to see with your clarity of vision. She will treasure every moment of every day with you, as I treasure every moment of every day that we have loved. I hope you still feel the love I send to you with every breath I take. This life you lead is right for you, for her.*
> *Romesh.*

She reread it every night whilst she was in the hospital, putting it, with the others he had sent, in the box which Boy had given her but not understanding, because Romesh's love was dead, wasn't it?

In March 1940 she went again to the hills with the station, taking the ayah. Each day she pushed Emily in the pram and she didn't know such love could exist and it was now that she truly understood how good Belle had been to let her come to India, for how could she ever allow this child to leave her? She cursed the war because she wanted her mother here, to see the first smile of her grandchild.

Sometimes David was with them, sometimes he was in Lahore, or Kashmir, or Madras – a million places. She took Emily to coffee mornings where the baby kicked her legs in the pram alongside the other children. As a member of the war committee she made more sweets. They packed up clothes for Britain, then they changed and dressed for an evening of dancing in the club.

In June they were quiet when Dunkirk was evacuated and that night Connie couldn't sleep as she thought of Boy in his plane, in the sky. Not Boy, not her Boy, she prayed.

In August she didn't listen as David ranted in the club because he had not obtained the most recent posting to Britain. She sipped her rum and lime and thought of the *Luftwaffe* hitting Britain's airfields, but not Boy. Please not Boy.

In September they were down on the plains again and now the German bombers were over British cities and Belle and Helen had taken in four evacuees and most of the pregnant mothers from the mission. Young Joseph had joined the air force. To be like Boy, Mary wrote.

David was at the Motor Transport School in Lahore when the telegram came from Belle informing her of Joseph's death, and Connie was glad because she could weep in peace. She told him on his return a month later.

'I'm missing it,' he said, splashing tonic into his glass.

'It will be here; it might get you yet.' She knocked the glass from his hand, watching the splinters skid across the floor.

Ben returned towards the end of 1941 and was posted to Burma. Dora stayed in Delhi.

'Of course she would,' Connie said, rustling her newspaper.

'That was uncalled for.' David leaned forward, shaking out a cigarette, lighting it. Emily sat on the floor. She raised her hands to her father. He touched her head and Connie warmed to him.

'She's growing so fast. I can't believe she's nearly two. I thank God we're here, and she's safe; thank you for that, David.' Her voice was gentle and she realized how little they spoke to one another any more. He looked up, then back at Emily.

'What's happening to us, Connie? It's all going wrong. I can't think straight. Do you remember the houseboat? It was easy then, simple. I thought everything would go so well.'

Connie knelt by his chair, and held him in her arms. 'It could go well, David. We are all safe, healthy. It could go well.'

They made love that night, as they had not done since the houseboat. They made plans to go again, and laughed gently at the thought of the creaking and groaning. He talked of Emily and how she must go back to England to school when the war was over.

Connie said nothing, because she knew that the British would all leave, once the war was over. Couldn't he see that?

In December Hong Kong fell to the Japanese. In January Singapore fell, and the Japanese fought their way up through Burma, and now Connie wanted to clutch her child to her because there was panic in the bungalows and jeering now that the British had been shown to be unable to defend what it was their duty to defend. Would India rise up against the British? Would the cantonments be stormed?

21

Belle showed Marion how to pull on the cow's teats again. 'There, you see, squeeze and pull.' The milk hissed into the pail; the child giggled. 'You have a go.'

Marion took her place on the stool. 'Won't she mind me cold hands on her?'

Belle laughed. 'She's used to it, don't you worry about that.'

She looked along the line of cows and exchanged a glance with Helen. 'Four eager milkers,' she mouthed. 'Won't the squire be pleased?'

When the milking was finished they and the evacuees tramped back through the fields, over the beck and into the kitchen of the vicarage. All the rooms had been opened up again and they would open the wing tomorrow, in readiness for Boy who had been shot down last week.

Mary was stirring the porridge, her face pale and drawn. The girls from the home were laying the table or feeding their babies. Belle put her arm round Mary. 'Did you sleep, bonny lass?'

'A bit, Belle.'

'Time heals, my dear – a little. When someone dies, you never really lose them,' Helen said, her eyes straying to the photograph of her son Philip. It seemed so faded and dated. What would he look like now?

'Thank God that Boy, at least, will never go up again,' Mary said. 'His war is over and though I'm glad that one of them is coming back I just can't stop thinking of Joseph, of the battles he fought and won – that we all fought and won for him. It's so damn stupid for it all to end in a burnt-out plane.' She ran from the room.

Helen shook her head at Belle. 'Let her be.'

Belle picked up the spoon and stirred. 'Connie's war isn't over,' she said. 'Hers is only just beginning and I want to be there, to hold her child, and my grandchild, and bring them home.'

There was no sound in the kitchen except for the scrape of the spoon against the pan.

'We'll win, now that the Americans are in; at least that is something,' Helen said at last.

'But how long will it take, and what will it cost?' Belle asked, hearing peals of laughter from the dining-room. 'Life goes on for the bairns,' she said, ladling the porridge into bowls, calling to the children to carry them through, giving Marion the jug of milk. 'Don't spill it, mind.'

'The doctor is coming at midday. Little Sarah's baby is ten days overdue, so he's getting anxious.' Helen dragged the pan beneath the running tap. 'It's a Polish serviceman's child, and soon we'll be getting Americans over here.' She raised her eyebrows. 'Some things never change, do they, Belle? It makes me feel rather tired, somehow.'

Belle laughed quietly. 'No time for tiredness until the war is over, then we can sleep for a million years.' But only if her daughter was back safely, she thought to herself.

David paced the floor; his boots squeaked. Would he never stop, Connie thought, watching his gin slopping as he shouted and raged as he had been doing all evening.

'With the Japs at the bloody gates these Congress wallahs have the bloody nerve to send Cripps and his offer home, and still wail on about independence now, not later. They've been guaranteed they'll get it once the war is won, and they've turned it down. What more do they want – bloody bells on it?'

Connie ran her fingers along the arms of her chair, up and down, up and down, in time with his pacing until she was able to bear it no longer. 'They want it now because they don't trust us – not after the last war.'

David peered over his glass. 'How the hell do you know that?'

She hesitated. 'I just do. Anyone can understand who wants to.'

'So you want to then?' His lips fumbled over the words. In a moment his hand would bunch into a fist. 'Each time I talk about them, you defend them. You love them, don't you? You should be out there living with them, like you used to. Go on, why don't you get out there in amongst their stinks and their temples?'

Connie asked, 'Is Ben safe? Has he got back over the border?' She had been stupid; she must only agree with him, his blows had taught her that, but rows were all he ever wanted these days.

'And that's a bloody disgrace, whites running from the Nips. That's what's started all this.' He nodded his head towards the town. 'They think the myth is broken, that we're not invincible any more. Well, we'll show them, just you wait; we'll show your bloody friends that we've a long way to go yet. We'll beat back the Nips, and them too, then they can see where their riots, their disobedience has damn well led them.'

Connie gripped the arms of her chair. He was coming nearer. 'Is your friend Alan a bloody disgrace? You know, the one who we've just heard is dead? For God's sake, David, I thought we were going to try hard to make this marriage work but no, even though there's a war going on, we scream and yell at one another, night after night.'

He glared at her, then walked towards her, kicking a stool away. 'It's your fault I'm stuck here, when there's a bloody war on, when others have gone.' He was leaning over her, stabbing his finger at her. 'It's because they think you're unsound.'

'No, it's nothing to do with me. It's because you're lucky, that's why. You're in the Service Corps, you're

doing what you are trained to do. Believe in yourself.'
Her voice was calm, her body still. It had to be or he
would strike.

He shambled towards the gin bottle. He poured, then
drank it down quickly, neat. 'Ben was always the lucky
bugger,' he mumbled.

'Is it lucky to be fighting your way through the jungle,
scared, hurt, defeated?'

'At least he's been blooded, at least he's tried.'

'But you are trying too, David. The front-line fighters
couldn't function without you.'

'I'm sick of the sound of your voice. I'm sick of it all,
the heat, the dust. I'm sick to the back teeth of instructing
a load of damn squaddies, black and white.'

'There you are – you complain about the Indians, but
they're volunteering in droves; it's only the activists who
are making a noise.' She stopped at the sight of his face.
Why had she brought up the Indians again; would she
never learn?

He turned, picked up the decanter and threw it. She
flinched as it crashed to the floor, exploding near her
feet.

'Shut up. I told you, I'm sick of the sound of your
voice.'

She sat quite still looking at the crystal nuggets which
lay all over the tiles, looking at the stool which lay on
its side, looking at the wreckage of their marriage.

'You must drink less, David. It's this that does all the
damage.'

He was rocking on his heels. 'No, it's this country. If
I wasn't here, I'd be in the war. Maybe I'd be fighting in
North Africa, making something of myself; I'd be doing
my duty, proving myself. But I'm not; I'm sitting here,
while Alan gets killed. He was a good man and my friend.'
He was maudlin, holding his glass to his cheek.

She heard a jeep pull up outside, and then the sound
of a horn. She ignored it. Then there were footsteps along
the path, a banging at the door. Ahmed padded in his

bare feet across the hall, not looking at them. Connie straightened the room. No-one must know. 'Sit down,' she urged David. 'Just sit down and be quiet.'

She followed Ahmed to the door. She would say David was ill, that he was lying quietly. A migraine again. God, how many migraines could a person have in a week?

It was Dr Pearce. He stood there, his hand on the door-frame. 'Connie, I've got to get a team up by tomorrow. I'm needed in Assam. I need to—'

Her heart leapt; she put up her hand, interrupting him. 'I'm so glad you came. David will come, just give him a moment, he has a headache.'

David came into the hall behind her, his footsteps were crisp, his voice too. He had straightened his tie, smoothed his hair. 'No, I'm quite all right, Jack. What's this then? Come in and talk about it.' He waved towards the sitting-room.

Dr Pearce shook his head. 'No, not you, David, you're needed here. It's Connie and her languages I need. It's chaos up there with the troops and refugees coming over the border; no-one can understand a bloody word. There are too many to cope with. Sally Masters is coming too.'

Connie felt the panic rise at the rage and disappoint-ment in David's eyes. She said quickly, 'No, I can't, there's Emily.'

Dr Pearce shook his head. 'No problem; my wife will have her to stay, your ayah can come to the house. Sally's kid will be there too. Come on, I need confirmation now.' His face was drawn and tired. 'I'm taking a team of nurses too.'

David said, 'Of course you must go; what is there to keep you here?' His voice was still crisp, his smile bright, but his eyes were hard.

In bed that night he said, 'It might do me some good if you are seen there. It might remind someone that I exist.' He turned from her then, as he did every night.

* * *

In Assam Connie worked alongside British planters and their wives in emergency hospitals and welfare centres. She distributed food, clothes, blankets. She guided refugees to the narrow-gauge trains that then came back loaded with men and ammunition.

She wrote to David, *You see, transport is vital. I know that you exist, I know that what you do is important, and these men know it too.*

She and Sally doled out curry and rice to the Indians, the Burmese, cringing when the Japanese planes flew over and the air-raid sirens rang in their ears. Mosquitoes bred in the slit trenches, electricity and water supplies were cut off, then came on again, whirring the electric punkahs into life, making the dust lift from the dried mud floors.

They were transferred to the casualty clearing stations which reeked of rotting humanity, of despair, of pain. Mrs McMasters, another helper, said as they finished for the day, 'I remember when wild turkeys used to do their courting dances here, in the spring.'

They watched the light planes flying off on reconnaissance and raids over enemy territory. They grabbed bully beef, bacon, beans and cheese fritters at the officers' mess, before returning, talking in Hindustani, Urdu, Punjabi, to men white with dust. To women with red eyes and thin bodies, to children who were too tired to cry. They handed out cigarettes, toothpaste or sweets and saw the canna lilies splashing the world with colour.

They talked to pallid exhausted soldiers. Three died in one day of cerebral malaria. Supplies of quinine were short. Cholera sufferers were isolated in separate tents on intravenous drips. 'Not many recover,' grunted Dr Pearce as they ate together in the mess one night.

A letter came from Romesh and she read it as the butterflies hovered over the lilies, the bushes, and she remembered in amazement that there was a world outside this chaos. She read his words impatiently.

What did she care that he thought Gandhi was wrong to be so obdurate in his immediate call for independence?

What did she care that it would lead to a stand by the Congress leaders against the British?

What did she care that their actions would open the way for the Muslim League to become close to the British in their support for the war effort? What did she care that this would lead to a divided country, because the Muslims would be repaid with their own Islamic state?

There will be such bloodshed, my Connie. I can see my nightmare coming true.

She looked across the clearing station. 'What do you think this is, Romesh, if it isn't already a nightmare?' She tore up his letter and watched the pieces drift to the ground, as the butterflies had drifted onto the bodies of the men who had died on the Burma Road.

She worked all that night, all the next day, interpreting, comforting. Belle's letter reached her the following morning. Boy was hurt, her own Boy; his leg was burnt, his arm broken, his cheek-bone smashed. Her hands shook and she couldn't read the words any more. She wanted to be home, in Rempton, holding him as she had done when they were children, not to be here in Romesh's India.

'Boy, darling Boy,' she whispered, and now, suddenly, her mind was clear. She would work at her marriage, she would make David happy. She would cut herself off from her past. She would not open Romesh's letters. She would take control of her life, a life which had been in chaos, as this area was. It was all so simple, so terribly simple. It was as simple as this rage which swept her at the thought of Boy, and the distance between them.

She worked day and night, as everyone else did, and there was no more thinking; there was just the effort of getting from one hour to the next and she became too tired even to miss Emily, even to worry about David, even to think of Romesh who still wrote every week and whose letters she destroyed, as the soldiers and refugees were being destroyed.

She was almost too tired to read the letter she received from Dora in the middle of May. *Well, I find you quite*

*extraordinary, Connie. I heard on the grapevine that
you had packed your bags and were off doing good
works in Assam in spite of your child, leaving her.
As her godmother I am now with her, and David.
Really, you should know where your priorities lie. This
is outrageous. I am needed in Delhi, I cannot take over
your responsibilities indefinitely. Incidentally, Ben is safe
though I find the whole retreat a disgrace. I can't think
what has come over the British.*

David enclosed a letter in the same envelope and his
writing was clear and neat, his words were short and
sharp. *You were wrong to go, I can see that now.
Whatever possessed you? Thank God for Dora; she has
brought Emily back into our own home. Dora is quite
right, a child needs her own things around her, her own
people. People who put her first.*

Connie left on the next train, her ringworm itching,
her jungle sores weeping, her anger gone, seeping away,
her confusion returning. She sat up all night, holding her
aching head in her hands, guilt pounding along with the
sound of the wheels.

'How am I going to grab hold of my life? How am I
going to think clearly, ever again? How am I going to
get the world to stop, so that I can think? Oh Mam, I
need you.'

The train pulled in at nine in the evening. She took
a tonga from the station. She walked up the path. The
lights were on. She opened the door and walked into
the sitting-room. Dora and David were playing chess
and she saw, as though through glass, Binnie and her
father. She couldn't see past the image for a moment,
it was so strong. She shook her head.

Dora looked up. 'I thought you'd come,' she said,
blowing smoke up into the air. 'Really Connie, as though
a major's wife hasn't enough to do without running
around looking after girls like you. Now, Emily is tucked
up in bed, and I have just been teaching dear David how
to play chess. You should have taught him long ago.

What have you been doing with these long evenings you spend together; surely you realize men need to unwind from the stress of their day?'

Connie wanted to throw the board in the air, hurl the pieces around the immaculate room and tell Dora that what they had been doing every night was destroying one another, and she hadn't known how to stop it. So she had gone with Dr Pearce; it was easier than staying.

Instead she sat down. 'Yes, you're right, I should spend more time with my husband. That is something I decided while I was away. Now, I am off to bed and then to the hospital in the morning to get my sores treated, and my ringworm. Have you blisters on your fingers from moving the knight, or perhaps the king?' How strange that her voice sounded so calm, when rage was nearly blinding her.

She left them, and lay in bed, but still she couldn't rid herself of the image of Walter and Binnie together, as Dora and David had been. She turned over, and Dora and David were replaced in her mind by Romesh and his uncle, then Dr Pearce and Sally, mud-streaked, exhausted. There was the whine of the air-raid siren which went on and on. She sat up and took the sleeping pill Dr Pearce had given her.

In the morning Dora left, kissing Connie. 'Take care, darling, but look, one tiny thing before I go. I need some money, something I simply have to get done. Could you? After all, I came up from Delhi to take care of your little family for you, as a godmother should.'

Connie shook her head. 'I have no money.'

Dora clicked her tongue. 'Oh come on, Connie. You can get hold of plenty. You've that first-class return ticket you won't be needing now.' There was anxiety in her eyes.

'No, really, I traded that in for Revd Williams's scholarship bursary years ago. Ask Ben, he's back.'

Dora's eyes were fierce. 'No, and neither must he know that I need money.' The jeep was waiting, David smiling in the driver's seat. Dora waved. 'I'll get it from somewhere else, don't you worry; don't even feel the tiniest bit of guilt.'

Connie watched her leave, then wrote to her mother, asking her why Walter and Binnie had spent so much time together. But then she tore up the letter because it was all so trivial, and she had her daughter to wake, her marriage to mend, her ringworm to cure. She didn't even look after the jeep as David drove off. Her head was aching too much.

Dora felt the hot wind in her hair as she watched David's stubby hands on the wheel. Bloody Connie, she'd banked on her having that little nest egg, that's why she'd got her back from the front line. She felt the nausea again. She hadn't much time left if she was to get rid of the baby. Ben would be back any day and she wasn't going to have him walking out on her.

Whose was it? That big ape of a Yank, or the civil servant? They'd both been good, whichever one it had been. She grinned to herself, then looked at David. She'd have to try him, he was all that was left.

She sobbed then, into her hands. He pulled into the verge as she'd known he would. His hand was on her shoulder. 'Oh no, what's wrong?'

'I've been so foolish, David, and I don't know anyone else who would understand. You're so kind, so intelligent, so sympathetic, not like Ben. He'll be so cross. I need a special friend, David.'

David left his hand on her shoulder, feeling her warmth, remembering the touch of her body all those years ago, the things she had done to him, her mouth on his thighs, her tongue—

'What's wrong, Dora. I'll help if I can.'

She told him then of the refugees she had helped, the British who had come to her, destitute.

'What could I do? I had to lend them money. I'm not like Connie, I can't just leave my responsibilities as she can. I owe it to Ben to live up to his position, act as his rank would expect. I did what I could for those who asked, but I've left myself so terribly short. In fact, I owe the bank. I shouldn't have done it, we can't afford it and I don't want to worry Ben. He has enough to do. You understand, don't you?'

David wiped her tears with his handkerchief. Ben was such a lucky bugger. 'How much do you need?'

She told him.

He wrote her a cheque. It was the money he had put in a separate account for their leave in England, but they wouldn't be going until the war was over, so why not?

'This will be our secret, won't it, David?' Her hand held his. 'Just between you and me.'

He wanted to bury his face in her breasts, but he only smiled, cleared his throat and restarted the car, holding close the thought of her trust in him, envy of his friend searing him.

22

By 1944 the tide of war was beginning to turn in Europe and the Pacific, and in February the British were on the offensive in Burma. 'Spirits are high, but rationing is tighter still,' Belle said, as she and Boy sat either side of the fire in the sitting-room of the wing. Belle pulled up the blanket which she had wrapped round her. She'd put layers of newspaper in her slippers and beneath her vest.

'Poke the fire, Boy, there's a dear.'

He grinned at her. 'It won't make it much warmer.'

'Perhaps not, but it will certainly be brighter – now humour an old lady, young man.'

He used the poker to lift the coal and let the air in. 'Grandma's good and warm in bed anyway. Do you think she'll get over this influenza?'

Belle laughed gently. 'Helen is the toughest old bird in this building, and that includes all the bairns running riot in the main vicarage even as we speak. She's determined to see the war out, and so she will. It's doing her a power of good to have you here on leave, and to have you behind a desk when you go back on duty.'

'I don't know what I'll do when she does die. With Mother and Tim in America it'll seem very lonely.' He eased his leg backwards and forwards as he sat.

Belle frowned. 'Is it hurting?'

'Not really, it's just the cold getting into it a bit.'

They fell silent, listening to the shrieks of the children next door. 'I'm glad you and Grandma came into the wing. The noise is too much for her when she's not well.'

Belle looked at him. 'You mustn't think that you'll have no-one when Helen does go. There's always me. I shall stay on in the wing when the war is over, if you agree. Your grandparents bought it for us years ago, but I'm quite prepared to leave, you know.'

Boy spun round, his face concerned. 'No, you must never leave. It's yours, it's all legal, you know. Did Grandma never tell you? And besides, I don't want you to go, ever.'

Belle picked up her knitting again, the needles slippping a little with her fingerless gloves, but not too much. 'Because one day, Connie will come, do you mean?' She didn't look at him but at the pearl stitch she was knitting into the back of, but all the time she was waiting. Would he answer at last?

Boy's voice was low. 'Yes.'

Still Belle didn't look at him, but concentrated on looping the wool round, slipping one stitch through, and then another. 'There can be more than one love in a person's life, you know. What about Fiona?'

Now she looked up. His eyes were dark, nervous. He ran his hand through his blue-black hair. His cheek was barely scarred and the bone had been rebuilt.

'Fiona was fun, and so were all the rest, but Connie is the love of my life; there will only ever be her. I just want to see her, to know that she is happy. She has always been everything to me but she always thought of me as a child. She went too soon for me to show her that I wasn't. Is she happy now, Belle? I thought at one stage that she wasn't.'

'Yes, my dear. I think she is. Does that please or distress you?'

He looked shocked. 'The only thing that would distress me is if she was ever anguished or unhappy.'

Then, thought Belle, you truly love her, and her heart broke for this young man.

Connie sat on the arm of Sally Masters's chair listening to the Queen Alexandra's nurses laughing with the officers in the club. 'It makes me feel old,' she murmured to Sally.

'You? What about me, I'm hitting forty and they think I'm someone's grandmother. You are only old enough to be their mother.'

The two women laughed, then looked round at the raucous call for more beer. David was laughing and he lifted his glass to Connie and Sally.

'He seems so much happier these days,' Sally said. 'I was worried at one point, he seemed to be going off the rails.'

Connie ran her finger round the rim of her glass. 'I think that was my fault. I always seemed to do and say the wrong thing.'

Sally put her hand on Connie's knee. 'Listen, my sweet, everyone said and did the wrong thing as far as David was concerned. Why do you think Jack Pearce asked for you to go to Assam? We wanted you out of it for a while. David was behaving atrociously – inadequacy causes the most appalling ructions. He's always been the same and it's such a shame because underneath he's a nice man.'

Connie looked at her husband. He no longer drank too much. He played chess with her in the evening. He played tag with Em. 'It's helped having the emergency commissions here; he's been the guiding light for the poor young men. My God, how he's enjoyed showing them the right fork to use, the correct way to dress. It's made him feel that, for once, he is the one who is experienced and King Bee. Now he's got this posting he's in seventh heaven. Men!'

Sally said quietly, 'This is the big one, isn't it? He's up for Air Supply, Tom told me. David's quietly excellent at organization and that's what General Slim needs as they chase the Nips down through Burma. There should be a promotion in it too, so he'll doubly feel he's proved himself once and for all.'

Sally took a sausage roll from the tray the bearer carried; his red sash was brilliant against the white of his tunic. ' "Inglorious but totally essential" Tom insists on calling himself and the other Service men. Did you know he's been posted too, but back to Balgaum where they were in December? Poor soul, he hated it; said the red dust was impossible. We'll be a couple of grass widows, Connie, but at least it should be plain sailing for you and David from then on.'

Connie sipped her rum and looked round at the panelled room, the tiger's head on the wall, the cricket and polo cups in the cases. It was home now. How strange when once it had seemed so alien.

Sally said, as a verse of 'For He's a Jolly Good Fellow' ended, 'Then when all this is over and the war is won, we'll be out of India.'

Connie shrugged. She had trained herself not to comment, not to think of the world out there. This was her husband, these were her friends. It was safer that way; it left her mind clearer, it stopped the ache which had surprised her when news came of the Congress leaders who were still imprisoned, and the Muslim leaders who were rising in stature.

Now she pushed away the thought of the blood bath there would be, the pain that Romesh must be feeling as hopes of unity faded. After all, her father's dream of a peaceful world had died too. She told herself, as she did on these occasions, that these things happened, she couldn't be responsible for everything and everyone, and sometimes it worked.

'Are you sure we'll win the war?' a nurse asked.

'How could we fail, with my husband supplying the great 14th as they avenge 1942?' Connie stood and bowed as Sally called for a soapbox.

The women laughed and talked of the heat which would soon stalk the plains, and Connie sat down again, marvelling at how adept she had become at talking of nothing serious.

She and David walked back to their bungalow, waving to the nurses as they headed for the hospital tents pitched behind the lines. There had been another influx of sick and wounded troops today. Her arm was linked in his; she replied to his comments and laughed at his jokes.

They looked in on Emily before Connie showered then lay in bed, waiting for him, lying naked on the sheets, as he had requested she should after he had returned from Balgaum.

She shut her mind, counting her breathing, as she had learned to do. She heard him pad across the tiles, she felt his weight on the bed, his hands on her body, on her head. He forced her face down to his thighs.

'Lick me,' he murmured. She did, hearing his moans. 'Again, again,' he ordered, his hands rough on her body, in her hair. He dragged her up, kissing her mouth, tasting himself, pushing her on top of him, then beneath.

She felt him in her and still counted her breathing, knowing now that it would soon end, as the chess matches ended, as the aimless talk in the evenings ended.

'You're a good wife, Connie,' he murmured as he rolled off her onto his side, and soon she heard the snores, and now she counted these, because sleep seldom came to her any more.

David stared out across the plain as he entrained for Burma, excitement making him restless. The fan was whirring, the other officers were talking, sleeping, or reading newspapers. Would there be a letter from Dora at the depot?

He rested his head on the headrest, her visit to Balgaum still fresh in his mind – how could it ever fade? He could almost feel her body, her tongue all over him, licking, sucking, then her mouth on his, her hands in his hair, pulling it, tearing at it, then her hands on his buttocks, pushing him deeper, deeper. He heard the train's whistle, and opened his eyes, clearing his throat.

Oh God, Dora was so wonderful; imagine anyone coming all that way just to repay money they had borrowed. The train picked up speed. He closed his eyes again to recapture how her hand had touched him, how he had heard her indrawn breath, seen the trembling of her fingers, the loosening of her mouth, the sagging of her body as she had leant against him, murmuring, 'David.'

'I say, old man, would you care for the newspaper?'

David jerked, opened his eyes, shook his head, not wanting to talk. Would there be a letter? God, he hoped so. Would he touch her body again? No, he had promised himself that he would not, he was a married man, for God's sake. It wasn't the done thing and Ben was his friend.

He smiled slightly as he remembered her voice.

'Please take the money, David.' Her hands were sliding up and down his thighs, her mouth was on his. 'No, it's yours,' he had said. How could he possibly take anything from her, after they had slept together? How adorable of her not to realize that.

In the middle of February Connie went with Emily to the hills, taking a house owned by Sally Masters's friend.

'You need the hill air after the malaria, my darling,' Connie said, as they exchanged the train for the narrow-gauge railway which chugged and puffed up the winding gradients into the hills. Connie held Emily in her arms, kissing her forehead which was too pale, holding her hand which was too thin. 'We'll go out in the snow, bring some roses to those cheeks.'

The air was pine-scented, and there was a breeze as Emily pointed at the bazaar she could see in the distance. The train stopped at the solitary platform. They took a tonga into the town. Connie pointed out the bungalows, the golf-course which was still under snow, the church.

'Listen to the goat bells,' she whispered to her child, hugging her as she sat on her lap, smiling at Ruth, the ayah, who pulled the blanket around her. Emily's hair was pure gold against the grey of the blanket.

They travelled between snow banks which had been heaped to eight feet when the track was cleared, and

Emily gasped, and tried to reach them. 'Ice, Mummy. Ice,' she said.

They sat before a roaring fire that evening and Connie and the ayah sang in Urdu *Talli Talli badja baba.* Clap, clap hands, baby, and smiled when Emily laughed and clapped.

Connie carried her to bed, and sat with her until she slept, then she walked to the veranda and drew the cold clear air deep into her lungs, and slept that night, and the next, and the next.

She wrote to Belle. *Emily is so much better, and the hills are working their magic as always. I think of nothing, I just am. I suppose this is happiness, is it?*

On the fifth day she walked Emily along the high banked paths then climbed to the clear clean snow, sitting on a tray with her and sliding down the slope, hearing Emily's laughter and remembering her own and Boy's. They walked into the town and through the bazaar. Emily chose a silk scarf for Belle.

'Paint Grandma a picture and we'll send it,' Connie said as they ate lunch in the dining-room which over-looked the valley. There was wire netting at the windows.

'Take it down,' Emily said, pointing.

'No, because the monkeys who live all around will come in like some naughty little girls do, and poke and prod and knock things over.' Emily giggled as Connie tickled her.

After lunch the bearer brought a telegram on the tray they had used as a sledge. It was from Sally.

Dora is here in a dreadful state. Ben has been killed and she came to find you. I've sent her on to you. This warning should arrive before her.

There was a later telegram, from David. He had been promoted to Major. Connie left both on the sideboard, looking out across the valley, wanting to push the outside world away, already feeling her peace slipping from her and trying to feel sad at the loss of Ben, but he had been such a snob and she could not.

She tried to feel sympathy for Dora, but she disliked her so much it evaded her. 'Oh damn,' she swore. 'Why does she have to keep turning up?'

Dora arrived the next day, as the evening was drawing in. She hugged Emily, crying over her. Connie eased the child from Dora's arms, handing her to the ayah. 'Take her to bed, please Ruth. I'll come soon or perhaps you could bring her in.'

She led Dora into the sitting-room, her arm around the heaving shoulders of the woman whose face was tear-stained and bloated. 'Sit here, by the fire. I'll fetch food, and a drink.' She plumped up the cushions, and eased Dora down into them.

Dora shook her head. 'No food, just some rum. No, gin. I'd prefer gin, and tonic.' She sat back. The fire played on her red hair, her luscious breasts, her gold bracelets which jangled as she wiped her face.

Connie brought her the gin, and poured tonic, hearing it hiss. Dora grabbed it, cradling it in her hands. 'I can't believe it. How can he be here one minute and gone the next – how could it happen?'

Connie sat on the arm of the chair, her hand on Dora's shoulder, remembering the small girl who had come to their mission, the girl who had risen so high.

'I'm so sorry, I really can't tell you how very much it's upset us. Poor Ben, poor you. I'm just glad you came to us.' Did she sound sincere? She said again, 'I'm so glad; we go back such a long way.' Was that better?

Dora clung to her. 'You are the only one I wanted to come to, Connie. I have been such a bitch. I've said horrible things to you about David. I even broke your doll, years ago. I'm alone here now, I had to come.' Tears rolled down Dora's face again. 'Can you forgive, can you help me as you have always done?'

Connie held the grieving woman, and remembered when Romesh had turned her away – the pain, the self-exploration, the endlessness of the grief, and felt that the same had happened to Dora. 'Shh, shh,' she said, wanting to take away her pain. 'It's all right, you're here, with me. The past is over. We just have to get you through this. Oh Dora, I'm so sorry.' And she really was.

'Poor Ben, I loved him so much,' Dora said, her voice muffled by Connie's blouse, her breath so warm and damp that Connie almost recoiled. 'He was shot, you know, as he was lighting a cigarette. I mean, how careless.' She peeled into hysterical laughter, breaking free from Connie's arms, hugging herself. 'He should have given up smoking years ago. They say it kills you. They're right.'

Connie gripped her hand. 'It will be all right, Dora. I'll look after you.' She nodded to the bearer who brought chicken curry on trays. 'Leave it, please,' she directed quietly, soothing Dora, talking gently to her.

At last they ate, and all the time Dora drank gin.

When the trays had been cleared, the ayah brought Emily in and she ran to Connie, climbed on her knee and stared at Dora through her fingers.

'Come to me, sweetie,' Dora called, beckoning. Her bracelets jangled. Emily looked at her mother who nodded. 'But bed in five minutes. I'll read to you, I promise.'

The child was warm on Dora's lap, her fingers were light on her arm as she played with the bracelets.

Emily said, 'My daddy's a major. It says on that paper.' She pointed to the tray on the sideboard.

Dora paused, looking at the sideboard, then across at Connie. 'I'm so glad one of us has had good news.'

Connie flushed. 'It is of no importance, not beside poor Ben.' Connie held out her hands to Emily. 'Bedtime, madam.'

Dora watched them go. She looked round the room at the chintz wallpaper, the matching curtains, the huge fire, the gleaming fire-irons and hurled her cigarette into the flames. Goddamn you, Ben, being shot for a bloody cigarette. She rocked backwards and forwards, hating him for being so stupid, for taking her position away from her. How bloody could he?

She looked across at the telegram and poured more gin. Thank God she had heard about the promotion or this would have been the last place she'd have come. She walked to the window, looking down into the valley. All she had to work out now were the details.

I've slept with Connie's husband to hurt her, but this will be so much better. I've always been watching and waiting, but it's never been the right time. This is.

Connie told Emily a story about the spirit who lived in the snow and whose heart sang with joy when the swallows returned to the hills, and the butterflies too.

'Will they come here, Mummy?' she asked.

'Oh yes, very soon, and we'll picnic with Ruth and we'll have curry puffs, and hard-boiled eggs which we'll roll down the slopes like Boy and I did.'

'Will I ever see Boy?'

'Oh yes, when we go back to England, which could be soon.'

'Will he want his metal box back then?'

Connie laughed. 'Perhaps.'

'Will he want the letters you keep in it?'

Connie shook her head. 'No-one wants other people's letters, and those will be thrown away soon anyway.' She knew she should have done so long ago, but somehow she couldn't bear to let Romesh leave her entirely.

Emily put her arms behind her head. 'Will Dora come on the picnics too?'

'If she's still here then.' But please God she won't be because I want this time with you, my love. Just you and me, Connie thought.

She kissed Emily, feeling the soft warm arms hugging her neck. 'Sleep tight, darling.'

She left the nursery light burning, lighting up the teddies and the doll that Emily took with her to all their postings. She turned at the door and smiled at her daughter. 'I love you with all my heart,' Connie said.

She sat up until midnight while Dora paced the room, crying, talking of Ben, asking how life went on when a husband died, asking how anyone bore the loneliness.

Connie said, 'You fill it as you have been doing while he's been away, I suppose.'

Dora flared. 'What do you mean by that? I've been busy, doing work he would have wanted me to do. Someone has to circulate.'

Connie poured herself another drink. 'I'm so sorry, I didn't mean anything by that. I meant you must fill your days.'

'But I need friends; I can't be alone in a country like this.' Connie drank her rum. They were back to this. She looked around the room at the prints on the wall, the brass picture hooks gleaming, the Royal Worcester in the cabinet, the horse brasses. No-one but an Englishman could live here. And no, Dora, I can't have you with us, she thought.

Dora fell on her knees by Connie's chair. 'I can't live alone. Please help me, Connie.'

The rum was making Connie's head swim. She looked past Dora to the range of mountains which were stark against the moon-drenched sky. She should have her, she was being unreasonable, but though Dora had cleared the past, she couldn't like the woman and she hated herself for it.

'Dora, my dear, you will love again. One day, you will love again. I promise.'

'But I might not, and what do I do in the meantime?'

Connie drank more of the rum. This had been going on since she had put Emily to bed and it would go on and on, she knew. So what did it really matter if Dora stayed? She was alone here with Emily, it could be fun, and she had come here for help. She had changed, she had talked of the past and recognized it. Connie shook her head, lifted her drink to her lips again.

The glass was sticky, she must have spilt some. She giggled. Messy girl, worse than the monkeys that came in the windows. She looked across at the desk, at the metal box.

'You'll love again,' she slurred to Dora. 'I did. I'm sure I love David and I thought I never would love anyone again.'

Dora stayed at Connie's knees, her smile in place, her voice coaxing, because Connie had never spoken of her private life before. 'But I don't think people do, when their hearts have been broken,' she said, pouring more rum into Connie's glass. 'Come on, drink up.'

As Connie drank, her glass slipped in her hand; more spilt. Dora mopped it up with her handkerchief, saying, 'Tell me something to give me hope, Connie.'

Hope, oh yes, everyone needed hope, Connie thought, her words corkscrewing round her head. She tried to catch the word, hold it steady in her mind. There it was; she'd caught it, as she'd wanted to catch Romesh's love.

She said, 'Hope, oh yes, hope. You can love again, because I did. I loved a man and he broke my heart and now I have David.' Connie frowned into her glass. 'I don't love David the same, I don't ache for him, but he's Emily's father, he's a good man, everyone says he is.'

Dora wanted to shake her, scream at her to go on because this might be something useful. Instead she said, 'David is a good man. Was your other man good? Was he a friend of David's?'

Connie put her finger to her lips. 'Oh no, he was my lover before I met David, when I was in—' She stopped. 'It's a secret. It's always got to be a secret.'

'Not between you and me,' Dora said, smiling.

'Oh yes, always. Romesh made me promise.'

23

It was June 1947 and at last the long hard winter was over. Belle cut a slice of newly baked bread while Boy perched himself on the end of the kitchen table. 'Grandma would have said, "It'll give you the gurgles and put me off my crossword."'

Belle pushed over the plate. It was heaped with butter and jam. 'We're celebrating so I've lashed out with the last of the jam – there's too much butter as well.'

'You think Connie's really coming home then?' His voice was carefully controlled as he looked at the letter on the mantelpiece.

Belle poured the tea, holding the lid. 'Wretched thing lobbed itself off the other day.' She pushed across the cup. 'Do sit down, Boy, it's like having a hen trying to roost with you perched there. And yes, I'm sure they'll be home soon. Partition has been announced to try and avoid further uncertainty and bloodshed. Mountbatten has set the date as 14 August at midnight, as you well know, or are you so deep in this new manuscript that you no longer know what's going on in the world?'

She watched as he sat in the carver at the opposite end to her. 'Will she come here?' he asked.

'Could you bear it?' Belle watched as he tore off the crusts and then ate them. 'That is a disgusting habit.'

He smiled absently. 'I don't know. I shall simply have to; if I can't I'll just bury myself in the new novel – the deadline is Christmas so I've a good excuse. You won't tell her how I feel, will you? I just want to see her, know that she's well. Oh, I just want to see her.'

Belle clasped her cup, remembering how she and Helen

had cheered when Labour had been elected after the war. 'It will mean independence for India,' Helen had crowed. 'The anti-imperialists will offload as quickly as they can. Our girl will come home, at last.'

They hadn't offloaded India quickly enough for Helen, though. She had died at the height of the coldest winter for years. Perhaps it was as well. Belle couldn't drink because of the tension that gripped her.

'Dora still hasn't left them, you know. Connie says that David feels they owe it to Ben to keep her with them until they leave. It's been three years, Boy. It's not good for a marriage.'

Boy reached across for the milk. The clock chimed five. 'Is Dora still spoiling Emily?'

Belle frowned. 'Connie didn't say, but at least the wretched girl can't take Em out riding now because of the unrest, so something good has come out of the mess that seems to be brewing. I don't know, somehow independence seems to have been rushed through by Mountbatten. Connie seems to have this thing about retaining the unity, and now the division of India has been announced she's distraught. She worked hard for that at the mission school, she says. I didn't know that.'

Boy finished the last of his bread, shaking his head when Belle offered him more. 'I must get on. Thanks for the tea, Belle. See you tomorrow, same time, same place.' He was grinning, though it didn't reach his eyes.

He pushed his hands deep into his pockets as he walked back into the main house. It was so quiet now that the evacuees and Mary's girls had gone; far too quiet. He leant against the door-frame, looking into his study and the paper that waited in the typewriter for him. Connie was coming home, along with the rest of the British.

He strode to his desk and dragged the paper from the machine, crumbling it into a ball, throwing it away. God, he longed to see her, but he knew it would tear him apart, because David would be there.

*   *   *

Connie lay in bed, feeling the humid heat even as dawn came up. David stirred beside her. 'You have remembered to order the food for the party tonight?' he mumbled. 'We must make sure it's a success for poor Dora.'

She wanted to scream at him, to shake him and ask how he could care that a party was a success when Lahore, that beautiful, integrated city, was in chaos, with Muslims killing Sikhs and Hindus, with Hindus and Sikhs burning and beating Muslims to death. How could he be thinking of parties when all around them it was the same? How could anyone? But there'd been so many, with people leaving.

She rose, looked out of the window at the smoke over the town. But what had she done that was better than the other people here, and for her there was no excuse? Yes. What have you done, Connie Symmonds, or French, as you now are?

She turned to look at David. That's just it; she had done nothing since the mission and she hated herself for it. She had turned her back on Romesh. Oh yes, she had read his letters which had begun again after he was released from prison, but she had never written back.

She had had her daughter to bring up, to drag away from Dora who always seemed to be between them. She had had her husband to nurture. She dressed. So what could I have done, Mam, Da, Romesh? She brushed her hair, not wanting to think about it.

She took Emily with her for a walk around the cantonment, and then for morning coffee with Mrs Mathers and some other wives. Dora was lying down when she and Emily returned, and Connie was glad. She and Emily ate lunch alone, for once.

'Where's Aunt Dora, I drew her a card for her birthday while Mrs Mathers was talking? I was bored. Aunt Dora could have played with me.'

'Aunt Dora should have been at the coffee morning too, but she was at the hairdresser.'

'I like Aunt Dora's red hair, it's pretty.' Emily pulled

her plaits over her shoulder. 'She said she'd make me lots of curls for the party tonight.'

Connie put down her fork. She was no longer hungry. 'I'll make you lots of curls, darling, I promised I would, remember?'

'Where's ayah, Mummy?' Emily looked round.

'I don't know. Perhaps she's with her friends; she asked if she could go and see them.'

'Aunt Dora said wogs don't have friends, they just have enemies whom they butcher. She says they're all animals.' Emily looked at her mother, and there was fear in her eyes.

Connie somehow kept her voice neutral. 'Emily, you are now eight years old. You know very well that we do not call Indians "wogs". You also know that Indians are people like us, with problems like us. We killed people in the war; some of the Indians feel that they are in a war. It happens. It shouldn't but it does and it's very sad. Think of ayah, the songs she sings to you, the love she gives you. Is she an animal?'

Emily smiled at her mother now. 'I didn't think Aunt Dora was right, but Daddy says the same thing too, doesn't he?'

'Daddy gets angry sometimes; we all say things we don't mean. I seem to remember you saying that you hated Frances Mathers, but then you shared your sweets with her.' Connie grinned at her daughter, trying to keep calm. Perhaps *this* is what I am doing, she thought – waging a battle of my own.

By evening Ruth, the ayah, had still not returned, and now, as she arranged the tureen and the punch bowl, she asked Ahmed where she was, yet again. Once more he shook his head. 'I do not know, memsahib. But the *chaukidar* say she gone to family in town – perhaps.'

Dora called through from the bedroom. 'It's really too bad. It is my party, surely she knows that we haven't time to fiddle about with Emily tonight.'

Connie resisted giving instructions to add arsenic to

the curry puffs. Emily who was wrapping napkins around the knives and forks flushed and looked at her mother. 'I'll keep my hair in plaits, Mummy.'

Connie smiled at her. 'You certainly will not. I've been waiting for this all day. Come along now.'

She took her to her bedroom, damped her hair and pinned it into curls while Emily sat on her knee and dabbed face powder on her nose. 'I like the smell of your things, Mummy. It makes me feel safe.'

Connie hugged her. 'You'll always be safe with me, Emily. I love you more than anything else in the world.' They sat listening to the monsoon rain pouring down outside. It would damp the fires that still burning in the town.

'Ayah will get wet when she comes back. I'll miss her, when we go to England,' Emily said.

'I'll miss India, but I want to go now,' Connie said. 'You will see Grandma and Boy, and the village where I lived, the mission in Newcastle. You can meet Mary and Sandy. Oh, it will be wonderful, so much simpler.'

Emily leaned against her, her arms coming up, her hands stroking her mother's face. 'Will Aunt Dora come too?'

Connie shook her head. 'No, Aunt Dora will not come with us to Rempton. Once we leave the boat at Tilbury, we will be together, as a family, and Dora must start her own life.'

Dora stood outside the door, listening. She strolled into the dining-room and lit her cigarette with the lighter David had given her.

She had smiled at him that night and touched his thigh. 'You are so kind, and, you know, I can't bear the thought of no more chess, of no more Emily, and no more Connie, of course,' she had said. 'But David, I have found it so difficult because I have become too fond of you. You are everything I need in a man. I was a fool all those years ago, to let you slip through my fingers.'

He had looked straight ahead, the flush rising from his neck to his face. 'You know how I feel about you, but I have a wife, and a child. It would not be honourable to leave them. Besides, I love Emily too much.'

Dora drew deeply on her cigarette now, looking at Emily's card which she had put on the mantelpiece, anxiety gnawing at her. She hadn't managed to get David to sleep with her again, he was too damn proper. If she had done, she could have arranged for Connie to walk in on it, but then Connie would keep the child, and she didn't want to leave her anything.

Were those letters in Boy's box enough? After all, the damned wog only talked of love in one, but at least it was undated. Could she tell David that Romesh had visited Connie in the hills? But no, it had to be more definite. Knowing David, he'd want to see something like that with his own eyes. These bloody men wouldn't accept that their wives preferred someone else.

She touched up her hair. Or there was always that Yank. She'd kept on writing and he'd have her, like a shot. Yes, maybe she'd have to change direction, but there'd be no kid then. She looked at the photograph of Belle and Connie together in the garden of the Newcastle mission and wanted to throw it to the floor. Damn them – how she wanted to wipe the smiles off their faces once and for all.

'I've a few more weeks,' she said aloud. 'Who knows what will turn up?'

At seven-thirty, just after the first guests had arrived, Dr Pearce sent a chit across to Connie. '*Come to the hospital at once; I have your ayah.*'

She looked across at David who was talking to Colonel Mathers. 'I must go. I'll be back soon.'

He looked at his watch. 'For Christ's sake, Connie, it's Dora's birthday.'

'I told you. I have to go. It's Ruth; Jack Pearce has her.'

Tom Masters took her arm. 'Come on, I'll run you in the jeep.'

The rain was drumming on the roof of the car; it soaked her as she ran up the hospital path, into reception. 'Straight through,' the Eurasian receptionist said. 'They're waiting.'

Connie turned to Tom. 'You go back. I'll be all right.'

She hurried down the corridor, seeing Dr Pearce at the end, his stethoscope hanging from the pocket of his white coat. 'In here,' he said, leading the way into a darkened room. It was Ruth – her hair was matted with blood, her arms were bruised and cut.

'She hasn't long,' Jack said as Connie held the small fine-boned hand, crusted now with blood.

She stroked Ruth's brow and remembered this sweet gentle girl holding Emily in her arms, watching her first steps, hearing her first words.

'My dear,' she whispered. 'My poor dear Ruth.' Ruth stirred. Connie kissed her cheek, her hand.

Jack Pearce stood behind her. 'She was worried about her family and went to see them. They had been burned in their house. Unfortunately, she was found by Muslims. The police came across her by the church, recognized her, and brought her to us. She was on her way back to you, and judging from the state of her knees, she'd crawled most of the way. I don't know how she managed with those wounds.'

Connie sat with her until she died. It took a mere half an hour and when Ruth drew her last breath Connie clung to her. 'Oh Mam,' she called as Jack Pearce prised her from the girl and held her in his arms.

'Soon we'll all be home,' he said. 'It wasn't your fault, you could have done nothing to stop it.'

She walked from the hospital to her bungalow. The rain had stopped; she could smell the earth, the grass, hear the music, see the lights as she walked up the path. She opened the door and walked into the sitting-room. She stood there until silence fell.

She saw Dora's face, David's, she heard the gasps of their guests. She looked down at her dress; it was blood-stained, so were her hands. 'Ruth is dead. The party is over,' she said. 'We have no right to dance and laugh when out there a continent is being destroyed. You will all leave.'

Dora stepped forward. 'Connie, how could you?'

'Very easily, Dora.' Connie called to the bearer. 'Umbrellas, please, Ahmed.'

Sally Masters stepped forward then. 'Connie is absolutely right; come along, Tom.' Connie had known that Sally would agree; so would Daphne, and Celia.

Others moved then. Connie didn't wait to see them go. She walked towards the bathroom but Emily was at her bedroom door. Connie smiled at her. Emily paled, then ran into her bedroom. Connie followed.

'Go away, Mummy, you're all bloody. Go away.'

Dora came into the room. 'It's all right, Auntie Dora is here.'

Emily ran to her.

Connie stared at them, then walked into the bathroom, showered, put on her robe. She put on her powder, her lavender-water, and then she held open the door of Emily's room.

'You may leave her now, Dora.'

Dora looked up from the book she was reading Emily and glared at Connie.

'Now, Dora.' Connie's voice was gentle because she did not want to frighten Emily ever again. 'Now, Dora,' she repeated, her eyes hard.

Dora left, her eyes raking Connie. 'You will regret this,' she raged.

'No, not this; perhaps the past years, but not this,' Connie said, moving towards her daughter, sitting by her bed, holding her.

In August as the date of independence approached, Connie travelled with David, Dora and Emily to Bombay. They had sold what they could and had already kissed their friends goodbye as week by week the British had left, their luggage piled high on the station. Now it was their turn to travel through the Punjab where the harvest had been wonderful.

She looked out at the irrigation canals, the bullocks lurching along the dusty road, the crowds of Muslims heading towards the north on one side, the Hindus streaming towards the south on the other, the refugee camp in the distance.

How could anyone divide this land? As the British have just done, by drawing a line on a map, Romesh had said. '*By giving a desk to one, a typewriter to another – perhaps it always had to be this way,*' he had written. '*I was chasing a dream.*'

They passed through a station but didn't stop. There were bodies lying on the platforms. Poor Da, poor Romesh. She looked at David. Poor David. His Muslim officers and men had had to choose whether to stay in India or go to Pakistan when they had only ever thought of themselves as one regiment. She fingered the garland on her lap which Ahmed had draped around her neck, tears in his eyes. Poor Ahmed.

She thought of the churchyard at the cantonment which held the graves of so many British who had served India with love. She thought of successive governments which had held tight for too long. She thought of the Indians, their dream at hand.

If only it had happened earlier, with less haste, more structure. If only the Muslims hadn't feared the Hindu majority. If only Congress had been prepared to share power. If only Jinnah— Oh, what was the point?

She looked at Dora as the train rattled and groaned. Soon India would be free of the British, and her family would be free of Dora. She put her arm around Emily.

'Soon we'll be in Rempton, darling,' she said, looking across the land she loved but longed to leave, for that way she could start her life again.

At Bombay station she walked beneath the red-brick neo-Gothic arches and remembered the young girl she had once been. There was the same smell of spice and urine, the heat, the jostling crowds, the baggage, sacks and bundles scattered on the platform, the beggars.

'Goodbye India,' she breathed, stopping, turning, looking, until Emily pulled her on, out into the streaming light and heat of the day.

In the streets their taxi hooted at buses, cyclists. They passed overladen trucks, jay-walking pedestrians. They were held up in a jam caused by a broken handcart piled high with live fowl. A horse-drawn doolie was behind them. Emily laughed as a chicken escaped.

They were clammy from the humidity and as they waited outside the hotel for their luggage to be unloaded they could smell the sea.

'I'll check us all in, then get off to the Booking Office,' David said, leading the way into the hotel. They followed the porter to their rooms.

As David left, Connie looked out at the light over the *maidan,* watching it fade from pink to purple. She was leaving, but how could she bear to?

Emily lay on the bed, sweat on her forehead.

'It's so hot, Mummy.'

'Soon we'll be cool,' she said. 'There will be a breeze on the ship, and we can throw our topees in the water, and see if they sink or float. If they float we'll be coming back.'

She returned to the window, wanting to soak in India until the last moment, wanting to remember every detail of the mission, the hills, Romesh.

It was then that she heard the knock on the door. She took the chit.

Connie, I must see you before you leave. Yes, I know you are going. Come to the Raj. Room 16. I will be waiting.
    Romesh.

Connie told Emily that she was going for some air. She knocked on Dora's door and told her the same.

Dora watched her go, then opened Emily's door, sat with her. 'Where has Mummy gone?'

Emily said she didn't know. 'A chit came.'

Dora asked at reception who had taken the chit up to Mrs French. The receptionist pointed out the porter. She bribed him knowing he would have read it. He told her its contents and so she waited in her bedroom for David to return and tore up the letter of love she had been writing to Johnny O'Malley in the States.

She smiled because she had thought it was too late, but oh no, it wasn't. 'The timing is perfect, Connie dear.'

Connie took a rickshaw to the hotel. The lift creaked as it rose. Her mouth was dry. She wanted to see him, but she wanted to run far from him. It had been so long but she didn't know if she could bear to say farewell to him, as well as to India.

She knocked on the door. Romesh opened it. 'It's not locked; you could just have turned the handle.'

He was thinner, older, but the smile was the same and so were the hands that pulled her into the room, but then he stood back, letting her go. 'I just had to see you,' he said.

There were pictures of the *maidan* on the wall, and of the harbour, and the room smelt musty. He gestured to a chair. She shook her head. There was Indian music playing on the radio. 'I can't stay. I just wanted to see you one more time.'

He nodded, standing quite still. 'You are so beautiful; you are the only woman I have ever loved.'

The words seared through her. She felt the pain of

them, the glory. She said nothing for a moment, remembering his uncle's house, the love he had rejected. 'So, Romesh, you have independence, but my heart breaks for the end of your dreams.'

He shook his head, putting out his hand. 'I don't want to talk of that. I want to talk of us. I love you, Connie. I always have, and I always will.'

He reached out and touched her cheek. She replied, 'But you have a wife.'

He shook his head. 'No, I lied. I wanted to set you free. How could I ask you to wait until independence? But now I ask you to stay, to live your life with me, to look within your heart and know that you love me.'

His hands were grasping hers, those fine hands which she had loved, and she repeated in her mind the words she once longed to hear. He lifted her hands to his lips. He was so close. 'I love you, Connie. Don't go. I thought I could bear life without you, but when I heard you were really leaving, I realized I could not. Stay with me.'

She wanted to hold him to her, to feel him against her because there was love in his eyes, as she now realized there wasn't in David's. She pulled away.

'No, I'm going home. I have a daughter I love, I have a husband whose love I can rebuild when we have some peace.'

'But do you love him, Connie, do you love him as I love you?' He walked to the window, looking out across the sprawling city. 'I realized how much I cared for you when Gandhi refused to save his wife's life. A penicillin injection would have meant the piercing of her skin, the invasion of her body. It would have been an act of violence. It could have saved her life. I knew then that I would have moved heaven and earth to save your life and that I should never have sent you away. Stay with me, Connie?'

She walked to the window, looking up into his face, soaking up the love she saw in it, making it last the lifetime it would have to. Could he see the love she still held for him, and always would?

He said, 'You do love me, don't you?' She nodded, unable to speak. He touched her face again. 'But you are going to England, aren't you?'

She nodded and this time whispered, 'I love my child, I care for my husband. He is a good man. We are going home, to Boy, to Belle.'

'I had to try.'

They were so close now; she could feel the heat of his body. 'Where will you go now, Romesh?'

He smiled gently, his eyes sad. 'To Amritsar.'

She had known he would say that, and now she held him. Because Amritsar was in the path of the migration, it would be swallowed up in the panic, it would be a place of death, anger, fear. But of course he would be there, as his father and mother had been. He had to be.

He said, 'Again, you have made my life simpler for me, Connie. If you had stayed, I could not have gone. I could not have completed the circle. I would have wanted to be safe. I would have avoided my duty, and then how could I have lived with myself?'

Connie said, 'And how could you have borne to look at me after that? We have loved one another at the wrong time and in the wrong place, Romesh, but it is no less strong, or true, because of it.'

It was her hands that touched his face now, and then she kissed his cheek, his lips, so gently, wanting to weep her farewell, wanting to beg him to strive for safety, but knowing she must do neither.

'I will always love you, Romesh,' she said softly. 'I will always love India, but now we must both go home.'

He held her, and she him, and neither spoke, but for the first time in years they both knew true peace and that it would have to last them for eternity.

It was then that the door burst open. Connie saw David and Dora, and Dora was pointing at her with one hand and waving Connie's letters from Romesh in the other.

'Now will you believe me, David? This is the Indian she has been whoring with for years, leaping from your bed to his.'

24

Belle stared at the bacon in the frying-pan, then looked out into the back garden. It was December 1947, the snow was heaped high against the house, reflecting white light into the room, making it seem even colder. She poked the range, shook the pan. She'd thought bacon for breakfast would lift the worry for a moment but it was a waste of the one ounce they were allowed on the ration.

'Would you like mine?' she called to Boy, lifting the rasher from the pan and holding it over his plate.

Boy shook his head. 'I doubt that I shall manage the piece I have. It smelt good cooking but somehow my appetite's gone. You have it; pretend to enjoy it, you might come to believe it.' His smile was tired, his face was drawn, as hers was too.

She eased herself into her chair, shaking pepper, salt, cutting the bacon, eating it. She put down her knife and fork; it was no good. 'Where is she, Boy?'

He didn't answer because they had been asking one another that for three months, ever since Connie's ship had docked, ever since the telegram which read, '*I won't be coming to Rempton. I'll write when I know my plans.*'

She hadn't.

'Perhaps there'll be something in the post today; David's club must have forwarded our letters.' Belle poured tea for them both, unable to relax. It was as though her daughter and family had disappeared. What was wrong? Oh God, Connie, what are you doing to us?

She looked up at Boy as she heard the letter-box slap and the letters tumble to the floor. 'You go this time, please, Boy. I can't bear it.' He rose saying, 'Neither can I.'

She listened to his footsteps on the tiled floor, then looked again at the snow against the windows – how bleak it all was. She couldn't bear to look as Boy brought the mail, but she listened as he leafed through it, stopping at one. She turned. He held it out to her. 'This one has a London postmark.'

She couldn't move. 'Open it. I can't.' The bacon fat was congealing on her plate, the fire was hissing. He opened the envelope. His lips moved. 'Louder, Boy,' she demanded, her voice fierce with impatience.

'It's from David's solicitor.' His eyes scanned the page. 'He's given us Connie's solicitor's address.' He read it out, then looked at Belle. 'What does it mean? Why a solicitor? What the hell's going on, Belle? What have they done to her?' He was shaking the letter in Belle's face.

She gripped his hand. 'We'll ring him, ask him.'

She did, but he would say nothing beyond the fact that the matter was confidential. 'Give me her address then,' Belle said. He refused, saying, 'Mrs French has asked that no-one should be informed of her whereabouts.'

Boy took the receiver. 'Please will you give us Mr French's address, or do we get that from his solicitor?'

Mr Smith replied, 'I cannot give it to you, and I would imagine that Sandford Booth & Masters will not either.'

They rang Sandford Booth & Masters. Smith had been right.

Boy stared at Belle. 'I'm going down. I'll make Smith tell me.' He wrenched open the door and ran along the cleared path to the vicarage, the snow crunching beneath his boots.

'I'm coming too,' Belle called, pulling her shawl around her shoulders, following him out into the cold.

He stopped. 'No, Belle, you stay here, in case she comes.' Of course he was right, but she wanted to do something, for heaven's sake; she was Connie's mother. He could stay here, she would go. She ran into the vicarage, watching as he threw clothes into a holdall.

'Boy, I must—' she began, then stopped as he looked up. There was such desperation, and hope, in his eyes that she said, 'You will ring me, won't you?'

She left, angry with herself for forgetting that Boy's love for Connie was so great that he would not stop until she was found.

Boy wouldn't think of Connie as he travelled on the train, listening to the shriek of the whistle, the drumming of the wheels, looking out at the bomb-damaged houses as they approached London.

He wouldn't think of the long years since she had gone. He would only think of today, of the solicitor. He crossed his legs, grasping his hands together. No, he mustn't think of her but here she was, breaking through, her smile, her laugh, the way she tossed her head, her voice. Oh God, Connie, where are you?

At Euston he took the underground, jostling his way through the crowds to his club, cursing the ending of the day, wanting to be at the solicitor's. He didn't sleep that night, but lay listening to the sounds of the capital and to the echoes of Connie.

He arrived at the solicitor's office as the secretary was taking the cover off her typewriter.

'I need to speak to Mr Smith. Mrs French's mother will have rung yesterday.'

The young woman nodded. 'I believe she did. Would you wait one moment. Do sit down.' She smiled.

His face was too stiff for his lips to move, his hands were trembling. He pushed them into his pockets as the secretary walked down a corridor. He wanted to run past her, push his way into the office, but he forced himself to sit.

She returned. 'Do go through.' She pointed to the corridor. 'Mr Smith's office is straight ahead of you.'

There was worn carpet on the floor, but then everything was worn after years of war. He made himself think of this as he opened the door because at last he was about to find Connie.

Mr Smith would not tell him where Connie was, or anything about her.

'But that's ridiculous,' Boy protested.

Mr Smith sat back in his chair, buffing his nails.

'Those are the instructions of my client. If she had wanted to see you, Mr Driscoll, she would have contacted you.'

'But she's obviously in trouble. She needs us. You must tell me.'

Mr Smith shook his head again. 'There is no must about it. My client has issued instructions and that is all there is to it.' Mr Smith pressed the intercom on his desk. 'Miss Andrews, would you show Mr Driscoll out, please.' Mr Smith stood, stretched out his hand. Boy shook it, turned and left as Miss Andrews held the door open.

He walked down the corridor, his shoes silent on the carpet, the damned worn carpet, and now he was shaking.

They reached the reception desk; Miss Andrews walked ahead and held open the door. 'Have a good journey back, Mr Driscoll. I'm sorry we could not have been of more help.' Her face was pale, thin and pinched as were all their faces after the war, and now in this austerity.

He looked at the door, shook his head and sat on the leather settee. 'I'm staying here until Mr Smith tells me where she is.'

He stayed until the office closed at 6 p.m. He was there again at 9 a.m.

'I shall call the police,' Mr Smith said, sweeping past him, hanging his umbrella on the stand, his coat, his hat.

'Then I would write it up in a newspaper,' Boy replied. 'That would do you no good at all.'

Mr Smith turned to him. 'Then why don't you use your contacts to help find Mrs French and leave us alone?'

Boy shook his head. 'Do you think I haven't tried? There is nothing, the trail is cold.'

He sat whilst clients came and went and all the time he thought of Connie. At 1 p.m. Miss Andrews passed him sandwiches and tea once Mr Smith had left for his lunch.

'You keep at it,' she said quietly. 'When you love someone like you love Mrs French nothing should stand in your way. I loved my husband like that.' She stopped, and started to type again.

Boy walked across to her. 'Did he survive?'

She shook her head. 'He was in a Japanese camp. I wanted to go over there and storm the gates, make them let him go. I couldn't do anything, but you can.'

Boy looked at the tears that were dripping off her cheeks. He wanted to ask her to show him Connie's file, but how could he now?

He sat down again, drank his tea, returned the flask, placing it on the desk, reaching forward and touching her hand. 'You are very kind, and I'm very sorry.'

She looked up at him. 'I am too. I should show you the file, but I need my job.'

Boy said, 'I know.'

He sat until six and was there again at nine the next morning. At 5 p.m. Mr Smith called him into his office and waved him brusquely to a chair.

'I can't tell you anything. I'm explaining this to you for the last time.' Mr Smith was tapping a file. 'But now I have an urgent and private telephone call to make. I shall return to this office in ten minutes. Is that quite clear?'

Boy looked at the man, who was not looking at him, but at the file. It was now that he saw the name – Mrs French. He nodded, his breathing quickening. 'Quite clear.'

Mr Smith rose but Boy wasn't watching; he was reaching for the file, opening it, reading, and the words of David's statement stunned him.

He read of Connie's black lover, he saw the letter

that Romesh had sent her on the birth of Emily, Dora's statement telling of the ongoing affair after Romesh's release from prison, Revd Williams's statement which provided evidence of the start of the affair. He read Connie's statement refuting the charges and contesting David's claim to sole custody of Emily.

He read Mr Smith's notes, one of which stated, *My client is in a distressed state, and will not consider any contact with her family or friends – perhaps out of fear that they will be repulsed by these revelations. She will need their support, however, since it seems more than likely that the custody case will go against her.*

Boy copied out her address, closed the file, left the office, stopping by Miss Andrews' desk. 'Thank him for me, will you?'

She nodded, then put her hand out to him. 'Don't believe it, not all of it. I met her. She's an honest woman. Don't let all this nonsense destroy your love.'

He turned and left, walking through the streets, breathing in the special London smell of charred ruins. He stopped beside a water-logged crater and all he could think of was her with a lover, and a husband, and neither had been him, and he hated her.

He ordered beer at the club, then Scotch, whatever they had. He drank it all and wanted to wipe her from his life, his mind, and cursed himself for his wasted years of love.

Connie sat in the pub at lunch-time the next day stroking the chair, the table and smiling at the old woman who played 'Danny Boy' on the piano. Then she looked across at the nice kind man who had bought her drinks yesterday and the day before, and now he was here again, bringing her another from the bar.

'You are such a nice kind man,' she slurred. She lifted the glass. 'And this is nice and kind too. I didn't know it could be so kind. David did. He's always known. My rum and lime didn't do what this does. Do you know, I threw my topee out into the water as we left and it sank so I'll never return to India. I wrote though, to Romesh, to get him to tell them the truth.'

She peered at the man. 'Colin, it is Colin?' She smiled as he nodded. She drank her Scotch. She didn't like the taste but it dulled the images. 'They took my daughter, you know. We came off the boat and they pushed her into a taxi and took her off. Dora and David took her off.'

She was crying; she knew she was from the taste of her tears, but then she was always crying. Colin touched her hand. 'I'll get you another,' he said, leaving her.

She didn't want to be alone – and today she had never been more so. She looked after him; he turned and smiled. So she wasn't alone, here. But yes, she was. Oh God, yes she was. She drank the last of her whisky.

'They say I've been an unfit mother all along,' she mumbled to herself, wanting the whole world to hear her. 'They said I left her to go and help the refugees and neglected my child. Dora came and was a mother to her. They took her from me at the docks. I saw her face, I heard her cries.'

The barman came across. 'Go home, Connie, you've had enough. This has been going on long enough, you're too good for this. Just come back tonight and play the piano for us again. Stop tipping this stuff back. Go on, go and have a lie down.'

His face was red, he had a white tea towel slung over his shoulder. He turned as Colin came back. 'And you, clear off; I don't know you, I don't trust you. Leave her alone. She's been out of her mind the last three days, it's daft.'

Connie put out her hand for the Scotch. 'Don't be rude, Roy. He's a nice man, he's kind, and I want to be out of my mind.'

Roy shook his head. 'You watch him, Connie. There's something about him I don't like. He's not from around here, so what's he doing?'

Colin sat down, sipped his beer and said quietly, 'I've got business here, that's all. I'm buying your booze, the black market stuff, at twice the price, so put a sock in it or I'll tell your boss.'

Roy walked away and Colin nodded at her. 'Go on Connie, drink up, then I'll take you home. You look as though you could do with a bit of help.'

She lifted the glass. It felt so heavy; her lips were numb, her tongue, but it still burned her throat. So, she was still alive. 'Romesh is dead,' she told Colin. 'His uncle wrote. I received it three days ago. He died at Amritsar. I knew he would. He knew he would.'

Colin said nothing and she was grateful to him. She didn't want to hear his voice, anyone's voice, not when she was thinking of Romesh who had stood between her and David in the hotel room and taken the blows meant for her. She had screamed at him to go. 'Just go.'

'Come with me, Connie,' Romesh had pleaded.

'No, he won't hurt me. We haven't done anything wrong. Go.'

Romesh's eyes had been full of love, of pain. 'I'm sorry, I have to be there, Connie.' He had pushed past Dora whose face had been alive with joy as David brought his fist down onto Connie's cheek and nose.

Connie put down her drink. 'I've got a bump now. He broke it. I didn't notice the pain. Did Romesh when he died? His uncle said he was calling for calm.'

'Finish your drink,' Colin urged.

She shook her head. 'I don't want any more.'

He reached across and lifted it to her lips. 'Drink it, I said. I'm looking after you now, so do as I say.'

His voice was kind, his eyes were too. She drank, then stood. She staggered. 'I'll fight to get my lovely Emily back,' she said. 'I don't want David, not now, but how can they take my child away?'

The daylight was harsh but Colin's hand was firm on her elbow. 'Come on, I'll help you back.'

The air was cold. She felt sick, her head was spinning. She clutched him as he put his arm around her, holding her tightly to him. It was good to be held. Oh Mam, I wish it was you, or Boy.

'I'll fight for my child,' she cried as Colin helped her across the street. 'I can't live without her.'

He was leading her along Travers Avenue, into Gladstone Square, then along Swan Alley. 'You know so much, you even know the way,' she said, leaning into him, putting one foot in front of the other, then stopping at her door.

'Your room's up the stairs, isn't it?' Colin asked.

'First on the right.' She felt so ill. 'I can't go up the stairs,' she protested. 'I want to stay here.' She pulled away from him, and leant against the damp and torn wallpaper in the hallway.

Colin half-carried her, opening her door with the key she gave him. He laid her on the bed. 'I said I'd look after you. Now let's have these cold damp things off.'

She rolled onto her side, trying to lift her arm to pull him close so that he could hear her. She wanted to thank him, but all she could think to say was, 'Is it raining? I didn't realize.'

He nodded. 'Now just lie still, there's a good girl, and let me help you.' The room was going round and round. She clutched him. 'Shh,' he said gently, 'just pretend I'm your mother.'

His hands were so gentle as he undid her buttons, his voice as soft as Belle's would have been. Oh Mam. She closed her eyes and saw her mother and heard the softness of her voice. She opened her eyes and saw Colin's bare chest above her; she felt the cold on her skin and the sweat on her forehead. She was quite naked.

The room was still going round, and she couldn't lift her arms to push him away as his head came down onto her belly. She looked past him to a man in the doorway. Oh no. He held a camera. It flashed again and again. She struggled free, pushing at Colin, who called to the man, 'Did you get enough?'

The man put his thumb up, and was gone. Colin

grabbed at his clothes, dragged the sheet up over her and laughed. 'Message from Dora. "See you in court." It's watertight now.'

At 2 p.m. that day Boy was still at the club, knowing he should ring Belle, but unable to do so, because of the hate that was in his heart for Connie.

The porter coughed beside him. 'There's a telephone call for you, sir. Perhaps you would like to take it in the lobby.'

It was Miss Andrews. 'I remembered that you said you were staying at the St Albans. I think you should know that Mrs French has called in. She's been stripped and photographed by a man sent from Dora. She knows that there's now no hope of Emily's custody. I should hurry and find her. She's desperate. Though I'm surprised you haven't already.' Her voice was high with anger.

He dropped the receiver back onto its cradle, and leant his head against the glass alcove. Was he mad, quite insane? How could he have believed that Connie could ever have been dishonest? Bloody, sodding, Dora. He brought his fist down. What had he done?

He rang Belle now, telling her briefly all he knew, then took a cab to Connie's room, urging the taxi driver to hurry, but a bomb-damaged building had collapsed and they had to retrace their route and try again.

Connie thanked the bus-conductor as she got off the bus near the corner shop. Miss Andrews had been so kind. She had started to say something about a Mr Someone or other, but Mr Smith had stopped her. Connie shrugged. Emily was lost to her, and it was her fault.

She bought paraffin in the shop. The can was heavy, the handle dug in as she walked back to her room. She removed her clothes and took a sheet from the bed. She slopped paraffin over it; her eyes stung as she wound it round and round her body. She sat in the centre of the room.

'White for mourning,' she said, looking at the matches she held. 'I am becoming suttee, Romesh, Emily. I am expunging my sins. There is nothing more I can do.'

She took a match from the box, lowered her head and prepared to strike.

Boy slammed the taxi door shut, and ran up the stairs. He tried the handle. It was locked. He barged against the door. The wood splintered, the door opened. The smell of paraffin made him reel. He saw her, moved, knocked the match from her hand, and fell to his knees, holding her to him, feeling the paraffin soak into his own clothes. 'Oh Connie, what have we all done to you?'

25

Belle held her daughter tightly when Boy led her into the kitchen and it was only now that Connie wept.

'She needs to rest,' Boy said quietly to Belle who nodded.

'Wait here for me,' she told Boy. 'Make some tea, or there's a whisky in the cupboard.'

Boy shook his head. There'd been enough drinking done to last a lifetime. He watched Belle lead Connie from the room, then removed the whisky and the brandy from the cupboard, taking them back to his own house, the cold gripping his throat, the snow clinging to his boots. He put them into the sideboard and locked it, remembering her pleas on the train. 'Give me a drink, let me have some. It helps, I've discovered it helps.'

Belle tucked the bedclothes in around Connie, stroking her hair. 'You're safe now,' she said. 'You've come home,'

Connie clutched at her mother. 'On top of everything I could have killed all those people in the house if I had burned myself. There is nothing left in me that is any good. Do people die of grief?' she asked. 'I hope so.'

Belle stayed with her until she slept, then drank tea with Boy in the kitchen whilst he told her all he knew.

'I failed her,' he said. 'I believed it all, for a while. I hated her and it was jealousy. I love her; I always have and I always will – but for a while I failed her and it could have killed her.'

Belle stirred her tea. 'We've all failed her. I was the one who kept Binnie on at the mission and then sent Dora across to India, just because it was easier than keeping her here and now that damn woman has taken all that Binnie wanted from me. Somehow I've got to live with the knowledge of that.'

Boy listened to her then as she told of Binnie's attempted seduction and there was only the ticking of the clock to be heard when she had finished.

At last he stirred. 'All we can do now is to try and help her fight the case, and if we fail, to try to make her life worth living.'

Connie barely noticed Christmas come. She shook her head when Belle handed her a coat and scarf. 'Come along, it's the carol service. They'll all be so pleased to see you.'

'No, Mam.' It was such an effort to speak.

Each day the snow grew higher and each day she sat at the window and looked out onto the whiteness and thought of the hills – the trays she and Emily had slid down on – the valleys they could see when the mist rose – the snow-tipped Himalayas.

But each time Dora slid into the image. Why hadn't she seen it, why hadn't she realized? She should have done. This woman was the one who had deliberately broken her doll. She should have done. Was she stupid?

Each day she walked out into the village but Belle or Boy were there, with her, steering her beyond the pub, pulling her away. How did they know? She searched the cupboards when they were in bed because the pain tore and split her body apart, but there was no alcohol. Emily, oh Emily.

At the end of January Connie was informed of the date for the hearing of the divorce and custody case. She said nothing, just smoothed the letter out on the table, again and again. Belle reached over and held her still. 'We haven't given up. Boy's been in daily contact with Mr Smith; just try and cling to some hope.'

Connie stared at her mother, at the grey-white hair, the lines which were etched deep, and the pain in her eyes. 'You will never see your grandchild, Mother.' Her voice was brutish and cruel and she wanted to strike her, again and again, because of the pain she was feeling.

Belle said nothing for a moment, then pulled her daughter to her. 'Oh yes I will and so will you. If not now, then someday, Connie Symmonds, and shout at me all you like, if it helps you, my darling.'

Connie wanted to sink into her mother's arms but even there there would be no comfort. There never could be until Emily was home, and it was driving her mad, quite mad. 'I'm sorry, Mam,' she whispered.

'You need never say that word to me.'

They sat together listening to Boy on the telephone in the hall.

'But Mr Smith, surely we can get David and Dora on living together. Has that private detective turned up anything?'

Boy tapped his foot in frustration as Mr Smith said, 'Mrs Bailey returns to her own flat every evening and takes care of the child only when Mr French leaves in the morning. Their behaviour is exemplary. It is Mrs French who appears to have been – shall we say – indiscreet.'

Boy gripped the receiver. 'Trusting, not indiscreet. Connie would never be indiscreet,' he shouted, slamming the phone down. He was getting nowhere. They'd written to David explaining the truth, sending copies of Romesh's other letters but they were all so nebulous, it was infuriating. They had told David of Dora's lies about her past. The only reply had been an acknowledgement from his solicitor.

Belle watched him, then looked at Connie whose eyes were fixed on Boy. She left the kitchen. 'I'm going to sort out the bedlinen, it's time there was order out of chaos somewhere.' Her voice was light, and she wondered how it could be. She touched Boy's shoulder. 'Go and sit with her.' Her daughter needed love.

Boy sank onto the kitchen chair. Connie was so thin, so haunted. He couldn't bear it.

She reached for his hands, his long fine hands. 'Little Boy, you are so kind to me, but do I deserve it? I met my old lover and allowed myself to lose my child. I drank myself stupid and ruined my chances. Dear Boy.' His eyes were so brown, his cheek-bones so fine, like—

She wanted to rest her head on his shoulder, be near him, but if she bore the pain herself perhaps no-one would take Emily. If she paid for her stupidity perhaps she could keep her child.

Boy said, 'Let me get you some tea?'

She shook her head. 'No, I'll get some for you.'

He pushed her back down. 'I'm the one looking after you now. You looked after me for so long.' She watched as he poured water from the kettle into the pot.

'You've grown into a man, Boy. You've grey hair—' She tailed off, moved out of the kitchen into the sitting-room. She stood at the window, feeling the cold. She must not relax, she must not for a minute feel comfort or pleasure or she would lose Emily.

The hearing was so quick. The divorce was granted and Connie lost custody of her child. She stood outside the court with Belle and watched David drive away. He hadn't looked at her once.

'At least you have access for two hours once a month,' Belle said, her gloved hand gripping her daughter's arm.

'Under their supervision,' Connie said slowly. 'Do they think I will corrupt my own child?' Why wasn't she crying? Because she was dead.

They stayed at a hotel that night and it was Belle who rang Boy, it was Belle who arranged with David that they would see Emily in the morning, and then not again for a month. It was Belle who offered Connie a brandy. 'No, Mam,' Connie said, because nothing would dull what had happened.

Nothing, nothing – and it was this word that played all night in her mind and danced amongst the shrieks of laughter from her daughter as they played in the hills, or rode their ponies over the Punjab plain, or sat together over a book last thing at night in the cantonment.

Nothing, nothing, nothing was left to her, but the loan of her daughter every month for two hours, and she didn't understand what had happened, and why. 'For God's sake, why, Mam?' she screamed as dawn broke.

They took a taxi, then walked down the path past pruned rose-bushes and otherwise empty flower-beds to the house that David had rented. He opened the door and was shocked again at Connie's appearance; she was so thin, so pale, so hopeless. He had wept last night until Dora had taken him in her arms. 'Don't forget what she did to you, and is still doing.'

He felt the anger rise again and ignoring Belle's out-stretched hand said, 'I had to resign my commission because of the scandal.' His voice was dry and hard.

Connie looked first at him, then past him to Dora. 'So you didn't win a major's rank as well. But surely it is enough for you that you took my family. Is this in repayment for the doll my mother didn't buy you?' Words were coming but where from? They were distanced from her.

She turned back to David. 'I will tell you again that I am innocent. You have taken my child from me, a grandchild from my mother.' She reached for Belle's arm. 'And you insult me by insisting that I am chaperoned with my own child. Please David, reconsider. Remember us as we were.' She saw the hesitation in his face. 'Please, David.'

Dora said, 'Yes, do remember, David, all of it.'

The hesitation was gone. He said, 'Bring Emily, then in two hours all this will be over.'

Dora disappeared and David moved back from the door, watching as Dora led Emily out into the hall. Connie held out her arms and moved towards her child.

'Em, it's me, it's Mummy, my darling.' She hadn't known joy and pain could mix as they did at the sight of her child. 'It's me.' It had been so long.

But Emily clung to Dora's hand, pulling at her skirt, hiding her face. Connie called, 'Emily, it's me, Mummy. I love you. What has she done to you? What has she said?'

She pushed against David's hand. 'Let me in. Let me hold her, explain. Why is she looking at me like that?'

She turned to Belle. 'Mam, why?'

Connie turned again to Emily who was clinging to Dora, horror on her face as she looked at her mother. She was trying to get behind Dora. 'Get away, get away,' Emily shrieked and she was crying now and the noise rang through the house, through Connie, Belle.

Connie stood still, looking at the child she had not seen for four months, and at Dora whose face was shriven with concern whilst her eyes were full of satisfaction, and at David who was trembling, his arm still across her chest.

He said, 'Please, I beg of you, don't distress our child further. Haven't you done enough? You chose a black instead of her. Who knows what she witnessed.'

Connie grabbed his arm, wanting to push him away, and Dora, wanting to clasp her child to her and run so hard and fast that they would never find her.

She shouted into his face, 'She witnessed nothing. There was nothing to witness.'

David shook his head and shouted back, 'That is a lie, look at her. Why else do you have this effect on her?'

Connie looked at the horror on her mother's face, at the whiteness of her skin, then back at David, at Dora, and lastly at Emily and she wanted to weep. But she mustn't cry, not here, not in front of her child. She backed away, out onto the porch, onto the path and just stood there, still hearing Emily's cries, and watching another woman comfort her.

Belle held the door-frame, feeling weak, looking at Dora, then at David. 'What have you allowed this woman to do to your family? How can you believe her? You know Connie. She is honest, truthful.'

David shook his head, looking from Dora to Belle, to Connie, then to Emily. 'I thought I did, but she lied.' He was crying.

Connie watched as Emily ran to her father. She moved towards her daughter again. Again Emily shouted. 'Make her go, make her go. I hate her.'

That night Dora kissed Emily good night, sitting on her bed, stroking her hair. 'I'll keep you safe from her. I kept you safe when she had blood on her clothes at my party, after she had been with that black man she loved. Who knows what she did while she was with him? Who knows where she got that blood from? There was so much killing then, wasn't there? She was on their side, wasn't she? Poor Daddy, poor you. I won't ever leave you like she left you.

'Do you remember how I looked after you and Daddy while she went off to look after those refugees? She was probably with her boyfriend then too. But I'll always be here for you, always. You are my daughter now. I won't let her take you back. She only wants you because her boyfriend is dead, she just wants you to fill the gap until someone else comes along.'

She kissed Emily on the forehead and Emily hugged her, then called as Dora went out, 'Don't shut the door. I don't like the dark.'

Dora called back, 'I know that.'

Emily reached for her teddy and her doll. She was too old at eight but no-one could see her, here in her own room, her own bed. No-one, especially not that horrid woman who had come today and who had left her and Daddy to be with another man.

She was glad she had gone. She didn't want to see her ever again, she didn't want to hear the voice which dug deep inside her and twisted something and made her want to be back when she was young.

She looked at the door, at the light which was lying across the carpet, and slept, though again she dreamed of the smell of powder and lavender, the softness of someone who left her, while blood came under her door, across the light on the carpet, making it all dark, letting the man come and hold her mother, before she ran away with him, laughing.

Dora came later and looked down at the sleeping child. Sweat had drenched her hair though the air in the bedroom was cold. She saw the likeness to Connie but if she changed the child's hair it would not be so noticeable. She looked round the room. Then down again at Emily. So much better than a doll, eh, Connie?

In June 1948 Connie received a letter from a panel of psychiatrists asking that she cease her monthly attempts to see Emily because of the effect on the child's mental health. In the same post was a letter from David, asking her to stand aside until Emily requested a meeting.

She took both letters into the garden and stood looking over the fields to Longdale where the buckets churned up the slag-heap as they seemed always to have done. She heard Boy and Belle behind her.

'What will you do?' Belle asked.

Connie didn't turn and face them but kept her eyes on the buckets. 'I shall not visit.'

Boy said, 'You will write, though, make that a condition?'

Connie smiled bitterly. 'Oh yes, I shall write every week but do you think she will see me in black ink on white paper? Do you think you can kindle love in an envelope? Love is born out of touch and sense and feel and laughter.'

She shredded the letters, dropping them onto the lawn, grinding them beneath her heel.

Belle felt more sadness than ever before in her life. 'I blame myself. I should have told you that Binnie tried to seduce your father, to take my place, to take from life always what she felt she was owed. I never dreamt that Dora would feel the same. I should have warned you. I should have done something. I should do something now, but there is nothing.'

The wind tugged at the trees, at the sweet-pea canes, at the young green wheat in the field. Connie turned now and put her hands out to Boy and Belle. 'What do I do now, where do I go until she sees me, if she ever wants to? It hurts so much. It hurts too much, I can hardly breathe.'

Boy took her hand, Belle the other. Belle said, 'You can either wait and live an empty life, or you can fill it – and wait. One day Emily will know the truth. Write, as Boy says, tell her the truth again and again. Tell her of your love, remind her of the years you've had. One day she'll grow up and see Dora for what she is.'

Connie shook her head. 'But what if Emily becomes another Dora, as Dora has become another Binnie? What if the pattern repeats?'

Boy gripped her hand too tightly. It didn't matter, the pain couldn't touch her. He said, 'The Jesuits say that if you give them the child for the first seven years, they will give you the man. Emily is eight. Trust her, trust all that you have given her. Give her time.'

Connie looked down at his hand, then up at the thin, kind face. 'How much time, though, Boy?'

'As long as it takes. Love will wait a lifetime.'

Belle looked at them both, and kissed first Connie, then Boy, and could have wept for the children they had once been, the laughter they had shared, the hopes they had held and it was as though it had all turned to dust but somehow they had to go on.

26

Connie left for Back Dock Mission on the following Monday after Mary and Sandy said they needed her. She hadn't slept since she had agreed not to visit Emily, but then again, she hadn't cried. She had walked, talked, but not smiled.

Boy watched her leave, wanting to travel with her, carry her case, hold her close but it was as though no-one existed for her.

'Will the mission help?' he asked Belle.

'Perhaps, that's why I asked Mary to create a need for her, otherwise we shall have to leave it to time, and love.' She deadheaded the marigolds, breathing in their pungent scent. Please God, let it help, and let Boy be steadfast for a while longer because she was convinced by now that Connie loved Boy, though she hadn't recognized the fact.

Connie secured the train window and watched the countryside turn from wheat to collieries, smelling the sulphur from the engines, forcing herself to remember a time before Emily, when she had travelled with her mother from Rempton to the mission to meet her father. Would it all seem dark?

Central Station was so busy still; so many people, so much noise, so like Bombay. But of course it wasn't. There were no betel stains, no Hindus, Sikhs, Muslims, and she felt a pang of loss for India, for Romesh, but it was as nothing against the greater pain.

She took a tram; it rattled and clanked past bomb-sites. There was dust and desolation. She got off and walked, unable to sit still any longer, weighed down by despair.

Her case was heavy. She changed it to the other hand, then stopped, smelling the charred ruins. She watched the children who were scrambling over the rubble and skimming round the craters. Emily, Emily.

Their voices were loud.

'Pirate ship coming up on the right. Fight off the boarders.'

'Take the men round the point.'

'Aw, get off me back, man.'

She picked up her case again, looking at the children one more time, seeing their excitement, their energy, their ability to use desolation to create something better. 'Canny little beggars,' she murmured and as she walked on her bag didn't seem as heavy.

She reached High Road and now she would have known her way blindfold. The houses crowded even closer, it seemed so dark. A woman scrubbed her doorstep, another wiped the grime from the window-sill. Had nothing altered in all the years she had been away? Life went on; it had to.

She stopped. 'Mrs Gribble? It's Connie Symmonds.'

Mrs Gribble turned. Her hair was quite white, her hands gnarled. She held Connie's hands. 'Bye, bonny lass, it's been a while. How's your mam? Haven't seen her for a couple of months. How're you? Had your troubles, I hear.' Mrs Gribble looked around and nodded at the rubble where Newsome's sweet-shop had been. 'Some more than others. You just remember that.'

Connie stood with her. 'Ay, some more than others. I'll see you again.' She moved on; Mrs Gribble called after her. 'It was dreadful that Mary's bairn was killed. Joseph was a grand lad, a credit to her, to your mam and your da. But it's grand that she's got the new boy.'

Connie waved, then walked on, hearing the echoes of the gang running out of the alley, hearing the neighbours berating Mary's coloured son, then accepting him, and finally loving him. Poor Joseph, poor Mary and Sandy.

She saw the church and stopped. No, she wouldn't go

in that way. She retraced her steps and walked down the back alley, ducking beneath the washing. She opened the door into the mission yard. Would the garden still be there?

It was just as they had left it. Sweet peas on their canes, the grass they had sown, the cinder path. She walked down, stopping halfway, looking at the spot where her doll had landed. She thought she heard Dora's laugh. She dropped her case and clutched her arms, thinking she was going to faint with pain. Emily, Emily.

'Connie, you've come, at last you've come.' Mary ran down the path and held her, talking of the taxi they should have sent, the lunch that was nearly ready, and old Matt who was still in the mission carving nativity figures.

'He remembers you, and wants to talk to you about India. He was there years ago.' Mary took her case and pulled her into the kitchen. 'Ignore the windows, they need cleaning, but it's so dusty everywhere out there. It'll be better when they've rebuilt.'

The kitchen was just the same. Connie ran her fingers along the grain of the table. 'I remember making toffee with the gang.'

Mary said, 'Sit down, lass. Sadie's coming to see you tomorrow.'

Connie shook her head. 'I don't think I can bear to see anyone.'

'Perhaps they can't bear not to see you.' Mary's voice was gentle. 'Sadie's husband was killed, you know that, do you?'

Connie shook her head. 'Poor Sadie. Romesh, my lover, was killed. My daughter is lost.' Her voice was harsh and for a moment there was silence, then the door burst open and a young boy ran in.

'Mam, Mam, I want to go the rec., please, with the gang.' He stopped when he saw Connie. His socks had rolled down round his ankles, his knees were dirty, his face was almost identical to Sandy's. 'And can I take some bread and dripping so I don't have to come back until tea-time?'

Mary grinned, and cut some bread, passing Connie the dripping. 'Get that ready for him, will you, Connie, while I put some water in a flask? Now, the whole gang are going, are they, Alex?'

Alex nodded.

'Fine, then be back by five, and no further than the rec. Your 'da'll check, but say hello to Connie, Belle's daughter, before you go.'

The boy waved and was gone, running out through the door, through the yard, slamming the gate behind him. Connie licked the dripping off her fingers, then said, 'I'm sorry, Mary. I just feel so hopeless. I shouldn't have said what I did.'

Mary hugged her. 'You can say what you like here, bonny lass. Get it all out, then start to live again. There are so many having to do that.'

Connie put the dripping back in the meat-safe. 'Has young Alex helped to replace Joseph?'

Mary hung the tea towel over the fire-guard. 'How can you replace a child? But he has helped to heal us, and bring us joy again. And one day you'll feel that, with or without another child.'

'Will she ever come back to me?' Connie blurted out, leaning against the wall.

Mary paused. 'I don't know, but whether or not she does, you have survived the war, you are one of the lucky ones. You must rebuild as so many others are having to do. You are not alone in having to bear grief, Connie. Look outside and remember that.'

Connie walked all afternoon because she couldn't face the new babies that needed bathing. She checked on Alex, she watched the children playing on the bomb-sites, the women working. She sat in the park and thought of nothing. She returned to the mission in the evening. She wouldn't put Alex to bed, she wouldn't bath the babies but lay in her room and listened to the sounds of life in the house, and wondered how laughter could still exist.

In the morning Sadie came and drank coffee in the kitchen with her, talking of the hospital she was now working in, her mother who had been bombed out and was living with her. 'I just wish she could cook,' Sadie groaned and laughed. How could she laugh when her husband was dead?

They talked of the gang. 'Flo married a Yank. She lives in Texas, in the lap of luxury,' Sadie said.

Connie shook her head. 'Such a long way.' She looked at the clock. How much longer would Sadie stay? Couldn't she see it was time she left?

Sadie leaned forward. 'Let's make toffee. Mary's got enough sugar – just don't ask where it's come from. The kids could do with a treat; Alex can give it to the gang this afternoon.'

Connie just wanted to sit here in the kitchen, in a place which had never known Emily.

Sadie dug out the pan, the ingredients, hauled Connie to her feet, threw her an apron. 'Get stirring, girl.'

The spoon seemed too heavy, the toffee too hot, but she stirred while Sadie talked of the day Walter had come in and sent them packing, of the stones the gang had thrown at Connie, of the fight she and Connie had, of Dora who had always tagged along, of Dora who had dropped Connie in it by telling her mother she knew about the facts of life, of Dora who had broken the doll. Sadie's voice went on and on. For God's sake, would she never stop, would she never go?

'Do you remember Dora—' Connie picked up the pan and hurled it across the room. She screamed, 'For God's sake, shut up about Dora. She's taken my child, she's taken my family. She's a cow. I hate her, I hate her.' She was pummelling Sadie. Mucous ran from her nose, tears from her eyes. 'I hate that bitch. She's destroyed me, like she's always wanted to do. I wish Mam had thrown them out. I wish Da had never taken them in.

I wish she'd been killed by a bloody bomb and never come out to India.'

Sadie was gripping her hands, pushing her back warding off her blows, saying nothing.

'Why don't you bloody well say something, you've never stopped since you got here, you stupid woman?' Connie shouted, pulling away from Sadie, standing still now, with her arms hanging at her sides, her chest heaving.

Sadie rubbed her arm. 'Well, they say it's better out than in, bonny lass, and you owe me a belting or two. Somehow we had to get you to break.' She waved towards the toffee which was splashed across the room. 'Now you'll have to clean up that mess – good for the soul, they say.' She was smiling but her eyes were watchful and now Connie began to laugh and she felt the load lifting from her shoulders, the darkness easing.

'Not so fast,' Connie said. 'Alex needs his toffee. We'll both clean up and make some more. Remember I owe you a few beltings? You'll get one if you don't agree.'

But then tears were coming, racking Connie's body, and she hugged Sadie because they were streaming down her friend's face as well. 'I'm so sorry about your man,' Connie said. 'So sorry I saw no further than myself. So sorry any of this had to happen to any of us.'

Connie worked all week with the new babies, and though it hurt her more than she could imagine to bath a baby as she had once bathed Emily, somehow the rawness faded. On Sunday, as she was packing her case, Mary told her that next week they would be taking the pregnant daughter of one of their old mothers.

'We didn't do enough to break the pattern,' Mary said.

Connie continued to force her clothes into the old suitcase. 'I've been watching the kids on the bomb-sites. They're wonderful, they find hope where there seems to be none, but it's not enough. They need time out of it to see another world, to breathe deeply, to have a change. Mam had evacuees. Some loved it. Their mothers came. Some of them loved it too. It just gives them a break, lets them recoup, rethink.'

She pressed the lid of the suitcase down. 'Sit on that, Mary.' She laughed as Mary lay across it and snapped the case shut.

Mary rested her chin on her hands. 'I'm not getting up until I know whether you are coming back to help, or whether that look on your face means what it used to mean with Belle, that there was a plan brewing?'

Connie pushed her from the case. 'It means, madam, that we have a great big vicarage with most of the rooms closed off. It's simple logic. They need to be filled. What do you think?'

Mary dusted herself down. 'Couldn't have put it better myself. I'll be sorting out families here, you'll be sorting out accommodation there.' Mary smiled, then said, 'But can you cope with the children? Will it be too much of a reminder of Emily?'

Connie picked up the suitcase. 'Everything is a reminder of her, but look around, there's so much that needs doing – and I have nothing to do. I've sat in the house since I returned. I haven't even been to the beck; it's as though I died for a while.'

'But would you rather do something for yourself, re-train, get away from helping others? It might be good for you.'

Connie shook her head. 'It comes back to patterns. I can't change mine, and I really don't want to. It's one I wanted my daughter to know so she could choose which way to go.' She stopped, her voice failing.

Mary said, 'She will remember; there have been enough years with your voice pounding in her ear 'oles.' Mary was grinning, but her eyes were serious. 'She will re-member. It will surface one day.'

Boy and Belle listened to Mary the next morning, sharing the receiver. 'It worked, she arrived at the idea herself.

Sadie was wonderful. Connie will be back in the early afternoon. I suggest you take her straight out for a walk, to the beck.'

The air was so clean, the sun so strong as Connie walked with Belle and Boy out along the lane to the beck. The clouds were scudding across the sky, the wheat was cracking in the heat, the leaves were rustling as the branches above them rubbed together in the breeze. There were blackberries ripening. The children would like those, the mothers too. They could make jam to take back.

Connie looked at Belle and Boy. When should she ask Boy? Not yet, wait until the beck. It had been their favourite place as children – they had slid on trays down the slope, they had paddled, caught minnows. The beck was where she had told him she was going to India. The beck was their place. Yes, that was where she would ask him. Would he agree? Surely he would, but then it was a lot to ask.

They were out of the lane now, into the sunlight, walking across the rock-dotted ground. She looked towards the beck. It was dammed, down beneath the willow.

Connie said to Boy, 'How long has that been there? It must be perfect for children to swim safely.' Should she ask him now?

He was hesitating, slowing. She caught at his arm. 'Who made it?'

Boy shrugged. 'I don't know.' He strode on ahead of them.

Belle said quietly, 'He hasn't been here since you left.'

Connie stared at her mother, then back to Boy. Confusion made her stand still. 'I don't understand.'

Her mother shaded her eyes and watched Boy sit on the bank. 'Don't you?'

Connie began walking again. 'How strange men are,' she said, wondering if she should ask him immediately. When she reached him she flopped down, watching as he flicked stones across the still pool, counting the jumps the pebbles made.

'Bet I can beat you,' she said.

Boy handed her some pebbles. 'Best of three,' he challenged.

She looked at his fingers, so long and thin, so like Romesh. She remembered that hot night in the mission when Romesh had held her box, the feeling of coming home, the warmth. She turned away, unable to bear the image of the man she had loved.

'Come on,' Boy made her take the stones. 'Best of three.'

He threw. She watched the stone jumping, then another, then the third, and by that time the blurring had left her eyes. Two of hers sank and the last only bounced twice.

Boy turned to her. 'You see, I have grown up. You always used to beat me. Can you see that?' He was smiling, but his eyes were not and she couldn't understand. She didn't reply, but instead looked at the pool. 'I have something I need to ask you.'

She then explained to Boy and Belle the need to bring children and their parents out to the countryside for a break. 'You know how much your evacuees enjoyed it. I will do all the work, I promise I will. But we'd need to open up the vicarage and that is a big thing to ask of you, Boy.' She stopped and then continued. 'I thought I could work at the school, to fund it. I'd make sure the children would be no trouble. I thought we could follow up on the unmarried mothers and their children too. Have them out here for a holiday to try to break the patterns—'

Boy shook her. 'Shh, let us get a word in edgeways, will you? You always did talk too much.'

Connie pulled at the grass while Belle laughed.

Boy said, 'Yes, you can open up the rest of the house, but you or your mother would have to move into the vicarage in case the children need you in the night. I use only the kitchen and small sitting-room, a bedroom and my office. Those are the only places which will be off limits.'

Belle groaned. 'Well, I am certainly not going to move

anywhere; I'm far too old to be getting up and down for children. It'll have to be you, Connie.'

Connie hugged and kissed Boy. 'You are the same wonderful person you always were. How can I thank you?'

Boy wanted to tell her that she could hold him, kiss him, press herself against him, and love him for ever but instead he said, 'Don't work at the school, work for me. I need someone to organize me, type up my notes, help with my research, my manuscripts, hassle my agent, protect me from my publisher and his boozy lunches, organize my diary. It needs to be someone I can trust, someone who knows me. I'll pay you, it will provide some funding. I suggest you try the squire for the rest. He's a mellow old boy now, isn't he, Belle, and his life wouldn't be complete without some member of the Symmonds family trying to touch him for a worthy cause.'

He laughed at the joy in her face and wanted to reach out and draw her to him, but it was enough that she would live in his house and work beside him. He must be patient for a little longer, he must discover if Connie felt love for him, as Belle had said she did.

But what would he do if there was no love? What he'd done so far, he supposed, feeling her hand on his knee. He looked at her. No, he could not go on as he had done. He would have to leave if she didn't love him – it would be too much agony to stay.

27

Connie and Boy had spring-cleaned three bedrooms by the middle of the next week, washing down the walls, drinking the tea that Belle brought, hanging sheets on the line, and blankets too. When they finished the women decided that one bedroom needed painting.

'Cream?' Connie suggested.

'What else?' Belle agreed. 'Do you remember the mission hall all those years ago?' Mother and daughter looked at one another. How could they ever forget? And how could Connie forget the mission school?

'There's some in the shed,' Boy offered.

The two women painted all Thursday while Boy worked on his novel, his sleeves rolled up, a pencil behind his ear. Connie brought him tea, her hands smeared with emulsion. 'Do you need turps for that?' Boy asked, holding her hand, turning it over, wanting to kiss her palm.

'Little you know, bonny lad – that's for gloss. You just get on with your work and leave the important stuff to the women.'

She laughed as she left and that night wrote to Emily, telling her how she had spoken to the squire who had promised his support, how they would be able to take several children this very weekend, how they would not be replacements for her, how she loved her daughter. She described the beck, the mission, the paint they were putting on the walls, the paint she and Belle had put on the mission walls so long ago.

The next day she rang Mary and said, 'Let's have three children and one unmarried mother and her child on Saturday morning. The following weekend we can take more, when the rooms are all finished.'

That evening Boy helped her to make up the beds, three in one room, a bed and crib in the other. The third bedroom smelt of paint.

'Sleep in mine, I'll take the camp-bed in the study,' Boy said. 'You can't sleep there, not yet.'

She shook her head. 'You're doing enough, Boy, I can't ask you to do that. I'll have the camp-bed.'

She wouldn't let him argue, but carried her bedding through to the study. 'Anyway, I like it here, there's a sense of you.'

The evening sun lit up her hair, her eyes, her lips. Boy argued, 'But I want you to be comfortable.'

She said, 'I will be, I feel safe anywhere that you are, or have been.'

He carried through the camp-bed, erected it, and watched her make it up. She was aware of his eyes and turned. 'Would you rather I left it until they come? Will it be in your way?'

He shook his head. Nothing she did, or was, would ever be in the way. 'Leave it, I don't notice things around me when I'm working.'

He would notice her, though, the shape of her body on the sheet after a night's sleep, the scent of her in his room.

She looked towards his desk. 'On Monday I will start work, clear up that huge pile of correspondence, type up the notes, earn my keep, earn your generosity. You are so good to involve yourself.'

He shrugged. 'No, I'm not good, I'm just following in James's and Helen's footsteps, supporting good ideas. Mother and Tim do it over in America too; old habits die hard. I'm just wondering whether we can cope with the onslaught of your typing.' He laughed. 'Can teachers type?'

She looked out at the setting sun which lit up the oil-lamp on the desk, the typewriter, the ink-well, and, as clearly as though they were here in the room, she heard the croaking of frogs and the clicking of geckos, and felt the sultry heat of an Indian evening. She moved to the typewriter, touched its keys. She saw Romesh and felt his heat against her. 'Oh yes,' she said softly. 'I can type.'

She and Boy picked up Alice, her baby and the children in Tom Willis's cart, bumping Alice up, laughing as the three boys vaulted on board. 'We don't need help, we're canny buggers,' the eldest shouted, standing up with his chest pushed out.

Connie handed the baby to Alice and somehow kept a straight face as Boy's mouth gaped. She put her hands on her hips. 'You'll walk the whole way, young Danny, if I hear any more of that talk, now sit down and behave yourself.'

Boy climbed up onto the seat, took the reins, shook them over the horses and whispered, 'My God, three years without the evacuees and I'd become quite civilized.'

'Writers should make sure they keep their fingers on the pulse, bonny lad,' she murmured. 'Think of it as research.'

Boy clicked at the horses, glanced behind at the boys, then back at her. 'Just you make sure you make a note of it all and stop sniggering – research assistant.'

That afternoon the sun was soft, the heat gentle, and the sound of the harvester loud as they stood with the boys watching the rabbits fleeing the machine, feeling the dust in their throats.

'It's so big, missus,' Danny said. 'I didn't know the world could be as big as this.'

She touched his shoulder. 'It's even bigger, you know. It stretches for miles over the horizon.' She pointed. 'Beyond that are oceans bigger than the sea which reaches Newcastle. There are people who speak a different language, who need a different colour to deal with the heat of their countries.'

'Aye, there are darkies at the docks,' Paul said,

straddling the stile. 'I never thought of where they came from.'

On the way to the beck they told the children of the hares, the pheasants, the partridges. Samuel found the gamekeeper's gibbet and he shrank back at the sight of the vermin strung on the wire. He clung to Connie's legs.

'It's all right. Old Tim's a bit of a devil and hangs those up to show the squire he's doing his job. It's time he stopped, but it's an old country habit.'

Samuel said, 'It can stay here, an' all.'

In the lane Danny said, 'Eeh, it's as dark as the back alley beneath them branches.' He whipped the blackberry bushes with a twig.

Boy put his hand on the boy's shoulder. 'If you leave those alone, you'll be able to come back and pick them in a month or so. We can make a pie with the ones we don't eat.'

Danny looked up at him, his face alight. 'Can I take some back to me mam?'

Boy nodded. Danny ran on, catching up with the other boys, pointing to the bushes, swaggering. Connie looked at Boy. 'Oh, so you're cooking, are you?'

Boy stuck his hands in his pockets. 'Well, when I said we, I think I meant you.'

'No deal, we means we.'

Boy laughed. 'I don't think I care for this American slang. As a writer I protest, and as a writer I need to look after my hands. I can't be mixing up flour and rolling pastry.'

Connie picked up an old branch and waved it about. 'I think it would be better if you looked after your head. Give in, say "we", and you'll live to write another day and it's me doing the typing anyway, remember.'

Boy ducked, weaved, and ran along the lane, shouting at the boys. 'Come on, get away from her, she's just a witch in disguise.'

Samuel looked startled and grabbed at Danny but he wasn't fast enough and Boy scooped him up instead and ran on, with the boys whooping and laughing behind. Connie chased them but slowed, laughing too much, feeling the sun on her face as the lane ended and the meadow lay before them.

She dropped the branch, panting, holding her sides. 'I'm too old for all this, and you are a cruel wicked young man, Boy Driscoll.'

Boy was whirling Samuel round and round. He looked up, brought the boy into land, called to the others way over by the dammed beck. 'Go on, stay in the shallows, look for the minnows.' He too then held his sides. 'We're both too old for this, but my guess is, it'll make us young again.'

She ran down to him. 'If only it was Emily,' she said.

He put his arm round her as they walked on. 'One day, it will be.'

That night the boys were dragged, complaining, to the bathroom. 'Less of that,' Belle said. 'It'll be a bath every night.'

'Then I won't come again,' Samuel growled.

Connie hauled his shirt off. She'd wash it that night, hang it on the airer; it would be dry by morning. 'Oh dear, then who will eat the blackberry pie that Boy is going to make?'

Samuel looked at her, his face creased in thought, then put his toe in the bath, pulled a face and clambered in. She handed him the soap. 'Put your head back, I'll wash your hair.' He did so, his eyes tightly shut. Was Dora washing Emily's hair? No, she mustn't think of that.

Samuel said, as she rinsed his hair, 'Is Boy really helping with the cooking, did he give in?'

Connie squeezed the water from his hair and said, 'Come on, young man, those feet are still dirty. And yes, he gave in, *we're* going to make it.'

'Is he your husband?' Samuel asked.

Connie laughed gently. 'No, he's like my brother. I grew up with him, he's part of me.'

She sat while Belle read *The Secret Garden* to them but

they were asleep before she had finished the second page. They crept downstairs and in Boy's kitchen Alice was brewing tea, her baby asleep in the pram. Belle handed a mug to Connie. 'Take this through to Boy, he's trying to catch up with some work.'

She watched her daughter leave. She hadn't seen her so young, so carefree, since she had left for India and now, as she sat with Alice, she dared to hope.

Connie knocked, entered and stopped. Romesh! But it was Boy, at his desk, the half-light catching the line of cheek and chin, the colour of his hair, the set of the shoulders. She couldn't speak because of the catch in her throat.

He came towards her, smiling as he took the mug. 'I could do with a break,' he said, his voice soft and so unlike Romesh's, but now she realized that she couldn't quite remember the sound of the man she loved. She put her hand to her forehead and Boy led her to the sofa. 'Sit down, talk to me, tell me of your life, the shadows and the sunlight.'

The light was fading as she told him of the mission, the heat, the promise of it all, the children, Revd Williams; but it was only when darkness fell that she could tell him of Romesh, of the glory and the pain of their love, of his rejection of her, of the years of hope, of the marriage she had had with David.

'There was never love, I can see that now. But there was fondness. I could have built on that.' She fell silent at last.

Boy wanted to hold her, stroke her hair, feel the weight of her body against him as much to assuage his pain as hers, because the thought of her with Romesh, in the ruins by the river, feeling the heights of passion, was a slow death.

She said, 'Tell me of Fiona; I thought you might marry her. Who else has there been?'

He gripped his mug, telling her of Fiona with whom he had laughed and lost his virginity, of Mary, Celia,

Pauline, but wanting to tell her that there had never been anyone but her; never had been, never could be.

They fell silent and in the darkness Connie pushed away the images of the women he had known, glad that he had stopped, not wanting to hear of Venice and the hot bedroom, of Crete and the rocky hillside, feeling angry with him, and not knowing why.

There was a knock on the door. Samuel called, 'Connie, I can't sleep; those nasty things on the gamekeeper's gibbet keep coming into my head.'

'I'm coming.' She turned to Boy. 'Shall I turn the light on, when I leave?' She could see his face in the dim light from the moon and wondered why his eyes were so sad.

In December she travelled to Surrey to take Emily's birthday and Christmas presents. She had written to her every week, and to David at the beginning of the month to say she would be coming and she hoped that her patience would be rewarded.

She walked up the path and David answered the door. 'I'm sorry, Connie. She still won't see you and has only just started sleeping well.'

She could see that he was telling the truth and smiled. She would not cry. She handed him the parcels, talking loudly, hoping that Emily would hear, not wanting her to lose the sound of her mother's voice, as she had lost Romesh's.

She walked back down the path seeing the frost that still clung beneath the rhododendrons. Were such bushes still splashing their colour across the foothills of the Himalayas? Of course they were.

When the bush bloomed again, would Emily remember the hill station, the years together? She turned and saw the net curtain move, then Emily was at the window. Connie smiled, waved. The curtain dropped. She waited outside the gate for an hour but her daughter did not reappear.

That night Dora lay beside David. He was asleep but

how could she rest? She'd argued, pleaded, wept, but he would not stop Connie coming next year as she had promised she would. 'It's only fair, not just for her, but for the child. Who knows, Emily might want to see her again. It would be more healthy if she did.'

Dora pulled the sheet up and over her head. It was so cold in this damn country and she had to do her own cleaning; it wasn't what she had planned. Damn woman, taking her rank from her. She bloody well wasn't going to come back into their lives in any way, shape or form.

She'd managed to stop all but a few of the letters getting through to Emily. Those that had, had been picked from the mat by David. She'd told Emily quietly that she must burn them and Emily had told her she'd put them on the fire. She was a good girl, a lovely child, and Dora felt a tug at her heart. She'd never felt love like this before.

She rolled over onto her back, feeling David's warmth. One day they'd need to get further away – when Emily was old enough to leave home. That's when Connie would try and get her claws into her, that's when the truth might come out. Anxiety gnawed at her, but then she relaxed. There were years to think and plan for that.

Connie couldn't read in the train on her return to Newcastle. She just sat, trying to draw Emily's face in close to her. Why was her hair so short? It had always been long like hers. Oh God, my child.

She changed trains at Newcastle and Boy met her at Longdale, his breath visible in the chill. He was alone; thank heavens they had taken no children this weekend. She smiled at him.

He shook his head. 'You don't have to pretend.'

Could he read her mind? He took her arm. She felt safe. 'Shall we walk?' he said. 'She'll come back,' he said. Yes, he could read her mind.

There were oil-lamps in the windows of the cottages and a Christmas tree in one. By the co-op, children were carol singing, shaking their tins. She groped in her pockets, her gloves made her clumsy; she dropped the six-pence, tried to pick it up, couldn't get a grip. Boy scooped it up, dropped it in the box, tipped his hat to the vicar.

'Will I see you in church on Christmas Day, Philip?' the vicar asked. 'And you too, Connie?'

Connie bent her head, then nodded. Boy said, 'Oh yes, and we might have some of the children from Back Dock, and their parents, of course.'

'Of course,' the vicar said. 'Children shouldn't be apart from their parents at Christmas.' He stopped abruptly. 'I'm so sorry, Connie.'

She walked on. Boy ran after her, she felt his arm round her. Oh God, he would feel her body shaking from the sobs, he would hear this stupid mewling noise which she couldn't stop.

He said nothing, just held her as they walked between hoar-frosted hedgerows. As they entered Rempton her shaking stopped. She said, 'I don't know what I would do without you, Boy. You are better than a real brother could have been. I don't want anything to ever change between us.'

28

The next day Connie woke to the sound of church bells. She checked her watch. How could she have slept so well? Her daughter was in Surrey, she was here, but somehow the darkness didn't press on her as it had done.

She listened to the wind in the eaves, the creaking of the house. Below her Boy would be sleeping, keeping her safe. She looked at the clock again. No, he wouldn't, he'd be up boiling eggs, toasting bread, simmering the kettle and he'd laugh at her as she entered. He'd point to the chair. 'Might as well keep that warm,' he'd say. 'Then can you have a go at the typing this afternoon, when I'm editing the day's work?'

She swung out of bed, changing into her clothes, hurrying to the bathroom. There was ice on the windows. She scratched *Boy* in it then hurried along the landing past his bedroom, the room where she and her mother had always stayed. The door was ajar. Yes, he was downstairs.

There was no sound in the hallway. She walked to the kitchen, her footsteps slowing. Something was missing from the house, a calmness, a sense of belonging.

She opened the door, calling, 'Boy, there's something wrong.' He wasn't there. The fire was low in the range. The eggs were in a bowl on the table, the pan beside them. Bread was cut, the toasting-fork was near by, on top of a note.

Connie touched it. Her name was scrawled on the envelope. She read.

Connie,

My agent has rung. I have an earlier deadline for the manuscript. I have gone away to work. Perhaps you could continue with the filing and deal with my correspondence.

Boy

She read it again. It was so curt. She looked out across the garden to the bare vegetable patch where Revd Driscoll had worked in his panama. Why wouldn't those damn bells stop? She picked up her coat and ran round to Belle's wing, bursting into the kitchen, waving the note at her.

'He's gone. Boy's just upped and left and I don't know when he'll be back and we've Christmas to organize.'

Belle was buttering toast. She pointed to the chair. 'Sit down, but shut the door first; I don't care to live in a barn.' Her voice was crisp.

Connie shut the door but ignored the chair, pacing backwards and forwards instead. 'I don't understand him; I'm supposed to work for him and he just barges off.'

Belle watched as Connie fidgeted with her hands and her hair which was in a long plait. It was usually rolled high on her head. Belle said, 'He won't be back for Christmas. It's as he said, he needs some peace.'

Now Connie sat, bereft, angry. 'He said nothing last night.'

Belle shrugged. He might not have said anything to Connie but he had come in to her when Connie was asleep, sitting where Connie was now, his shoulders slumped in defeat. 'She thinks of me as a brother and never wants that to change. I can't bear it. I am going away. I might come back if I can cope with the truth, but I love her so much I fear I can't. I will make provisions through the bank for the holiday scheme to continue.'

Now Connie's shoulders were also slumped as she sat,

her eyes dulled. Belle said, 'Perhaps Boy has a lover to go to. It is difficult to live without passion, without companionship, love.'

Connie jerked upright and stared at her mother. 'But he never told me when we were talking. Surely he would have done?' Her voice trailed off and now there was darkness all around, and panic. She would lose him to someone else, he would not be here for her. She looked at her mother. 'She'll take him from us.'

Her mother turned away, wanting to shake her daughter. She said, 'Have the toast on the table if you like. I'll make some more for myself.' There was just the slam of the door in reply.

Connie tied the scarf tighter round her throat, pulling it up over her head against the east wind, walking along the edge of the fields as she and Romesh had walked along the narrow earth bunds.

She looked across to Longdale and could no longer remember the hot, humid path to the river, she could no longer remember the smell, or the structure of the ruins. She tried to pull it back to her, and the love for Romesh with it. The wind whipped it away.

She walked through Longdale, past the cottages, then alongside the slag-heap, smelling the coal. She strode on and on across fields, over stiles, and only when the light was fading did she turn, hearing the coughing of the bullocks as she neared Rempton.

She stopped by the school where she had hoped Emily would go, leaning on the hard cold stone wall, remembering the laughter of children. She walked past the cricket field; 'Oh, Da.' She passed the baker's, looking up at the light in old Mrs Green's window. Would the grandson take over one day?

She walked up the path to the church, opening the door; the hinges growled. She sat in the front pew and remembered Boy picking up the sixpence, talking to the vicar. 'I'll miss him,' she murmured. 'I'm trying not to be angry with him, but he's my brother, God. He's mine and I can't bear to share him.'

Belle was waiting for her in the kitchen of the wing. 'I knew you'd come here. The big house is too empty with no-one in it.'

She hung up Connie's coat, draped her gloves on the guard, propped her boots at the bottom. 'It'll smell like the classroom in here any minute now.' She smiled gently at Connie. 'Have you been reminding yourself of the hills, the hawthorn hedges, the cold wind?'

Connie nodded, looking at the geraniums on the window-sill. They would bloom again in the spring.

'Does spring always come?' she asked, looking at the plates on the dresser, the Christmas cards that had arrived.

'Always,' her mother replied.

Connie leant her arms on the table. 'It won't be home without Boy. Somehow I never thought of him having a life without us. I don't want anything to change, Mam. I need him here, I need you.'

The heat stole into her, thawing her hands.

Belle opened the oven door and checked the pastry. 'A few minutes more, I think.' She looked at the cloth in her hands, striving to be patient. She said, 'Did you love Romesh very much?'

Connie said nothing for a moment, then sat up, looking at her hands. 'Yes, very much, almost from the first moment. He filled an ache in me.'

Belle folded the cloth, smoothing it. She said, 'Tell me about it, that first meeting.'

Connie counted the lines on her hand, not wanting the pain of remembrance but then she said, 'I came into the school hut and Romesh was holding Boy's box and for a moment it was as though Boy was there. They have the same hands, cheek-bones, hair, the same eyes. I felt at home, safe. Romesh was the love of my life.'

Belle stood quite still and looked at her daughter and now her patience was at an end. 'For heaven's sake, you stupid, stupid girl, hasn't it occurred to you that your love for Romesh was born out of your love and need for Boy, that it is Boy you have always loved, as he has loved you? Can't you see the obvious?'

Connie couldn't sleep that night, and as dawn broke she crept to Boy's bedroom and climbed between his sheets, smelling him.

She thought of the ruins. Had she never loved Romesh? She shook her head; she had loved him deeply, but again she thought of that first evening, his hands on the box, and now she buried her face in Boy's pillow, knowing the truth at last.

Over breakfast she asked Belle, 'How can I love anyone when my daughter is not here? It's as well Boy has gone. I don't deserve happiness; it might bring me bad luck. I might never see Emily again.'

Belle slammed her hand on the table. 'How can you sit there and be so damn selfish and sanctimonious? That young man loves you. He has stood quietly at your side and waited for love, just as you wait for Emily, but he can bear no more. Connie, you are in danger of casting love aside. It is too rare and precious for that to happen. I won't allow it for either of you. There has been too much unhappiness.'

Connie leant away from her mother's fury, then stood up, pushing back her chair. 'It is so easy for you to say this when your life is over, your husband is dead. You've never lost a daughter, Mam.'

She stalked out of the house. Belle paled and sat down. She pressed her shaking hand against her mouth, then Connie came back into the room and held her mother. 'I'm so sorry, I didn't mean it. Your life's far from over. It's just that I don't know what to do.'

Belle hugged Connie, then said, 'The first thing you can do is to take the pie out of the oven, I can smell the burning pastry from here.'

Connie laughed, picked up the cloth. 'There you are, I told you you were getting on a bit.' She stooped over the

351

oven and Belle slowly felt the shaking subside. Connie brought the pie to the table. It was black at the edges and the gravy had bubbled out.

'What shall I do, Mam?' Connie asked, all laughter gone.

'He's at the Richmond Hotel. I have the number or you could go and bring him back, if you feel you love him.'

Connie said, 'I know I love him.'

The next morning Connie walked to the station; the ice crunched beneath her feet and a robin perched on the hedgerow. 'You should have mitts on those toes, you silly creature,' she said.

She was almost into Longdale when she saw Boy. She stopped as he did, and then they walked towards one another; his coat was swinging. They stopped again. She could have touched him if she had reached out. She did not.

He said, 'I couldn't stay away from Rempton at Christmas.'

She said, 'I was coming to find you. I can't bear it when you are not here. Oh Boy, I thought you had hands like Romesh, I thought you had his cheek-bones, his eyes, his hair, but it was he who had yours. I love you; I always have, I always will. I loved Romesh too, but you are the one deep in my heart; you always have been, you always will be.'

His face was soft, joy lit up his eyes as he reached for her, taking her hands in his. 'We will have lots of time, whilst we're waiting, to find out how bottomless our love is.'

Connie pressed his hands to her lips. Oh yes, now she knew just how much she loved this man who clearly knew that Emily was the point of her being, the focus of her life, and that Connie would always be waiting for her return.

They walked back, hip to hip, saying nothing. They

walked through to his study. He poured brandy, saying nothing. They stood close together, sipped, their eyes never leaving the other's. His were so dark, his lips were so full, he was so close and now the glass flipped from Connie's hand as their bodies touched. His mouth came down on hers, his arms were round her, and at last he felt her along the length of him, at last he could kiss her neck, her eyes, her hands, at last he could murmur into her soft rich skin.

'I adore you, I love you, you are my life.'

At last he heard, 'I want you, Boy, I can't bear to live without you.' She held his face, kissed his eyes, his cheeks, his hands. 'I will never leave you again.'

BOOK THREE

29

Emily leant against the rail of the ship, looking at the harbour they were approaching – Herakleion, Crete. Good God, she was sixteen; it was 1956 and her dad might have lost his job, but why did they have to move out here? And why hadn't they told her Crete was to be their new home, that this was not just a holiday? Why did they just drop it into the conversation over dinner last night? She pulled away as Dora put her arm round her.

'Oh for goodness sake, you're not still sulking. You'll turn me grey at this rate.'

'You already are,' Emily whispered.

Dora pretended not to hear, but made a mental note to rinse her hair again the moment they were settled. It simply wasn't fair; there were grey hairs every time she looked in a mirror, and what could she do about the bags under her eyes? Cucumber was supposed to tighten the skin; perhaps she should try it.

She took out her powder compact and dabbed her nose, looking at the fine lines around her eyes and the deeper ones to her mouth.

'I told you, Mother, it's not fair. I thought this was just a holiday. What about my A levels? I had plans, I wanted to go to university.'

Dora snapped her compact shut. 'Nonsense, only ugly girls go to college and that's because they won't hook a man and will need to earn a living. Now we can find you a nice husband when the time comes. Just think of Crete as a finishing school. Pinkie's wife will school you in cordon bleu cookery, in etiquette, and deportment. Put your shoulders back.'

'I don't care about etiquette,' Emily shouted, glaring at Dora.

'Don't frown, it creates lines, especially with your pale skin, and where is that blue chiffon scarf I told you to wear? The salt will ruin your hair and that colour does flatter your eyes, deepens the blue. And while we're here you must put some weight on – you're too slight. Men like cuddlesome girls. You must listen to me, my dear, because I haven't put my life on hold all these years for you to throw it away on riff-raff.'

People were lining the rail, gazing across to the harbour. The sea was dark blue and the sun was coming up behind Mount Dikte but in Emily the anger was still burning. She turned towards the ship's bridge, wanting to snap off the radio which was churning out folk music. Who wanted bloody lyres? She wanted skiffle. She wanted to go home.

'Look over there,' Dora insisted. 'Go on, look. Where would you get such lovely white buildings in England, or such clear blue skies? We'll have help in the house here, we'll have Pinkie as a neighbour. He's all set up, he has expatriate contacts. We'll have a bit of dignity and be able to hold our heads up and live well on your father's army pension. It'll be like India again.'

'It's still not fair,' Emily said, almost in tears. 'It simply isn't fair.'

Dora shook her arm. 'I'm afraid life isn't fair. It certainly wasn't fair when your father's firm was taken over and he was sacked, but one just has to make the best of things. Just think about that and stop moping. I think it's as well anyway – look at the company you were keeping, and after all we've spent on your education too. Yes, it's time we all had a change.'

Emily strode to the prow of the ship. By riff-raff Dora meant the youth club and Geoff. She heard Dora's heels clicking on the deck behind her, then her voice in her ear. 'You wouldn't have wanted to take that boy to the Conservative Club Dance, would you?'

Emily flared. 'He wouldn't have wanted to come

anyway – and he's not what all this is about. You lied, you said it was a holiday.'

Her father came up then, holding his panama firmly on his head, his jacket buttons strained across his large stomach. He frowned, his grey eyes concerned. 'No, Dora didn't lie, she just softened the truth. We didn't want you to be upset.'

'But can't you see what you've done? I didn't say goodbye to any of my friends, they'll think I just ran away – I just don't understand why you didn't tell me.'

The dockers were cursing and swearing on the quay now, hauling the hawsers, securing them. She left David and Dora, and leaned over the side, not wanting them to be near her. Grown-ups were such idiots. Why panic over someone like Geoff? Of course he wasn't marriage material – of course she wasn't going to throw herself away on someone of that class. Did they think she had no sense?

She glanced across at her parents, then down at the people who were waiting. Some called to relatives on board. At least that woman who had once been her mother hadn't been there when they boarded at Southampton. Emily had looked – she'd kept looking back and she hadn't come, thank God – and now she wept and it was for her friends, that was all.

David and Dora watched Emily from the prow. David rubbed his chin and said, 'We should have told her; she wouldn't have created, you know.'

Dora shook her head. 'Nonsense, you know how difficult she's been. Teenagers are impossible these days, and there was more than enough to worry about as it was. Just remember, David, *we* decided it would be neater this way.'

David nodded. 'You're right, I just don't like lying.'

Dora tucked her arm into his and they walked towards Emily. 'Neither do I, my darling, but sometimes it's necessary.'

David stopped. 'You did post that letter to Connie, didn't you? I promised her when she gave her permission that I would let her know in good time. Who knows, Emily might just have said goodbye, spoken to her at last. It would have tidied the whole thing up somehow. I warned Emily her mother might be there – perhaps Connie couldn't face it.' He shrugged and continued to walk until he stood behind his daughter.

Dora watched them. Of course she had posted the letter but not until too late. She had no intention of letting Connie anywhere near Emily – who knew what she'd blurt out? It was for this reason that she'd told Emily this was a holiday. God knows what the child would have done if she'd thought she was being taken from that butcher's boy. She might even have demanded to see her mother – just to be difficult.

Dora lifted her head and breathed in the sea air and felt the sun on her face. At last she was to be free of that bloody Connie. The nerve of the woman, coming down each Christmas, with her husband, and then that son of hers. She looked across to Herakleion and sighed with satisfaction. Here, the truth could not come out, the fear could die.

David called to her. 'Come along, Dora, we're disembarking. We should be in Ayios Nikolaos soon.'

The car they had ordered did not arrive and David was white with anger as they sat in the bus which rattled along the coast, climbing a pass through the mountains, then stopping near a small chapel. They watched other passengers scrambling off the bus, and hurrying to the chapel.

'For pity's sake,' David shouted to the driver. 'Drive on.' The sweat was pouring down his face and soaking into his collar which felt too tight.

The driver shook his head. 'Oh no – they come back. If no stop, have accident as punishment. They give offerings to St George.'

David half-rose, then sat down, fanning himself.

'Bloody natives. What the hell have we done, moving here?'

Emily laughed. 'You see, Mother – it's all been a mistake.'

Dora reached across the aisle and slapped her arm. 'Nonsense. When we get to Pinkie's it will be fine. We'll be among our own sort and you, my girl, will make sure you don't mix with these people. We don't want any more Geoffs, is that quite clear.' It wasn't a question.

The passengers were clambering onto the coach again, talking and laughing. Emily stared out of the window. Her arm hurt, she missed Geoff, the youth club; she wanted to go home, but Dora and David would not be there. This was her new home and she didn't know what to feel.

That evening Dora and David sat on the balcony with Pinkie and Marjorie and clinked glasses as they looked out over the sea.

Pinkie said, 'Tomorrow we'll introduce you to Phil and Betty Erley. They've been visiting friends in Herakleion for a few days but are due back by lunch. You'll like the circle there. Perhaps you've already met the Erleys though? They were in Ooty. He was in tea, came home in 49. He's put on a bit of weight since then, but haven't we all. He couldn't settle under the wogs. Took to teaching. He said he'd help your girl.'

Marjorie smiled. 'He's such a laugh – knows several people in Boston. That would be a good place for Emily to go, once she settles down. I feel for you Dora, having to cope with all these histrionics – one wonders if she takes after her mother, of course.'

There was a silence and Dora said coldly, 'I am her mother. I have eradicated any reminders of Connie. Emily has just gone through a normal streak of independence which is now over.'

Marjorie flushed. 'I'm so sorry. I didn't mean anything by that remark and I have to say she looks remarkably like you, Dora, even to the tinge of red in her hair, and the same short cut.'

Dora touched David's hand and he smiled at her, then at Marjorie. 'Dora has been a marvellous mother, a wonderful wife and support.' He looked towards the sea and the moon which loomed large and bright. 'I doubted the wisdom of this move, but again, she was right. I'm going to be very happy here, we all are. Thank you, my darling.'

Emily unpacked in her room, thinking of the small lake by the harbour, the dusty squares, the narrow alleys. It was all so different and she felt frightened, lost, abandoned. She wanted to go to Dora but she was on the veranda, talking and laughing.

She sat back on her heels, then started on another tea chest, dropping the newspaper, then picking it up again, wanting to read something English. It was torn; she threw it down. How could Dora have taken her to Cornwall while the packers came in? How could she have taken her straight to the boat? She delved into the crate, throwing newspaper around the room.

She found the metal box her mother had sent her. Inside were the few letters that had come from her. They were unopened. Why hadn't she burned them? She threw that across the room too, watching it hit the wall, fall, skid on the tiles, stop at her feet.

'Why should I even bother to burn them, let alone open them? I just kept them to remind me how much I hate you, how much it must have strained you to write such a few measly letters,' she whispered, picturing the woman who had come each year. She had seen her hair grow quite grey.

This Christmas she'd lifted the curtain as her mother had walked away following her husband, holding the hand of her son, who must be six now. She'd turned at the gate, seen Emily, and smiled. Emily dropped the curtain. Bitch. First she'd run away with a black man, and now she had another, younger husband, and a son. 'Flaunting her husband,' Dora had said, 'flaunting her son, the cruel woman.'

That night as the water lapped at the rocks below their house Emily dreamed of her mother covered in blood, coming at her, and she woke, calling, 'Mother.'

Dora came, sat by her bed and held her. 'It's all right, I'm here, but this can't be a nightmare. You haven't had it for years. Why, Emily? oh, why?'

Emily didn't tell her of the letters but lay down when Dora left and as she drifted off to sleep she smelt face powder and lavender and was puzzled, because neither were the scent of Dora.

The next day Marjorie gave her lessons on deportment, making her walk with a book balanced on her head, showing her how to sit, how to shake hands. That evening she sat with them all on the veranda, smiling, listening, resenting them all. They were so old, she was so bored. She excused herself, went to her room and wrote to her friends and then to Geoff, wanting to rush to Dora and wave his letter in her face. She didn't.

At the beginning of the next week they drove to Knossos. They passed orchards of plums, pears and olive trees as the heat beat in through the windows.

'Why are we coming here, it'll be as boring as everything else?' Emily moaned.

Dora sighed.

Emily slumped in the back. 'It's just a load of old stones.'

Dora's voice was crisp. 'It is not a load of old stones. It is an example of what an Englishman can do. Pinkie said we must come.'

'That explains it then,' Emily said. 'An old fogey like that would like old stones.'

David shouted at her. 'Emily, I've just about had enough of all this – will you stop being so obnoxious, so rude and childish. You are here to stay and that is that. You will walk round Knossos with us and then you will write about

Sir Arthur Evans's reconstruction as Mr Erley requested, as though it were a letter to an old aunt.'

'I haven't got an old aunt.'

Dora spoke now. 'But one day, next year, I will be taking you to Boston for six months and you must have social skills, and letter-writing will be one of them. Now, be good with Mr Erley because he can give us lots of contacts over there.'

Emily ran her fingers through her hair. 'It's just a marriage market. What if I don't find anyone I like?'

'You will, and that is that.'

Emily leaned forward now. 'But why can't I just go back to England?'

Dora shouted at her. 'Because I say so, because England has sacked your father, because we want something better for you. Now I don't want another word.'

Dora gripped her dress. It was all so difficult. Why couldn't Connie just die or something? She didn't know what to do next, how to keep them apart. It had to be Boston. Oh, why couldn't the child just do as she was told?

They parked, then walked in the shade of cypress trees to the edge of the ruins where a guide was talking to a group of tourists.

'Please, join us if you wish.'

David looked at Emily. 'Come along and listen carefully. You have that letter to write.'

Emily fanned herself with her hat, listening to the Americans who talked amongst themselves as the guide led them up the slope. She didn't want to go to America, she wanted to go home. She kicked at the ground; dust rose and caught in her throat.

They stopped, the guide began to speak. She couldn't hear but didn't care, then Dora took her shoulder, saying in a loud voice which cut across the guide, 'I'd like her to come to the front. It's important that she takes it in.'

The Americans parted as Emily was propelled between them. The guide looked at her and smiled gently. 'I'll start again.' He was young; he raised his voice and said, 'The question that perhaps should be considered when looking at Knossos is whether it was a temple or a palace. Sir Arthur Evans felt it was a palace, and as you can see, he has imposed his interpretation for all to see, for ever and ever.'

He stood aside and pointed to the concrete reconstruction that had been erected on top of the excavated site. 'As we go round the site you will be able to make up your own minds as to the accuracy of his reconstruction, or indeed, whether he had any right in the first place to impose his ideas on centuries-old ruins as he has done.'

'Damn cheek,' Emily heard her father say. The guide heard as well and he glanced towards her. She flushed with embarrassment and looked at the ground. They moved on and he told them of the three hundred chambers on the ground floor and a similar number which had made up the upper floors before it was destroyed by fire.

'They say a south wind was blowing when Knossos burned in 1400 BC,' he explained. 'And though we may argue over whether it was a palace or a temple we all agree that Knossos is a symbol of an entire ancient culture, one that was ruled over by a just and wise king, Minos.'

Emily looked at the harsh concrete. How could anyone build on such history? Dora's voice cut across the guide's again. 'Such lovely views.'

The Americans tutted. The guide stopped, waited, said 'Have I the attention of you all?'

'Well, I say,' Dora protested.

Emily looked at the ground again, then at the large pots in a chamber which was open to the skies. The guide led them into dark interiors, pointing out the bull motifs.

'The cult of the bull reigned here. It is said that Poseidon was jealous of King Minos's control of the seas and inspired Minos's wife with an uncontrollable desire to mate with a white bull. She persuaded a friend to build a wooden cow and hid inside it. The cow was taken to the bull. I leave the rest to your imagination.'

Emily waited for Dora's or David's shocked comments. There were none. She looked round; they weren't with the group. The guide led them up and out into the sunshine again. Her parents were standing by a wall, looking out across the hillsides. And what would Mr Erley think about your lack of attention? Emily thought.

The guide led them down into the Labyrinth where it was cool, dark, and somehow sad. Her parents remained behind and Emily breathed a sigh of relief. The guide said, 'Myth has it that Theseus encountered the hideous bull-man at the centre of the Labyrinth and killed him in unarmed combat before finding his way out following Ariadne's thread.'

Emily heard the clicking of Dora's heels on the stone as her parents approached, then Dora's voice, 'It's too cold, dark, dreary.' Why couldn't they stay outside then?

They moved on to the Throne Room. The guide pointed to the fresco of griffins on the wall. 'As you can see, Evans not only rebuilt, but here he repainted. There is no evidence to suggest that there were originally griffins on this north wall.'

He led the way to the antechamber. 'As you can see, there is a bowl in the middle. It is the focal point of the room and the wooden throne seems to preside over it. Very much a confirmation that this is a palace. But wait, perhaps not. Sir Arthur Evans placed it this way. He had such a sure sense of what Knossos was and what the culture was, or perhaps we should say, what it should have been, that I feel perhaps he was too anxious to prove the fact.'

They emerged into the light again and now Dora gripped Emily's arm. 'We're going. I'm not listening to this nonsense from a damn native. This is an Englishman he's talking about. It's purely his own point of view and totally outrageous.'

Emily shook herself free. 'He's almost finished and I have to write this letter for Mr Erley; surely you want me to get good marks, Mother?' She hurried after the group, slipping to the front, listening closely.

She understood when he explained how Evans had been right to reconstruct in many places for the safety of the excavators, and the preservation of the chambers.

'But in such a permanent manner? In such an ugly, certain way? Let us think of the Throne Room. Couldn't it have been the burial chamber of a temple? It could only have seated eighteen people – is that sufficient for a king who ruled much of the Aegean, would it satisfy his sense of self? And what about the sunken "bathroom" of the Throne Room? Surely this was more appropriate for a religious function, rather than secular?'

'Bloody nonsense,' David said from the back.

The guide shrugged. 'I am not dictating either way, I'm just suggesting that we think about it. Perhaps it was a temple, perhaps a palace. But because of all the reconstruction it is difficult to avoid being forced to accept just the one vision.'

The Americans applauded. 'Well done, young man, plenty to think about,' one called. The guide smiled towards the voice, then at Emily. His eyes were warm, his hair too long. 'And you, will you think too, for this letter I heard you speak of?'

David caught at her arm. 'We're going home. We're not listening to his impudence any longer.'

Emily pulled from him. 'Dad, how can you, in front of everyone?' she whispered.

'You're coming home, right now,' Dora said. 'It's getting far too hot anyway.' She put her hand round Emily's shoulders. 'I'm quite sure you have enough material for any letter.'

Emily looked back towards the group, towards the guide. Damn them, did they think she was a child, hustling her away from everyone just because it suited them? It had been interesting but she hadn't seen all the rooms and this boy had rattled her parents as she had often longed to do. She heard the guide say to the group, 'I shall be here every other day for the next two weeks, if you need to know more.'

That evening she was sent to her room in disgrace, having told Mr Erley that Sir Arthur Evans had imposed his ideas when he had no real right. Dora followed her in, pushing her down onto her chair, shaking a finger at her.

'You are still a child. You do not presume to contradict your elders. You know nothing of Knossos, nothing of anything. That's why Mr Erley has, out of the kindness of his heart, offered to instruct you in the arts and culture of the world. It will be useful in drawing-rooms and at dinner parties later on. Now go to bed, and let us have no more of this impudence.' She slammed the door as she left.

Emily broke the pencil she was holding. She was sick of being called impudent, sick of them, sick of everything. She wrote another letter to Geoff, then looked at herself in the mirror, then back at the letter. No, it wasn't enough. If Geoff got up their noses, what would a Cretan guide do? She pulled at her hair; and neither would she put that stupid red rinse through any more. Childish? When would they realize she was nearly seventeen?

Connie helped the mothers of the families they had staying that week, cutting up the vegetables, rolling out the pastry, but all the time her mind was on Emily. Had Boy managed to find an address yet? She washed her hands under the tap and laughed as Mrs Kelly made a pastry doll out of the pie-ends. How could one function at two levels like this? But she must.

She looked up as Philip came in through the back door. 'Mam, we caught four tiddlers but we put them back, didn't we?' The other three boys nodded, while their jam jars dripped on the floor.

'Where's Grandma?' Connie asked.

Philip grinned, 'She's gone back to her kitchen to make herself a cup of tea, and she says if anyone goes in and disturbs her they'll be rammed into a jam jar and fed to the sticklebacks.'

Connie smiled and nodded to Mrs Freely who was shaking the kettle at her. 'Yes, I'd love a cup, and you boys stop dripping all over my kitchen floor. Go on, all of you, put everything back in the shed, then come in and wash your hands or I'll beat Grandma to the jam jar stuffing. I think we've a cake or two for you, haven't we, girls?'

The women nodded. 'Aye, but get those jars in the shed as Connie's told you, pets.'

They ran off, then came back, and took the cakes. Philip said, 'Is Da in the study, Mam? Has he finished his chapter, can I go in?'

'Scoot, take the cakes outside, finish them off, then you can.'

She walked along the corridor and knocked. Boy called, 'Come in, my love.'

He put the receiver down as she entered and shook his head. 'That Dora is a bloody bitch. She left the address off deliberately and of course no-one will let us have it. I'm working my way through the shipping companies, seeing if they are on any of their lists, then at least we'll have the country. David said Rhodesia, South Africa or Greece, didn't he?'

She nodded, wondering when the hate she felt for Dora would end, when the waiting would too; but one day she'd find her daughter, and she'd continue to write every week as she had always done. But this time, instead of sending the letters, she would have to put them in a parcel to post once they had the address, hiding nothing from her, trying to win her back with the truth.

30

The next day, and the next, Emily worked with Mr Erley who finally rejected her letter, telling her to spend time on facts, not conjecture. He then asked her to study the history of America, and its constitution, saying drily, 'Far more appropriate, I feel, young lady. In fact, you can take the book with you and work at home tomorrow, since I shall not be here. I shall, of course, test you on it.'

She said nothing, just put her head down, read, and seethed.

The next morning she left the house as usual, saying nothing to Dora of Mr Erley's instructions. She caught the bus to Knossos, feeling the sharpness of fear and anticipation, half expecting Dora to come after her, looking behind as she left the bus. There was no-one.

She walked up the slope towards a group of tourists and sidled to the front. It wasn't the young guide. Disappointed, she moved towards the cypress trees and looked out towards the sea, hearing the breeze in the branches, not knowing what to do, but then she heard him, over by the large jars.

She moved across and listened as he said, 'These jars were found in the west front storage block, and also in the north-east section. In Mallia the storage block extended along the east front as well, but at Phaistos they were restricted to the west wing.' She liked the accent and the tone of his voice; it suited the site, the cypress trees, the gentle sun.

He turned and led his group down the slope, then saw her. He stopped, bowed, and said, 'Sadly we are finishing.'

'I just wanted to ask a few questions.'

He hesitated, before saying, 'I will return shortly. Please remain here.'

He led the way to the cars parked alongside the road. Emily strolled towards the jars. She heard him approaching but didn't turn round. Should she shake hands? But no, he was only a Cretan, he wouldn't expect it.

He said, close behind her, 'So, you are interested in the jars?'

She stepped to one side. He was too close. She looked at the open chamber. 'Yes,' then paused, unable to think of anything more. 'Very.' She waved her hand towards them. 'I missed most of what you were saying and I didn't hear you talking about them when I was with my parents.'

He smiled. 'I think a few people missed what I was saying that day. I seem to remember I had a little competition.'

She flushed, not wanting to talk about her parents with this stranger. Her father was right; he was impudent. 'I'd better go,' she said.

He put out his hand. 'No, I'm sorry. I will answer your questions since you have taken the trouble to return.' He stood beside her. 'You see, storerooms with large storage jars are common in Cretan temples and I was telling my group that many were found at Knossos, which rather supports my temple theory. The jars could have held produce which was collected as a sort of tithe. Perhaps the Labyrinth was the storage point.'

She looked towards the Labyrinth. 'It's more believable than Theseus following Ariadne's thread.'

He looked surprised. 'You were listening properly then?'

'Of course. Why ever shouldn't I?' Her voice was crisp and annoyed.

He shrugged. 'No reason, it's just that many don't. Perhaps you would like to see over Knossos again?'

He led her, talking quietly, thoroughly, and half the

time she didn't take it in, but listened to his voice and looked at his face because it was young and alive, like those of her friends. Her sense of loneliness made her stumble.

Eventually he stopped, shrugging his shoulders again. 'That is enough, I think. My voice is parched and your ears must be tired.'

They were in the shade of trees again and she said, not wanting him to go, 'Your English is very good for a native. Do you speak other languages?'

He looked at her, and his eyes were cold. 'No, most people understand English; after all, there is a great deal of pink on the map of the world, you know. The British have imposed themselves on a great many places, just like old Evans.'

Why was he so angry, what had she done? She struggled to find more words which would keep him with her. 'How do you know so much, stuck here? Perhaps you should think of travelling. There are lots of jobs in England; waiting on tables, that sort of thing. I mean, there are a lot of Cypriots in London. You'd feel at home with them.'

He threw back his head and laughed loudly. He said, 'Yes, perhaps I would, just as your parents feel at home in their compound. No, my little English girl, if I travelled I'd want to explore the country and its customs.'

He turned, looking out over the countryside, lighting a cigarette, drawing on it. His fingers were so dark against the white of it. He removed a fleck of tobacco from his lip. It was deplorably rude to light up in front of her without asking. She waved away the smoke. 'You could still do that as a waiter.'

Now he looked at her, his eyes remote, his face calm, his voice slow and clear. 'I think I might be overqualified. I am at university in Athens studying archaeology. What are you studying – anthropology perhaps – the study of the origins of man, starting with the Cretan native?'

There was silence and she didn't know where to look,

what to say. She felt humiliated, shamed, and angry. She glared, then walked away, down the slope, wanting to run, forcing herself not to.

He called after her, 'You could be a pleasant person and it would be nice to meet again. I shall be at the ruins beyond Ayios Nikolaos next Thursday if you want to pursue your tour of the island, or will you have made your parents angry enough with today's slumming?'

She stopped. How could he know? How dare he speak to her like that? She groped in her purse, turned and threw some drachmas at his feet. 'There, that's for your services. Now go to hell.'

He just looked at her, his hand in his pocket, his shirt so white against his skin, his face so alive, damn him. She marched off, wanting to kick and scream.

He called, 'No, I won't go to hell, but to Gournia which has a tiny temple, or is it a palace? It's past Ayios Nikolaos as I've just said and it may interest you, once you have stopped sulking.'

'I said, go to hell,' she shouted back, ignoring the shocked looks of the Americans who were climbing past her.

The bus took hours and hours to return and Dora was waiting for her in the sitting-room, her foot tapping, disturbing the fringe of the rug. 'Where exactly have you been?' she shouted at Emily who didn't stop to answer, but walked to her bedroom. She shut the door, wanting to lock it, but there wasn't a lock, of course, here in this pit, was there?

She leant against it, listening to Dora running down the corridor. The handle turned, Dora shouted. She braced herself but Dora pushed harder than she could cope with and slowly the door opened.

Dora grabbed and shook her, her newly rinsed hair gleaming. 'How dare you lie to me? How dare you go heaven knows where when Mr Erley said you were to study at home?' Dora pushed her to the bed. 'You're being ridiculously difficult and getting so like your mother

373

and it's not fair on your father or on me. What repayment is this for all our care and love? Now, where have you been?'

Emily glared at the woman who was looming over her and now she leapt up, pushing Dora back. 'Don't you dare say I'm like her. I'm not, I'm not.' Her face was in Dora's. 'And how dare you bring me here, stuck in this stinking flea-pit, and how dare Dad lose his job, how dare he affect me like this? I hate you. I couldn't even say goodbye. And you've got a red stain on your temple.'

Dora slapped her face so hard that Emily thought her nose was broken. 'I hate you all,' she wept, falling onto the bed. 'Just leave me alone.'

She spent all week confined to the house, and most of the time she stayed in her room, playing her gramophone too loud, ignoring Dora when she called, 'Turn that thing down.' Eventually Dora came in and broke her Lonnie Donegan record.

On the following Tuesday evening her father sat in her wicker chair, leaning forward, his paunch straining against his shirt, his stubby hands clasped loosely. He looked tired and for the first time she noticed how grey his hair was, how far it had receded. He said, 'Are you really so very unhappy? We thought it would be a fresh start, a relief after all the difficulties of the loss of my job. We two just felt so tired, so frayed. What can I do to make it easier for you, Emily? You do know I love you very, very much, don't you?'

Emily went to him then, kneeling on the floor, leaning against him, holding one of his hands. His skin was always so tanned against hers. 'I'm sorry, Dad, I just feel so confused. I hate everyone, but I love them. I don't know what I'm thinking or feeling half the time.'

He stroked her hair. 'I'm glad you no longer rinse it. It has a lovely sheen of its own, and a natural wave. I never quite knew why you did it.'

She wanted to tell him that it was because Dora had told her she must, but why bother? It was trivial and he was here, stroking her hair, talking, listening.

She said, 'I love you, and Dora, but somehow everything's going so fast. I'm lonely.'

'Mr Erley's grandchildren will be out in August; that will be company for you. Dora said she'll arrange a party for you then; how about that?'

'Thanks, Dad, that will be lovely.' He was wriggling now and she sat up as he stood and walked to the door, and knew that it wasn't lovely. It was nothing; it didn't touch the anger and confusion.

On Wednesday she told Mr Erley of Gournia and explained that she wanted to visit it, to explore more deeply because his teaching had exposed an interest she hadn't known existed.

'Excellent idea. Unfortunately I cannot accompany you, but I will draw up a list of other sites you can visit as well.'

'You'll tell Dora you agree?'

Mr Erley smiled. 'Of course. Who knows, your parents might even be able to go with you.'

That evening she heard Dora and David arguing long into the night and in the morning Dora said, 'Your father feels that it will enhance your prospects in America to have conversational pieces. But keep your hat on, we don't want a wrinkled skin. And you are to be back by six, at the latest.'

David winked at her and she hugged him, then Dora, before running out of the house, down to the bus, then rushing back for a flask, bread and cheese, pad and pencil. 'Don't forget your hat,' Dora shrieked. 'We'll be out with the Erleys visiting friends towards Herakleion but we'll be back by six, so be warned.'

The bus was piled on top with freight; there was even a case of chickens strapped onto the rack. Inside there were not enough seats but wooden stools had been placed in the aisles. She sat on one of these. They had let her come, they were letting her grow up. She stopped and looked at her pad. Then why was she going? There was no need to get back at them any more. She didn't know, or care, she just wanted to.

They drove along the coast, past fields of eggplant, olive groves, chapels, and always the blue, blue sea, and all around her was laughter, talk, gesticulations, and she longed to be part of it.

The driver called out, 'Gournia.' She returned the passengers' smiles and stepped out into the baking heat, jamming her hat on her head. She heaved her bag over her shoulder and waved as the bus moved off, turning her face from the dust, looking around her for him. Would he come? It was more than a week.

There was no sign of him and now the happiness was dampened, the heat was oppressive. She shifted the bag and looked at the hill where ancient streets led up to a small square. There seemed no point any more. She would have been better off listening to the gramophone out of this stinking heat, in this dusty, dirty country. She looked down the road. How long before another bus came?

He called then, and she turned, shading her eyes. He was standing in the square; she waved and walked up the hill, feeling uncertain, foolish, excited. 'I just thought I'd come. I didn't think you'd be here; I thought I could look round in peace,' she said as she approached.

He grinned. 'I can always go.'

She shrugged. 'Why not?' She felt the sweat running down her back, her chest. Was it staining her clothes? She looked quickly. No.

'On the other hand, I could stay and explain a few things to you. I see you have your notebook.' He was taking out a cigarette again, lighting it, blowing the smoke up into the air. He offered her one. She shook her head. He said, 'I'm having a look at the palace, or is it a temple? Come along if you like.'

She watched as he walked across the square then crouched, smoking, his backbone ridging his shirt. He called to her. 'This is a complete Minoan town; there would have been carpenters, coppersmiths and potters in the narrow alleys. Their tools are on display in Herakleion. It's not like Knossos where jewellery was found. This must have been very like any Cretan village today.'

She crouched beside him, looking over the town, imagining people working, living, talking, loving. 'I like the feeling that people were here, doing what others still do. It makes me feel safe, as though the world goes on, no matter what I think or feel.'

He nodded, and together they listened to the bells of the grazing sheep and goats. 'Would they have grazed animals?' she asked.

'Probably. The town was built on the slopes of the ridge to leave the bottom ground free for farming – they would have had goats at least. Look over there, the buildings could have spilt over onto that flat ground.' They walked over the cobbled streets, winding along, and down the hill.

She said, 'I can almost feel them here, farming, weaving, fishing perhaps?'

He nodded. 'Oh yes.'

'Would they have used donkeys? The streets aren't wide enough, are they?' She stretched out her arms; her bag slipped. He took it from her; she barely noticed, picturing the people, the donkeys, and almost hearing the sounds of that life.

They talked, explored, and argued about palace or temple, and forgot about lunch until three o'clock, and it was only when they were tearing apart their bread, breaking up their cheese and drinking the water which was almost hot that she said, 'My name is Emily.'

'Mine is Nikos, and I think you should study anthropology; you are very interested, very intelligent, and nice, especially – nice.'

She looked down at the Bay of Mirabello, listening to the bells of the grazing animals, and wanted today to last for ever because for once there was no confusion.

She said, 'I'm sorry I was so rude at Knossos.'

'We were both rude.'

He handed her his flask. 'It is water with wine, very weak.'

She drank, but refused the cigarette. He said, 'The bus comes in twenty minutes.'

'I must get it. I must be back by six.' She looked over the town, over the sea, not wanting to go, wanting the two of them to stay on the hillside for ever, outside real life.

He said, 'Next week I could take you to a modern Cretan village, only if you would like to continue to explore "the people" angle, of course.'

She was folding up the greaseproof paper, shaking out the remains of the water from her bottle, packing her bag, hanging it over her shoulder. 'I'd like that, it would be interesting. I could take notes. It would help my work; just that, of course.'

The next week Dora and David were in Herakleion with the Erleys and Emily met Nikos on the bus this time, in the early afternoon. They sat squashed together on the seat, his thigh against hers, and neither spoke until they jumped down from the bus into the sunshine and he pointed to the hills. 'We'll walk.'

She nodded. He had been so close that she had smelt his skin. Had he smelt hers?

She strode ahead; he caught up. 'It is too hot to walk too quickly, take time to look around.' He pointed to a German gun emplacement. 'What will future archaeologists think of that I wonder, or anthropologists?'

She laughed. 'That we were people who needed to live without light, or culture.'

He nodded. 'I wonder if that is true?'

They argued about that now as they walked on, and now she was no longer frightened of his closeness or the fact that she had not been able to sleep properly all week because she couldn't push his voice, his face, his hands, from her mind.

He told of the almonds which would blaze here in February, filling the air with scent and the world with their beauty. He told her of the bees drowning the senses with their noise, and the poppies and daisies covering the slopes in the spring.

He pointed to the mountain peaks. 'Even when they are tipped with snow, the anemones will bloom here.'

She looked up at the mountains and for the first time for years she thought of the Himalayas, the smell of cow-dung fires, the mist, the shriek of laughter, the feel of a tray beneath her, the sensation of speed, arms around her, a smell— She stopped, shaking her head. What smell? She couldn't remember, she didn't want to remember, and now there was an ache, a drenching misery which had come from nowhere and she could not understand the tears that filled her eyes.

Nikos took her arm. 'What is wrong, Emily?'

'I don't know, I must have kicked some dust into my eyes.'

The sound of his voice had pushed away the ache and she could see the hill-slopes, the olive trees, and feel the heat again. She brushed her eyes with her hands. 'There, it's fine.'

They were at the village now, and Nikos was greeted with smiles and they were gestured to chairs which had been set up beneath trees. 'A son of the village has returned from America. There is to be a party,' Nikos said, then spoke to an old man, slapping him on the back, kissing an elderly woman.

'I have known them for years. They know my family. My father is a doctor in Athens, but we have roots here. My father is the one who led me to archaeology. One's family is of importance, is it not?'

She nodded, not wanting to think of families, not here, not now, not ever.

She watched as fruit and bread were set on the table whilst children laughed and shouted all around. Nikos reached across. 'The best bread in the world is that made in the villages. Here, taste it.'

He pushed some into her mouth, some into his own.

His fingers brushed her lips, and it was suddenly difficult to breathe suddenly, and she barely tasted the bread, but nodded when he said, 'Isn't it wonderful? It's made in their own ovens from wheat ground at the nearest mill, then baked into thick, round, heavy loaves that will last for weeks. I always take some back to Athens with me.'

The black-clad woman brought milk while the younger ones looked at her from a distance and the men smoked, talked, laughed. 'When are you going back to Athens?' she asked.

'In October. Do you mind?'

She shrugged. 'Of course not, why should I?'

A large pot was brought to the table. Nikos pulled her to her feet. 'Come on, taste some.'

They were given a bowl of beans and lentils with tomatoes, parsley and garlic. It was still so hot, it was almost bubbling. It burnt her lips, and she winced, then laughed as Nikos did the same. 'Don't they mind sharing with us?'

He shook his head. 'No, however poor Cretans are, they never doubt their value as human beings, therefore they are confident enough to share, to listen, to be unafraid. Perhaps you could do to think about that.' He was too close; she could smell the wine he had drunk on his breath.

She said, 'I came here to learn about the people, not about myself from someone who knows nothing of me.' Her voice was hard and he nodded, handing her a glass.

'Of course, how remiss of me,' he said.

He pointed to an old man with a beard. 'That is Nikolaos. He is a shepherd and sells his milk to the villagers. He wears a beard because his uncle died, to indicate grief, but also respect.'

He pointed out the cobbler who had a shop in Ayios Nikolaos. 'He will drag you into his shop when he next sees you and give you coffee because you will now be considered a friend.'

The wine was easy on her throat. Men were playing

lyres and the villagers were singing, eating, laughing. An elderly woman brought them a plate of fried fish called marides. 'Eat them whole,' Nikos instructed, showing her how before he was dragged to his feet by two men. 'Excuse me,' he called to her. 'I have to share wine with the returned prodigal.' She watched as he was surrounded by young men, as arms were thrown over shoulders, and laughter burst from the group. Women talked and laughed in clusters. Children played in groups. She was alone. She belonged nowhere.

She looked across to the mountain range which was bathed in moonlight and again she heard laughter and knew it was hers, and her mother's.

A boy ran out from a group of dancers, a child of about six. The dance ended. Nikos broke away from the group of men and came across, shooing the child out of his way.

She said, 'My mother has a son that age.'

Nikos said, 'Oh, I didn't notice him at Knossos. Is he as noisy as that?' He was laughing, moving his body to the rhythm of the music which had begun again.

She said, 'I've only seen him, I've never heard him.'

Nikos looked at her, a question in his eyes, but she said, 'I must go. Thank you for this, I have learned a great deal.' She put out her hand. He looked at it, then at her. She turned, thanked the old lady, the old man. They wanted her to stay. She shook her head. 'No, I must go.'

She began to walk down the track. Nikos came after her, walking with her. She said, 'No, I'm fine alone. I can find my own way.'

'You can't, and I would not allow you to.'

He steadied her on the downward path, his hand was on her arm. In the moonlight there was no difference between their colours. Had her mother noticed that, as she was doing?

She was silent as they walked for an hour and a half along the tracks that Nikos knew, until they reached the town, then her street. There was no light showing from the house. Her parents were not home. Yes, that's right, her parents. Not that woman who called herself her mother. She stopped, turned.

He said, 'There is a wedding in July and you are invited. But only if it helps your studies, of course.'

'Of course,' she said. 'Perhaps.' And ran into the house.

'I'll contact you,' he called after her, 'then you can decide.'

Boy had at last tracked down the shipping line and the destination of Mr and Mrs French. Connie parcelled up the letters she had written. They didn't know the address in Crete but Boy sent it to the local newspaper, and knew, as fellow journalists, they would somehow forward the parcel. That night he took Connie in his arms and they lay, smelling the honeysuckle, seeing the moon so large and light.

She said, 'I love you, Boy, I love Philip and I love Emily. Will she ever come home? Will it do any good to find her?'

'Of course,' he said. But in his heart he had almost given up hope.

31

Each day Emily leafed through the post. Would Nikos write to her about the wedding? Did she want him to? She wasn't sure as she walked around the squares with Dora, but not near the cobbler – Dora would guess.

They shopped, she ate, or sat on the veranda playing patience, or writing to her friends, but no longer to Geoff. Somehow all that seemed so far away, part of another life, childish, left behind.

The next week she returned to Gournia with Mr Erley because the waiting was too hard. Perhaps he would be there? She and Mr Erley rambled up the steep entrance passage, past foundations and segments of walls, through the main portal, then into the old market place and she looked all around. Nikos was not here. She realized she was half relieved.

Mr Erley explained the basics to her, but she already knew, and more besides, though she hugged this to herself along with the memory of Nikos's voice, and his face as he had become animated, his body as he had moved to the music, his hands as he had torn bread for them both.

Mr Erley took Emily and David to Lato Etera the next day. As they drove she looked for Nikos down every street, then across every olive grove. She didn't see him. Would she ever again? Why had he said he would contact her, if he wasn't going to? Perhaps he only remembered her rudeness, the drachmas she had thrown at him. She half hoped that was the case.

Lato Etera was perched high above the plain.

Mr Erley parked the car and pointed up the saddle of the twin-peaked hill. 'The ruins are all along there, and around the crater. Let's go and have a proper look.'

'Oh, must we?' said David fanning himself. 'It's so damn hot.'

'Then stay down here, Dad. We'll go up and I'll tell you all about it.' Emily was already starting up the hill. Why had he come if he didn't want to see it?

'Now, hang on, Em. I'm coming, of course I am. Just needed a bit of a breather.'

David plodded after his daughter and Mr Erley, tasting the dust that they kicked up, making it halfway, then turning back. 'I'll wait by the car for you. I'm just not used to the heat.'

Emily waved and for a moment she looked just like Connie, and his heart seemed to stop. He gazed after her. How could he be unused to the heat after those years in India? How could Connie not have come to wave goodbye to her daughter? How could a mother write to her daughter so seldom?

His feet slid with every step, and now he hugged his good fortune to him, thanking God that he had Dora, someone he could trust, when Connie had shown herself to be everything that he couldn't.

Emily pulled Mr Erley the last few paces and when he'd recovered they looked at the huge cistern though he was still panting as he said, 'It's more of a fort, with those walls and these cisterns – they could obviously outlast any siege. It's a strange atmosphere, isn't it – different to Gournia.'

She looked across the plain, imagining hostile forces. 'I can smell fear,' she murmured.

Mr Erley nodded in agreement. 'But how strange – you should be too young to know what fear is.' He looked at her intently.

She said, 'Come along, it's time we had our picnic, Dad's fed up.'

They ate bread, olives and tomatoes under an almond tree and she looked·up at Lato. He was right; how could she smell fear?

She searched the hall table when she returned. He hadn't written. She was pleased, but hurt, angry, abandoned.

The next evening Dora insisted that she pass the drinks round at the party they were giving. The ice clinked in the glasses and in the water jug that she carried. She smiled at the guests noting how very old they seemed, glad because it made them safe.

She refreshed Mr Erley's drink, splashing soda onto the whisky, handing it to him, smiling as he said to Mr Davies, 'We had a most interesting day in Lato, did we not, my dear?'

'Yes, but I prefer Gournia. It's much more like a modern Cretan village than either Knossos or Lato. At Gournia you can imagine the crafts of today, the same bread making, the leather workers, the peace.'

Dora joined them, holding a plate of cheese straws. 'And how do you know what modern Cretan life is like?' Her eyes were sharp, her voice crisp. She thrust the plate into Emily's hands. 'Take these round now, but first, answer my question, please.'

Mr Erley held up his whisky glass. 'Conjecture, my dear Emily, but this time accurate, unlike your comments on Knossos, eh?'

Emily smiled. 'Absolutely.'

David laughed, and put his arm round his wife. 'There you are, you see – what a clever daughter you have.'

Dora snapped, 'Clever girls don't catch good husbands; men're frightened of them. Anyway it's high time you were in bed.' She moved on to the Wards, pointing out the views from her veranda, feeling the rage and the fear in her. Didn't David listen to her, didn't he understand that they must marry Emily off to a nice American man who would keep her safely away from England? She must not be thought to be clever, just sociable.

The next day Emily took the bus to Knossos. Nikos

was not amongst the guides who all looked so foreign and dark. 'I've made a mistake, I need to go back,' she said to the bus driver.

The third week she received a note from Nikos.

Emily,
  I have borrowed a car. I will pick you up at noon tomorrow, if you would like to come – purely to extend your interest in our customs, in village life, in the people of the area – of course. Wear walking shoes, but carry high heels. I'll collect you just after noon. Try and stay as long as you can, the party goes on all night.

She read the note again. No, she wouldn't go. She worked all morning at Mr Erley's house, then Pinkie's wife made her walk with a book on her head again, sitting down with it. She was taught how to lay a table, how to talk to each guest.

She lay on her bed after lunch, as her father and Dora were doing. How could she go? It was safer to stay here, doing as she was told. Safe? Why did that word keep emerging?

That evening, on the veranda, Dora said, 'Your father and I have been invited, along with the Erleys and the Robinsons, to Herakleion by Mr and Mrs Davies. Mr Erley's housekeeper will move in here for three days – just to keep an eye on you.'

Emily stared out across the sea. 'Can't I come with you – I don't want to stay here alone?'

'You won't be alone, I've just told you,' Dora said.

'Next time, my dear.' David joined her by the rail. 'Next time.'

They left the next morning and she bathed, brushed her hair, seeing the glossy sheen of rich blonde. All the red had gone. Her hands were trembling. She would go – purely for the knowledge, of course. She found white high heels, and wore sand-shoes.

'Goodbye, Kyria Irene, don't wait up. I will switch the lights out when I return.' But she wouldn't be late. She walked to the main road. She would meet him here where they could not be seen, just as she had always had to meet Geoff.

They drove along the road, then a track, and there was little talk because the car rattled and jerked, knocking the breath from their bodies. He parked at the foot of a hill and pointed to the village above them. 'Now we walk, I'm afraid. Keep your sand-shoes on, and we can change at the gate.'

She walked behind him, but he reached for her, pulling her to his side. 'Come along, you will eat my dust. I don't bite.' His smile was wide, his eyes gentle. 'I've missed you,' he said as they climbed. 'I've missed our talks. I had to go to Herakleion Museum and work there. I didn't know whether to tell you, or perhaps you didn't even notice.'

She shook her head. 'I've been busy. I've been to Lato, all over the place, and so many parties.'

'Ah,' he said, then nothing more. They continued to climb towards the village and now she could see two figures waiting by the gate. 'Wait, my high heels,' she panted, trying to catch her breath.

'That's all right, just put them on now.' His hand steadied her, warm against her flesh.

'I can manage,' she snapped. He stepped away, looking at her quietly, then back at the figures by the gate. They were waving.

'The parents of the bride,' Nikos murmured to her, taking her sand-shoes from her. She snatched them back because they were sweaty. She dropped them under an olive tree. 'I'll pick them up when I leave.'

Nikos clasped the hands of the elderly couple, kissing their cheeks. He introduced Emily who shook hands with a stiff arm. Nikos led her to a grape arbour where others were drinking. A girl with a tray of glasses stopped them.

'Try some tsikoudia, and a wedding biscuit,' Nikos said, raising his voice as musicians started to play. Immediately a circle formed. 'Sit on the chairs and get your bearings.' Nikos waved first to one person then another. 'This is the Chaniotikos – just see them leap.'

She held her drink, then sipped it. It was strong, harsh in her throat. The dancers were slapping their thighs now, their skin shiny from the heat, their faces alive, so different to the British, the music so different, everything so different. Why was she here? She was stupid to have come, she wanted to go home.

She turned to tell Nikos, but a young man was dragging him into the circle. He shrugged helplessly. 'I'll be back,' he shouted as he picked up the rhythms, turning his head, his legs moving so quickly, his hands slapping his thighs.

She watched, and drank, and he was better than the rest; his face was more alive, his body more fluid, wheeling, turning, stamping. The music stopped; he returned, flopping onto the chair beside her, picking up his glass from the ground, wiping his face with his handkerchief.

'So, you are seeing Cretan customs but at least you are not having to perform in them.' He was laughing, his head thrown back, his shirt unbuttoned at the top, sweat gleaming on his throat, his dark smooth skin.

She sipped at her drink. 'You were very good. I can only do the waltz and then I step on people's toes – I'd probably bowl the whole circle down.' She was smiling nervously, and now he turned to her.

'That is not a Cretan custom, but if it was done by you, it would be beautiful, and should become part of our culture.'

He reached for her hand, lifted it to his lips, and she felt a shaft of pleasure and then fear, and she wanted to cling to him but also to break from him, and for a moment it seemed the world stopped – the colour and the noise ceased – but then they were dragged to their feet and taken to a village house, being jostled amongst others as they went.

The bride was wreathed in tulle and lace, her dowry was laid out in a seperate room and Emily saw the woven work.

'The bride has spent all her spare time for years working on these.' He was so close behind her that she could feel the heat from his body, but then he was pushed away.

She felt his hand reaching for her, dragging her out, and as he did so she thought of the etiquette lessons, the art of conversation lessons, all leading to America and now she could hardly breathe in the cluster of bodies and she wanted to fight free, to hit out at everything and everyone.

They were out into the open, and it was cooler beneath the vines, quieter, and the music was playing and the dances were slow. Nikos spoke to the leader of the group and he began to play a waltz. Nikos came to her, held her, danced with her until the music stopped.

They ate at a long table, and drank wine.

'Not too much of either,' Nikos warned. 'There'll be another feast later at the bridegroom's house.'

'I'll burst,' she murmured.

'I do hope not; it's so messy when that happens.'

They both laughed and couldn't stop, even when they trooped down the lane to the church losing one another in the crowd. He found her again, leading her into the church, holding her hand as they stood near the old priest in his flowing robes. She watched as the white crowns linked by a ribbon were placed on the heads of the couple and then exchanged three times by the best man but all she could feel was his hand.

He whispered, 'The best man will be the protector of the new family, and his relation to it will be as strong as a blood tie in the eyes of the church. His is a very important role. Now, the couple is considered to be united for ever, to belong to one another until the end of time.'

The priest joined hands with the bride and groom and performed the ancient Isaiah Dance around the altar. Then Emily was handed walnuts mixed with honey, along with everyone else, but all she could think was, 'There is no such thing as for ever, or belonging, is there, Mother?'

She turned as Nikos touched her arm. 'What do you mean?' he asked and it was only then that she knew she had spoken aloud.

Outside the bride and groom danced together, then the two fathers danced with the bride, then all the male relatives in turn held the girl's white handkerchief and led her round and round, throwing money on the ground for the newly-weds. On and on it went for over an hour and now Emily drew back to the edge of the crowd, leaving Nikos there, smiling, clapping his hands.

What was she doing here? These were not her people, the boy that had held her hand was a stranger, everyone was a stranger. It was better that they remain so – as Geoff's friends and family had been. She started to walk towards the gate. Where had she left her shoes?

'Emily, Emily.' She heard his voice, the sound of running. She felt his hand on her arm. She pulled away. 'I can't stay, I must go back. Mr Erley's housekeeper will be waiting.' Her voice was aloof. Yes – it was better this way.

The gate was warm beneath her hand. She opened it, closed it, walked to the tree, changed her shoes, walked down the hill. It would not be far to Ayios Nikolaos, she would be home before dusk. She could sit on the veranda looking out across the bay to the Sitia mountains, alone. Yes, it was better that way.

She passed the car, touched it. It was hot. Yes, it was better that she walked. She tasted the tears that were pouring down her face – why? She didn't know.

'Emily, Emily.' He was grabbing her arm, turning her round and she wanted to be held, but no, she couldn't bear the pain that would follow.

'Leave me alone,' she shouted. 'Leave me in peace.'

'You are safe with me,' Nikos said, grasping both arms. She looked at him, at his soft eyes, his mouth, his dark skin, the white shirt which clung to his body.

'But you are leaving in October.'

'I'll be back at Christmas.'

She could taste the wine still, her head was spinning. 'My mother came at Christmas. She won't this year. She did not even come to say goodbye.' Her mind was running on, finding these words – but where from, and how could they hurt as they were doing? How could the tears just keep running down her face, falling onto his arms which still held hers?

He pulled her to him now, holding her so close, but she mustn't let him. She musn't let herself love and belong with anyone. She struggled, pushing him away. 'I don't understand,' Nikos said, not letting go completely, holding on to her hands, pain in his eyes.

'Do you think I do?' she shouted. 'She left me and Dad for another man, an Indian, years ago. She didn't care about me, or anyone. I know because then she slept with someone else in England when her lover died. Now she has someone else again, and a son too. Do you think I understand anything about love?'

He said quietly, 'But I think I love you, and I think you love me.'

'But love hurts too much.'

'I said you were safe with me.'

'There's no safety anywhere,' she said quietly, slowly. Her tears had stopped. She just felt tired.

He pulled her towards the car. 'I'll take you home.'

The car was like an oven. It rattled and clanked down the lane. He stopped in the shade at the end of her road and neither moved. He said, 'I think you love your mother still. I think you need to talk to her.'

She shook her head. 'No, she chose him, not me, not Dad. Him, and others.'

'Why, and did she really? What has she said to you?'

She shook her head. 'I haven't spoken to her, ever again. She hasn't spoken to me.'

Her hands were too heavy. She should open the car door, leave this boy. She looked at him; he was staring ahead. He said, 'Why hasn't she spoken to you?'

'Listen to me,' Emily hissed. 'It's me that won't talk to her. She comes every year, parading her new husband, her new son. She writes, but hardly ever. I don't read them. Why should I? A few measly letters to a daughter she used to play with in the snow of the Himalayas, a daughter she used to hold and sing to, and laugh with. Why should I? I keep her as far from me as possible.' It was almost a scream.

He gripped her hand. She tried to pull away. He held tight. 'Listen to me. Remember Knossos. We talked of explanations, ideas, broadening the argument. You have only looked at this from one side; yours. And perhaps that of your present parents.'

She couldn't fight him any longer; she let him hold her hand but her lips were almost too tired to form the words. 'But this isn't Knossos, this is my life.'

He shook his head. 'Perhaps it is mine too because you push me away in case I hurt you. You push love away and I don't know how to help; I don't want to say the wrong thing, I don't want to lose you before I've even known love with you. Did you sense the fear at Lato? I sense the same with you but I am not an enemy. Love is not an enemy.' He was whispering as he finished.

She looked at him. 'Leave me alone.'

She left him, not looking back, finally hearing the car start, move away. She opened the door. Kyria Irene came to meet her, surprise on her face.

'You are back, so soon. I will prepare a salad.'

Emily shook her head. 'No, I'm not hungry. I'm going to lie down.'

She walked along the corridor, her shoes making marks on the clean tiles. She opened her bedroom door, then

Kyria Irene called, 'Something came for you. Our post is truly wonderful. They found you.'

She turned, watching as the housekeeper padded along the tiles, her hand outstretched. She took the package. It was from her mother.

In the vestry Belle cut the stems of the dahlias, arranging them in the brass vases. Soon it would be Harvest Supper, then she shook her head. Well, not soon, but in six weeks. Would Mrs Green help again? She smiled. They'd have to hand over to the younger ones soon, it was all getting too much.

She called across to Connie, 'Do you think you'd have the time to take on the flowers – sharing a vicar with Longdale is all very well, but his wife just can't cope with this parish too, and we old-timers are just creaking these days.'

'Nonsense, we'll just oil you from time to time. But, yes, I'll certainly help you, though good grief, you're only in your late sixties, Helen Driscoll was going strong until her eighties.'

'Helen was of sterner stuff, and she didn't feel the cold so much. These stone floors have a really vindictive streak where I'm concerned.'

Belle scooped the remains of the stalks into a carrier bag, wondering how they could talk about trivia when they had still not heard from Emily. Had Connie almost given up hope? She certainly had.

Connie stood back looking at the flowers in the vases.

'Will we ever hear?' Belle asked, though she had promised herself that the question would never pass her lips.

Connie picked up the vase. 'I do so wish they had a scent.' She nodded to the other vase. 'Come along, we've the children coming off the twelve-thirty train. We must see how many from the mission want to come for the service and the supper – and I won't answer that question, Mam, because we *must* hear.'

393

Connie lifted her chin, and walked into the church, the light shining blue and red on her hair and her dress as she moved beneath the stained glass window. Belle picked up her vase, her joints aching, and that night she prayed, as she always did, that her granddaughter would return.

32

Emily sat on the bed, fingering the envelope, turning it over. Why was it addressed to a newspaper, not to her? She threw the letter unopened into her cardboard box, along with the others, dusting her hands, wanting her skin free of the feel of anything to do with her mother. She walked to the window, wanting Nikos, but not wanting him, hearing his voice, seeing his eyes, feeling his hands. That night she couldn't sleep.

When her parents returned she walked with Dora in the afternoon heat to the rocky cove and lay on the flat rocks. 'Put your hat over your face; we don't want lines do we?'

'I don't know what I want,' Emily whispered, looking out to sea.

She lay down, the straw hat over her face, but the heat was too much. 'I'm going for a swim,' she said. Dora did not reply. Emily raised her voice. 'I'm having a swim, Mother.'

Dora half-raised herself. 'Keep your hat on; the sun reflects dreadfully off the water.' She lay down again.

Emily stared at Dora, then dropped her hat on the rocks and eased into the warm sea before stroking through the water until her chest heaved for breath; then she looked back. So many rules, so many problems, so many everything.

She closed her eyes and dived down and down, where it was silent, where all she could hear was her heart and Nikos's voice. She surfaced, wiping the water from her eyes, looking at the mountains, the coves, the rocks where

Dora lay and then beyond to the other side of the outcrop where a boy stood, looking towards her.

It was Nikos. He waved, dived, and swam towards her, his arms slicing through the calm sea. She was glad, and she was sorry.

She looked back at Dora. She was still asleep. She swam towards him, then trod water, as they met. The water was dripping from Nikos's hair. It was so black it was almost blue. 'A raven's wing,' she murmured.

He shook his head; water flew off. He wiped his hair; water dripped down his bare arm. 'Do you mind me finding you?' His voice was gentle. 'I waited until your mother was asleep. Your stepmother, I mean. Come, let's swim back behind the rocks into the other cove. It would be better for you, I think, if you are not seen with me?'

He didn't wait for her acknowledgement but swam off, his feet moving steadily beneath the water, his arms slicing, glistening, his head turning, his mouth opening then closing as his head went beneath the water.

'Stepmother,' she repeated. She hadn't thought of Dora as that. She turned to look at the still sleeping figure, then back at Nikos who was so far away, disappearing behind the point. She was alone, with so much water beneath her, so much water all round her. She was alone. She felt her arms go numb, her legs too. Oh God. She was alone. She raised her head to call, but Nikos was already swimming back towards her. He stopped, beckoned, then came on again, reaching for her hand, pulling her along.

'Come along, you have trod water for long enough. Come along, lazy girl, I will tow you in.'

His hand was so warm, so strong, and now she kicked and smiled as he turned and grinned at her. 'You swim now?' he said.

'I'll race you,' she replied, surging forward, leaving him behind, but only for a moment because then he came abreast of her but he didn't pass, just kept to her pace, guiding her into the cove.

The rocks were slippery and he steadied her as they

waded ashore and now she saw how long and strong his legs were, how flat and brown his stomach was, how a line of hairs ran from his belly button to the top of his trunks.

She looked away to the rocks that lined this cove, wanting to cover up her own body. 'I can't be long. Dora will wake, and she is my mother, not my stepmother.' Her voice was crisp, hard.

She sat on a rock and looked out to sea, picking up pebbles, throwing them, feeling the sun harsh on her shoulders.

Nikos sat near her, his arms resting on his knees. 'I am trying to help you,' he said.

'I don't need help. I am all right. I was tired, drunk – oh, I don't know. I was stupid. We talked nonsense. I don't want love. We're too young for love.'

He was throwing pebbles now, flicking them with his wrist, trying to make them skim across the water. 'You just want to extend your knowledge of our customs, our ways?'

His voice was low, gentle.

She turned to him now. He understood. She said eagerly, 'Yes, that's right. That's all I want.'

'Then, my dear Emily, that is what you shall have.' He threw one last pebble and she watched the muscles ripple beneath his skin and then relax as he let his arms flop on his knees. He looked at her, a slight smile on his face which didn't reach his eyes. He repeated, 'That is what you shall have.'

She looked out to sea again. 'I'd better swim back. My mother will wake.'

'Indeed *your mother* will wake.'

She swung round but his face was blank. She walked towards the water, wanting him to call her back. Why? What was the matter with her? She'd got what she wanted, hadn't she?

The water was cold, she waded out, stopped, brushed water up and over her arms, her shoulders. He called softly, 'You could climb the rocks. It would be quicker; safer if you are frightened of being out there alone.'

She stood quite still, looking at the horizon. 'I'm not frightened of anything; I told you I was being stupid. I don't need you to make me feel safe. I'm all right alone.'

She plunged into the water, swimming, trying not to think of the depth beneath her, the distance to go, just ploughing on through the waves, round the point, into the bay. She looked behind her, wanting to shout her defiance to him, but he was not on the shore. He was three yards behind her. He looked, waved, turned and swam back to shore.

She worked all week with Mr Erley, and told herself she was content. It was easier this way, not thinking, not feeling, but her sleep was poor, and on Saturday night the nightmare came again. This time she did not call for Dora, but walked to the veranda and leaned against the balustrade, and remembered the slippery rocks and Nikos's hand on her elbow, his form in the water when she thought she had been abandoned.

On Sunday morning she received his note and met him at the harbour in the evening. He was in a suit, watching the fishing boats which tied up at the quay. At her approach his smile was as gentle as it always was.

He shook her hand. 'I thought we should continue your education. Your parents did not object?'

'They don't know. They think I have just come for some evening air.' She didn't look at his eyes as she spoke, just at the collar, so white against his neck, at the tie he wore, then at the hand which had shaken hers but now held the rail.

He pointed to the men, women and children who were strolling out along the harbour boulevard.'This is our *volta*, or promenade. Shall we join them?'

As they walked with the Cretans towards the beach he pointed out the Club, the tavernas. 'In the tavernas you will find the real Crete. In the Club you would find perhaps Mr and Mrs and Miss French.'

Her voice was sharp as she said, 'And just what do you mean by that?'

'Nothing that need bring this edge to your voice, to your mind.' His voice was level, quiet. 'It is the place for professional and business men. In the tavernas there will be dancing, singing, laughter. Here there will be newspapers, Turkish coffee – the important things of life – perhaps. You will also find bank clerks who come to meet the daughters of important men, so like marries like.'

Silence fell between them. She rubbed her forehead thinking of America, her parents, her mother. No, no thinking.

She said, 'Why do they walk and do they walk every Sunday?'

'I'm surprised you haven't seen them, or do you not venture out when the natives are abroad?' His voice was hard now and she recoiled. He put his hand on her arm. 'I'm sorry, I don't know why I said that, forgive me. It's been a long week, the hours have dragged.'

She looked at his hand; he dropped it. She missed it.

He said, 'They walk in summer and winter. Always the best dresses, the best suits.' He said gently, 'It is good to mix with others, to talk, to laugh. It makes the problems grow smaller, do you not think?'

'I must go,' she said.

He walked her to the end of her road, and then shook her hand. 'Good night, my dear Emily.'

'Good night, Nikos.' They stood together for a moment and then she walked away, not turning to see if he still stood there, not acknowledging the pain which swept over her when she heard him leave.

She worked for another week with Mr Erley but while Dora and David were at the Robinsons she left the house to meet Nikos outside the taverna as he had suggested. He was late. She looked at her watch. He wasn't coming. She thought she would faint from disappointment and leaned back against the wall, wanting to bury her head in her hands.

'I'm so sorry I'm late. My scooter broke down.' People turned as Nikos shouted. He was running towards her, shaking his oil-drenched hands.

When he reached her she said, 'It's quite all right. I could have come another night, it wouldn't have mattered. I could have asked Mr Erley to bring me next week; I expect the taverna would still be here.'

The smile faded from his face. She said, 'Would you rather we left it for another time? Can you eat with those?' She nodded towards his hands.

'I was thinking of using a knife and fork,' he said.

She stared at him, and then they both laughed, clinging to one another, and there was oil on her arms and then she was in his arms, against his chest, breathing the smell of the nape of his neck. 'I've missed you,' he whispered.

'I've missed you too.'

They entered the taverna and the light and noise hit her. There was sawdust on the stone floor. There were only men in here, in dark high-necked sweaters. They looked up from their cards, saw Nikos, hailed him, nodded to her, then slapped down their cards again.

Nikos pulled out a chair for her, then disappeared to wash his hands. She traced the grain of the table. Bazooka music came from the gramophone by the bar. The air was rich with smoke. She rubbed at the oil on her arms with her handkerchief, not wanting to wash it off in this strange place.

Nikos returned. 'I have ordered our food. Is grilled octopus, some tomato, cucumber and some cheese sufficient for you?' He put two glasses on the table. 'And some ouzo, but you don't have to drink it.'

He sat down and showed her his hands. 'They'll do,' she said, clinking her glass to his. He ran his finger over the remains of the oil on her arm. 'I'm sorry.'

She said, 'It'll come off.' The ouzo was strong; she took tiny sips.

'I mean, I'm sorry.' He was holding her arm. 'I don't know how to deal with any of this.'

She swept her eyes over the taverna. 'They all look quite harmless to me.'

Nikos finished his drink and called for another, leaning back in his chair, nodding at her. 'I understand.' But there was as much confusion in his eyes as there was in her mind, because she knew he hadn't been referring to the room, but to their relationship, to her, and she wanted to discuss nothing, to think of nothing.

She drank another ouzo and ate the octopus when it came. It was fresh, there were herbs on the tomatoes, there was salt on the cucumber; the music was pounding, the seamen were dancing, gyrating in a circle with their hands linked, and then their arms, then they danced separately. She tapped her foot; the music was too loud for speech.

The circle reformed and now she thought of the village wedding, of Nikos whirling, leaping, and of his body on the beach, so taut, so slim, and his face, so gentle. The seamen were calling to him. 'Nikos, Nikos.'

He shrugged at her, stubbed out his cigarette, and joined the circle, twisting, turning, laughing and then he broke the grasp of his neighbour's hand and waved to her. 'Emily, dance with us, for me, Emily, and for your work, of course.' The circle was dragging him round; he was still waving and laughing but his eyes never left her face.

She joined the circle, linking her arms with him and an older seaman, hearing the music, the clapping, the laughter; finding the rhythm, letting the music into her mind, her soul, moving with Nikos, making errors, catching up, relaxing, keeping time, stamping, moving her feet, turning to him, her eyes clinging to his, their smiles fading as their love met, clung, broke away, met again, wordless.

They sank into the background, breaking the link with the circle, but not with one another, sitting at the table, their fingers joined, their heads together, their thighs touching. His eyelashes were so long, his skin so smooth, his lips so close, his eyes so kind, so deep, so full of love, and now they kissed and it was as though she didn't exist any longer, it was as though she was floating; there was no pain, no confusion, only warmth, and love, and desire.

A voice cut in on them. 'So, Nikos, when you go back to Athens – soon, eh?'

The man was grinning at her. His teeth were stained; he had spilt coffee down his shirt. His arm was round her, and Nikos. She drew away from them both. She had forgotten he was leaving. She tried to disentangle her hand. Nikos wouldn't let her.

'Yes, Cristos. But I am coming back at Christmas, if not before. I do not leave those I love.' He was looking at Emily, not at the man. 'Come along, we'll go now.' He pulled her with him, out of the taverna into the soft warm quiet night.

'I'm coming back,' he repeated, his arm around her shoulders. 'I *am* coming back.'

She said nothing, trying to lose herself in his closeness, trying to blank out her mind.

Belle buttered the bread. 'Just put jam on those, please, Philip.' She counted. 'Will twenty be sufficient, Connie?'

Connie was passing the flasks of tea to Mrs Jenkins. 'Yes, with the jam as well. Boy, can you make sure that we've enough trays for the slope above the beck?'

Boy grinned and put his pencil behind his ear. 'How am I supposed to finish this first draft with all this carry-on?'

'Prioritize, my darling – mission picnic first, then earning a crust.'

Belle and Mrs Jenkins laughed. Mrs Jenkins said, 'I can't believe it's our last day. We've had a grand time again, Connie. It makes such a difference to the kids, keeps them going all year, especially with the weekend top-ups.'

'Not just the bairns either,' Sally Stuart called through

from the scullery. 'It keeps us sane an' all. Will six jam jars be enough?'

Belle answered, 'Yes, but let them put the string on themselves, they prefer it that way. And just make sure they know they're to put the minnows back afterwards, will you, Sally?'

Connie helped Philip with the last of the sandwiches. 'We mustn't forget to tell the kids that this is the jam they made last year. They can do some more when the plums are ripe, which should be any day now.' The phone rang in the hall. 'Can you get that, Boy?'

He was already on his way. 'I'm expecting a call from my agent. He'll be nagging me again, and how do I tell him it's held up because I'm sorting out trays?' He laughed as he left the room.

'All right, Philip, and you too, Jamie, you nip off and make sure the others have finished their chores too, then we can go,' Belle instructed.

Boy came in. He was no longer laughing. He said, 'That was Carl. He's heard from his contact in Herakleion – the package was delivered three weeks ago. The newspaper are forwarding us the address.'

Connie sat down. She felt cold. 'Three weeks,' she repeated. 'And I've heard nothing. I did so hope—'

Boy put his arm round her. 'Don't give up, not yet.'

Connie said, 'But it seems so hopeless.'

Belle shook her head. 'No, nothing is hopeless. You know where she is – you can go out there, at Christmas, as always. That's what you must do.'

The other women left the kitchen, shooing the children before them. 'But what do I do until then?'

Belle said, 'You write this evening, as always, but now, we have children to take for a picnic. Life goes on. It must.' Her voice was firm, but her eyes were sad as she met Boy's.

33

Nikos and Emily walked away from the taverna, and though his arm was round her, it was as though they were miles apart. In a month he would leave and not return. She knew he would not. People didn't return.

There were others on the streets, laughing, holding hands, one group was singing. She wished she was one of them, not Emily French. They reached the end of her road. He held her hands, leaned forward and kissed her lips but this time it didn't reach her soul.

She was stiff; she smiled. 'Thank you, Nikos.'

'I will meet you again?'

'Yes, that would be nice. It would be interesting. I have learned a lot.' Too much, she thought, leaving him.

In the middle of the following week Pinkie Robinson phoned Dora who talked for ten minutes, then came into the sitting-room, touching her hair, looking in the mirror, checking her rinse. She wiped her eyebrows with her finger, then called Emily to come in from the veranda.

'We'll take you into the town today. We must buy you new shoes, a new dress, even a new swimsuit. Pinkie's Boston friends are in Herakleion, and coming to Ayios Nikolaos this evening. So inconsiderate not to give more notice, but they have a suitable son with them. It's a chance we can't miss.'

Emily looked at David, who rustled last week's *Times*. 'Quite right. Good idea. I suppose we should have cocktails here this evening.'

Dora picked up her handbag, checked her purse. 'No need, thank God, Pinkie's doing the honours. You might have been right about Emily and this culture thing.

Apparently this boy, Francis, is keen on that sort of stuff so at least she can talk him up tonight, and take him to places tomorrow. What did you say that place was, begins with a G?' She was looking at Emily.

'No, I can't take him to Gournia.' Emily was gripping her glass of orange juice. Not Gournia – Gournia was Nikos.

'Nonsense, you can and you will. Now come along.' Dora fixed her with a hard stare.

Emily looked at the sea. What did it matter what she did? She joined Dora, walking beside her into town, thinking of the dance in the taverna last night. It had been a dream. Dreams didn't last.

They passed the cobbler. Levandis waved and called to her. She looked away, scared that Dora might see. Last week and the week before when she had been shopping alone, she had stopped, chatted, drunk coffee. Levandis called again. She looked straight ahead, then glanced back and saw his bewilderment, then his hurt.

They shopped, bought clothes, food, and a red rinse for Emily's hair. Dora insisted, and it was easier to do as others told you.

Dora kissed her as they left the house for Pinkie's. 'There you are, your hair looks so much better and I'm pleased to see you're quite over this awkward phase; I knew you would grow up, see sense. Now, make sure you behave with decorum. This is important to us all.'

Pinkie and Marjorie gave them Pimm's. It was weaker than ouzo. Emily shook hands with Francis Jones, wondering what it felt like to stroke a crew cut. Nikos's hair was smooth and dark.

As he talked to her in his soft drawl of Athens, of Corfu, of Boston, she listened, smiled, saw herself in the mirror. Her hair was red; she was Emily French, Dora's and David's daughter again.

She drank another Pimm's, the ice clinked. Marjorie said, 'So glad you could come, Emily. Now, Francis, did you know that this young lady, when she is *finished* here, is thinking of travelling to Boston to complete her education? She's most interested in these funny old ruins we have all over Crete. Much as you are, I believe?'

Francis smiled at her over his glass. 'Sure, fascinated. I thought I'd try and get to Knossos tomorrow.'

Dora's chiffon floated in the fan's breeze. 'Emily can take you.'

Emily looked at the ice in her glass. It had almost melted. She shook her head. 'I have Mr Erley's class, I can't let him down.' How could she go to Knossos? Nikos would be there, and Nikos was leaving.

Dora pinched her arm. 'Nonsense, Mr Erley will be pleased to release you for the day. Then there is that G place.'

'I can't take you to Gournia, but I will take you to Lato Etera.' She forestalled Dora's protest. 'It's nearer and it's different to Knossos. Gournia would be a sort of repetition.'

Francis touched his glass to hers. 'It's a date then. Knossos tomorrow, then Lato Etera the next day. It'll mean extending our stay, but I guess Mom and Dad will be only too pleased. They're pretty tired.'

Emily looked at the hand which held the glass so close to hers. It was so pink, so smooth, and she wanted to slap it away from her.

She moved across to Mr Erley, ignoring Dora's frown. 'Will you come with us to Knossos tomorrow, you know so much more about it? It would be more fun too.'

Mr Erley smiled at her. 'I'd be delighted.'

Dora nudged Emily's elbow. 'We wouldn't dream of dragging you away from your well-earned rest. Good heavens, Knossos in the heat of the day, when you could be putting your feet up.' Dora's laugh was light, but her grip on Emily's arm was tight. 'Emily can escort our visitor; indeed, he's looking as though his drink needs freshening, Emily.'

The evening was interminable, and Emily felt too tired to talk, but she did, sparkling, smiling, and wiping the smile momentarily off Dora's face when she invited Mr and Mrs Jones to Knossos. 'You too, of course, Mother.' Emily ignored her glare.

At Knossos, Emily walked with Mr and Mrs Jones, searching for Nikos, not wanting him to be here, not wanting him to see her with Francis, but what did it matter if no man was ever to be important to her? She pointed out the view, the concrete reconstruction. Dora urged Mr and Mrs Jones to come into shade. 'Emily, you stay there with Francis and wait for the guide,' Dora ordered.

Don't let it be Nikos, she prayed. But there he was walking towards her, his face alight with pleasure. She looked away and when she looked again his face was blank.

'Is there no-one else?' David's voice was curt, rude. Emily wanted to shout at her father and tell him Nikos was everything, but she said nothing.

Nikos led them round, talking of a palace, not a temple, his voice neutral, courteous. Dora said in Emily's ear, 'Well, at least the young pup has been taught some manners by someone, and not before time.'

Francis said to Nikos as they approached the Throne Room, 'My teacher said something about an argument over whether it was in fact a temple?'

Nikos looked past Francis to Emily and she wanted to smile, to reach out and touch the hair that fell across his forehead. She didn't and Nikos shrugged. 'Perhaps,' he said.

Francis stepped back to Emily. 'Some kind of guide this is. You'd have thought someone at this level would know what he was dragging you round.'

Nikos heard and looked at her again. Again she said nothing. She walked back to Dora who was saying to Mr Jones, 'You can't expect natives to have the same sort of brain as a son of yours. I mean, it's quite clear young Francis has far to go. You must be so proud of him, just as we are of Emily.' Dora put her arm round her daughter, loving her, proud of her. Emily smiled at Mr Jones. It was so much easier this way.

The next day she took Francis to Lato Etera, walking in the heat of the day, wanting him to sweat, wanting her own shoes to rub.

As they approached across the plain she pointed to the ruins on the saddle of the twin peaks. 'It's very different to Gournia which is built with an eye to productivity, to peaceful pastoral life. Here it is as though Lato is guarding itself, protecting itself against all comers.'

Francis was panting, his baseball hat was pulled low, his ears were burning. He looked ridiculous. 'Who was the enemy?'

'What does it matter? Enemies are enemies, fear is fear; surely all you need to know is that it exists.'

Her voice was curt, crisp, as she strode on, climbing the hill, hoping her dust was in his face, his mouth.

'Hey, hang on, you're not leading a Goddamn charge,' he called, his breath loud as he hurried and caught up with her. 'With your kind of speed you'll do well in the States, it's all rush, rush, there. I tell you what, I'll take you skiing when you come over; how about that? Maybe we can catch a game of tennis in the summer?'

She kept her eyes on the path ahead. 'Fine, we'll do that.' Her voice was no longer crisp. Francis was talking about the future but only this minute existed, only this heat, this climb. It was the only certainty.

That evening he called round to the house, shaking Dora by the hand, giving her flowers. David poured him a drink. Dora said, 'I'm sorry you're going. It's given poor old Emily some company, hasn't it, my dear? She was only saying to me this evening over dinner how much she had enjoyed showing you – oh dear, I know it begins with an L. Anyway, she enjoyed it so much.'

Emily looked at her. How you lie, Dora.

Francis said, 'I was just wondering if she'd have the time this evening to walk me round Ayios Nikolaos.

Seems kind of ridiculous to come all this way and not see the bottomless lake, and the locals.'

'Oh yes,' Emily said. 'You must see the locals, the natives in their natural habitat.'

'Emily,' Dora said. 'You have such an odd sense of humour sometimes.' Her body was rigid with rage.

Francis laughed. 'Sometimes this British way with words just flies straight past us.' He raised an eyebrow at Emily. 'I take it that was a yes, to the guided tour?'

'Come along, we'll go now.' She picked up a cardigan and hurried out. He caught up. The shops were still open. She said, 'I expect you know that they close for siesta, then open well into the evening?'

He smiled at her. 'Sure do.' He touched her arm. 'Look, I'm sorry if I've said something to upset you. I feel you're not altogether over the moon about me being here.'

His face seemed suddenly young and vulnerable. She shook her head. 'I think I'm just not over the moon about myself.'

She pointed out the square, leading him past the leather shops, the woven work. 'The Cretan crafts have changed little since the Minoan times,' she said.

They passed Levandis. He waved again. She strode on. Francis might tell Dora. They looked at the harbour. She told him of the promenade. She pointed out the bottomless lake, then walked back via the Club, explaining who used it. They passed more shops and tavernas. She hesitated outside the one she had been in with Nikos.

Francis said, 'It looks kind of dirty. I can see why people like us wouldn't use it.' He was craning his neck to see through the window, his face screwed up in disgust.

She listened to the rhythm and the laughter which was rising and falling. She looked again at Francis and it was as though everything fell silent for a moment, and at last she had time, and peace, to think and to feel. She took his arm, anger making her voice harsh and loud.

'Come this way,' she ordered, heading towards the

cobbler's. Levandis didn't wave this time as she approached; he looked past her, beyond her, but she strode up to him, letting go, at last, of Francis's arm. She kissed Levandis on each cheek and went with him into the shop, calling back to Francis, 'Come in here with us. Levandis is my friend. Have coffee, or will it keep you awake?'

Frances stooped beneath the doorway, his face puzzled. 'Dora said you knew no-one.'

'Dora knows nothing,' Emily said, passing him coffee. Her voice was still loud with anger, and it was at herself as much as at Francis.

He checked the cup carefully.

'It's clean,' she said. 'Or if it isn't it has only been touched by lips that are the same as ours.'

Francis put down his coffee untouched. He listened as she and Levandis talked of the day, of Lato Etera, of the winter which would come.

Emily finished her drink, leaned forward. 'Please ask Nikos to meet me at the taverna, tonight. He's close, I know he is.' Now her voice was gentle.

Levandis said, 'Yes, he is near by. He cares for you. He can't stay away.'

She stood up, walked out, calling to Francis, 'Go back, Francis. I have someone to meet. You can find your own way.'

Francis followed her, running to catch up. He grabbed her arm. She shook him off. 'Go back, and tell whomever you like that I'm going to a taverna, to meet Nikos, the boy I love, the local boy I love.'

She didn't turn as she walked away, hurrying to the taverna. Only when she arrived did she glance over her shoulder. Francis hadn't followed, so no-one would interrupt the hours she would spend with Nikos.

The seamen looked up, then back down at their cards. She nodded as Cristos brought over a glass of ouzo and said firmly, 'Please bring another, Nikos will be here soon.'

He came as she finished her drink, approaching from behind, his hand stroking her hair. 'I liked it the colour of wheat,' he said as he kissed her neck.

'I will be washing it out.'

He sat, held her hand, kissed it, kissed her, drank the ouzo. 'I love you,' she said. 'I don't know anything about anything else. All I know is that I love you.'

He led her from the taverna, down to the beach and they sat on the sand which was still warm from the heat of the day and felt the breeze in their hair, felt their bodies touching. They watched the moon rise and the sea lapping on the sand.

'If only this beach, this hour, was all there was,' she murmured.

'But it isn't,' he said, 'and I'm glad. It means that we have time to grow, explore, come to know one another.'

She leant into his neck, holding him tightly. 'I'm frightened – not of them, but of me.'

He held her, his hand stroking her hair. He kissed her forehead, her nose, her mouth, her neck. 'I know,' he said. 'I'm frightened of you too – in case you decide you can't love me, or trust me.'

They sat in silence again, clutching one another.

It was only when the singing died in the tavernas that they rose, walking from the beach to the street, arms around one another, not wanting to be parted, not even by an inch. She stopped in the square. 'Go home, Nikos. I'll walk by myself now.'

'No.'

She kissed him. 'Please. I have things to do. Please, Nikos, or there will be no future.'

He touched her face, running his finger round her mouth, kissing her. 'I will be near if you need me.'

She walked on, down the street, into Dora's and David's road. The lights were still on in the house, as she had known they would be. She turned around. She couldn't see Nikos, but she knew he was there, somewhere.

*　　*　　*

Connie finished writing her letter to Emily. The range was dying down. She riddled it, then shovelled out the ash, tipping it carefully onto the coal. All she could hear was the ticking of the clock. She gripped the mantelpiece, looking at the photographs of Emily and Philip. She looked at the clock, then back at the photograph, her mind made up. She couldn't wait until Christmas. She would travel to Crete next week. There had been too much waiting.

34

Dora and David were standing in the entrance to the sitting-room as Emily opened the front door. Their faces were suffused with rage. Dora darted forward, grabbing Emily. 'How dare you, how bloody dare you send a message by a decent boy to say you are meeting a peasant? How dare you consort with such people?'

Emily stood quite still. 'I said I was meeting Nikos. He is the boy I love. He is a Cretan, he is the guide you were rude to, the guide I ignored today.'

Dora slapped her across her arms. David's hand was also raised as though to strike her.

He shouted, 'Get to your room and we'll discuss this tomorrow. Go on, you disgust me, go to your room. You are no better than your mother.'

Emily looked at him, then at Dora, smelling the gin they had been drinking. She walked to her room, shut the door, leaned against it, trembling. Oh God, what had she done? She bit her finger, forcing herself to be calm, thinking of Nikos somewhere near, thinking of him at Knossos allowing her to turn away from him.

She hugged herself, looking at the cardboard box on the top of her wardrobe. So, *Mother*, I'm like you, am I? But you left me. Would I leave my child for Nikos? She felt that she would not. Why did you do it, Mother? I need to understand if I'm ever to be free.

She took down the box, opened it, took out the package that had come via the newspaper. She wondered again why it was addressed to a newspaper, not to her. She opened it. There were many letters, one for every week since she had left England for Crete. All had news of Rempton, the mission, the family.

She read through them, not understanding until finally she read the letter which told her that her mother was sending all the letters in one parcel because Dora had not told her the Crete address.

Her mother also said, *I can't bear to think that for the first time since the divorce you will not receive my weekly letter.*

Emily began to tremble again. She remembered Nikos saying, 'You need to listen to all sides of the argument.' She read through them again, and then the few letters which had lain in the box year after year.

She read one from Romesh's uncle, confirming her mother's love for his nephew, and his certainty that their relationship had ceased long before Connie's marriage to David. She read others referring to earlier letters and other news that had never reached her.

She read one which talked of the photograph snapped when she was on her way to school and which was on the mantelpiece with that of Philip. She read another which talked of Connie's love for David, though it had been a different kind. Another which talked of Philip and how he was not a replacement, of Boy and the love she hoped her daughter would one day feel for a man.

There were two from her grandmother, from Boy, even one from Philip. All mentioned previous letters.

The ink was faded on some – they were so old. She counted the letters. Fifteen – where were the rest? How many questions have been answered? How many words of love had been written which she had never received?

She opened again the letter from Romesh's uncle, then shut her eyes, remembering how she had lifted the curtain as her mother had walked down the path at Christmas. Recognizing now that her mother's smile had been one of infinite love and understanding.

She rose from her knees and walked into the sitting-room where Dora and David sat close together on the settee, huddled over their glasses. They looked up. 'I said get to bed,' David shouted, banging his glass down on the table. He had loosened his tie and his top button was undone.

Emily held up the letters. 'These are from my mother. I've just finished reading them.'

David looked confused. Dora paled, stood up; her knuckles were white as she gripped her glass. She slopped her gin down her green dress as she moved towards Emily.

Emily said, 'Don't come near me, either of you.' Dora stopped. David looked from her to Emily, then he too started to get up, his face still flushed, and now shiny with sweat. 'Now look here—'

Emily shook the letters, not looking at Dora, just at him. She shouted, not letting him finish, 'No, you look here. I want to go to England. I want to talk to my mother about these, and those that are missing.'

He was upright now. 'What the hell—'

Dora pushed past him. David spun round, knocking her arm. Her glass crashed to the ground but Dora took no notice as she snatched the letters. 'Where did you get these? I thought I'd intercepted them or told you to burn those your father picked up from the mat. What has she said, the bitch? Don't believe her, not a word, it's all lies; she was a harlot, a cruel, vicious harlot.'

David grew pale, then walked slowly towards his wife. He put out his hand for the letters. She ignored him, glaring at Emily who stood quite still, watching as Dora scanned the letters. Silence fell. Dora lifted her head as David reached out again and took them from her, reading first one, and then the next, and the next.

He lifted his head eventually and his voice was old as he said, 'When these letters arrived I thought they were the only ones Connie had bothered to send.' His hands were trembling, his shoulders sagged. Dora was hugging herself, rocking backwards and forwards.

Emily looked only at her father as she said, 'I couldn't

bear to read them until now. I've kept them in a box. My mother said she has written every week since the divorce.' Now she looked at Dora. 'You said, Dora, that you'd written to her with our Ayios Nikolaos address in good time for her to come and say goodbye. She received the letter after we left. There was no address but they've tried, dear God, how they've tried to reach me.'

She watched the envelope flutter to the floor, then looked up. 'Go on, Dora, pick it up. You were the one who said we were coming here on holiday. That was a lie. How many more lies have there been? I want to go and talk to my mother. I don't believe any more that she just left me.'

Dora rushed and kicked the envelope aside. 'I won't have you consorting with her. I won't have this, do you understand? You are my child, not hers.' Her voice was a scream.

David moved now, gripping his wife's arm, shaking her, shouting, 'For God's sake, we said she could go whenever she wanted to.'

She shrugged him off, her voice dropping to a whisper. 'I won't have her poisoning this child's mind against me. I won't have her talking to her.'

Emily moved into the room, feeling indescribably tired. She spoke slowly, her voice was low. 'I am not a child. I told you this evening that I love Nikos. But you see, there's too much in the way. I *need* to know about my mother. I need to hear her side.'

Dora slapped her now, hard across her face, and then again and Emily reeled from the blows hearing Dora screeching, 'You're just like her, a tramp. How dare you? You're just as dirty as she is.'

David came up behind and grabbed her. 'Dora, stop it, pull yourself together. How dare you hit my child?' Dora was sobbing now, loudly, as though she were demented.

Emily moved back, her cheeks stinging. She shouted to David above the noise. 'My mother says the affair was over long before you met. She says the man in the pub was a put-up job. She admits she shouldn't have left me when she went to the border. She says she was visiting a sick person later on when she came back to that party and made me scream because she was covered in blood. She hadn't been with Romesh at all.'

David was still struggling with Dora, but now the wailing stopped and Dora sagged, her hair dishevelled, her lipstick smeared across David's shirt. David looked at Emily, sweat dampening his hair; a button had been wrenched from his shirt. 'Of course she wasn't with him. We know where she was, she was with the ayah. The doctor was with her. Why did you—?'

He stopped and looked from Emily to Dora, horror dawning, and his lips barely moved as he said quietly and slowly, 'Go to your room, Emily.'

First she stooped and picked up the envelope, then walked to the table, avoiding the broken glass. She dropped the envelope on the table, turned, looked at Dora, her face expressionless. She looked at her father but his eyes could not meet hers. She walked past them both, into the hallway, into her room.

David watched her leave, feeling the weight of Dora's body all the time. He led her to the sofa, lowered her into it, easing the strap of her dress back onto her shoulder. Then he stood above her as she looked up at him, her eyes swollen with crying.

'Why did you lie about the ayah?' he said quietly. 'You obviously told Emily she was with Romesh. Why? And what else have you lied about?'

Dora clutched at his trousers, reaching for his hands. He stepped back, looking at the floor. 'I wanted you. I'd lost everything. I could no longer have a child; Ben was dead. She, Connie, had a husband, just like her mother. Her mother had everything, you know. My mother told me that. They drummed Mam out of the village, took all hope from her. Everything afterwards was charity.

'I could see that happening to me, so I took you. I wanted you to give me security. I wanted to give her pain to pay her family back. I wanted her child, I wanted the divorce watertight. I lied, and I kept on lying because I grew to love you, to truly love you and Emily, and I couldn't bear the thought of living without you.'

Dora was weeping again, but silently now because it was the truth and she would die if he left her.

'Is this another lie?' he asked, looking at Dora. Her lipstick was smeared, her mascara had been washed down her cheeks by her tears, her dress was wet and stained from the gin and had ridden up round her thighs. He caught sight of himself in the mirror, sweat-drenched, overweight, his shirt gaping. They looked what they were, and he could have wept. 'Tell me, is this another lie?' he repeated.

She opened her eyes. 'Would I have stayed with you throughout the redundancy, helping to spin out our income here, if it was? I love you both, I always will.'

David sent her to bed and sat on the veranda all night, smoking, thinking, remembering, and as the dawn came up he said aloud, 'Oh Connie, what have we done to you and Emily?'

He went to the bedroom and looked down at his wife who was asleep, her arms flung across the bed, as though searching for him. He thought of the dances in India, of her body which Ben had known, of his wedding to Connie, and knew that he had always loved Dora, and always would. But how could they live with what they had done?

He knew that somehow they would have to.

After he had telegraphed Connie he drove Emily to Herakleion. They said little on the way and Dora remained behind.

As they approached the harbour he said, 'Forgive us. I was weak, Dora was desperate. Try and forgive us.'

She kissed him when he stopped the car. 'I love you, Dad, I love Dora too, in a way, but I want to go home.'

He hugged her, saying nothing. What could he say? He took her cases from the boot and they walked to the ship further apart than they had ever been before. As they approached the gangway a young man detached himself from the crowd and walked towards them. It was Nikos.

Emily looked at her father, relief pouring through her. Her father had promised he would leave a message with Levandis. She hadn't checked; she hadn't dared. She wanted to know she could trust David.

Emily held out her hands. Nikos kissed them. David reddened, began to move between them, then stopped. Hadn't he done enough?

He said, holding out his hand, 'I'm Emily's father. We've met before and I apologize for those episodes.'

Emily watched as Nikos smiled, shook hands briefly, then turned to her again.

He asked, 'Will you return?'

'How can I not? I love you but I have so much time to make up with my mother. Dora was lying.' She stopped. 'I'll miss you, it seems that we've only just begun.'

He kissed her fingers, slowly, one by one. 'Perhaps at Christmas you would show me the archaeology around your mother's home?'

She was closer to him now. 'You'll need a vest.' They were silent. He kissed her, on the lips – softly, gently, then on the cheeks, the eyes, the mouth again. His arms were round her now, and she felt safe, as though she belonged, but perhaps she belonged at Rempton too?

Emily clutched the rail, looking back at Crete, feeling the swell beneath the ship. She could still see Nikos and her father as they stood together, waving. She lifted her hand, then turned her face into the wind. Soon she would be at Rempton.

That night she sat on the deck, holding her mother's letters, gazing up at the stars, feeling the warm September breeze. Would it be cold in Rempton? She had never been to the north which Dora insisted was cold and dark and ugly. Therefore it probably wasn't. She hungrily reread yet again her mother's letters.

No, at Rempton there were wheatfields and Connie said that the harvest had just been gathered. There was a colliery, though, in the next village. Did that mean there was coal dust and ugliness? There was the church. Dora had said her mother Binnie was buried there. What was it like? The letters didn't say. Who was Mrs Green? Her mother obviously thought she knew. It must have been in a previous letter. And what did she mean about Grandpa's cricket team? She pushed the letters into her bag. Oh God, there was so much she didn't know.

She paced the deck, nodding at fellow passengers but not really seeing them, thinking, digging deep into her memory, wanting to know this place which was her mother's home, but there was nothing, except the bits and pieces in the letter.

That night she barely slept, longing for Nikos, longing to know her mother, to see her, but afraid too. At dawn she walked the deck again, then stopped and gazed down into the sea, watching it rush beneath the prow of the ship. What was her mother like? She dug deep into her mind and remembered her mother's laughter in the Himalayas, the trays they had slid down, the stories she had read her. There must be so much more. But what?

The prow was surging through the waves; the ship was lurching, rolling slightly. She watched the water break and the light catch it, and now out of her tiredness and longing she remembered another sea, another ship.

She closed her eyes. She saw her mother weeping, her father and Dora taking her from a cabin. She heard her mother's voice calling, 'She's my daughter. I must be with her.'

She remembered the confusion of the docks and being pushed into a taxi with just Dora and David. Her mother was left outside, crying, running after them, her face tormented. 'Oh Mum,' Emily whispered. 'Oh Mum.'

She opened her eyes and looked out to the horizon and now as the sun climbed in the sky, she remembered standing with her mother in the Himalayas watching the sun come up behind them and the mist in the valleys, and the rhododendrons all around them. She'd forgotten those. She remembered the crispness of the air, she heard the sound of their voices.

She remembered the small train coming up the hill, and the blanket she had been wrapped in, the walls of snow as they travelled in the tonga to their house. Ayah had been there. What was her name? She couldn't remember. She must ask her mother.

In the house there was wire at the windows. Yes, to keep monkeys out. And the trays they had slid down. And now she could hear her mother's voice, 'This is so wonderful, my darling.' It was clear as though her mother was beside her. She spun round, then back to the horizon. She mustn't break the spell.

She remembered the heat of the plains, the large halls where she had played with other children while their mothers cut sandwiches. Why? Now she remembered. They were for the troops that passed through the stations. She could taste the dust as they drove in jeeps, and the noise as the train came in. She could feel her mother's hand on her shoulder, always close. There was something else, not a sound, not a sigh, but something else she could almost remember.

Emily shook her head; the images were fading and she wanted to weep. She tried to claw them back but there were others on deck now, talking, laughing, calling her to breakfast. She went, then played deck quoits, then wrote to Nikos, then dozed in the afternoon sun, then dined as the sun went down.

That night she dreamed of sledging on trays and woke in the morning remembering her mother's stories of Boy sliding down the hill at Rempton to the beck, in the snow. And in the summer they would slide down on the grass. She remembered her mother's face as she told her, and

421

her voice, and there was something else, just on the edge of all this, but no, it was gone.

The days passed and with each one came more images, sounds, memories, and always there was something that she couldn't quite see, or was it that she couldn't quite hear? She didn't know. But as England grew closer she remembered the river at Walton-on-Thames where David and Dora took her on Sunday afternoons. She paddled whilst they lay on the bank. She remembered Brownies, Guides, her school, the youth club, Geoff. How long ago it seemed, and almost unreal.

Again she slept badly because she seemed almost in limbo, suspended amongst memories of India, of Surrey, and Crete, and torn between people, and love, and anticipation, and fear of the unknown. What if she didn't love her mother? What if she could no longer bear to belong to David and Dora? What if—?

Belle laid flowers on Binnie's grave. She had been unable to do so for years, but now Emily was almost home and her hatred was dying. David's telegram had been received a week ago. She clipped the grass around the grave, pushed herself up from her knees, then stood and stroked Walter's stone. 'The bairn's coming home, Walter, at last she's coming home.'

She walked down the fields, to the cricket field. The oaks had grown bigger and stronger with every passing year. 'She's coming home,' Belle murmured, hearing again the sound of leather on willow as she had just before the young men had gone to war. 'We are so very lucky.'

She walked back through the village. 'Is Emily back yet?' Mrs Overton called from the scullery of her house.

'Not yet. The ship should be docking now. Connie rang from the hotel last night and no delay is expected. They'll be arriving at Longdale on the four-thirty.'

Mr Richards came running down the path with cabbage. 'I know you grow them, but this is specially for the bairn.'

Mrs Evans was waiting by the gate with a pot of strawberry jam. 'I hear the squire's brought down cream for your tea, and Mrs Green will be stopping you with some scones, so take this from us, and give Connie our love, and the lass.'

Mrs Green came out of the baker's, flour on her cheeks, and scones in a bag. 'Take these for your tea, though I doubt there'll be much eating done, just a grand lot of talking.' Mrs Green was crying as she passed the bag to Belle. 'I never thought she'd come back. It makes everything all right, everything.' She nodded, and looked back through the village in the direction of the cricket field.

Belle hugged her. 'You're a generous woman, Vera Green,' she whispered.

Mrs Green wiped her eyes with her apron, and flapped it at Belle. 'Get along now.'

Boy and Philip were folding up the best tablecloth as Belle staggered in with the beans, jam, scones, and flowers that the postman had given her. Her hair was falling out of its bun and she smiled as she put them on top of the cloth.

'I don't know, talk about a high day and a feast day.'

Boy shook his head, pointing at the cabbage. 'Well done, Belle. Petals all over the cloth and mud from the cabbage.'

Philip leant against the table. 'Yes, Grandma, we've just checked that it's clean. Now we'll have to wash it again.'

Belle laughed, took the cloth to the back door and gave it a shake. 'There you are, perfect.' She carried it to the dresser as Philip asked, 'Are we having tea in the dining-room?'

Boy answered, 'No, Emily is family, not a guest.'

Belle couldn't speak for a moment because Boy had said what was in her heart. Instead she hugged her son-in-law. 'You're so wonderful, what would we all have done without you?'

Philip said, 'Urgh, I hate all this slobbering. *She's* not going to do it when she comes, is she?' He pointed to the photograph on the mantelpiece.

Boy and Belle laughed. 'I hope so,' Belle said sitting down suddenly, her shoulders shaking as the tears came. 'How silly, I'm just so anxious, so pleased, so terrified. How will they feel? It's been so long. I couldn't bear it if Emily rejects her.'

Connie watched the men dragging the hawsers, securing them. She heard the excitement of the crowd as they waved at the ship. The sound seemed to roll over her again and again. She searched the distant figures at the ship's rail. No, she couldn't see Emily. She stared around her. It was here Emily had been taken from her. She bunched her hands and looked again at the ship.

Passengers were disembarking, disappearing into Customs. She stood motionless, not moving from foot to foot or talking, laughing, gesticulating, as those others who were waiting were doing. Her daughter was going to come to her after all these years and she didn't know what to do.

The passengers were coming through now, waving, their skin tanned, their hair bleached. The crowd surged forward. Connie stood still, waiting, watching, but there were too many people in front of her and now she forced her way through, as though her life depended on it.

She scanned the passengers as they walked forward, waving, and shouting greetings. There were none that she recognized. She looked past them, holding tightly to the image she had glimpsed so briefly through the glass last year. Either side of her, relatives called or beckoned to those they were waiting for. All around, people were hugging, kissing, exclaiming.

Emily carried her two cases as she followed the other passengers. She wanted to slow down, to stop, think, go back, but the others were pushing her on, eager to be met, eager to go home. Where was home? She looked ahead of her, to the mass of people waiting. Should she shake her mother's hand? Should she run to meet her? Would they recognize one another?

She remembered her mother's look of love and understanding through the glass. Yes, she would recognize her. She looked around, at the faces of the people waiting. Perhaps she hadn't come? As she hadn't come to see her off. She shook her head. No, that was Dora's fault. Her mother was the woman who had held her as they slid down the trays. Her mother was the woman who had written every week, and never lost faith.

She looked again, first this face, then that, and then her eyes locked with others that were violet and she stopped and now there seemed as though there was no-one else in the world but this slight, tired, beautiful woman in a pale blue dress, whose eyes held the same anxiety that she felt, whose hands were reaching out to her, whose lips were moving. 'My darling Emily. You've come home at last.'

Emily dropped her cases and there was no uncertainty as she ran towards Connie. 'Mum, oh Mum.' Her mother's arms were round her, and they were both weeping, and her mother's voice was soothing her, and then Emily smelt face powder and lavender, and knew now that this was what had been at the edge of her memories. It was the scent of her mother, of her comfort and of her love.

As they travelled up in the train, they talked, then fell silent, then talked again. They held hands, then sat apart, then came together. They travelled through the south of England, the Midlands. England seemed so huge after Crete, but so small in comparison to the India she was discovering through her mother's words.

They talked of Rempton, of Belle and Boy and Philip. 'Who is Mrs Green?' Emily asked. Connie told her. 'What about Grandpa's cricket team?' Connie explained. They talked of Nikos, then of David and Dora, and

Connie felt the tension flare at the mention of their names but forced it away. Her daughter was with her, her voice was the same as it had once been, and love was there, she knew it was, though it had not yet been spoken aloud.

They travelled on through chimney-spiked towns, wide moors, collieries, sweeping hills and drystone-walls. They changed trains. 'Not long now,' Connie said.

The wind was much colder than it had been in Southampton. Emily nodded and sat silently as the train took them between hills dissected with drystone-walls and fields and pit villages, onwards to Rempton, her mother's home. Would it also be hers?

Connie said, 'We've had our Harvest Festival. You might like to help with next year's if—?' She stopped and looked at Emily who had turned away. Connie looked down at her hands and wished she had not asked the question. It was much too early. She said, 'I mean – we've had our Harvest Festival. Your grandmother helped with the flowers. She always does.'

Emily smiled at her. 'There are lots of Cretan festivals too. People need to celebrate sometimes. Nikos said he will take me to more when I go to Crete again. He said he would like to explore England too.'

Connie smiled gently. 'Then I'm sure you will.' But she said nothing more.

They were approaching Longdale. Connie pointed. 'Rempton is just over there, just a short walk from here.'

Emily craned forward, looking out over the mine to the terraced houses, and to the village beyond it. 'Rempton,' she repeated.

She and Connie walked from Longdale Station each carrying a case. 'I asked your grandmother, Boy and Philip to wait for us at the vicarage. I do hope you don't mind. I thought it would be less of a strain if you absorbed your surroundings in peace, before being deluged with the rest of your—' she paused, then plunged on, 'your family.'

Emily looked over at the slag-heap. She heard Connie but didn't know how to reply because she didn't know how she felt. She walked steadily on, looking across at the winding gear, the back-to-backs, the dog which ran down the street in front of them. It isn't dark and ugly, Dora.

They entered Rempton, walking past the cricket pitch where young oaks were growing.

'These were planted in memory of your grandfather's cricket team,' Connie said quietly.

They walked down the main street. People were in their gardens, picking flowers or leaning over their walls or standing in shop doorways. 'Hello Emily,' each one said. 'It's grand you're home, my bairn.'

Emily gripped her case and smiled at them, though she said nothing, because she didn't yet know if this was her home.

They walked on. A church was over to the right. Beyond it was a large house. Rempton Vicarage. Emily stopped, looked at the church, then at the churchyard. 'This must be where Dora's mother is buried. She said it was near the yew.' Emily put down her case. Connie stood and looked at her.

'Would you like me to take you to it?' Connie said gently, not wanting to, but knowing she must, if it was what her daughter wanted. She smiled at Emily. 'I'll come with you, if you wish?'

Emily said nothing for a while; she just stood and watched the rooks fly from the trees and listened to their cawing, then she turned to her mother and there was still that look of infinite love and understanding that she knew there had always been. At last she spoke, knowing now what she felt.

'I love Dad, and Dora too, in a way. She loved me, you see. She was wicked, but she loved me. I don't know, though, whether I can forgive her because she has kept me from Rempton, and from you – and all this. We've lost years – all these years of love. All these years of the village and harvest suppers, and Mrs Green, and being called "bairn". Oh Mum.'

She held out her hand and Connie grasped it. They looked at one another, picked up the cases and walked on to the gates of the vicarage.

Belle stood by the front door. Philip wriggled and she pulled him back against her. 'Just be patient for a little longer, I know it's been a long wait – it has for us all, longer than you could ever imagine.'

'They're here,' Philip shouted, pointing down the drive.

Belle looked towards the gate which had been open all day and saw Emily and Connie walking hand in hand towards her, as though they had always been together, and she felt Boy's hand on her shoulder. 'Thank God,' he said, just as Emily called, 'Hello, Grandma, Boy, Philip, I'm home at last.'

THE END

A DISTANT DREAM
by Margaret Graham

It is 1920 and Caithleen Healy, as beautiful and spirited as her Irish homeland, dreams of fighting back against the Black and Tans, and of avenging her mother's brutal death. Caithleen is unsure how best to serve Ireland's cause. It is her childhood sweetheart, Mick O'Brian who shows her the way: she must strike up a friendship with an English Auxiliary and distract him from the work of the Volunteers. But the English Auxie Caithleen must betray is a decent man. Ben Williams believes her tender words, and all too soon Caithleen finds herself believing them too.

Determined to escape the Troubles, Ben leaves Ireland and heads for Australia. And soon Caithleen follows him, fleeing her home to help save Mick O'Brian's life. But her hopes for a happy future are shortlived, for both Mick and Ben, each believing himself to have been betrayed by her, abandon Caithleen.

In the dust and heat of the Australian gold mines, Caithleen becomes Kate, turning her back on Ireland and forging a new life for herself. Yet even in this newly established community Kate finds prejudice and division which turn neighbour against neighbour, friend against friend. And the echoes of past treachery resound still. For as the years go by, and Kate begins to prosper, the figure of Mick O'Brian, as embittered and impulsive as ever, returns to make her pay once more the price of betrayal.

A Doubleday Hardcover
0 385 405537

FOREIGN AFFAIRS
by Patricia Scanlan

Four women, Paula, Jennifer, Brenda and Rachel. All at a crossroads in their lives. All with choices to make.

PAULA: Beautiful, ambitious and successful, she works hard and plays hard. Men find her irresistible . . . except for the one man she really wants and is determined to have.

JENNIFER: She's a true friend. Paula comes to her with man troubles. Rachel tells her of family woes. Brenda her sister, is deeply envious of Jennifer's high-powered career and successful marriage. Then tragedy strikes. Will Paula, Brenda and Rachel be there for Jennifer when she really needs them?

BRENDA: In her late thirties, she longs for glamour and excitement. Tired of being a housewife stuck at home with her children, Brenda is determined to make changes in her life. Then the unthinkable happens.

RACHEL: Shy and timid, she has always been dominated by her cold, intolerant father. But beneath the surface she is bubbling with suppressed rage. This is her last chance to break free, but does she have the courage to finally become her own woman?

When Paula, Jennifer, Brenda and Rachel stay together in a luxurious villa on a Greek island, they soon realize that they have embarked on more than just a foreign holiday. Amidst rows, arguments, laughter and fun they come to see each other in a different light, and questions are raised. Can their friendships be sustained? Indeed, will their lives ever be the same again?

A Bantam paperback
0 553 40947 6

THE DAFFODIL SEA
by Emma Blair

The summer concert in St Petroc, Devon, was never intended to be a life-shattering event, yet for fourteen-year old Roxanne Hawkins, one of the local farmer's daughters, it is the evening of a lifetime. Entranced by the lights, the magic and the greasepaint, she suddenly realizes that she wants to become part of this fascinating world.

So it should have come as no surprise to her parents, when, on the day of the St Petroc's Autumn Fair, Roxanne disappears. Taking all her worldly possessions, she runs away to London where she meets the music hall comedian Harry Bright – a suave and sophisticated fixer who, she knows, will act as her entrée into showbusiness. Roxanne adopts the stage-name Annie Breeze, and it isn't long before they begin to make a name for themselves as the highly popular double act, Bright and Breeze.

But at the height of her career, disaster strikes and Roxanne is forced to return to Devon. There, despite family pressure, she establishes a new life, miles away from the bright lights of the big city and, amid the peace and serenity of her own daffodil farm, she begins to accept that love is a thing of the past – or so she likes to imagine.

'Heart-warming . . . Emma Blair is a dab hand at pulling heartstrings' *Daily Mail*

A Bantam Paperback
0 553 40614 0

A SELECTED LIST OF FINE NOVELS
AVAILABLE FROM BANTAM BOOKS

THE PRICES SHOWN BELOW WERE CORRECT AT THE TIME OF GOING
TO PRESS. HOWEVER TRANSWORLD PUBLISHERS RESERVE THE RIGHT
TO SHOW NEW RETAIL PRICES ON COVERS WHICH MAY DIFFER FROM
THOSE PREVIOUSLY ADVERTISED IN THE TEXT OR ELSEWHERE.

☐	40727 9	LOVERS AND LIARS	*Sally Beauman*	£5.99
☐	17632 3	DARK ANGEL	*Sally Beauman*	£4.99
☐	17352 9	DESTINY	*Sally Beauman*	£4.99
☐	40429 6	AT HOME	*Charlotte Bingham*	£3.99
☐	40497 0	CHANGE OF HEART	*Charlotte Bingham*	£4.99
☐	40427 X	BELGRAVIA	*Charlotte Bingham*	£3.99
☐	40163 7	THE BUSINESS	*Charlotte Bingham*	£4.99
☐	40428 8	COUNTRY LIFE	*Charlotte Bingham*	£3.99
☐	40296 X	IN SUNSHINE OR IN SHADOW	*Charlotte Bingham*	£4.99
☐	40496 2	NANNY	*Charlotte Bingham*	£4.99
☐	40171 8	STARDUST	*Charlotte Bingham*	£4.99
☐	17635 8	TO HEAR A NIGHTINGALE	*Charlotte Bingham*	£4.99
☐	40072 X	MAGGIE JORDAN	*Emma Blair*	£4.99
☐	40298 6	SCARLET RIBBONS	*Emma Blair*	£4.99
☐	40372 9	THE WATER MEADOWS	*Emma Blair*	£4.99
☐	40373 7	THE SWEETEST THING	*Emma Blair*	£4.99
☐	40614 0	THE DAFFODIL SEA	*Emma Blair*	£4.99
☐	40504 7	FLOWERS ON THE MERSEY	*June Francis*	£4.99
☐	40719 8	FRIENDS AND LOVERS	*June Francis*	£4.99
☐	40820 8	LILY'S WAR	*June Francis*	£4.99
☐	40400 8	A SEASON IN PURGATORY	*Dominick Dunne*	£4.99
☐	40321 4	AN INCONVENIENT WOMAN	*Dominick Dunne*	£4.99
☐	17676 5	PEOPLE LIKE US	*Dominick Dunne*	£3.99
☐	17189 5	THE TWO MRS GRENVILLES	*Dominick Dunne*	£3.50
☐	40730 9	LOVERS	*Judith Krantz*	£5.99
☐	17504 1	DAZZLE	*Judith Krantz*	£4.99
☐	17242 5	I'LL TAKE MANHATTAN	*Judith Krantz*	£4.99
☐	17174 7	MISTRAL'S DAUGHTER	*Judith Krantz*	£2.95
☐	17389 8	PRINCESS DAISY	*Judith Krantz*	£4.99
☐	17505 X	SCRUPLES TWO	*Judith Krantz*	£4.99
☐	17503 3	TILL WE MEET AGAIN	*Judith Krantz*	£4.99
☐	40206 4	FAST FRIENDS	*Jill Mansell*	£3.99
☐	40361 3	KISS	*Jill Mansell*	£4.99
☐	40360 5	SOLO	*Jill Mansell*	£3.99
☐	40612 4	OPEN HOUSE	*Jill Mansell*	£4.99
☐	40682 5	THE GOOD MOTHER	*Sue Miller*	£5.99
☐	40642 6	FOR LOVE	*Sue Miller*	£5.99
☐	40816 X	IF WISHES WERE HORSES	*Francine Pascal*	£5.99
☐	40720 1	MALINA	*Penny Perrick*	£4.99
☐	40947 6	FOREIGN AFFAIRS	*Patricia Scanlan*	£4.99
☐	17630 7	DOCTORS	*Erich Segal*	£5.99
☐	17209 3	THE CLASS	*Erich Segal*	£5.99